$29.99

DAT

Girl on the Golden Coin

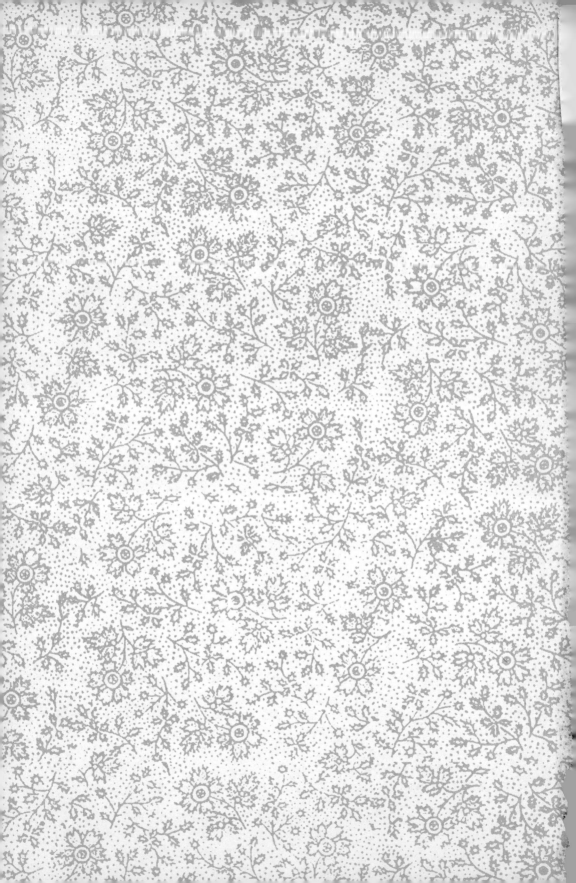

Girl
on the
Golden
Coin
A Novel of Frances Stuart

Marci Jefferson

THOMAS DUNNE BOOKS
ST. MARTIN'S PRESS
NEW YORK

THOMAS DUNNE BOOKS.
An imprint of St. Martin's Press.

GIRL ON THE GOLDEN COIN. Copyright © 2014 by Marci Jefferson. All rights reserved. Printed in the United States of America. For information, address St. Martin's Press, 175 Fifth Avenue, New York, N.Y. 10010.

www.thomasdunnebooks.com
www.stmartins.com

Design by Jonathan Bennett

Library of Congress Cataloging-in-Publication Data

Jefferson, Marci.
    Girl on the golden coin : a novel of Frances Stuart / Marci Jefferson.—First edition.
        pages cm
    ISBN 978-1-250-03722-0 (hardcover)
    ISBN 978-1-250-03721-3 (e-book)
    1. Richmond and Lennox, Frances Teresa Stuart, Duchess of, 1648–1702—Fiction.
2. Louis XIV, King of France, 1638–1715—Fiction.   3. Charles II, King of England, 1630–1685—Fiction.   4. Courts and courtiers—Fiction.   5. France—Kings and rulers—Fiction.   6. Great Britain—Kings and rulers—Fiction.   7. Great Britain—History—Restoration, 1660–1688—Fiction.   I. Title.
    PS3610.E3655G57 2014
    813'.6—dc23

                                                                        2013030272

St. Martin's Press books may be purchased for educational, business, or promotional use. For information on bulk purchases, please contact Macmillan Corporate and Premium Sales Department at 1-800-221-7945, extension 5442, or write specialmarkets@ macmillan.com.

First Edition: February 2014

10 9 8 7 6 5 4 3 2 1

To Kevin,
Dalton, and Delani.
Without you, all is nothing.

Map was provided by Knowledge Quest, Inc. You can find more historical maps on their Web site at www.knowledgequestmaps.com.

DRAMATIS PERSONAE

England

Royal House of Stuart

King Charles I of England—*Descendant of the Fourth High Steward of Scotland*

Henrietta Maria de Bourbon of France—*Married into the Stuart royal family as queen to Charles I*

Their children:
King Charles II—*The restored king, no legitimate heir*
Catherine of Bragança—*Queen to Charles II*

James Stuart, Duke of York—*Later crowned King James II of England*
His wives:
Anne Hyde, first Duchess of York—*Died before daughters Mary and Anne succeeded to the throne*
Mary of Modena, second Duchess of York—*Became queen when James became king, son denied succession to the throne*

Princess Henriette Anne Stuart—*Married into the French royal house of Bourbon as duchess to Philippe of France, Duc d'Orléans*

Henry, Duke of Gloucester—*Died just after the Restoration*

Prince Rupert of the Rhine—*Nephew to Charles I*

The Blantyre Stuarts

Walter Stuart, First Lord Blantyre—*Descendant of the Fourth High Steward of Scotland*

Walter Stuart, Master of Blantyre—*Nephew of Frances, recipient of Lennoxlove Estate*

The Honorable Mr. Walter Stuart—*Youngest son of the first Lord Blantyre, physician*
   Mrs. Sophia Stuart—*His wife, of unknown parentage*

  Their children:
     Frances Teresa Stuart—*Queen Catherine's maid of honor*
     Sophia Stuart—*Married Henry Bulkely*
       Anne—*Their daughter, wed Duke of Berwick, illegitimate son of James II*
     Walter Stuart—*Served Lord Douglas's regiment, volunteer on the* Montague

The Lennox Stuarts

Charles Stuart, third Duke of Richmond and sixth Duke of Lennox—*Descendant of the Fourth High Steward of Scotland, possessed numerous additional titles*
  His wives:
     Elizabeth Rogers—*Died after the Restoration, daughter died young*
     Margaret Banister—*Died without children*
     Frances Stuart
  His retainers:
     Roger Payne—*The steward*
     Lee—*A footman*

Ludovic, Seigneur d'Aubigny—*The duke's uncle*

Dramatis Personae

The Hamiltons

Elizabeth Hamilton—*Maid of honor to Queen Catherine, wed the Chevalier de Gramont,*
George Hamilton—*Admirer of Frances Stuart, wed Frances Jennings*
Anthony Hamilton—*Author of the Gramont Memoirs*

The Hydes

Henry Hyde, Earl of Clarendon—*Lord chancellor to King Charles II*

His children:
    Anne Hyde—*Married James, Duke of York of the Royal house of Stuart*
    Henry Hyde, Lord Cornbury—*Lord Chamberlin to Queen Catherine*

The Jermyns

Sir Thomas Jermyn—*Nonresident governor of Jersey, father to Earl of St. Albans*
Henry Jermyn, First Earl of St. Albans—*Vice-chamberlain to Queen Henrietta Maria*
Henry Jermyn the younger—*Nephew of the Earl of St. Albans*

The Villiers

George Villiers, first Duke of Buckingham—*Reputed lover of James I and Charles I*

His children:
    Lady Mary Villiers—*Sister to the second Duke of Buckingham*
    George Villiers, second Duke of Buckingham—*Son of the first duke*
    Mary Fairfax, Duchess of Buckingham—*The second duke's wife*

Barbara Villiers—*Granddaughter to the older half brother of the first duke, wife of Roger Palmer, first official mistress to Charles II*

Eleanor Villiers—*Daughter of the first Duke of Buckingham's half brother*

Other Courtiers and Characters

Queen Catherine's ladies:
   Lady Sanderson—*Mother of the maids of honor:*
      Katherine Boynton
      Simona Cary
      Mademoiselle La Garde
      Jane Middleton
      Helene Warmestry
      Winifred Wells
   Elizabeth Frasier—*Queen Catherine's dresser*
   Lady Mary Scroope—*Queen Catherine's dresser, mistress of Henry Bennet*
   Lady Mary Wood—*Queen Catherine's dresser*

Maids of honor to Anne Hyde, Duchess of York:
   Arabella Churchill—*Mistress to James II, their son became Duke of Berwick*
   Frances Jennings—*Married George Hamilton*

Henry Bennet, later Lord Arlington—*Secretary of state to Charles II*
Earl of Carlingford—*Irish peer*
Earl of Chesterfield—*Upbraided his countess after her affair with the Duke of York*
Samuel Cooper—*Miniaturist painter*
Oliver Cromwell—*Protector of the Commonwealth, death prompted the Restoration*
Moll Davies—*Actress*
Nell Gwynn—*Actress*

Dramatis Personae

Louise de Kéroüaille—*Maid of honor to Duchesse d'Orléans; second official mistress to Charles II; their son is ancestor to Lady Diana Spencer, Princess of Wales*

Sir William Killigrew—*Vice-chamberlain to Queen Catherine, Member of Parliament*

Elizabeth Mallett—*Northern heiress, married John Wilmot, Earl of Rochester*

Admiral Sir William Penn—*Member of Parliament and admiral in the Royal Navy*

William Penn—*Son of Admiral Penn, founder of Pennsylvania*

Samuel Pepys—*Diarist and secretary to the Admiralty*

John Wilmot, Earl of Rochester—*Rake, kidnapped and later married Elizabeth Mallett*

Roettier—*Engraver to Charles II*

Gilbert Sheldon—*Bishop of London, Archbishop of Canterbury*

Prudence Pope—*Quaker maid fictionalized as daughter to historical figure Mr. Pope*

Mary—*Fictional Catholic maid given to Frances Stuart by the Queen Mother*

Sir Isaac Newton—*Scientist*

France

The House of Bourbon

Henrietta Maria de Bourbon—*Daughter of Henri IV of France and Marie de' Medici, sister to Louis XIII, aunt of King Louis XIV, queen to Charles I of England*

Anne of Austria—*Married into the house of Bourbon as queen to Louis XIII of France*

Her sons:
Louis XIV of France
Marie-Thérèse of Spain—*First cousin and queen consort to Louis XIV; their great-grandson succeeded to the throne*

Dramatis Personae

Philippe of France
  Henriette Anne Stuart—*First cousin and duchess to Prince Philippe, Duc d'Orléans*

De Gramonts

Philibert, Chevalier de Gramont—*Married Elizabeth Hamilton*
Guy Armand de Gramont, Comte de Guiche—*Nephew of Philibert, Chevalier de Gramont*

Other Courtiers and Characters

Nicolas Foquet—*Superintendent of finances*
Father Cyprien of Gamache—*Capuchin friar serving Queen Henrietta Maria*
Chevalier de Lorraine—*Lover of the Duc d'Orléans*
Lully—*Composer*
Cardinal Mazarin—*Advisor to Anne of Austria, possible biological father of Louis XIV*
Molière—*Playwright*
Françoise-Athénaïs de Rochechouart-Mortemart—*Maid of honor to Queen Marie-Thérèse, later Marquise de Montespan, called Athénaïs, second* maîtresse-en-titre *to Louis XIV*
Louise de La Vallière—*Maid of honor to Henriette Anne, Duchesse d'Orléans, first* maîtresse-en-titre *to King Louis XIV*

UPON THE GOLDEN MEDAL

Our guard upon the royal side!
On the reverse our beauty's pride!
Here we discern the frown and smile,
The force and glory of our isle.
In the rich medal, both so like
Immortals stand, it seems antique;
Carved by some master, when the bold
Greeks made their Jove descend in gold,
And Danaë wond'ring at their shower,
Which falling, storm'd her brazen tower.
Britannia there, the fort in vain
Had batter'd been with golden rain;
Thunder itself had fail'd to pass;
Virtue's a stronger guard than brass.

—Edmund Waller

Girl on the Golden Coin

PROLOGUE

Richmond House, Whitehall Palace
London
July 1688

Fireworks from St. James's Park lit the night sky as I stood outside my home, Richmond House, the finest at Whitehall Palace, and waited for one of my oldest friends. He was the Earl of Clarendon now that his father, the old lord chancellor of England, had died in exile. But I would always remember my friend as simply Lord Cornbury, one of the gallants in my reigning circle when Whitehall belonged to the Merry Monarch.

I glanced down at my niece, Anne, as she sat on the portico, studying the Britannia side of a copper farthing. She knew it was my image on that coin. She knew why, too. Light crackled and rained overhead, and chatter from my guests, who'd come to celebrate the birth of a newborn prince, carried from my bay windows. Anne flipped the coin over to the king's profile. "Was it this exciting when King Charles the Second was restored to the throne?"

"You know I wasn't in England then."

"Tell me the story again."

I knelt beside her so my skirts draped into a silk puddle around me and recited the tale she'd come to cherish. "I was about your age, ten years. Exiled English Royalists filed into the great hall of the Queen Mother's French château to greet our king, who'd been forced to wander Europe since we'd lost the civil wars. I told my father I was hungry.

1

He studied me with the sharp eye natural to a royal physician and said in his Scottish brogue, 'Ye know there's nothin' to be had. But when the king is restored to 'is throne, it will change everythin' for us.'

"'What need have I for a king?' I'd asked.

"'You've Stuart blood in ye'r veins, lass. Ye'r fortune, if ye ever have any, will begin and end with the Stuart royals.'

"And when Charles the Second of England, Scotland, and Ireland filled the doorway, he was the tallest man I had ever seen. Behind me someone spoke, just loud enough for me to hear. 'Let us see if we can fool him.' A shove between my shoulders propelled me forward. 'Your Majesty, here is your sister, Henriette Anne!'

"The hall fell silent. King Charles appeared before me on one knee, lifting my chin to catch my eye. I should have dipped a deep curtsy to show reverence. It was a subject's duty. Everyone in the hall waited in silence to see if the king would fall for this little jest. Then he pulled me close and kissed me. Laughter. The room shook with it. The king glanced around, then back at me.

"*He knew.* The edges of my vision blackened. I had not curtsied. What punishment might he dole out for such disrespect? He stood and then . . . laughed. I forgot my hunger that day. For the first time, I hoped he got his kingdom back for his own sake, not only for mine. Three years later, he did." I stood at last, shaking out my silks and ending my story, though there was so much more to tell.

Anne sighed, content. "I want to have a life like yours. To become a duchess and provide for my family."

God, please let her path be nothing like mine. "One must be clever to marry a duke." She glared at me and I laughed. "I'm sure you will, someday."

Then my friend appeared, trudging through the Bowling Green looking more strained than I'd ever seen him. Almost. He presented his leg and bowed low. "Your Grace."

"You don't seem in a celebratory mood."

"Nor is London. Nobody believes King James really has a son. Rather, they don't want to believe it."

"They know this prince will be raised a Catholic, and they haven't the stomach for another Catholic rule."

"It's just as our late king predicted. Men are already stirring up talk." He hesitated, glanced at Anne.

"She's trustworthy. Go on."

"They want to depose King James. You'll have to choose a side. I know you disagree with his policies, but it's no small thing to side against a king." He paused as he registered my expression. All our years of intrigue in the glittering court at Whitehall seemed to pass between us. "Though, when it comes to the courage to reject a king, you've proven that *you* have it."

He was right in more ways than he could know. It *was* no small thing. Yet he only knew of *one* king I'd rejected.

CHAPTER 1

Palais Royal, Paris
March 1661

S ettle, Frances," my mother whispered over her shoulder. "Don't draw attention to yourself."

Henry Jermyn, Earl of St. Albans, who rarely deigned to look directly upon me, glanced in my general direction, seemingly displeased.

I was straining my eyes in the candlelight, searching the wedding guests in the gallery of the Palais Royal, seeking out one English duke in particular. Now I fell back on my heels and slouched. I had gotten a good look at the guests waiting for the royal couple to return from the chapel. The French nobles, in impeccable silks and jewels, politely averted their eyes from the chipped murals of our dilapidated palace walls. No jewel hung from my neck, only a blue silk ribbon. A gift from my older cousin Princess Henriette Anne, it was the prettiest thing I owned. Members of the exiled English court, like me, wore sensible clothes, repurposed with outdated lace. Although we weren't exiles anymore, now that King Charles had possession of his kingdom. Most of the members of our court had returned home—at least those who had something to return *to*. Our monarch had won his throne and restored place and power to as many Royalist families as he could, but my family had no prior claim on anything. My father was the third son of the first Lord Blantyre in Scotland. Third sons get nothing: no title, no estate, not even the right to be styled "Sir." A third son's eldest daughter gets even less, and when my father died two years ago, his death left me with less than less. My family was still in France with the Queen Mother because we had nowhere else to go.

At last I spotted the one powdered face that was neither French nor exile. George Villiers, second Duke of Buckingham, was King Charles's lifelong friend. *His* clothes were not repurposed. His brown woven-silk doublet and pantaloons, embroidered with scrolls of gold thread, glimmered in the candelabra's light. Favor with King Charles had gained him much with the Restoration: income rights, property, and court offices. He'd escorted Princess Henriette Anne back from her recent visit to England, and he'd gained popularity at the French court, too. After her wedding, he would return home to his wealth and his duchess. I had to talk to him. Tonight.

Buckingham glanced at me, as if he sensed my stare. I felt a blush creep up my cheeks. He muttered to the French ladies in his circle. Then he moved across the hall toward our threesome, scabbard flashing at his hip. He spoke directly to St. Albans. "I expect your court will follow me to England shortly, now that Princess Henriette Anne is married."

St. Albans shook his head. "The Queen Mother will delay her return."

"Parliament will never cough up her allowance while she's on French soil. If you expect her to pay you for your loyal service, you'll encourage her to sail soon."

St. Albans was the Queen Mother's lord chamberlain and the only courtier she kept in comfort. Though he wasn't as ostentatious as Buckingham, his black silk ensemble certainly wasn't shabby. "She's not one brought to heel easily."

I suppressed a smile. The Queen Mother was notoriously headstrong, thoroughly French, and supremely Catholic. England was the last place she wanted to go.

"She wishes to see Princess Henriette Anne settled into her marriage before she leaves," said my mother. "The prospect of leaving one's child is heart-wrenching, you know."

I tensed at her hint that *she* wouldn't want to part with *me*, either. Buckingham turned to me. "I believe this lovely creature is your child, Mrs. Stuart?"

My mother made no move to present me. "One of my children, Your Grace, yes."

I held my breath. She had to introduce me so I could talk to him.

St. Albans intervened. He gestured toward me and said, "Your Grace of Buckingham, may I present Frances Teresa Stuart, daughter of the late Honorable Walter Stuart." My mother looked stunned but joined him as he stepped aside. When my father died, St. Albans was the man my mother turned to as an advocate. She deferred decisions to him—apparently she believed him to be the most suited at court to protect a penniless widow and her three children related to the Stuart crown.

I dipped into an expert curtsy, just as I'd rehearsed.

"I've long wanted to meet you, Frances," Buckingham said. "Everyone praises you as the most beautiful girl at the Queen Mother's court."

I felt the blush creep up again. Then I wondered how much beauty might add to the value of my Stuart blood. "Thank you, Your Grace. Though our princess, Henriette Anne, is the prettiest." My mother relaxed, satisfied with my response. Buckingham had declared himself my cousin's *champion*. Everyone said he was devoted to her, even in love with her.

Buckingham grinned. "I have a secret for you, if St. Albans and Mrs. Stuart would excuse us."

Mother stepped in front of me. "What could you say to a girl near four-and-ten that you wouldn't say in front of her mother?"

Buckingham frowned, and St. Albans took her arm. "What Mrs. Stuart means is, remain in the hall while you talk to her eldest daughter."

My mother shot a furious glare at me, and I tried not to look too happy. She did not protest as St. Albans steered her away.

When I turned to Buckingham, he was grinning again.

I opened my mouth to speak, then closed it. What, exactly, was I going to say? *Do you know any unmarried English noblemen willing to wed me and so save me from my miserable life?* I shifted, toes pinched in my secondhand boots. "Tell me of England," I said instead.

"Have you never been?"

"No, I was born in Scotland. My family escaped the Civil War by joining the Queen Mother here in France when I was a babe. I know little of my homeland."

He shrugged. "The wars took their toll on her, and Oliver Crom-well's Puritan rule drained her spirit for a time. But King Charles is reviving her with all the enthusiasm of youth."

I knew all this, of course, but nodded my head trying to think of what else to say.

"Aren't you going to ask about the secret? Princess Henriette Anne is not the prettiest."

"Wh—I thought you declared yourself her *champion?*"

"That was before I met you."

Me? I couldn't respond.

"Surely you're used to people complimenting your beauty?"

"Well, no. I live within the Queen Mother's court . . . we are but a small household."

"The princess told me what a dear friend you are to her. Now that she is married to the French prince she shall have a court of her own, and you will have ample opportunity to meet gentlemen. They will fall at your feet."

This was my chance. "French girls are entitled to every official posi-tion, and my mother won't permit me to accompany her court. I must continue serving the Queen Mother."

His lips turned down in an exaggerated frown. "Oh, but how dull that will be."

I thought of my mother's scorn when I'd made that very complaint. "It is positively beyond dull, Your Grace."

"Think of the balls you'll miss." His expression seemed almost mocking now.

I hesitated, wondering if he was teasing me. "It is more than that. I am tired of being in captivity."

"Of course." He nodded. "But you can endure it a short while longer. Surely your mother has plans for you to marry soon?"

"She does not. She desires me to stay with her for several more years. She married young herself, you see."

"How unfair." He clicked his tongue. "You should be allowed to em-brace life, enjoy England's return to favor."

"Your Grace, I agree." I cleared my throat. "That brings me to a point I hoped to discuss with you this day." I was trying my hardest not to look embarrassed. "If you know a decent man from a noble English family, would you consider recommending me to him as a possible bride? I have no dowry, but I am a Stuart, and that must be worth something now."

"Forgive me." He bit his lip, suppressing a laugh. "Why leap from one captivity to another?"

"My other choice is to live in the Queen Mother's convent. Chaillot is no release at all."

He stepped closer. "There is another possibility you haven't considered." I leaned in, willing to hear his wisdom. "Come back to England with me. I'll make you my mistress."

I gasped so hard my head lurched back. He was more than twice my age. "Your Grace," I said as calmly as I could, "you must think I care nothing for honor and virtue. You insult me, and you do your wife no credit."

He leaned back on his heels, frowning sincerely this time. "I take that as a no."

"I'm not so foolish that I'd sell myself, sir!"

This time he didn't try to suppress his laugh. "You're sure you won't run away with me?"

I glanced around, looking for someone else to talk to, refusing to look at him.

"Perhaps I have a better offer. Frances, you know I am King Charles's most favored friend?"

I made no reply.

"He trusts my advice, and in some matters, I can speak for him. Your royal cousin has excellent taste in women and a . . . fondness for them."

I faced him again with astonishment. "You wouldn't dare suggest—"

He held up his hand. "I guarantee he will take you as his mistress at first sight. You could have a house of your own, jewels, silk gowns, money, horses, carriages. He might even grant you a title. And you'd escape from here." Buckingham grabbed my arm, enthusiastic. "I should have thought of it before. Your beauty, your poise, you are exactly what he'd want."

I shook my arm free, not believing a word. "No."

"Suit yourself. Stay in captivity with your mother and St. Albans. Your secretive little family."

The doors of the great hall opened, and everyone turned. A herald presented the newly wed couple, Monsieur Prince Philippe, duc d'Orléans and Princess Henriette Anne of England. They proceeded in, followed by the groom's brother, the French King Louis XIV and his queen, Marie-Thérèse of Spain. King Louis and Philippe's mother, Anne of Austria, entered next, followed by the English Queen Mother. The bride, my cousin, smiled and waved when she saw me. *She* was beautiful. She loved me, and now she must leave with her husband and I would be alone. I dipped to curtsy, slipping into misery, as Buckingham bowed beside me.

I caught my mother's eye. She watched me with a cold expression. The royal family took their places at the banquet table and signaled for us, the court, to be seated. "You hold rank," I said to Buckingham, barely moving my lips. "Command St. Albans and my mother to allow me to join court with the princess."

"Why? You will capture the heart of every man there—including the man the princess is in love with. You will unknowingly heap disaster upon your head."

How did he know whom the princess really loved? And what made him think I could attract men of such high status? I saw my mother marching toward us. "How hurt do you think the princess will be," I said quickly, "if she learns your affection for her is all pretend?"

He narrowed his eyes, registering my threat, then glanced at my mother fast approaching. "I will do it only on this account, that you repay me in one way: when disaster befalls you, you will ask me to introduce you to King Charles. No one but *me*."

I nodded just as my mother gripped my arm. She stared at Buckingham's back as he headed to his table. "He looks displeased. What did you do?"

I lifted my free arm in a helpless gesture. "Nothing, Mother. We were only talking."

"I could see you were talking." She moved us gracefully to our seats.

Even with a bear's-jaw grip on my arm, my mother's steps were light and elegant. "You should never talk with someone so highly ranked. You could embarrass us all."

Ranked. My cousin's marriage now ranked her the second-highest woman in France. Permission to stay with her would bring freedom enough. We sat at our assigned table, but I was lost in thought. *She can help me find a suitable husband, and a French marriage is as good as an English one . . .*

"Frances, sit up." Mother jabbed me with her elbow.

But I was already sitting perfectly straight. I tried not to watch Buckingham and St. Albans as they conversed at the high-ranking English table and glanced at me from time to time. *Oh, please let him keep his word.*

Tradition dictated that the royal couple be escorted from their wedding banquet to bed by their families, Catholic officials, and the most important wedding guests. I was not included in this group; instead I was sent to my family's tiny chamber.

"Tell me of the bride," said my sister, Sophia, pulling our quilt up to her shoulders.

"A beautiful flower." I kissed her good night. "She must be the happiest girl in the world."

"Frances, you won't wed, right?" said my little brother, reaching for me. "You won't leave us, will you?"

"Shhh," I soothed, mussing his hair. He was the youngest, they were both under ten years, and I could hardly bear the thought of being without them. "You know I'll always love you both. Now climb up, time for sleep." He crawled into the bed he still shared with our sister and curled up, yawning, and I drew the bed curtains.

Mother returned hours later.

"How was the princess?" I asked anxiously as I unlaced her bodice.

"We did not see the couple to bed. She had her monthly flux and felt unwell. Monsieur went home to the Palais des Tuileries without her." She eyed me suspiciously. "I don't want you talking to the Duke of Buckingham again."

"I said nothing to embarrass us, I promise."

"It isn't that. He—the Villiers family—I fear they think they have the right to take you from me. To use you in some way. They aren't . . . honorable."

I was stunned. "Why? Why would they think they have such a right?"

She turned away, stepped out of her petticoat and smoothed the front of her linen chemise. "Just stay away from him."

I sat on our old wooden chest. Battered and worn, it was one of the only items of furniture my family owned. Every bed we slept on, every table we ate upon, belonged to the Queen Mother or the French royal family who housed us. Mother once told me that this chest had belonged to her family. It was a vivid memory because it was the only thing she'd ever told me about them. I traced the little scrolling *V* adorning the front.

"Mother, are you a Villiers?" I pointed to the initial.

"That initial isn't mine. Don't ask personal questions."

This was the cage that closed me in. I was told nothing, allowed to ask nothing, and expected to achieve nothing with my life. If my mother were a Villliers, why wouldn't she tell me? "Well, I'm a Stuart." I stood. "I'll talk to whomever I please, for they've no rights to me at all."

"Stop acting so foolhardy. The chest isn't from my family. It—it's from your father's."

"Wouldn't my father have an *S* painted on the chest?" I countered brashly. Then it slowly sank in. "You mean my father wasn't . . ."

"Stop pushing, Frances. It will only humiliate us both." She stepped into her bed and let the curtain fall upon my shock.

CHAPTER 2

He is unable to resist the temptation of showing himself in clothing which, by displaying all of his graces, makes him appear one of the prettiest people at court.

—DUCHESSE DE MONTPENSIER,
describing the younger brother of King Louis XIV

Two nights later the princess summoned me to stay the night in her chamber. I crept over the freshly beaten carpets to her bed. "What's the matter?"

"Ma cousine," she said in French, the only language this English princess knew after a lifetime of exile. She reached for my hand. Puffy blond curls framed her rosy face, but I could see she'd been crying, and I crawled under the coverlet with her. "My flux has ended. I can't bring myself to go to Monsieur. I can't do it."

"You must stop pining for King Louis. You knew you would marry his brother."

"King Louis might have chosen *me* as his queen if my brother had been restored one year earlier." She wiped her eyes. "He might have chosen me if I were pretty like you."

"Nonsense." The princess was generous. She'd taught me how to dance, how to ride, and every stitch of my clothing had once belonged to her. But this was a subject about which I'd learned my place. "Only a man in a blindfold would think me beautiful."

"Men were blind to me until my brother's Parliament granted my dowry."

"Blindness enhances a man's other senses." I poked her ribs. "They can smell money."

She giggled, then fell quiet. "My new husband has an affinity for men."

"What do you mean?"

"He beds them. His mother encouraged his effeminate ways so he wouldn't be inclined to usurp his brother as he grew older. You remember the Fronde wars, when the people tried to limit the French king's power? If Monsieur were to join forces with the noble frondeurs, France would have more civil war. So he is not man enough to be a king. But is he man enough to be a husband?"

I was shocked. I'd never heard of such a thing. "You should talk to Father Cyprien, he would know whether this is acceptable." The Queen Mother's old priest had been our confessor and tutor for as long as I could remember.

"He's the one who warned me. He called it the Italian vice, and of course it's not acceptable. The priests know, the court knows, my mother knows, and they ignore it. He advised me to ignore it, too." She looked at me sheepishly. "By any chance, do you have your monthly flux?"

How could Father Cyprien know *and* accept it? "I'm sorry, not right now."

She held up her arm and rubbed her wrist. "I thought about cutting myself enough to put it off one more night—"

"No!" I grabbed her arms and pulled her close. I would have cut myself for her if I'd had the courage. *My blood. Which may not be Stuart blood after all.*

The Queen Mother entered her daughter's chambers without the courtesy of an announcement early the following morning. I scrambled out of bed and curtsied. She frowned at me. "Your mother has changed her mind. You will go with my daughter."

Buckingham kept his word! I laughed aloud, then quickly lowered my head. "Excuse me, Your Majesty."

She turned to her daughter, still abed. She whipped the coverlets back and yanked my cousin's chemise up. "Not a bloodstain in sight. Monsieur will come before supper and take you to the Tuileries." The Queen Mother touched the crystal on her bracelet, which contained a lock of her late husband's hair. The White King. The Stuart Martyr. The father who'd only held his infant daughter once before his execution. "Your father would be ashamed at how you shirk your duties."

My cousin covered herself and remained silent.

"Remember how important your union to the French royal family is to your brother the king. You can be useful to us only by being above reproach in this marriage." She turned to me. "You have always been a good child, Frances. Remember all I've taught you and remind my daughter of her duties when she forgets."

I wondered why she used the word "when," but nodded. "I promise."

The Queen Mother pulled her prayer book from the folds of her skirt and turned, pacing slowly toward the door. "You must always retire early and rise early. You must not speak too freely with any man. You must report useful information to me. You must seek my counsel before making any major decision. You must devote your free time to prayer. And above all . . ."

Henriette Anne and I shot each other a look and mouthed the next words as her mother spoke them. ". . . you must never drink too much wine in the presence of men."

Henriette Anne's voice was honey. "Your instruction will guide me every moment," she called to her mother's departing back. She reached to me, and I clasped her hand. "Go, see to your things now, Frances, for tonight we shall have our supper at the Tuileries."

As I left, the Queen Mother's maids bustled in to prepare the princess for departure.

I fetched morning bread from the kitchens and broke it with my family. We spent the day playing marbles, sewing, and packing the old wooden chest with my few dresses. It seemed to mock me. *You're not who you thought you were.* Mother didn't look at it, and she didn't speak much, beyond murmuring over her rosary. She had shattered my heritage. Would she ever tell me of her family? Did she miss them? Would she miss me when I left?

When the time came, Sophia embraced me. "The maids say Monsieur plans to spend winter here," she said with hope. "We shall see you again soon."

I hated to release her, but our mother would never carve a place for us outside of the Queen Mother's service. If she or my brother were to have a better life, I would have to make it for them. Walter was upset. I squatted down to memorize his boyish face framed with red curly hair. "I'll still be in Paris, only one palace away."

My sister sighed. "If only I could go with you." She studied me with big blue eyes, the only feature we shared. With her plain features and no dowry, she would need my help to secure a good marriage.

"Go now. I shall see you downstairs." I watched her leave, Walter at her side, and turned to Mother. "Thank you for allowing me to go."

"I . . . no choice was left to me." She took one step toward me, and then studied my face for a long moment. "At all times remember: gossip always follows disgrace. We exist at court by the charity of Lord St. Albans and the Queen Mother. This will end if you force secrets into the open. Secrets about me. You must, *must* behave above reproach."

I nodded, confused. I could not reveal secrets I did not know! I lifted my arms to embrace her, but she dropped her rosary, and I caught the cold beads in my hands. The next moment she pulled the chamber door open and gestured for me to exit.

Princess Henriette Anne stood in the gallery holding her black velvet cloak. *"Bon,"* she said. "We can go down together."

My mother stepped from behind me. "Princess." She curtsied, then handed me a black wool cloak, frayed and worn. I placed it around my shoulders and tied its strings at my neck.

"It is Madame," said the princess.

"Pardon?" asked my mother.

Henriette Anne shot her a haughty stare. "Now that I am married to the prince, you must style me simply 'Madame.' It is my new title. An honorific."

Her tone surprised me. She had never spoken to my mother in such a way.

Mother lowered her head and curtsied like a practiced courtier. "Of course, Madame." When she rose, her face was polished marble. "Shall I go down to wait with the others for your farewell?"

Madame nodded.

Without looking at me, my mother slipped away.

"The one good thing about my marriage is power," Madame said, as she held her cloak out to me. I wrapped the garment around her shoulders and tied the thick silk ribbon at her neck. "My brother Charles lives as he pleases. Surely I can garner the freedom of my marriage and still capture King Louis' heart."

I tried to keep my tone light. "Your mother would beat you if you did."

"It's her own fault that I love my husband's brother. All my life she campaigned to form a betrothal between the king and me." She slumped. "Having that crown would have changed my life. It would have put me over my mother once and for all."

"This marriage does put you over your mother. It makes you the second-highest-ranking woman in France."

"She was a queen of England. Nothing is the same as being a queen."

Oblivious to my worry, she scanned the gallery, and I, too, gazed at the high walls, broken and bare. They still bore hack marks where sconces and carvings were once attached. I remembered waking one cold night to the shouts of frondeurs rioting in the Paris streets. I'd peeked out of my chambers to see two Royalists tear down an oil portrait framed in silver gilt. They lit a roaring fire in the hearth the next day and served a hearty stew: both were rare treats. I shivered and pulled my cloak tighter around me. "We can leave these cold memories behind."

She turned toward the stairs. "We need never be cold again."

Hand in hand, we descended the staircase to the hall, black cloaks slipping down gently from step to step in our wake. Madame made a great show of appropriate farewell tears at the threshold. There was weeping and clinging and kissing until Monsieur swept her away, ushering us into his massive white coach.

I sank into plush velvet in the far corner as Madame perched beside me. When Monsieur fell into the seat across from us, the crystal sconces clinked and chimed. He raised his jeweled fist to thump the wall and his flowery perfume filled the space. *"Allez!"* he cried.

The coach jolted forward. When I craned my neck for one final look at the palace, at my childhood of little happiness, I realized I could not see out.

Madame did not even try.

CHAPTER 3

Palais des Tuileries, Paris
End of April

I was the picture of *négligence*. Wrapped in a *robe de chambre* of mantua silk and propped upon a tufted bench, I had one servant rubbing almond oil into my toenails while another dotted rose water on my shoulders. It was nearly noon, and fruit tarts and dismantled pastry pyramids on silver platters were scattered about the floor. I soaked in the glow of the hearth's crackling fire, which Madame insisted on burning despite the warming spring season. I brought a dish made of porcelain, a delicate ceramic from faraway China, to my lips and sipped the costliest commodity in the chamber.

"Is that tea?" asked Françoise-Athénaïs de Mortemart, one of Queen Marie-Thérèse's maids of honor, visiting from Fontainebleau. She was one of many nobles who'd traveled to the Tuileries to pay her respects to the newly wed Monsieur and Madame. She sat up from her giant pillow on the floor and accepted the dish a servant handed her. "Thank God."

Louise de La Vallière, Madame's maid of honor, lifted her head from the rumpled coverlets of Madame's bed where she'd fallen back asleep after eating. "You drank too much wine last night."

"You should talk," retorted Mortemart, pushing wheat-colored curls away from her face. "You were so drunk the Comte de Guiche never left your side. I do believe he was trying to get up your skirts."

La Vallière stumbled out of bed. "I only spent so much time with him because Madame *asked* me to." She plucked a leftover sweetmeat from a platter near Mortemart. "She was too busy entertaining the other guests." She stuffed the bite into her mouth. "Madame bats her lashes at every lord and noble; you'd think she was trying to make the whole world fall in love with her."

Madame, sitting quietly at her toilette table while her maid applied cosmetics, laughed. "I don't need the whole world to love me. Just one man."

"*L'amour.*" La Vallière's dreamy smile matched the look in her eyes. "I hope to have true love when I marry."

But Madame didn't mean her new husband. I waved my attendants away.

Mortemart snorted. "You don't marry for love, stupid. You marry for money."

Mortemart was twenty-one years of age, from a French noble family nearly a thousand years old, and a member of a fashionable Parisian *ruelle*, a salon for intellectual women. She was so witty, so well informed with ballroom gossip, and had such a distinguished heritage, she expected us to hang on her every word. She'd abandoned the name Françoise and insisted her friends call her Athénaïs. She did not insist *I* call her this, which didn't bother me at all.

The cosmetics maid finished and Madame stood. Her mantua gown of pale green silk hung low on her shoulders and cascaded to the floor. A series of emeralds clasped it together at her chest, and her linen chemise peeked through, sweeping down to the tops of her slippers. "A woman can also gain freedom in marriage if she can rule her husband." She shot me a glance. "If she can rule him, she can find love with whomever else she pleases."

La Vallière made choking sounds. Mortemart slapped her on the back.

"Madame!" I said. "If your mother heard you—"

"What?" She waved her hand around the room to encompass the dozen dress forms, mounds of fabrics, stacks of shoes, piles of black face patches, feathers, and ribbons. "I couldn't have gotten us all this unless I knew how to rule him."

"She meant the part about having a lover." La Vallière plopped down on a pillow, white-blond hair fluttering on the breeze she made. She, too, was from an important French family. But with a deformed leg and a provincial upbringing, she had an unassuming air. She was most comfortable at mass or on horseback, praying or hunting. "Marriage or no, I shall have love in *my* life."

Given her limp and the lack of money in her family, she had about as much chance of marrying well as I.

"I don't know about love, but Madame is right," said Mortemart, not to be outdone. She held her tea dish above her head for the servant to collect. "If you can rule your husband, you can do any scandalous thing you want in this world."

I stood, wrapping my rich gown around me with the sash. "You said *if* you can rule. If you can't, a jealous husband will make you miserable."

Mortemart only smiled, reflecting the confident and careless demeanor of the entire French court. She pulled La Vallière to the toilette to brush her hair.

Madame moved to me, emeralds winking. "Do you want to know the real reason I wanted La Vallière to distract Guiche? Because my husband is attracted to him."

I glanced at the other girls, the servants. Father Cyprien foraged for gossip whenever he visited the Tuileries, and he'd certainly carry it home to our mothers. "Hush. They'll hear you."

"They will see it for themselves soon enough. And they will accept it as a matter of course," she whispered. "Guiche likes me. I have to keep him away from me to prevent my husband from growing jealous. Thus have I learned to rule my husband." She crossed the chamber and called through the door. "Send in the seamstresses!"

A train of women streamed in with pincushions, boxes, tapes, and ribbons. Everyone scrambled to pull out unfinished garments. Swirls of silk and the snip-snip of scissors filled the chamber. Box lids landed on the floor and the smell of fabric mixed with perfume-scented leather gloves blossomed. My favorite seamstress handed me a box and draped my latest bodice around a dress form. "Choose the *passementerie* for this."

I took the box and balanced it on the edge of the bench. Grosgrain ribbon spilled out when I opened it. I rummaged through a rainbow of bobbin and needle lace, gimp, eyelets, glass beads, tassels, and spangles. Finally, cream parchment lace wrapped itself around my fingers, and I handed it to the seamstress. I'd sent baskets of trinkets and cloth home with Father Cyprien for my family, but today's gown was just for me, fashioned after the important ladies flocking to pay court to Monsieur and Madame. "Cut open panes in the front of each sleeve, and cover the panels with this. Then apply it along the front boning of the bodice busk here." I traced the deep V where it came to a point below the waistline.

She shook folds from the petticoat, making a pretty whip-snap sound with the fabric, and waited with an expectant, ready-to-please smile.

I leaned down. "And some down the front and along the hem." Yet the cream tissue fabric, silk woven with silver metal threads to give it a moiré effect, seemed to call out for more. I tapped my lip. "Add a darker overskirt that I can pull back to reveal the lace-covered petticoat."

"Frances!"

I spun around just as Madame tossed a pantofle to me. I caught the flat slipper and inspected it. The light brown velvet covered in silver embroidery was a perfect match. "But I want higher heels. Can I order it as a mule?"

She nodded. "Now catch this!" She hurled two great handfuls of silver ribbon into the air.

Everyone squealed. I twirled around, laughing as the shimmering trim streamed down around me. I let Madame's confidence envelop me. She made everything fun. A herald cleared his throat and called from the door. "Son of France, Monsieur Philippe, Duc d'Orléans."

The chamber echoed with more squeals. Mortemart dove behind a screen and knocked over a box of feathers just as La Vallière whipped a gown over her half-finished bodice. Feathers fluttered across Monseiur's entrance.

"*Merveilleux!*" He planted his hands on his hips and smiled broadly at our tableau of fashion misrule.

The Chevalier de Lorraine and the Comte de Guiche entered behind him. Lorraine went directly to Madame's toilette and poked around for her ceruse pot, while Guiche leaned against the wall, studying Madame.

Monsieur's ensemble, more embellished than any gown, filled me with envy. The full sleeves of his blue figured-silk doublet were slit with long, thin panes. A shoulder sash with gold fringe held his sword at his back. I longed for garments as unrestrictive as his pantaloons. As he pranced around the chamber inspecting everyone's creations, he grinned and giggled. When he reached me, I noticed the fine texture of expensive cosmetics on his face. I wondered that a man, free to do whatever he pleased in this world, wanted nothing more than to dress and act like a woman. If clothes could truly change our place in life, I'd gladly trade my skirts.

"*Bon.*" He plucked up my cream parchment lace. "You should add this to the tip of each bodice tab around the waist."

"Your Grace, those tabs go under the skirt to make it flare out. No one will see the lace there."

"Oh, someone shall see it." He waggled his polished fingertips up in the air by his ear. A knot of ribbon loop *galants* around his shirtsleeve rustled. "Someday."

When he reached Madame, he twirled her around and kissed her cheeks. "It worked," he said to her, eyes twinkling. "Word of our dazzling entertainments has reached my brother. He summoned us to Fontainebleau for the summer."

Madame clapped her hands. "See! Our efforts give fruit. He knows you were wiser than he in choice of wife. He will realize you are far more fashionable, too."

"I'll rise to favor for certain." He practically skipped to the door. "Prepare for departure and spare no expense. None. I want him to see how spectacular we are."

When the door closed behind the men, Madame shot me a smug grin. "Thus do I rule."

I cringed. Her first days with her new husband had been a fête of tears. Monsieur was indeed man enough to be a husband, just not a very gentle one. I'd stroked her hair after their first night together, trying to be the comfort she'd so often been for me. Now she seemed so sophisticated I hardly understood her. She'd just steered her husband's weakness to her advantage.

"Don't look so worried. Every important French family will come to Fontainebleau this summer. We shall find a young man just for you." She eyed me. "Have you considered the Chevalier de Lorraine as a possible husband?"

Lorraine, with his mincing and his layers of point lace, who had just openly hunted for her ceruse pot! "I can't be involved in a scandal . . ."

She laughed and dropped something into my hands. "Order a mantua gown of light blue silk to match your lovely eyes." She kissed my cheek.

I peered down at six sapphire clasps set in gold. "These are beautiful. I can fasten mine just like yours."

"I want you to be happy. Just like me."

"I shall try." I kissed her back. Her words "just like me" unfurled in my mind. She was only happy in her pursuit of King Louis. How could my oldest friend think a reckless affair or an effeminate man would make me happy? But if she could steer people so deftly, couldn't I?

Before the month was out, plumed horses drove Madame's gilded carriage from Paris while Monsieur rode alongside on a white stallion. Drummers and heralds carrying the Orléans standard led the long train of coaches and carts, and peasants ran to the road, waving and scrambling for the coins Madame tossed from her window. The grounds and forests of Fontainebleau soon opened to us, green and glimmering, and we rolled through the gates into a fairyland palace.

King Louis and Queen Marie-Thérèse greeted Monsieur and Madame on the massive curving staircase, and then hosted an outdoor banquet in the Cour Ovale, where everyone was formally introduced to the monarch, and the households were introduced to one another.

Everywhere were women in voluminous satin sleeves and men with jeweled scabbards. Each young man, I noted with dismay, was already married or flounced about Monsieur too eagerly, feeding him cake or complimenting his clothes. The violinist Lully played for hours, lively and deep, even after we dined, and the two households replenished wineglasses as the stars came out. Ladies and lords broke into dance, maidens and gallants slipped into alcoves, and the fête went on still.

Queen Marie-Thérèse finally retired, and Monsieur departed with Armand, Comte de Guiche. Many noticed, whispered, and pointed. La Vallière leaned to me and muttered, "I fear we will not escape this summer without a scandal." As Madame and her brother-in-law, King Louis, fell into close conversation, I knew in my heart La Vallière was right.

W ake up! Madame ordered us to ready ourselves for a walk in the forest." La Vallière gestured for her maid to come in to my alcove, which was connected to Madame's bedchamber, to help. We had been at Fontainebleau for several weeks. "Why aren't you dressed yet?"

I threw back my coverlet, raced to my wooden chest, and opened it quickly. So empty when I'd left Palais Royal, it now sat full of shimmering splendors. I tossed the cream tissue bodice at the maid and stepped into the petticoat and skirts. "Madame usually opens our door herself to wake me."

"She couldn't be bothered today. She's been up since dawn talking to King Louis."

I poked my arms through the bodice, pulled it over my chemise, and turned for the maid to lace my back. Night after night, it was always the same. "What time did they retire last night?"

The maid knelt on the floor behind me to work my laces with quick fingers. La Vallière climbed on the chest and tugged an ivory comb through my hair. "After you went to bed, they ordered more wine, one bottle after the next. They called for dancing music well past midnight, but I had to sleep. I just can't stay up all night as they do. I hear," La Vallière whispered while twisting my hair into a knot, "she likes King Louis."

The maid gave my laces a final yank. La Vallière jumped down and wrapped lace trim around my bodice so it fell like a gauzy scarf from my shoulders. She pinned it together at my breasts with one of my sapphire clasps. "People are saying King Louis likes *her*. Can you believe it?" She sounded jealous.

The maid handed me a glass of wine and water. I gulped it down, then turned around to dig shoes out of the chest. How long did I have before word of King Louis and Madame reached the Queen Mother?

"You cannot wear high heels," La Vallière said when she saw my silver-embroidered mules. "In the woods? Put on your boots."

"No," I said firmly as I tossed the mules on the floor and slipped my feet in. "My boots are old. They pinch."

"So. Endure it."

"I will *never* wear those ugly boots again."

We raced down the curvy horseshoe staircase leading to the lawn where Madame and King Louis waited. A warm breeze lifted my skirt hem and carried the fresh scents of a new season. King Louis stood on the lawn while an array of pomp rotated around him. Footmen and musketeers and servants scampered, waiting or working, while his ministers vied for position. He had an angular nose and hawkish eyes, but what I felt made him attractive was his knowing look, his air of authority. Today a *justaucorps à brevet* hugged his frame. This blue silk coat, lined in red, was covered in gold embroidery. Only the French royal family and favorites could wear one. Diamond-encrusted buttons down its front dazzled in the spring sun.

Madame hung on his arm and batted her eyelashes as if he were simply too bright to behold. King Louis suddenly waved and men bowed, backing away. The pair set off for the woods together with only us ladies, known as Madame's flower garden, following in attendance.

I touched the back of my neck as we walked, rubbing out the anxiety I felt while watching them together. "What do you think they're talking about?"

La Vallière shrugged. "He's allowing her to arrange all the summer entertainments at Fontainebleau. Apparently pregnancy makes his wife too dull for anything but laziness. Perhaps they are discussing the ballet she's planning. Let's hope she orders us to rehearsals right away so she is distracted from her pursuit of the king."

I envisioned a summer-long rehearsal of Madame's downfall. And mine. We entered a glade of towering beech trees, and the train separated, trailing down different paths. Sunlight streamed through the budding coppices to dapple the mossy floor in patterns when a breeze swayed the branches. Little shoots peeked from the ground, the first happy colors of spring. It was a magical forest. Yet I was not enchanted wandering its trails. The Queen Mother had made me promise to warn Madame of her duties when she forgot. What was I to do if she refused to listen?

"Look." La Vallière pointed to a long-eared hare in the path a few paces ahead.

The hare studied us for a brief moment, then hopped away. We followed, but it rounded a corner at the end of the trail where Madame and King Louis stood in the center of a small clearing. Embracing.

La Vallière looked away and whispered, "Oh."

"Act nonchalant." I turned away, too. What if someone were to see them together? I wanted both to slap my cousin and shield her from prying eyes. "Pretend we're talking."

"We are talking."

"Right." I ignored the panic in my chest. "They're courting disaster."

"They're royalty." She sighed. "I suppose they do as they please. Do you hear that sound?"

"What?" I paused. "That little chirping noise?" I glanced around. At the base of an old oak tree, a baby bird sat perfectly still in a thatch of damp leaves. It opened its wide beak and chirped again. I knelt to pick it up.

"Get up," La Vallière hissed, horrified. "The dirt. You'll ruin your skirts."

"Look, here's the nest. Help me."

"Quiet. They'll hear you. And leave that thing alone. Have you no sense?"

"More than you'd guess." I raised my voice. "I'm going to get this little bird back in its tree if you help me or not."

"It won't do any good," said King Louis.

Aha! I stood with the nest in my hand as he and Madame came closer. I couldn't suppress a victorious smile even though my cheeks were burning.

"You can't reach up there." He pointed to the high branches. "Even if you could, the mother won't return to care for it. You've touched the nest." He dropped Madame's arm and joined me, peering at the tiny thing. "It's a regular sort of bird. Why not leave it to nature?"

I glanced to Madame, then back to the king. I wondered, fleetingly, how irritated Madame was that I'd interrupted them. "It deserves a chance."

King Louis' face softened. "I suppose we've all been given chances at one time or another. You're Frances Stuart?" I managed a nod. "You seem keen to bestow opportunity."

I cleared my throat and hoped I didn't sound childish. "It would be wrong to be selfish." He looked puzzled. "What I mean is, God has blessed me. Through Madame. Her generosity rescued me. If God's smallest creature here needs aid, who am I to withhold it?"

King Louis studied my face for a long moment. "A loyal friend is a rare prize."

Madame cleared her throat. "So. What of the bird?"

King Louis and I looked at the twigs in my hand. Without speaking, we both knelt. The king scooted the bird along the ground and I scooped it gently into the nest. King Louis called out, and a page, hitherto hidden from view, trotted to us. "Take this creature to the falconer. We expect to see the little thing healthy and flying by summer's end."

Two weeks later I led a horse to the opening of the park and pointed at an elderly groom napping on a nearby bench. La Vallière giggled wildly and shook her head. We had concocted a game. I indicated five noblemen during the course of each day. She explained who they were, and if all were married, I had to curl her hair into *confidants* around her ears the next morning. If just one of them were unmarried, she would give me a silver button and introduce us. Now at the end of May, my fingers had curling-rod burns, I hadn't a single silver button, and I'd given up searching for an unmarried nobleman in an attempt to find *any* unmarried man. I shrugged with a grin, and La Vallière mounted her horse.

"Mademoiselle Stuart, I need your help."

I turned to see Father Cyprien approaching from the stables. "Father, I was hoping to see you." I pulled a letter to my mother from my hanging pocket. "Is something wrong?"

"King Charles has chosen Catherine of Bragança, the Portuguese infanta, as his bride. The Queen Mother directed me to retrieve his last letter to Madame for more information, but she has refused to see me." He wrung his smooth white hands. "Do you know where Madame keeps such things?"

I thought of the treasured letter, hidden under Madame's pillow for safekeeping. I shook my head instead of lying aloud.

"It's worse each visit. Madame hardly says anything in confession and flies off to King Louis' side. She hasn't written, she is neglecting her mother."

I thought of the Queen Mother's letters, piled upon Madame's writing table unopened. "Fontainebleau is very busy."

He frowned, took my letter and inspected it. "No basket of goods today? You mustn't neglect your own mother. If you only knew what that poor woman has been through."

My breath caught. Might he know about my mother's past? Why had I not considered this before? I tried to think of a way to ask him about my true father, but Madame emerged from the stables before I could speak.

"Do leave her alone, Father Cyprien." She yanked on riding gloves, glaring at him. "Frances is a perfect daughter." An equerry bent, took her foot into his cupped hands, and lifted until she landed gracefully in her saddle.

Father Cyprien reached for her as the equerry lifted me onto my horse. "Anne of Austria has complained about the time you spend with King Louis. Your mother implores you to focus on getting your husband's heir."

She heeled her horse and called over her shoulder, "Tell her not to fret. The French royals need me for my connection with England, remember?"

We raced into the park, our skirts whipping behind us. Madame laughed and laughed, and I wished I could be so carefree. "Let's ride hard," she called to me and the other ladies. "I want to get back to the palace in time to sit with King Louis at tonight's ballet."

CHAPTER 4

The Duc de Saint-Aignan's Open Air Ball Fontainebleau

Mid-June

S ir, I must insist you release your hold of my backside." I reached around with my folded fan and smacked Philibert, Chevalier de Gramont's hand.

A Frenchman of noble blood, neither married nor betrothed, he yanked his hand away and pressed his shoulder against mine instead. "People say you have the finest *taille* in Madame's court. How can I judge if they are correct?"

I brought my fan up to my face and snapped it open, painted side out, to put a barrier between my nose and the heavy garlic on his breath. I gave him a coquettish look, one I had often seen my cousin deploy, over its laced edge. "With your eyes, monsieur. Same as every-one else."

He put his hand over his heart. "Am I just another hopeful lover spurned by the lovely Frances?"

"Spurned, nothing." I laughed. "I welcome your company."

"If only you'd welcome me to your bed."

A loud explosion followed by a screeching whistle erupted nearby, and we both jumped. Sparkling streams of color lit the sky. We re-laxed. It was only fireworks, lit in honor of Queen Marie-Thérèse's pregnancy. Gramont thrust his wineglass, full of Bordeaux, into my other hand. He circled my waist and pulled me behind a torch so we no longer faced the outdoor dancing floor where courtiers twirled and stepped. He traced my collarbone, pressed against me.

The strength of his grip alarmed me. "There are people nearby."

"No harm in a little love play." He put his nose on my cheek.

I turned my face aside to keep from smelling him and told myself that, though Gramont was near forty years of age, he was still quite handsome. "What if I prefer a different sort of love?" I asked, clinging to the wineglass. "The sort that would lead to marriage."

He ground his pelvis into me, groaning as his hardness rubbed between the pleats of my skirt and against my hip. "Why would one invest in marriage when the pleasure of love is free?" His words came out on a heated, foul breath. "Come to bed with me."

It caught in my throat. "I cannot play at love."

He reached past the top of my bodice and squeezed my décolletage. "Mademoiselle, you *are* playing at love."

I jerked away from his paw.

He pressed himself hard against me again. "You can't walk away after teasing me thus."

"I certainly can!"

His breath came short and heavy, his eyes heated. But he saw my determination and, to my relief, gave me a crooked smile. With one final grind, he released my hips. He downed the remainder of his Bordeaux as he reached to the front of his pantaloons to adjust himself.

Catching my fan back up, I snapped it open to cover the red marks on my skin.

"Gramont!" King Louis broke from a band of tipsy courtiers. Among them was Madame, looking slightly shocked and bleary-eyed. When the king reached Gramont, he muttered, "Don't touch her again." Then he turned to me, searching my face with an odd expression. His hushed tone was firm as he whispered in my ear. "You will reserve your kisses only for me. Do you understand?"

Gramont's eyes widened; he had heard.

King Louis turned sharp on his heel and jovially addressed the party. "They will join us for a gondola ride!"

The chevalier pulled me by the arm, dragging me along the grass in the procession of drunken nobles going for a ride to nowhere in the canal at midnight. I pressed my hand against my head. "I want to go up to bed."

Gramont snorted. "I'd love to, mademoiselle, but the king made himself perfectly clear. I had no idea you were spoken for."

"Nonsense," I hissed. "I am *not* spoken for. I have no idea of the king's meaning—"

"The king made it clear he wants you as a mistress. I will not impose on you again."

"Please do not say such a thing."

"What? That I will refrain from imposing on you?"

"Do not speak of the king and me in such a way." I shot him a nasty glare. "It would break Madame's heart if the king kissed me." I clamped a hand over my mouth.

"Indeed?" Gramont eyed Madame as King Louis handed her into the gondola.

"Please do not repeat what I just said."

"A word of advice. If you intend to rebuff the king, you had better forge some self-restraint." My face burned as he handed me over the canal's edge into a gondola seat near Madame. Then he promptly seated himself beside La Vallière and began flirting.

Madame draped her arm around my shoulder. "Congratulations, the Chevalier de Gramont is very a handsome man. And I hear he is an accomplished lover." She giggled, wine heavy on her breath. "Though he lives off his gambling winnings and will certainly require a dowry should he ever wed." She studied me for any reaction. "And you haven't any dowry, of course. Be more discreet if you do become his mistress. He tells the most awful stories about people."

I propped my elbows on my lap and dumped my head into my hands.

"Speaking of secrets," she went on. "Something's going to happen tonight." She cupped her hand around my ear to whisper. "The king is coming to my chamber."

I sat up, glaring.

She closed her eyes. "Don't look that way and don't try to stop me."

"Monsieur is just a chamber away. You have a duty to your mother, to your brother the king—"

"Monsieur sleeps . . . elsewhere. And you will be there to ensure no one finds out." I stared dumbly. "He's coming through the servants' passage. That means he'll pass through your little chamber. My other doors lock from the inside. You shall guard yours and proclaim I am ill if anyone tries to enter."

I turned away.

"What are you going to do? Tell Monsieur and ruin both our lives? Tell my mother? You won't because you know she'd come spend the summer here to watch me and bring your mother, too. If you don't want anyone to discover us, you're going to guard that door."

Three hours later, I paced my tiny alcove, still dressed. She'd roomed me here on purpose. She'd planned this tryst all along. And there was nothing I could do to stop her.

If he found me up, still dressed, would he think I'd been waiting for him? I crossed to the narrow bed alcove, slipped in through the curtain, and lay down.

Even worse.

I scrambled to a sitting position, opened the bed curtain, and sat on the edge with my feet on the floor.

Too inviting.

I started pacing again. *Why am I so nervous?* Was I afraid they would get caught? Was I afraid King Louis might try to kiss me? If Madame found out what King Louis had said to me . . . A soft creak at the door shattered the stillness. King Louis stepped in, still wearing his day clothes. I curtsied.

"I hoped you would be awake."

"I—I think I wanted to talk to you."

His face softened to an open, unguarded expression. "Truly?"

I whispered very low, hoping Madame would not hear. "I wish you would not do this. Think of the consequences."

"I am the King of France," he said. "I determine consequence."

"I fear it will turn out badly."

He stepped closer. "Could it be something else?" He leaned in so close I could see each fine hair of his soft mustache. I realized I was staring at his lips and quickly looked at his eyes.

"Yes," I blurted. "There is something else. I—I hope to marry soon and, if there is a scandal involving my name, I fear my prospects will diminish."

He studied my face. "Yet you kissed Gramont in front of the court."

"It was the wine. Poor judgment."

"Would this be poor judgment?" He touched his lips to mine. I felt his hand on my shoulder, and for a moment I became lost, let myself flow into him. I ached to feel his touch against more of me. It startled me. I stepped back. "How could you do this?" I asked. "I thought you cared for Madame."

"I do. But I have to," he said. "I need her to ally with England."

"Hearing that would devastate her." His indifference astonished me.

"So don't tell her. Her infatuation will burn out soon." Then he opened the door and slipped through. Whatever they shared that night, it could never amount to what she'd dreamed of for years.

CHAPTER 5

Madame had no timidity in affairs of gallantry . . . she did not foresee consequences,
but found therein all the pleasurable excitement of a romance.

— COMTESSE DE LA FAYETTE

People say," whispered La Vallière as we bathed in canvas gowns
in the forest spring, "Monsieur is made a cuckold by his own
brother."

Golden sunbeams trickled through the branches and danced on the
ripples while Madame laughed and splashed at the opposite shore as if
she gave no thought to her troubles, no heed to the gossip. Our bathing parties at the stream had become a daily ritual.

"Monsieur will be furious that people are gossiping about him," I
whispered to La Vallière. After that first night, King Louis had only
come through to Madame's twice. I tied my bed curtains tight every
night and lay with the coverlets clenched in fists at my neck. "Madame
must stop."

"I wouldn't stop," Mortemart cut in. Her wet gown clung to her
heavy bosom and curvy hips.

La Vallière gasped. "You would have an affair with the king?"

"If I had a husband to legitimize any child that might be conceived."
She shook her head as if we were fools, and it shamed me. She was describing what my own mother may have done to give me the Stuart
name. "Imagine how much power she'll wield with the king's heart in
her hand."

"Who cares about power?" La Vallière was irritated. "It's a mortal sin, you know."

I shot Mortemart a smug smile. "See."

"Though I probably wouldn't stop, either," La Vallière went on.

I turned. "What?"

"He's so handsome. So radiant." Her eyes glazed. "What French girl isn't in love with the Sun King?"

"Queen Marie-Thérèse is outraged that Madame spends so much time with the king. She tells me Madame's mother is coming to chastise her," said Mortemart boldly.

I waded to the shore, exasperated that Mortemart knew everything and shocked that both ladies wanted to be mistress to such a man. The flaps of Madame's taffeta and silk tent waved in the light breeze as I entered. No one spoke as the maids pulled off my wet gown, dried me with diapering cloths, and dressed me in a gold-laced gown. Instead of leaving, I sat on a footstool, eating her strawberries and waiting.

"Oh," said Madame when she came in herself. "Are you not finished?"

I noticed, for the first time, her shoulders were not exactly straight. I blinked, studying them, and realized her spine actually hunched forward a little below her neck. Why had I never noticed it before? "I wanted to talk to you."

"I see." She entered and held out her arms.

The maids untied her bathing gown. As they peeled it from her skin and she stood naked, I saw shadows of every bone in her body. I had seen her thus before. But in my love for her, I'd never realized how unhealthy she appeared. She never ate. She hardly slept. All she'd done since her marriage was chase King Louis.

I cleared my throat, took a breath. "King Louis doesn't love you."

"La-la." She snorted. "I'm sorry we haven't found a husband for you, truly. Why haven't you taken up with one of the married men who would be happy to have you?"

The suggestion coming from my cousin's lips was even more insulting than Buckingham's offer. "The sin, I suppose." *Because my mother is sure a scandal will expose a secret that will ruin our family.*

"My brother Charles says God won't mind if we take a little pleasure along the way."

"But the rumors—"

"Don't."

"Your mother is coming here."

Her eyes widened for a fleeting second. Then she shrugged. "I finally have the passion I longed for all my life. I'll never give it up."

Her mother did not come. Instead, her husband and his mother, Anne of Austria, packed her belongings and forced her on a sojourn into the country. "You must watch de Mortemart while I'm away," she said through clenched teeth on her way down the horseshoe staircase. "I don't like how she looks at Louis, and who knows how long I'll be gone?"

CHAPTER 6

Youth does not lend itself easily to reason.

—MADAME DE MOTTEVILLE

She'd only been gone a day when I received a summons from King Louis to meet him by the Diana fountain. I started to make an excuse to the page, but he informed me the king would take me riding to the falconry to check on our rescued bird. I was touched that he'd followed through. Perhaps he was not so careless as I'd thought.

Though I was wary, I pulled new boots over silk stockings. The Spanish leather was as soft as my own skin. I tied the ribbon laces grimly, thinking that these boots would never hurt my toes.

La Vallière was right. King Louis *was* handsome. And strong. As I breathed the jasmine-scented fountain water, he helped me onto a horse himself with one swift swing. When he touched me, I felt my cheeks burn.

"The Goddess Diana," he said, nodding to the statue in the sunken fountain. "Known as the Chaste Huntress. I wonder how she maintains her virtue so scantily dressed?"

I glanced at the statue's bare shoulders. Madame had stolen the Greek stories Father Cyprien kept in his library after he refused to teach them to us. "The divine have the power to rise above worldly desires."

"Unlike us mortals." He whisked his horse to a trot and we rode from the garden, two of his guards leading with torches. At the falconry, the chief ran out with his assistants and bowed low. "My page brought you an injured bird some weeks ago," the king called.

The man nodded and gestured to a boy, who ran back in. "*Oui*, Your Majesty. The creature heals. Would you like to see?"

The boy hustled out holding a shallow wooden crate.

"Show the lady," said King Louis.

The nest was pushed to one side, and the bird, larger now, sat by it on a lining of straw. The boy coaxed it to perch on his finger and lifted it up for us to see. It fluffed its dark brown feathers and opened its wings. Just then the bird relieved itself. A little white smattering of waste landed on the toe of the king's boot. His eyes opened wide with astonishment, and he looked at me. The falconer fell before the king, wiping his boot and apologizing, and the little boy flushed scarlet. I burst out laughing, felt my spirit lighten, and soon the king was laughing with me.

We rode back to the palace by way of the forest's edge. The full moon bathed the lawn in silver light and cast eerie shadows among the trees. The darkness heightened the whispered secrets of the rustling leaves, making the forest as mysterious by night as it was magical by day.

"You and I are just alike," he said.

"Oh?" I grinned. "You enjoy tea and have no dowry?"

He laughed. "We have both just been granted great opportunity."

"Forgive me, Majesty, but what could be greater than the kingship you were born to?"

"My mother has been my regent for much of my life, and Cardinal Mazarin helped her keep France intact. To their credit, the Fronde is over, my parliaments have little power, and the nobility are weakened."

I smiled. He was setting out on his own much as I was.

"I couldn't surpass Cardinal Mazarin's authority while he lived. God rest him, but with his death, I finally have absolute rule in France."

"Oh, I rule nothing. I may be out from under my mother's nose for now, but she won't allow it much longer."

"Are you close to your family?"

"I miss them terribly. But I needed this time away."

"I wonder what it would be like to have a regular family. A king must always give his younger brother something to think about other than the throne. And things with my father were . . . complicated."

"But you were so young when he died."

He eyed me. "Can I trust you?"

I nodded.

"I meant Cardinal Mazarin. He and my mother loved each other deeply. Though my mother won't admit it, I've come to suspect the rumors are true and that he was my real father."

Is this what he'd meant when he said we were alike? Does he know about my parents? "This must have caused you great conflict."

"I knew you would understand." He paused. We were reapproaching the fountain. "It would do me great honor if you would ride with me again soon."

I didn't respond but heeled my horse to move a little faster.

"Ah. Diana will resist worldly temptation."

"I'm no Diana." I was sorry the moment I said it.

Two days later, Monsieur stepped from one of Anne of Austria's carriages wearing a lace robe over his traveling clothes and a sulky expression. He dutifully handed Madame out, then marched up one side of the horseshoe staircase to embrace the Comte de Guiche. They disappeared into the palace arm in arm. My cousin gestured for her ladies and led us in a promenade to the canal. "Tell me all that happened," she whispered to me.

"We are nearly prepared for the *Ballet des Saisons,*" I said haltingly, and gestured to the workers erecting a stage beside the lake.

"Was there a ball? Did the king dance with anyone?"

"There was none." I turned my face. "Fontainebleau was perfectly boring without you."

She seemed to relax. "They think to control me, to make me the unhappiest creature in the realm, to make me the perfect little Catholic bride. It may be extremely useful to die in God's grace, but it is extremely dull to live in it," she said. "He will come to me again tonight." She stooped to flick her fingers in the canal. The splash sent little ripples in every direction. "I *will* be the king's mistress."

CHAPTER 7

July

King Louis said he loved Frances Stuart not as a mistress, but as one he could marry as well as any lady in France.

—SAMUEL PEPYS'S DIARY

On the night of the *Ballet des Saisons,* the moon illuminated the lawn at the bank of the lake at Fontainebleau. Thousands of torches lit the tree-lined avenues and sparkled their reflection in the canal. Clusters of candelabra glowed at the edge of the stage where we danced.

I formed a circle with ten other ladies. Clad in drapes of flowing green silk, we played the Muses and rounded Madame, tossing flowers at her feet and reciting verses. She played the goddess Diana in a frail white Grecian gown. With a silver crescent on her brow and her dainty bow and arrow poised, she looked majestic, innocent. A Chaste Huntress. I knew better on all counts.

Rising on my toes, I turned in time with the swelling melody of the violins. I leaned gracefully toward Madame and tossed a rose at her feet. Beside me, La Vallière began her twirl. As we continued our wide circle around Madame, she gloated in the pomp. I hurled another rose at her feet and forced myself to look into the crowd.

Queen Marie-Thérèse had emerged from her bed to sit a bit too close to the stage. With her dog in her lap and her dwarf and attendants at her sides, she did not watch the ballet. Instead, she glared at something with a severe frown.

Curious to see what vexed her, I turned with my next pirouette and followed her line of sight.

It was King Louis, offstage, draped in a cloak of woven flowers and wearing a diamond-encrusted crown. He stared intently at Madame with an unmistakable look of lust in his eyes.

My heart thudded, and I hated the rush of heat it sent through me. I had been avoiding him. Every rehearsal, while he flirted with Madame and cast me surreptitious glances, I busied myself elsewhere. At dances, I flirted with every man, married or no, to be sure I was never without a partner. I might be envious of the way he looked at Madame, but I would not be tempted into a trap.

We Muses pulled in quickly to Madame, fell to our knees, and lifted our hands to her in homage. The rest of the players danced onto the stage, skipping and circling around us in the final sequence. Then came the king's cue.

He was the best dancer at court. From where I knelt, it looked like his feet hardly touched the stage, and his silk stockings accentuated the muscles in his legs. At last, he dropped to his knees before Madame for his final line. "To you, the Queen of Beauty."

Queen Marie-Thérèse stood then. She yanked up her skirts, placed one hand on her burgeoning belly, and stomped away. Her attendants leaped and scrambled after her, glancing back at the stage and whispering.

The remainder of the audience stood and applauded. Half of them watched the queen retreat. The rest whispered and eyed the royal lovers onstage.

I looked back at the king and Madame. They gazed into each other's eyes, oblivious to the pregnant queen's anger. How could they be so heartless?

The violins pulled their last notes, spiraling higher and cutting to the nerves. We bowed and the curtains fell mercifully closed. The players scattered offstage, muttering and peeking back at Madame and King Louis.

I stepped up to them. "Your Majesties, please. People are talking. Your husband would be in a rage if he were not so preoccupied with—" I glanced at King Louis.

Madame threw her head back, laughing. "The king already knows my husband is having an affair with the Comte de Guiche. Everyone knows."

"The queen looked very angry watching the pair of you tonight."

"Even a queen must submit to her king. And Louis loves me more than that short, fat dullard."

I held my breath, fearful of how he would respond to such disrespect.

His features seemed carefully neutral when he met my gaze.

"Right, Louis?" Madame looked from him to me, then back to him.

At last, he turned to her. "She is nothing compared to you." He stroked her cheek. "And I cannot bear to see you scandalized by the wagging tongues of malicious courtiers."

She shook her head. "You know I care not what—"

King Louis placed a finger on her lips. "My brother grows jealous of my favor," the king said to her in a soothing tone. "You will suffer at his hand because of me. Can we not throw them all off somehow?" King Louis leaned toward her. "Put it out that I am conducting a dalliance with one of your ladies. I can continue keeping company with you under the guise of visiting her."

"How clever," Madame said. "No harm in a ruse for the days. And no one knows about your visits at night."

King Louis nodded. "Maybe Frances would agree to the task."

"No." Madame snapped out of her trance. "De La Vallière."

"As you wish, my love." Then he released her and slipped away.

She eyed me. I bit my cheek, replaying all that had just happened. "I'm good enough to guard your chamber door at night but not to serve as a distraction during the day?"

"Your beauty is a little *too* distracting." She stepped to me and lifted one of my long curls. "Your hair has streaks of gold in it now, streams of sunshine. Fontainebleau has changed you."

And not all for the better.

Watching them during the banquet supper and then as they danced together in the hall became too much for me. Whispers about them burned my ears. So I wrapped my arms around myself and slipped away early. I needed no maid to pull off my costume, and I donned my chemise and *robe de chambre* in solemn quiet. Propping my elbow on the high sill, I pushed my window open. It creaked softly. The lawn was deserted but for a few servants cleaning the mess we'd left behind. Cloaked in silver darkness, the geometric courts and canals of Fontainebleau stretched, splendid and vast. I felt small in its complexity. The only element keeping me here was the blood Madame thought we shared, and friendship with her was one thing I never wanted to lose. The passage door inched open behind me, and King Louis slipped in quietly.

"Pardon me," I said, curtsying. "It is earlier than I'm used to—"

"I love her as a tie to her brother the king. But it is you I truly want." He wrapped his arms around me, a warming embrace that tempted too much.

He kissed me so fiercely I leaned back under his weight. "Please."

He tugged the sash of my *robe de chambre* until it gaped open, and he pulled me closer. Our eyes locked and he put his hands on the shoulders of my *robe* and slid it down my back. He nipped my lips with his and pulled my hips with one hand. Without thinking, I ran my fingers across his cheek, stroked his curls. Our warmth grew hot, spreading, needing. He looked at my face for one agonizing pause, then pushed my *robe* to the floor, held me tightly and thrust himself into my hips. I did not stop him; I wanted to fall back onto the bed, let this be what it would. Then I saw the window, still open to the night air. *No,* my mind said. *I would ruin myself and destroy her.* I had to end this. I imagined the window inside of me. I pulled it until the diamond-shaped panes latched closed over my heart, separating us. "Stop," I said loudly, pushing his shoulders.

King Louis moaned into my ear and tugged my chemise strings, loosening it and exposing my breast.

I never heard the door open. She didn't make a sound. I only spotted her because I shifted to find my *robe*.

Madame.

I froze. Regret and my too-late resolve crashed around me. King Louis muttered some question, saw my horrified expression, and then followed my gaze. He released me. I nearly fell.

She was ashen, barely breathing. The shock on her face seared me. King Louis stepped to her, put his hands on her arms, and tried to turn her away. She stood firm, staring me down.

I lifted my rumpled chemise and held it in front of my chest.

For one fleeting moment the shock gave way to hurt in her eyes. The worst expression I'd ever seen on her. Then it was gone. She started to tremble, and her color returned as if her blood seethed.

The king gave up trying to turn her and just pushed. "Come away now. Come away."

She stumbled back but did not break her stare. I thought she would burn a hole right through my soul. I felt myself starting to sink, slipping against the bed.

He finally inched her out and started to pull the door behind him.

She reached out to stop it with force. "I save you and this is how you thank me? You grab at my heart's one desire for yourself? Pack for England tonight, you—you whore! If it is a royal lover you want, I will arrange one for you. Who will save you from your mother's wrath when *Charles* is through with you?"

"Enough!" King Louis pushed her back and slammed the door.

Behind it, I heard her retching. Then wailing. "I will tell Charles you betrayed me; you are not to be trusted!" Her muffled cries mingled with his low voice. Her skirts swished in hurried steps and then they were silent.

My knees hit the floor. What had I done?

CHAPTER 8

She opened, but to shut
Excelled her power; the gates wide open stood.

—JOHN MILTON,
Paradise Lost

The first summons came from King Louis. One of his guards appeared at my chamber the next morning commanding my attendance in the François Gallery. My hands trembled. I would tell King Louis, firmly, we must apologize to Madame and dally no more. I glanced around for something to hold and fished my mother's rosary beads from the wooden chest. I said a quick prayer and followed the guard.

Musketeers stood at the entry to the gallery and stepped aside to let me in. I squinted to accommodate the brightness. The carved wood and gilded stucco wall on one side of the deserted hall was awash in sunlight, streaming through the windows that lined the opposite side. Amber light bounced off the intricate details, statues, and paintings. It filled the room, the perfect setting for the Sun King to dwell in. I paced along the wall inspecting the frescoes and Italian paintings, lingering at one by Leonardo da Vinci, *La Joconde*. This palace was so unlike Palais Royal or Château Colombes. Here the art was intact. Here the walls did not peel.

When I turned to the windows, I paused. There a table stood that I had not seen at first. A large gray parrot sat on a perch beside it. It examined me with its head cocked to one side. Its tiny eyes were like black glass beads framed in a circle of delicate white feathers. I went to it. "Pretty creature, *bonjour*." I took an orange slice from a bowl and slowly lifted it to his beak. He cocked his head the other way and studied me. Then, gently, he lifted one claw, took the food from my fingers, and ate.

"Do you like him?"

I turned to see King Louis approaching and dipped in a low curtsy. He lifted me by the elbow. "Do you like him?"

"Very much."

"He is yours."

"Oh, no, Your Majesty, I cannot accept such an expensive gift."

"You cannot refuse a gift from me."

I clung to the beads in my palm. "Gift or no, we must not continue in this way."

"I agree, that is why I summoned you here. Look, there is more." He pointed to a velvet box on the table.

Perhaps these gifts were his way of severing with me? "Your Majesty, this is not necessary."

He opened the box to reveal a gold necklace with three tiered strands of rubies. It gleamed in the golden sun, reflecting little fiery dots on the king.

"This is far too valuable."

"You underestimate your worth." He lifted the necklace and stepped behind me.

"Your Majesty, may I ask, what is the purpose of these gifts?"

"To honor you," he whispered behind my ear.

The necklace lowered before my eyes and rested on my chest. The beads in my palm felt damp.

"Move your hair."

I lifted it carefully, holding my breath, refusing to feel his fingers on my skin or remember how they'd felt last night.

"There." He stepped around, one hand on my arm, and swept an approving gaze across my chest and neck.

I felt myself flush.

"Beauty enhances beauty."

"I do not require you to do this."

"I hope to do it often. And if you will accept me, you may ask for a gallery full of jewels, if it will keep you happy." King Louis released my arm and stepped back. The look in his eyes changed, softened. For a moment he appeared beseeching. Almost an average man. He smiled. A real smile.

It warmed me to my toes.

"Look about you." He swept his arm up and across the length of the gallery, and my eye followed the path of carved frames and marble statues. "I own the finest collection of beauty captured in the magic of artistry. Yet none of it reflects even a shadow of your perfect face."

I glanced at *La Joconde* and pictured myself trapped within the frame rather than the mysterious woman who smiled back. He wanted to own me like some gilded prize. The rubies at my neck glittered as I turned to look at him.

His gaze was pleading. "I want you. Please accept my heart. Be my love."

My eyes burned. "Be . . . your mistress? I cannot."

He stepped close and grasped my arms. "It is true we cannot marry. But you will have first place in my heart, first place in your own household. I only require you to love me in return and allow me to lavish you as I please."

"It would be wrong in the eyes of God." My tongue tripped over the real reasons.

He squeezed my arms. "I am God's appointed king. My cardinal will dispense pardons and prayers for us every day."

"*Society* would never forgive such adultery."

"They will when I give you a title, land, riches. No one would dare judge you." King Louis lowered himself before me to become just a man. "When I rebuild the Château de Versailles, it will be the grandest palace in Europe. You shall have your own apartments and rule my heart as I rule France."

Such a betrayal would shatter Madame and sever our friendship forever. And the Queen Mother would surely dismiss my family and humiliate them. "You offer an illusion of security." I looked away.

He gave my arms a sudden shake that startled my gaze back to his.

His face was panicked. "What is it? Do not think about Madame.

She is my subject and must answer to me. I will set it right. You have nothing to fear from anyone."

I shook my head. Even as I looked into his eyes, I could feel myself change. I closed my heart, like the window of diamond-shaped panes of glass. Separating my soul from his, shutting out his affection, and sealing my fate.

"No," he whispered. "Please."

I forced myself to be silent and stiffened my spine. I answered him with a gentle stare.

His eyes, so unabashed, expressed hurt. He released me and stepped back, averting his gaze to the safety of the floor.

I reached behind my neck to release the necklace.

King Louis raised his hand. "Keep the gifts as tokens of my lo—" His hand dropped. He took a deep breath, then straightened his shoulders. "They are yours. Please keep them."

I left the necklace in place and dipped in a curtsy of thanks. When I rose again, he had changed.

Lips in a flat line and eyes narrowed slightly, he smiled the Sun King's smile. "Part of me knew you would refuse. Loyalty is a trait I admire."

I studied my white knuckles.

"Look up, Frances. If you are going to burden yourself thus, you may as well do it with pride." His voice was soft. "You will have to grow strong, I think, to endure the path you've chosen." A shadow of sorrow passed over his face. Or was it a look of pity? Whichever it was, the man who had offered me his heart retreated, while the monarch slowly slipped back into place. "Loyalty such as you exhibit is a rare, strange thing," he said. "You cling to it without fear of offending me."

I dipped again to curtsy. "I am not without reverence, Your Majesty." I held my low pose.

He took his time. Finally, he spoke. "Rise."

When I met his glare, no shred of the man who'd offered me his heart remained. Now the Sun King, known for his meticulous planning and lofty goals, stood proud before me in his brilliant gallery. "Tell me, have you any affection for me?"

Tears stung the back of my throat. I swallowed them. *You woke my spirit, dominated my dreams.* "You have my utmost respect and admiration."

"You allow me to take liberties with you, inspire me to offer all I own at your feet. You made me think you loved me. You confuse me."

"If I have such feelings, I cannot allow them to develop. My obligations to—"

"*If* you have such feelings? I risked angering the crown behind the most fearsome naval power at sea for the sake of your love. Madame will tell her brother, the *King* of England, that I humiliated her. Do you know how many battleships I have? Not one! I didn't do this for respect and admiration, damn it." His voice cut through the shining room and echoed off the walls. "I risked war to have your love!"

My whole body trembled. I clung to the rosary beads in my palm.

"Tell me I was not wrong. Tell me."

Tears slipped down my cheeks because . . . I could *never* tell him now.

He walked away a few paces, then back again with calculation in his eyes. "Your tears are proof enough that I was not wrong." He paced away. "You put me at a disadvantage with England."

"I beg pardon." The ruby necklace seemed a heavy weight on my chest. My fingers stiffened over the rosary.

"Pardon she who shows loyalty to everyone but me? I have harbored your exiled family in France your entire life. Now you ask for more." He stopped pacing and stood directly before me. "Swear fealty to me."

"Pledge devotion to a French king?" I stammered. "Is that acceptable for an English subject to do?"

A bitter laugh escaped him, and he stepped close, his nose nearly touching mine. "That depends on who you ask, so be cautious who you tell. Because if you want my forgiveness today, I will at least acquire your precious loyalty to my crown. Now kneel."

"Sire, I am of Stuart blood."

"You'll need that connection to repair the damage you've done between Charles and me."

"Do you mean—I really have to go to England?"

His upper lip curled. "To England and to the English king's bed."

"You wouldn't!"

He put his hands on my shoulders. "You're more than just a Stuart. Your mother is a bastard. If I make that fact known, no husband will ever accept you."

My mouth gaped wide. *Mother.*

"I know everything about the powerful men I allow into my country. And your grandfather would be none too pleased if you exposed him." He pushed down on my shoulders. "Kneel. Or shall I call my guards?"

I slowly descended the length of his body until I was on my knees, my face before his groin. Still he didn't budge. *The English king's bed. What grandfather? Mother is the bastard, not me.*

"Repeat: I, Frances Stuart, once a subject of England, do hereby swear fealty to Louis the Fourteenth of France. I subject myself to his will and pledge to serve him faithfully in any capacity he requires for the duration of my life."

When I'd spoken the words, he released my shoulders but did not back away. Nor did he command me to stand. Refusing to crawl away on my knees, I rose back up the length of his body on shaky legs. I had to turn my face to avoid brushing his erection. Sparks of heat flashed between us like the fiery little beams from the necklace.

When I finally faced him, the arousal flaring in his eyes told me I should have crawled. I turned to the parrot.

He grabbed my arm and yanked me back. He pointed in my face with his other hand. "Do not test me again." He thrust my arm away and turned, walking to the exit.

I took a deep, shaky breath.

He called from the doors. "My first command is that you name the bird."

"Yes, Your Majesty," I muttered.

"You will call him Serment." He chuckled, a sound more sinister than merry. "To remind you." Musketeers pulled the doors closed behind him.

Serment. The French word for "oath." I felt a desperate need to say a prayer. I looked down at my hands as I opened them, stretching my tingling fingers. But as I pulled the rosary beads from the deep indents they'd pressed into my palm, I couldn't remember a single prayer.

I sat dazed in my chamber for the next hours, staring at the rubies. I'd gone in to apologize, been offered the world on a string, and emerged the daughter of a bastard, indebted to a king. Now I would have to go to England, and I couldn't stop thinking of Buckingham and his wretched words; "when disaster befalls you, you will come to me to introduce you to King Charles." I could never allow anyone to discover my mother's illegitimacy. My fate was uncertain, but my sister might yet make an honorable marriage . . . *No one can learn what has happened.* My new pet bobbed his head up and down and stared at me. Perhaps Serment could be taken for Sir Ment in English.

A scratch from the door to Madame's room startled me, and I scrambled to get up. I smoothed the front of my skirt and stepped through the door into the brightness of the larger chamber. My breath caught at the sight of the Queen Mother's footman. He stepped aside. The Queen Mother herself sat on a red velvet chair, with my mother standing behind her, both their faces as smooth as marble. My cousin reclined on the bed.

"Frances. Come in." The Queen Mother gestured servants away.

I dipped to a deep curtsy, as if into icy water. "Your Majesty, Mother, how pleasant. I didn't know you were here."

"It is not pleasant at all," she said calmly. "Anne of Austria demanded I come hedge my child's behavior. Imagine my humiliation." She bent knuckles around her prayer book and pursed her lips. "Tell me exactly what King Louis and my daughter share."

"Share?" I took a slow breath and thought carefully. "Well, they share a love for the *Ballet des Saisons* . . ."

The Queen Mother thudded her knee with her little prayer book. "Foolish girl. I know not whether to pity your simple mind or teach you the ways of this malicious world. I mean what sort of feelings do they share for each other? How can you live here at Fontainebleau and not have heard gossip about their love affair?"

I glanced at my mother and feigned a shocked expression. "Gossip? Oh, no, Your Majesty. I have heeded your instruction in this and avoided it. As you taught us."

"You are either a great simpleton or a great schemer. You risk sacrificing my good favor to protect her reputation."

My mother frowned.

"I would sacrifice much in my loyalty to Madame." Madame glanced at me, a fraction of a moment.

The Queen Mother narrowed her eyes. "I wonder, then, why she is so displeased with you."

"Let her be." Madame sat up and made to reposition herself on the bolsters. I moved to assist her, and she let me. "Frances still has my favor." She studied me briefly, with blank eyes, then looked away. "Such favor, in fact, I am recommending her for a coveted position." Madame went on. "Charles will prepare a household for his new queen soon. Frances should be offered as a maid of honor for the English court."

My mother stepped forward. "With respect, Madame, I do not—"

The Queen Mother held up her hand, silencing my mother. "He knows *I* will make the recommendations. He would ravage her, prey on her innocence."

"He would adore her innocence." Madame shrugged. "And he quite trusts my judgment, as his letters prove." The hauteur in her tone shocked me. "She is the prettiest girl in all the world, the most fit to adorn his court."

Mother and I studied each other. She looked helpless. I had to look away.

"Well, I am pleased to see you gain influence with Charles." The Queen Mother seemed genuinely satisfied. "If you continue thus, he will come to rely on you in political matters as well. Remember, in everything, you must encourage him toward the Catholic faith. Confer with me whenever he confides in you."

Madame frowned. "Charles hates your meddling. Perhaps I best deal with him on my own." She waved her hand dismissively as she often did to servants.

The Queen Mother blanched. "Daughter, you know as well as I of the mistress who grips Charles's heart. That crafty jezebel draws him dry as she wields his hand. Just how do you plan to become a greater force in his life?"

"Put your worries to rest." Madame's lips curled. "I learned how to control others from the world's most ruthless mother."

My eyes widened, but I dared not move lest they turn their venom on me. My mother lowered her gaze and the Queen Mother's neck turned red. She stood, stepped toward the bed, and raised one bony finger just as a herald cried outside the main door. "The king! The king! Make way for the king!" The door opened and King Louis filled the space.

"Dear aunt, forgive my not receiving you earlier." He put his hand out to the Queen Mother. "I knew nothing of your plans to visit."

"Beloved Majesty and favorite nephew." She gushed and bowed to kiss his ring. "Anne of Austria summoned me with urgent haste."

"Ah, yes. Philippe has been bawling at Mother's feet about my relationship with Madame again. He is jealous that his charming wife and not he holds my favor." He stepped to Madame and presented his hand.

She hesitated to kiss his ring. Glimmers of gladness, hurt, then desperation played upon her features as she searched his face. I realized this was the first time she had seen him since last night; she probably had no notion of his offer to make me his mistress. *Praise the saints.* She slowly lifted her hand and laid it on his, as if *she* were the ranking royal.

He paused, then brought her hand to his own lips and kissed it. "I suppose he has a right to be jealous. Madame certainly has my heart." He turned to the Queen Mother. "You need not get into such a fuss on Philippe's account. Though I love her as a cousin and a sister, the rumors are baseless. We are not lovers."

The Queen Mother studied the pair. They waited with pleasant, stone faces for her to accept their word.

After a long moment, she pretended to. "Of course not. Did you think I would heed malicious gossip? It is only born of envy, after all. But do use discretion, dears, when you are together. Give no one cause to criticize you."

Madame waved away her advice. "We have devised a way to deal with it already. Isn't that so, Louis?"

He smiled at her. "I just sent Louise de La Vallière a little gift before coming here." Then King Louis turned to me. "We made additional plans, Madame, did we not?"

She followed his gaze to me. "Oh?" Her tone was grim.

King Louis clasped his hands behind his back and began a slow walk around the bed. I tried to back away but found I was already against the wall. "Are you sure you do not mind losing the fair and loyal Frances Stuart?"

Madame snorted. "I am willing to sacrifice for my brother's sake." Then, as if she sensed she were missing something, she leaned forward. My mother, too, took several steps toward us.

"I have considered this since we spoke last night," he said. He was closer to me now. "And I find the idea appeals to me. Frances, would it please you to do my bidding?" He held out his hand for me to kiss.

Madame nearly sprang out of bed.

The hair at my nape rose. "Yes, Your Majesty." I put my lips to his ring.

He let his hand linger, took it back slowly, then turned to Madame. "Any king would find her fascinating."

Madame could not hide her pique and fell against the bolsters. "What made you change your mind?"

"She has proven herself *most* loyal."

She shot me a curious glance. "Has she, now?"

King Louis looked Madame in the eyes. "She will befriend Charles, be my liaison to him, and use his ear on my behalf." He turned and spoke to me. "You will convince Charles that I am his friend in everything."

After a pause he turned to leave.

The shock in my mother's expression was more than I could bear.

The Queen Mother jumped to the king's side. "Your Majesty, surely you realize that my services are at your disposal. If you must convince my son of anything, please rely on me."

"You? Didn't you threaten never to speak to your youngest son Henry, if he didn't convert to Rome? You turned him out when he refused. He had to beg just to pay his way to King Charles's court."

"I—I would have spoken to him in England last winter."

"He died without your pardon. I once saw Charles walk away as you ranted at him about policy. You exasperate your children." He shook his head. "No. You may seek refuge in France, but you'll take no part in my relationship with Charles. Your interference only wreaks disaster."

Numbness settled over me as I watched her bow, back away from him, then fumble into a chair. All my life, the Queen Mother had been the intimidator. King Louis, the monarch who now held *me* at his mercy, had humbled a queen in front of her own daughter. Was this the same man who'd offered me his heart hours before?

Mother leaned heavily against Madame's bed, ashen. She said nothing. But what could she possibly say to counter a king's command?

"Madame," he called as he walked to the door, "write to your brother and tell him you are sending Frances to serve his new queen. See that she is well treated in your court, well supplied, and well prepared. I want her delivered to his household just as she is. Perfect."

My poor friend covered her face with her hands.

He looked back. "And Madame."

Her fingers parted slightly.

"Tell Louise de La Vallière I will call on her soon."

She managed a false smile before turning into her pillow. She had lost him. I wondered if I'd ever known him at all.

That night I lay on a straw pallet and let Mother have my bed. "This is the worst that could have happened, yet I have no power to refuse it," she said, eyes wide with disbelief.

"An English girl could never get an official appointment at the French court, and I cannot expect Madame to support me forever. You would have to take me to England once the Queen Mother sets out anyway. I may as well seek a position in the English court to keep me occupied." I spoke with more confidence than I felt.

"At the English court the Villiers family safeguard themselves to the peril of others."

I thought of how complicated things might become if she discovered my promise to Buckingham. "Have you ever been to England? Have we any . . . family connection there?"

"Of course I've been to England. And you know better than to question me about family."

"One of my Stuart cousins just inherited the dukedoms of Richmond and Lennox. And there's Father's nephew, Lord Blantyre, surely they would be willing—"

"Lord Blantyre never comes down from Scotland, and the Duke of Richmond is an insatiable drinker. I will help you as best I can myself."

She hadn't refuted my relation to the Stuarts. "Mother, I truly am my father's daughter, aren't I?"

She lowered her gaze. "How did you learn this?"

"I must hear you say it, please."

She hesitated. "Yes, you are Walter Stuart's daughter."

"Why did you lie to me? Was *your* father a Villiers?"

She was silent.

"Don't try to protect me from things I need to know."

"Stop asking questions. The answers will get us into more trouble than you're already in." She turned to the wall and would speak to me no more.

After our mothers departed, I knew our days at Fontainebleau were limited. Madame and I would be back in Paris with the change of season, and I would be packed off to England in the new year. If I wanted to regain my cousin's favor, I had little time.

CHAPTER 9

Château de Vaux-le-Vicomte
Fête of the Superintendent of Finances,
Nicolas Fouquet

Mid-August

"This must be the finest palace in France," I said to Louise de La Vallière. As we strolled along the canal, a huge boat, shaped like a whale, drifted past. Over twenty violinists edged the stage where we had just watched Molière's new comedy, *Les Fâcheux*. Vast displays of fireworks periodically lit hundreds of courtiers who were on a nighttime promenade through the gardens.

"And the grandest fête," she replied. "And Nicolas Fouquet created it with *livres* stolen from the king."

"Did you ask me to walk with you so you could share state secrets?" I asked, surprised.

"I know how angry it makes King Louis. He is what I want to talk about."

"He tells you such things?" In the weeks since I'd refused him, he'd spent an increasing amount of time with La Vallière.

"And more. Oh, Frances, I love him so."

"Yes. I know. You've said this before."

"But now that he loves me back, I think I could die a happy woman."

I stopped in the center of the gravel path. "Did you say the king loves you?"

She pulled me along. "I was beginning to think he flirted with me to distract from his affair with Madame. But then Superintendent Fouquet attempted to bribe me for the king's favor, and he is positively *outraged*."

"The King of France?"

"Yes, silly. He says he loves me and wants to make me his mistress." *Had he truly loved me if he's changed so soon?* "Does Madame know?"

"She saw us together and was very piqued. Louis won't let her dismiss me. What can she do to me but not speak?" She pointed across a parterre, where Madame stood close to the Comte de Guiche. "No need to worry about offending her when she is lashing out at the king by taking a new lover."

As we watched, Guiche whispered in Madame's ear. She giggled, and they both glanced around before ducking through shrubbery and slipping down the path to a hidden grotto. She had been taking opium for a recent illness. She looked even thinner to me.

La Vallière went on. "What should I do about King Louis? I love him, but an affair would be a carnal sin."

I watched the Chevalier de Gramont, that gossiping troublemaker, peek toward the grotto, then make his way across the avenue to the Chevalier de Lorraine. "That is a matter between you and God," I said distractedly. Gramont muttered to Lorraine, who trotted across the lawn so awkwardly on high heels that his tall periwig tottered with every step. He was heading straight to Monsieur, who sat on a bench surrounded by fops and gallants. *I have to warn Madame.*

I left La Vallière, walking quickly around the parterre, dashed through the shrubs and ran down the path. I found them pressed against each other, leaning against the rocky wall among the little candles in the man-made cave. Praise heavens they were still dressed. Mostly. "Madame."

They cursed and scrambled to rearrange themselves. Madame shot me a glare that looked like one of her mother's. Guiche grinned at me. "You wish to join us?"

"Monsieur is approaching."

Madame paled, then smoothed her hair. Guiche fumbled with the ribbon ties of his pantaloons. I grabbed his arm and pulled him toward the path.

We were almost there when Monsieur appeared. He took one look at me holding Guiche as he yanked at his pantaloons and said, "I'm shocked, Frances. The Comte de Guiche is a notorious seducer." He glared at Guiche. "Of men and women." Then he turned to Madame. "I'm beginning to suspect he's seduced my wife."

She crossed her arms. "You're more ashamed that your *lover* cheated on you. Get out."

"So he can take you again, right here on the ground? He is leaving, not I." He lunged at Guiche and pushed him against the wall.

"You don't own me, Philippe!" Guiche shoved him. "You can't make me love you."

"How could you?" Monsieur fell on his knees before Guiche and wept. "With her? She is a faithless whore."

I grabbed Madame's arm and pulled her away, but she hissed over her shoulder, "You're not half the man your brother is." I pulled her down the path until she yanked her arm free. "You think to gain forgiveness by interfering?" she said to me.

"*Ma cousine*, I—"

"Stay away, traitor." And she flew back toward the palace.

CHAPTER 10

November

"I do not want to have a child! I want to die!" Queen Marie-Thérèse screamed, writhing and sweating. Her state bedchamber was crammed with courtiers. To support the royal claim that the child produced was really born of the queen's body and to ensure no one surreptitiously traded a worthless female infant for a male heir, everyone craned their necks for a glimpse of the queen's most private parts. The maids fussed to keep her modesty concealed with a sheet, but the men kept a wary eye. Courtiers chatted while she struggled, discussing her odds of survival and how much King Louis might reward her if she lived.

King Louis stood by the bed, unable to offer his wife solace. Madame lay propped on a litter, coughing incessantly and droopy with opium. She'd recently announced she was pregnant, and I would certainly never ask which royal brother was the father. I imagined her anxious over the queen's pain, but I stood by La Vallière's side, waiting for the queen to either die or bring forth life. Madame would only wave me off if I tried to offer reassurances.

The chamber door I shared with my cousin was now wide as an ocean distancing separate lands. I never told her I had refused King Louis' offer; it would only have deepened her wound to learn he wanted to make me his *maîtresse-en-titre*. I had started to change my

61

thoughts about England. I'd progressed from "when will they make me go" to "when may I finally just go?" Far away from France, from King Louis, from Madame's disdain, from the oppression of my mother's fear.

La Vallière tugged my arm, and together we slipped outside for some air. The browning lawn crunched beneath our shoes. Bare rose stems swayed in the breeze, thorns piercing the chill. The dark fur tippet tied at my neck wasn't warm enough, and I wrapped my arms around myself as we walked.

La Vallière's rosary dangled from her hand as her fingers moved from bead to bead, presumably reciting prayers in her mind. "For all that I know it is wrong, I cannot help myself," she said. "I love the king. And being loved by him is . . . irresistible."

I did not respond. La Vallière now suffered Madame's silence as much as I.

The upper windows of the West Wing burst open. King Louis himself leaned out and shouted, "The queen has given birth to a dauphin!" We applauded for the newborn prince with the others in the garden as the king ducked back inside without further mention of his queen.

"I must confess," La Vallière said, sighing, "I dreaded this event. Now both households must move to Palais Royal to spend winter in Paris. We will have to be more discreet to hide our affair."

"Won't you seek a marriage to excuse a pregnancy, secure your future?"

"Ah, but marriage would make my sin a mortal one." She sighed again. "The king tells me you are going to the English court. I shall miss you."

"Tell me," I said casually, for if anyone would know, it was she. "Does he know when the English marriage will take place?"

"Catherine of Bragança was the candidate King Louis promoted so England wouldn't form a marriage alliance with Spain. He believes King Charles will appoint the members of her household soon, for his bride will set sail come spring."

CHAPTER 11

Palais Royal, Paris

January 1662

B y Advent I was aching to leave for England. When the Ballet-Royal arrived to give a private performance in Madame's chambers, King Louis ordered my attendance. I dutifully reported to her bedside, hoping this would be the send-off I longed for.

Red velvet drapery fell in lush folds around Madame as she reclined. Her belly was slightly rounded, a contrast with her sunken cheeks and hollow eyes. Her hair and face were set and painted but couldn't hide her poor health. She ignored me, and greeted the gathering courtiers with false smiles. A herald called from the door, "The king! The king!"

Six young pages, liveried in red velvet, rushed into the room and stood in opposing rows, making an aisle. Everyone bowed or curtsied. King Louis walked through them straight to me. He presented his hand. As my lips grazed his ring, he squeezed my fingers softly. It surprised me, and I hoped my face didn't reflect this as I stood.

He whispered, "Remember, Charles must know I seek his friendship. Gain his trust and his ear. I will send ambassadors to you with further instructions when the time comes."

"Yes, Your Majesty. I will not forget." Nor could I forget the promise I'd made to Buckingham when I'd assumed it would never need to be fulfilled.

"You must gain a position of influence over him, so that when I want him to do a political thing . . . you can make him do it."

"He would follow my suggestions regarding political things?"

"Charles is easily influenced," he said. "Especially by the women who share his bed." He turned his face toward the chamber.

He pitched his voice for all to hear. "How I will hate to lose Frances Stuart to the English court. No offer of a dowry or a marriage arrangement will convince her mother to keep her here." He eyed me. "For I love her more than a man loves even a mistress." A frenzy of whispers and fluttering fans washed across the chamber. "Indeed, she is so rare I would marry her myself if I could."

Does he mean it? My throat constricted. *Even as he hurls me to another man's bed?*

The king found a flustered-looking La Vallière and settled down in front of the makeshift stage. She had heard him. Everyone had. They were all staring. I spotted the Queen Mother, studying me from the corner. What malice did she brew behind those eyes?

Madame hissed at me. "Get out of my sight."

Thus, instead of making my way to an open chair, I returned to my family and what little time I had left with them.

I have made many plans for you," the Queen Mother said the next morning, sweeping my figure with her eyes. I had been summoned to Madame's bedchamber, though she would not look at me from her lavish bed. "You are my daughter's dearest friend. I have a gift for you."

I hovered between fear and doubt.

"Mary," she called.

The door to Madame's closet opened, and one of the Queen Mother's longtime maids emerged. This woman, with gray hair swept under a mobcap, had always looked the same. The creased skin around her eyes and her perpetually pursed lips never seemed to change, making her age a wrinkled secret. Though she had always stared down her long nose at Madame and me as children, she never spoke, and I had no idea of her character.

"You know Mary," the Queen Mother said. "She is industrious, good at setting hair. A strong, trustworthy Englishwoman and a true Catholic. I have paid her a year's wages. She will accompany and serve you in England where you will keep her and continue to pay her yourself." She looked at me expectantly.

I knew that look.

Friendship with the princess had lent opportunities, and after every tutor's lesson, every supper, every outing in her carriage, the Queen Mother had looked at me this way. She expected gratitude, obedience, and good behavior. This time she'd appraised me with a woman's eye. Simple gratitude would not be enough. "How can I ever repay you?" I asked.

Her face registered pleased surprise. She turned to Mary. "Go now. Prepare her things."

As Mary marched dutifully away, the Queen Mother took my arm and pulled me down into a double chair beside her. "Since you are so willing, child, there *is* something you can do for me."

She produced her little black prayer book, settled herself, and held it up. "Cardinal Richelieu gave me this upon my marriage. When they sent me to wayward England, he made me promise to do everything I could to turn them back to the true faith."

I nodded. The Catholic Church had never had a more determined advocate.

"Henry the Eighth of England severed from Rome to take up with that heretic, Anne Boleyn, and Protestants have wrongfully triumphed ever since." She looked past me, remembering. "Pope Urban hailed *me* as savior to oppressed British Catholics. I did everything I could to turn England back. *Some*"—and here I could see she meant to say King Louis—"may say my efforts caused the civil wars that ended in my husband's beheading." She eyed me. "The English think they have the right to choose how to worship God! *They* denied the absolute right of kings, *their* mistakes brought bloodshed." She clenched the book with white knuckles. "What do you remember of my son King Charles?"

My mind tripped over the events she had failed to mention: her banishment, Cromwell's victory, our exile. What did I know of Charles II?

There was only one memory. A mistaken identity when I was still a child. He thought for a moment I was his sister. I glanced at Madame, who still would not catch my eye. "Little, I'm afraid."

"He is an easy man. Merry. Malleable." She studied me. "Prone to attach himself to any sort of woman, even the self-seeking sort. He is so forgiving, you see, he hardly notices a woman's flaws."

The hair at the nape of my neck rose.

"When Madame and I visited him in England last winter, we met one such woman, Barbara Palmer." A pink tint crept up the Queen Mother's neck. "She is the worst sort of creature: steering his decisions, scheming, vain, greedy."

The description reminded me, perversely, of the Queen Mother herself. Again I looked to Madame. She stared through me as if I were invisible.

"She passed her first child off as the king's bastard and humiliated her husband. Charles granted them a peerage. They are the Earl and Countess of Castlemaine, but only children of Barbara's body shall inherit the title. Which is as good as an announcement to the world that she is his official mistress." The pink spread to her face, and she struggled to maintain composure. "The worst of it is, Barbara Palmer is . . . a Protestant." Her hands trembled around the prayer book. "Under her influence, Charles will *never* return to the Church of Rome. I did my best to persuade my sons to be Catholic, but their father . . . He made them promise to remain Protestant."

"What has this to do with me?"

"Child," she said as she held out her little black prayer book. "Make Charles love you . . . and get rid of that whore."

The small book fell heavily into my hand. She had never spoken so baldly before. I could hardly believe she meant her own words.

"He will not heed his mother, but he will listen to a mistress if he loves her." She narrowed her stare. "You *must* make him Catholic."

I longed to throw the book down and run. "To be a mistress is to live in sin."

She reached out, took my hands, and wrapped them around the book. "You good, simple girl. Not a mistress. A king's mistress. You must pray for absolution. And you shall have it, for your sins are committed for the sake of saving England from eternal damnation. God will understand, child. You are doing it for Him."

Slowly, blankly, I nodded. "I—I would like to bid farewell to my family."

"There is no need," she said. "They are going with you."

I nodded. I'd feared they'd stay behind. Mother would not be easy about it, but I was relieved, for the closer they were to me, the easier they'd be to protect.

"I shall follow you to England come summer, after the birth of Madame's child. You will report your status to me then." She stood and actually *smiled* at me. "I have high hopes for you. God could not have made you so beautiful for nothing."

After she left and the door had closed, Madame sat up and finally looked at me. "First you steal my lover, then the love of a mother who rarely shows it."

I tossed the prayer book to the chair. "Please, Madame, forgive me."

Resentment clouded her eyes. "I don't know about forgiveness. Though knowing you face Lady Castlemaine satisfies my need for vengeance." She stretched her legs to the edge of her bed. "That woman will roast you for supper if you are not cautious."

"Do you think your brother could—love me?"

"My brother loves any female who opens her legs to him. They do not call him an enemy to virginity and chastity for nothing." Madame took a few steps to her cabinet. Her small, rounded belly pressed a curve against her mantua gown. "He is a whore of a man." With a quick flick, she tossed a small purse to me.

Coins jingled as my hand closed around the soft leather. "I cannot accept—"

"The purse is from the Earl of St. Albans. You shall have to fight to get maid of honor. Here." She extended a letter closed with her large black wax seal. "Have your mother present this to Charles. My recommendation."

I took the letter. Tears burned my eyes. "I wish you could have—"

She climbed back onto her ornamented bed. "There is no sense for a princess to wish. Politics determines our fate, not fancy. I shall take my happiness where I can."

I clutched the letter and the leather purse, the need to be forgiven sweeping through me. "Madame . . . I . . ."

She held up her hand. "Go. I cannot stand to look at you any longer."

CHAPTER 12

The English Channel
End of January

No royals had emerged for farewells. We'd simply climbed into the Queen Mother's carriage and rolled out of Paris. Mother seemed reluctant to fuss at me in Mary's presence, and the children chatted excitedly as we set out. "Why must we go to England?" asked my sister.

"We are Stuarts, and they have England's throne again." I scooted close to her and tucked both of our cloaks around us. "It's where we belong."

Walter tugged our mother's arm. "Have you ever been to England?"

"Yes," she said as I watched her carefully. "Of course I have." She snuggled Walter under her arm and revealed nothing more.

We'd slept at the inn in Rouen, and now my family convalesced in the cabin of the ship commissioned at the port of Le Havre-de-Grâce to carry us across the Channel. But I had sea legs, so the captain said, and I didn't mind the icy winds on deck. It blew my hair around my face as I looked back toward France: the coast had long since receded under heavy gray, along with everything I thought I was. Cold air filled my lungs, and I tried not to think about the future. Just for a moment.

I closed my eyes and turned so my ribs pressed the railing. The wood was thick, and I gripped its smooth curve as the waves tossed the ship. The icy blast now lifted my hair off my back and sent it swirl-ing in the air behind me. It pierced through my bodice and lifted the edges of my velvet cloak so it whipped around me like a black flag. I raised my arms just a little to feel the wind push them up and imag-ined I was flying. Up and up went my arms, until I didn't have to hold them up anymore. This must be how it felt to fly. To be free.

Then I opened my eyes, squinting against the wind, and saw it.

England. A thin, distant line on the hazy expanse.

As I lowered my arms, my thoughts fell to what I must do. Somehow I would win a place in the new Queen Catherine's household. Ingrati-ate myself with King Charles without becoming his mistress. As long as the Queen Mother thought I was cooperating . . . I must handle each task delicately for my brother's and sister's sake. If I incurred too much scrutiny, someone might uncover our mother's secret. If I could do all these things, I might even find a way to be happy. I balanced on my toes, trying to reclaim that soaring sensation, to greet my new home.

We entered the mouth of the river Thames and disembarked at Greenwich, the Queen Mother's palace. All along the river-bank, crumbling red brick walls and towers gaped hollow while workers pounded them with chisel and hammers. "Why is it being torn down?" asked Walter as an arched window tumbled in on itself.

"This is the old Tudor palace," said Mary wistfully. "These walls saw royalty's most glorious days. The wars and the Commonwealth let it crumble beyond repair, but King Charles is rebuilding it to match the Queen's House." She pointed toward a long, white house built in what the French would have called the Italian style. "Begun for the first Stu-art queen, it was completed for our mistress. But she didn't enjoy it long before the wars broke out."

She ushered us through the rubble and up the walk, then arranged our dinner, and saw us to bed. If Mother had ever served the Queen Mother here, she gave no indication that she recognized the place.

Next morning, we took a carriage up Old Dover Road to the Southwark side of the city, and the heavy London air filled my nose. The children propped themselves at the windows when Mary announced we were approaching London Bridge. I peeped around the leather curtain for a better view.

Royal arms marked the opening of the Great Stone Gate, but my eyes drew upward to a dozen spikes pointing to the sky. Each topped with a human head. My brothers and sisters fell back, eyes wide with fear.

Mary saw my shock. "Those would be members of Venner's rising."

"What was their crime?" I asked.

"They were Protestant Dissenters rebelling against the newly restored monarchy. Traitors' heads are preserved in a mixture of spices so they must show their faces in shame for years."

I'd never seen England's religious conflict firsthand, and its brutality shocked me. If this was their reaction to a Protestant rebellion, how might they respond to a Catholic plot? I shivered and wrapped my arms around myself.

A convergence of men herding cows, sheep, and geese, farmers with their wagons, and peddlers with their carts all jostled for passage through the gate, and our progress slowed. Once we lumbered through, I realized the bridge was lined most of the way with an array of buildings. Houses topped shops and joined overhead, making it feel as though we passed through a tunnel, and the chorus of common life echoed.

Mary said periodic fires had destroyed some sections of shops, and when we came to these openings, I could see the river Thames. Dozens of ships and small vessels dotted the blue. Men aboard sang or called to one another, pulling up nets, throwing out fishing lines, or struggling to maneuver through the arches of the bridge. Walter pointed downriver to a huge fortress on the north bank. "Is that the castle where we're going?"

But Mary shook her head. "That's the Tower of London, for prisoners, executions, and for punishing anyone who displeases the king."

As we emerged through the final gate of the bridge, into the city, a thunderous noise made me cover my ears.

"A waterwheel," said Mary. "To supply nearby homes and for putting out those fires."

Mother seemed surprised at Mary's explanations, as if she knew nothing of London. It made me wonder, quietly, if she'd truly ever been here, but I didn't dare ask in present company.

I once thought Paris smelled foul in the hot summers, especially compared to the sweet country air of Fontainebleau. But this was midwinter and still a grimy cloud, mixed with fog from the river, hovered over the whole of London. I could smell the fumes of lime factories, dyers, butchers, and tanners. Walter covered his face with his sleeve.

The street was a seething river of mud, dung, and kitchen refuse. It coated every woman's hem in filth. The carriage wheels bumped along the rutted road and jostled us in our seats. Muckrakers jerked out of our path, then returned to scraping, stirring the sludge around and scattering muddy rats. The poverty overwhelmed me more than the stench, and I felt a flash of relief that I carried St. Albans's purse and the ruby necklace. A fresh whiff of animal entrails decaying outside a butcher's shop made me cover my nose.

Children screamed or played, dogs fought, and people bartered, cursed, or laughed. Peddlers roamed everywhere, dodging chamberpot waste hurled from windows and shouting out their advertisements. They carried baskets of produce, boards of fresh bread, cases of fish, even barrels of ink for sale. One woman balanced piles of soiled clothes on her head for trade. Building was constructed upon building, and the crowded line of taverns and coffeehouses seemed never ending. I spotted a man urinating against a timber shop, and I shrank back from the window, stunned. Finally we rolled past the towering St. Paul's Cathedral and through Ludgate, part of the Roman wall that had surrounded the city in ancient times. We covered Fleet Hill, Fleet Bridge, and went through the timber arches of a gate Mary called Temple Bar.

"London is huge! We'll be lost here," said Sophia.

"No," Walter replied. "Frances will be a maid of honor. She'll take care of us."

Mother glanced at me and I saw the worry in her eyes. I clasped her hand and squeezed.

Mary nudged me as our driver maneuvered around a massive pole jutting up like a ship's mast in the middle of the road. "It's the great maypole King Charles brought in at the Restoration. But look there."

She nodded toward a distant curve and break in the road. "Whitehall Palace is down the Strand beyond Charing Cross. Farther still, through Holbein Gate and King Street Gate, is Westminster."

I looked at the street again, relieved to see this section of the city seemed cleaner and quieter. The carriage halted before a long arcade of stone pillars and arches on our left.

"Welcome to Somerset House," said Mary.

CHAPTER 13

Somerset House, London

Through the gatehouse arches, Somerset opened to a three-sided courtyard. The gardens within lay in a winter sleep, its huge fountains and grottoes empty. They stretched clear to the river landing where workers hauled stone to construct an arched gallery. Inside, years of neglect underwent slow repair. Drapers hung red velvet in the new presence and privy chambers, and joiners constructed furniture on-site. Painters had just applied the finishing touches to our apartment, and it lent the feel of a fresh start as we settled in. Mother didn't know her way around. She didn't seem familiar with any of the chambers, even in the older wings. It seemed apparent that she'd lied to me—she'd never been here before.

So it surprised me the next day when she ordered the Queen Mother's carriage to take us to Whitehall Palace. "Put on your best day clothes and bring Madame's letter," she said. "We shall see it into King Charles's hands and hope he'll be generous."

She made Mary go with us. A King's Guard approached as we turned off the Strand into the red brick archway of Court Gate. Mother introduced herself and flashed the black seal of Madame's letter. "We've come to present ourselves to His Majesty."

"His Majesty isn't like to receive in his regular rooms today. The privy gallery is under repairs."

"We will return at a more suitable time."

He nodded. "Try yer luck at St. James's Park, as His Majesty is like to take his daily walk."

Mother smiled patiently. "Just instruct our driver to enter the court and turn about."

He looked quizzically at us. "Ye can this once, but you're supposed to turn yer carriage out here in the street."

We rumbled through the gate, Mother looked embarrassed, and I fought my disappointment. Mary pointed out the many structures. Some tall, some wide, all were tumbled together in contrasting styles of differing generations. There was no center point, no main entry, but doorways, gates, and alleys leading in every direction. If Mother hadn't been here before, she would need Mary to guide us. Before the carriage turned in front of the Great Hall, it stopped. Mother gasped, and pointed to the long wooden terrace that stretched the length of the Great Court. Through the arched doorway walked King Charles, short cloak whipping around him, trailed by several gentlemen and a rowdy pack of spaniels. She pushed open the door and slipped gracefully toward him.

Mary pushed me. "Go, girl. Now is your chance."

King Charles caught sight of my mother. "Sophia Stuart?"

She dipped, right there in the middle of the Great Court, to a deep curtsy.

"It is you! Have you just returned from France?"

Mother presented Madame's letter. "To bring word from your sister and to introduce my daughter at court."

He glanced at me just as I stepped out of the carriage. I hardly knew whether to curtsy on the spot or approach. "Ah, the girl who was not my sister at Colombes those years ago!"

I went to them, disguising my fluster with a curtsy and a smile.

He took the precious letter and said, "Carry this for me, Bennet." A gentleman, with a narrow black strip pasted across the bridge of his nose, snatched it and tucked it into his doublet. The king grinned at us. His eyes—I'd forgotten how golden brown they were—crinkled at the edges, lighting his dark face with joy. "Thank you mightily and welcome to Whitehall. We're off to the park for a walk." He leaned close and whispered. "One can always tell which of my courtiers needs the most favor by noting who keeps up with me the longest. It's most amusing. Would you care to join us?"

Speechless, Mother and I glanced at each other before she replied, "Thank you, Majesty, not today."

He walked toward Court Gate and called over his shoulder. "I expect to see you at court whenever you have an excuse."

The band of men and pack of yipping spaniels followed close behind him. One man stopped to catch my eye. *Buckingham!* He flashed a wildly satisfied grin, pointed at me, and then followed the king out.

Mother noticed. But Buckingham couldn't dampen my delight. It had been unusual, but we'd gotten our welcome to court. A warm welcome at that. Now I needed an excuse to return to the palace and pursue my goal.

The sight of Buckingham made Mother so nervous, we didn't leave Somerset for a fortnight. She evaluated improvements at the house, and I secretly sewed St. Albans's silver coins into the hems of my sister's petticoats.

"It's so much," she said when I showed her. "We'll never be hungry as we were during the Fronde."

If I didn't get my appointment, we'd need this money to sustain us until the Queen Mother's arrival. But I wouldn't explain to Mother why St. Albans had given it to me any sooner than I had to. I didn't even know the reason myself.

The excitement I'd felt initially soon faded, as we received no invitations to engagements. Mother wouldn't even take me to Whitehall's presence chamber to meet the English courtiers. Our only glimpses of London were of watercraft navigating the frosty river beyond Somerset's garden walls. Until a letter finally arrived.

"An invitation to a ball at Whitehall." I held my breath. "The king is sure to be there."

Mother pressed her lips together and said nothing.

That evening, when I'd tied gauzy lace around the shoulders of my green velvet bodice, slipped the matching petticoat over the waist tabs, donned black and gold mules, and curled black and gold ribbon into my hair, I pulled King Louis' velvet box out of our old wooden chest. If I wanted to impress them, set myself apart, I had to stand out. I took a deep breath and opened the box. I extended it to Mother.

Her voice was a tight, slow whisper. "How did you get that?"

"King Louis gave it to me as a farewell gift."

She closed the box so hard it fell and clattered against the floor. "I wouldn't dare let you go to court if the Queen Mother didn't command me." Hot fury lit her eyes and I realized too late I should have lied. Her fingers reached into my curls and ripped a black ribbon out, pulling strands of hair with it. "No man, much less a king, lavishes such trinkets on a woman for nothing. Whatever you did with him, whatever he wanted you to do in exchange for that gaudy thing, you best never speak of." She looped the black ribbon around my neck and tied it at my nape. Hard.

I choked and reached up, slipping a finger underneath to take a breath. "Mother, I've done nothing—"

"Don't speak if you are going to tell lies." She took a shaky breath. "If people discover—your brother will be *shunned*."

"Mother, please tell me your father's name."

"That is a name no one can *ever* know," she whispered, resigned.

Afterward, our short journey down the Strand to Whitehall Palace in the Queen Mother's cavernous carriage was dark and somber. We alighted in the Great Court and passed through the arch of the long wooden terrace. Mother spied some old friends, Royalists who had been in France, and anxiously struck up conversation.

The Banqueting House at Whitehall Palace had white walls and tall straight windows. Inside, a glance overhead revealed heavenly gilt-framed murals by Rubens. Angels and seraphim frolicked among clouds with members of the Stuart royal family over candles that twinkled in huge chandeliers.

I hid behind one of the massive columns and faced a corner. With one swift move, I slipped the ruby necklace on and tucked the black ribbon away.

Praise Sophia, who had tucked it into my hanging pocket when she kissed me good-bye. I tried not to think of the trust, the hopefulness in her young eyes as she did it. I had to prove I was equipped to adorn a queen's train. *Let Mother rage. There will be far worse consequences for us if I fail to get this position.*

Men and women of upper rank knotted together, and I inched my way around them, hoping for a glimpse of the king. I had to press my request, inquire about Madame's letter. I would beg for the position if I had to. I backed into someone and quickly turned around to apologize to a girl who appeared to be my age. I took in her bodice, old-fashioned with its high waist and colorful pattern. I realized, under ribbon embroidery, the base fabric was simple wool. Like I used to wear. This was the face of noble pride subjected to poverty and suffering. One I knew too well.

"You just arrived from France, did you not?" She inspected my velvet and her eyes widened. "You certainly cut a fashionable figure here. I am Elizabeth Frasier. And you are Frances Stuart, cousin to the king. Everyone's talking about your arrival."

"Pleased to make your acquaintance," I said with a quick curtsy. A twinge of guilty prosperity made me blush. "Madame, the king's sister, is very generous to loyal servants." I tried not to choke on the words.

"Did you petition for a post in the new queen's household? I did."

"Yes." I squeezed her hand. "We can become friends if we both succeed."

Her face warmed to a pleasant smile. "There are so many Royalist families pressing the king for money or positions. I fear there is not enough favor to go around."

I nodded. "So many sacrificed for the king's cause during the Commonwealth."

"You've never seen such merriment as when our efforts paid off and King Charles was restored to the throne. Fountains flowed with wine; streets were carpeted in flowers. Now everyone has hopes to regain their place, better themselves. Praise God we are finally free from Cromwell, for those were dreary days indeed."

I was moved by her passion.

"Although," she went on, "there will be little left to spare us if Lady Castlemaine continues." Frasier peered over her shoulder, then whispered, "She is with child, you know."

All the breath went out of me.

Frasier went on. "Everyone believes this one is the king's bastard, though her first babe was probably her husband's get. We will all be better off if his new queen can oust the Lady."

The new queen might actually win the king's heart. "I wonder, what sort of woman is Catherine of Bragança?"

"She is Catholic, Portuguese," a young gentleman in fine silk said beside me. He bowed swiftly to Frasier. "But I think most can forgive her that since she brings such a rich dowry. Several hundred thousand pounds, it is."

"Frances Stuart, this is Henry Hyde, Lord Cornbury. Son of a real hero, Lord Chancellor Earl of Clarendon, who helped negotiate the terms of the Restoration."

"A pleasure, my lord." I dipped a quick curtsy. "What do you know of our new queen?"

He gave a stiff bow. "Little, I'm afraid. They say Catherine never left the convent where she was raised. I imagine she'll be dutiful." He raised a finger into the air. "But I know something of Bombay, the most important part of the marriage agreement between Catherine and King Charles. The trade of its ports will make England prosper."

"God, I hope so. England sorely needs it." Frasier tipped her head. "Lord Cornbury, did you see the king's portrait of Catherine?"

"She seemed small and dark." He shrugged. "No great beauty, I'm afraid. She'll have to be sweet as plum pudding or more shrewish than Lady Castlemaine, to capture the king's attention."

"You think it's possible, then?" I asked. "King Charles could be coaxed away from Lady Castlemaine?"

"I doubt it."

Herald and trumpet calls echoed off the high, glittering walls, and we stretched our necks toward the entrance. Excited mutters, curtsies, and bows rolled through the crowd like a wave. Gentlemen removed their hats, ladies pinched their cheeks. King Charles entered the hall, followed by his brother James, Duke of York, and his duchess, Anne Hyde. The Queen Mother had once bitterly accused her of entrapping her son by becoming pregnant.

"The Duchess of York is my sister," said Cornbury.

"Of course," I replied, and faces began to match the names in all the rumors I'd heard about the English court.

King Charles signaled for music from the upper gallery and danced a coranto with the Duchess of York to the appreciative *ah*s of the spectators. I stood on my toes to get a glimpse of him.

A hushed voice sounded at my ear. "I see you got my invitation."

Buckingham. Frasier seemed astounded at his appearance. Before I could introduce her, she backed shyly away, blending into the crowd. Cornbury peeked at Buckingham from the corner of his eye but pretended to take no notice.

"Did Madame throw you out when King Louis fell in love with you? I warned you."

"Your presumptions are insulting." How did he know? He was far too canny to be trusted.

"Either way you're here, and I'll wager you want to be a maid of honor."

"I'm here to take a position that ought to be mine by rights. As a Stuart."

"These things require persuasion. Finesse." He leaned in. "Let me help you."

I narrowed my eyes. "On what condition?"

"Simply gain the king's favor. Keep it. And remember it started with me."

Buckingham took my arm as the violins crescendoed, spiraling and rising to the end of the dance. As he guided me toward the inner perimeter, people bowed, curtsied, and backed up to make way. Everyone, I noticed, watched us circle the dancing area, their eyes upon me like talons. And one pair of those eyes belonged to my mother.

"I agree to nothing," I whispered.

A string of courtiers stood looped and knotted tightly around King Charles, affecting airs and prattling. They eyed us and reluctantly made way for my high-ranking escort.

Buckingham whispered, "No matter. The price for this will still come." He swept his arm, extended his leg, and bent forward before King Charles. I dipped in a low curtsy, waiting for the king's acknowledgment of us before standing.

"Bucks, you found my little cousin," the king said. At least one head taller than the others, and wearing a hat with a long white plume, he loomed above us. "I do hope you've done nothing that would upset her mother."

I had once looked to King Charles as my savior—all England had. Now I looked to him as such again. My entire future depended on what would happen with this man. His full lips curved in a grin, which deepened the lines beside them. I smiled back.

Buckingham gestured toward me, pitched his voice for curious ears to hear. "In all my travels through Europe I never saw a lovelier girl. I've dubbed her la Belle Stuart."

"The title suits her." King Charles eyed Buckingham. "But take care your cousin doesn't hear you."

Men standing nearby snickered. *Who do they mean?*

Buckingham waved his arm theatrically. "If you will appoint her to your queen's household and move her into Whitehall, I will let you dance with her tonight. Otherwise, I'm whisking her off to Wallingford House to make her my mistress, and you'll never have a chance at her again."

I smiled wider, hoping everyone would see this as sarcasm.

King Charles tipped his head back and laughed while the surrounding nobles giggled courteously. "I hear you were much in favor at the French court, and my sister spoke so highly of you in her letter. She's sorry to lose you."

"And I her, Your Majesty," I said, not allowing myself to be sad. "I love your sister with all my heart. Alas, there is no official position in her household that mustn't go to a French lady. That is why I hope to serve your new queen as maid of honor."

He leaned back on his heels. "You and every other eligible maid of a Royalist family in England."

I didn't miss a heartbeat. "How many of them share your same Stuart blood? How many of them so long to serve her royal Stuart cousin, that she would take a position serving his queen in order to serve him?"

The men snorted, as I knew they would. But King Charles did not. God forgive me.

"La Belle Stuart." His eyes twinkled. "I think I'd be sorry not to appoint you. The position is yours."

Victory! I dipped low again. "Your Majesty, thank—"

The swish of heavy skirts whipped hard against my own, and the first thing I saw were her red mules, with the highest heels imaginable, covered in gold spangles. They planted themselves in front of the king. She did not curtsy until she had taken his hand in hers. Only then did she dip and kiss his ring.

I rose, speechless, and looked to others to validate my shock, but they did not appear shocked in the least. I looked at King Charles, who I thought must be outraged at this informality, but he . . . smiled.

She swept the room with an upturned palm. "Why did any of you bother coming tonight? I'm the only one who can keep up dancing with the king."

"Don't flatter yourself, cousin." Buckingham stepped to kiss her upturned cheek. "You wouldn't be able to keep up with him, either, if not for those long pretty legs of yours."

Cousin?

A wicked grin spread across her face.

King Charles laughed. "The prettiest legs in the whole of England."

Buckingham called over his shoulder, "Did that sound like a royal declaration, Bennet?"

"No, Your Grace. It was a statement born of personal experience."

All the men guffawed.

"Quiet, rogues," called King Charles. "You'll ruin my good reputation."

"He already does that well enough himself!" She was witty, but they laughed and laughed to play into her obvious influence.

King Charles gestured. "We were talking with Frances Stuart, just back from France."

Turning her eyes to me for the first time, she inspected me from head to toe. The expensive, shimmery glass beads stitched over her red bodice emphasized the rose in her lips as she frowned. The king went on, "This is Barbara Palmer, Countess of Castlemaine."

She held rank. I dipped in a low curtsy as violinists in the upper gallery struck chords for an allemande. Before I had fully risen, she *stepped away.* She took King Charles's arm and walked toward the dancing floor, leading the king and leaving everyone else behind.

My face felt like fire. By protocol, without her first speaking to me, I could never speak to her. She had cut me. And effectively ended my audience with King Charles.

When Buckingham pressed my side again, I felt relief in spite of myself. "Now you must go," he muttered. "You will take my coach and I will send your mother directly."

"Go? Nothing is yet arranged," I said, turning toward him so no one else might hear.

"La Belle," he hissed as he dragged me toward the wall, through a door. "He liked you. If you go while he still wants your company, it guarantees he will send for you tomorrow."

"A Frenchman once told me that teasing is in very poor taste."

"A Frenchman would. I am telling you it is in your best interest tonight. And mine."

An hour later I made sure I was in bed with the curtains and my eyes closed tight. But when Mother returned, she peeked in, and she was crying softly. She muffled her sobs as she tried to undress herself, and I couldn't bear it. I climbed from bed to untie her bodice laces, and she let me. "You know I have to do this, and Buckingham is only helping," I whispered as I ushered her to her own bed.

"It is as I feared."

I kissed each of her cheeks. "Rely on me."

CHAPTER 14

Whitehall Palace

February

Buckingham sent his men to fetch me early the next morning. They presented sealed parchments outlining my formal appointment as maid of honor, which included quarters at Whitehall Palace, and they waited while I prepared to depart Somerset House.

"Let us come, too!" Walter pulled me into a dance.

I hugged him to me. "You shall in time!"

Sophia packed the last of my gowns into the chest. "Does this mean we can all come to court functions?"

"The ones you're old enough for," I promised.

But Mother gripped her hands together until they turned white. "You must be cautious with him."

I didn't know whether she meant Buckingham or the king. I embraced her, promised to send for them soon, and kissed them too many times. I felt very tense in Buckingham's coach.

King Charles greeted me as I stepped into the Pebble Court. "So glad you could arrive this early. I want to show you to your chambers myself." He offered his arm, waved off his followers, and pointed to a gap in one corner. "We'll go this way, through the Stone Gallery."

I clung to his arm and took two steps to each of his just to keep up as he guided me under another wooden terrace around the Pebble Court to the passage. We stepped into the wide corridor and my shoes clip-clipped on the long, paving-stone floor.

The king pointed to a door on our right. "The Privy Garden is on the other side and runs its length. I've just ordered a marvelous sundial to go out there, a scientific marvel." He gestured to the walls. "Most of the court has apartments on either side here. They cram into every coveted corner. Whitehall is an intricate maze." He stopped and pointed to the left. "Remember: turn toward the Thames to get to the maid of honor apartments."

When I stepped through a passage, my head buzzed with "scientific," "coveted," "maze," and then I was outside again in a narrow, jagged alley created by the high stone walls of the houses. I lifted my skirt to tiptoe around puddles in the cobblestone walk and turned a corner.

"Lady Sanderson is installed as mother of the maids to look over you since your mother is still at Somerset House, but she'll give you no trouble." He opened the door, startling a servant, and indicated a large chamber with several doors to antechambers and bedchambers beyond. "This is their area. But yours is separate." He led me farther down. "Step up, the Thames tends to flood occasionally."

I mounted a few stone stairs and walked through the door to my new home. Sunlight filled the space through a window overhead. It shone against a black-and-white marble fireplace and high, wainscoted walls washed in white paint.

King Charles walked toward the fireplace. "You can order tapestries for the walls, or paintings. Whatever you like." He pointed to the passage leading to the bedchamber. "The closets, with enough space for a maid to sleep in each, are between your chambers."

"This is . . ." I almost said it was more than I deserved.

King Charles appraised me and leaned against the fireplace, regal even in his casual stance. His simple brown satin doublet glittered with the diamonds of his garter star. "Where did you get off to last night? I wanted to talk to you."

"I am not used to attracting so much attention and thought it best that I go."

"I guess you wouldn't be. Serving my sister might make one feel second-best."

I realized he was right the instant he said it; I just hadn't attached the feeling to a name. His insight moved me unexpectedly. "Your Majesty is very wise."

"And not immune to flattery." He winked.

"I do miss her," I said with a pang of longing. "I love her so."

"You remind me of her, la Belle Stuart. Look." He pulled a small locket from his doublet pocket and opened it. It was a miniature of Madame. "Samuel Cooper painted it. Do you care for art?"

"Of course! I spent last summer at Fontainebleau. You've seen the collection there. My favorite is *La Joconde*."

"By Leonardo da Vinci! My father once tried to buy it. He collected art. I am doing my utmost to recover pieces Cromwell sold to feed his damn New Model Army."

"Do you have anything by the Italian masters? Nothing is more beautiful."

"You are wrong." He grinned, and I wasn't sure if he was flirting or teasing, but I found myself grinning back. He lifted his hand and traced the bone of my cheek with the tip of one finger. "I've never seen more beauty than I do here," he whispered. "So pure. Your face reminds me of the Virgin Mary in a drawing I have by Raphael. I grant it to you! I'll deliver it myself."

Three of Buckingham's footmen entered with my old chest and Sir Ment's cage. King Charles's gaze fell on my parrot. "What an excellent specimen! Does he speak?"

The parrot promptly replied, *"Oui, oui."* When I nodded, Sir Ment called, "Yes."

The king's laughter echoed off the walls. "This apartment will be perfect for you. Come." He walked through the passage between the closets, took my hand, and pulled me to the door on the far wall. "Look," he said, throwing it open.

Decorative ironwork birdcages were built into the courtyard walls—some so high they met my windows. Exotic, feathered creatures jumped from limb to limb on tree branches within, while a page in king's livery pushed dishes of seeds through a feeding gate.

"The Volery Garden," said King Charles.

I clapped my hands. "I love them. How did you know?" I brushed my fingertip against a silver gilt candle sconce on the wall. "Never before have I had so much for myself."

"Whatever you want, anything you need, you may have it. You are my cousin. My only living sister's friend. You shall have several hundred pounds each year. I shall commission Samuel Cooper to paint that face of yours and fill your walls with works by the Italian masters." He draped one arm across my shoulders. "My brother James is all the family left to me here. Let me treat you like a sister?"

"Very well." *A petted sister! Surely a wiser course than becoming his mistress!*

"I have something else. Actually, a favor to ask." He turned his face toward the closet. "Prudence," he called. A waif of a girl, dressed in wool, stepped out. She curtsied.

"This is Prudence Pope," said King Charles. "When I lost the battle at Worcester, I evaded Cromwell's army disguised as a servant escorting a woman to Abbots Leigh. Prudence's father was the head butler there, and he recognized me. Without his aid I never would have escaped England alive. He passed away before my restoration, leaving his daughter. She's been alone in the world, raised by—friends. If I provide funds for her, would you keep her as a handmaiden? Until she decides whether she wants to marry."

She was younger than I, wide-eyed and trembling. I crossed to the girl and took her hands. "Of course."

Prudence's huge brown eyes filled. "Milady, thank ye. Thank ye." She curtsied to the king and flew through the passage to my old chest and began unpacking.

"You should know one thing about Prudence." King Charles spoke in a hushed voice. "The friends that helped her after her father's death, I believe they are Quakers."

I frowned, not knowing what he meant.

"A new Protestant sect who believe all people are spiritual equals. Some are radicals bent on challenging authority in government."

"She's a Dissenter?"

His eyebrows flew up, surprised at my choice of words. "Yes. There is no need to fear her, of course. But if she herself is a Quaker, she might need your protection. Encourage her to practice her religion privately."

"You would house a Nonconformist?"

He glanced at her where she knelt, sorting my clothing. "Does she look dangerous to you? My subjects ought to worship according to their own tender conscience, as long as they remain peaceful."

I studied his expression, both gentle and strong, and saw he meant it. Never before had I heard a man, much less a king, show such acceptance of another person's beliefs. It exalted my estimation of him, and I decided I agreed with him.

"I promised toleration when I was restored."

Toleration. This word was not the choice of a man who intended to return his people to the Catholic Church against their will. *No matter what his mother might wish.* "You may rely on it. I shall advise her where I can, even protect her if needed."

"You are kindness itself," King Charles said softly. "I am so pleased you are here."

A few days after my move to Whitehall, Mary had appeared, insisting she wait on me. "My queen commanded it and I'll not be leaving," she'd said. Mary's real purpose had become clear: to gain information about my progress in bedding King Charles and report back to the Queen Mother.

"Milady," she called to me from the doorway.

"What is it?" I sat at my new toilette table and blotted Spanish paper onto my lips. The red effect was too garish, so I wiped it off with a bit of cloth.

"Prudence, milady. She's left your linen over in the laundry to dry when I told her she should stay with it lest it be stolen."

"Do you think you can cook, mend, dress me and my hair, and tend our fires all by yourself while Prudence is gone watching laundry dry?"

The wrinkles above her upper lip deepened.

"The court laundry maids can be trusted not to steal my stockings. You must find a way to get along with Prudence."

Her eyes bulged. "But she's a—*Protestant.* She never goes to mass.

You cannot trust her. She shouldn't be here." She huffed and stomped away. She would tell the Queen Mother everything.

Buckingham's voice rang from the door. "You should leave it on. The Spanish red."

I glanced at his reflection in my looking glass. It was from Venice, his own gift, and very expensive. "If you call on me this often, your wife will get cross." He'd come every day since my arrival, bearing gifts to embellish my chambers and to accompany me to a few court suppers. Today he would escort me to the St. Valentine's Day Ball.

"My wife doesn't get cross when I visit my mistress. She certainly doesn't care that I visit you." He pulled out his clay pipe and box of tobacco. "Put it on." He gestured to the Spanish paper. "You need all the help you can get to supplant Lady Castlemaine."

"Why do you wish to undermine your own cousin?" I longed to ask what he knew of my mother's parentage, but didn't dare. "I thought the Villiers family protected one another." I watched his response.

"We do." He sucked a flame into his pipe until he was breathing smoke. From the feather in his cavalier hat to the polished red heels of his shoes, his ensemble was perfect. Outside, four footmen and two guards waited to accompany him anywhere. He was admitted everywhere without question; his high rank and position on the Privy Council were envied by all. Yet, for all his wealth, he held no high government office. I knew what Madame's conclusion would be: he was buying me to gain more trust from the king. I stuffed the Spanish paper into its paper fold and tossed it into my jewel casket.

He took a long draw on his pipe and blew a series of smoke rings at me. "As you just pointed out, I'm a Villiers. Not one to be challenged."

"Well, I'm a Stuart. Not one to be underestimated."

The Great Hall was almost half the length of the Banqueting House and more than a century older. The lower portion of the plaster walls was painted in black-and-white checkers, with huge windows above. The central hearth crackled and glowed, and the smoke wafted to a great louver in the center of the hammer-beam ceiling. This part of winter was carnival season. The table was draped with lace and ribbon and boasted a huge urn from which valentines would be drawn.

Buckingham paraded me before King Charles, but as Castlemaine was fondling his lace bib, he barely glanced at me. She never looked at me, either. At length Buckingham retreated, leaving me to fend for myself. A familiar voice captured my ear. "She resents your beauty. Do you hate her yet?"

"Thank you, Lord Cornbury. I don't think so."

He shrugged. "She'll get her place in the palace if she has to tear the walls down herself. King Charles empties the privy purse into her very lap. At any rate, I came to tell you your cousin wishes to speak with you." He pointed toward the door, at a gentleman propped carelessly against the wall.

"Is that . . . Charles Stuart?" I'd last seen him with his uncle Ludovic, Seigneur d'Aubigny, two years earlier. He was living in Paris then.

Cornbury shook his head. "It is, but he's the Duke of Richmond *and* Lennox. Bit of a rake, in and out of favor with the king, but your cousin Charles Stuart is a baron and earl more times than I can count. Don't short one of the highest-ranking men in England. Go over—he's waiting."

"You've grown," he said as I approached. He bowed, kissed my hand. "Last we met you were as scrawny as I was and dressed in the same threadbare clothes that marked us as exiled Royalists."

I inspected him from collar to silk shoelaces. Now he wore enough finery to rival a prince. A row of rubies buttoned his black satin doublet, quilted in elaborate scroll and sunburst patterns. A red plume topped the cavalier hat he clasped at his side. "Heavens," I said. "You're suited to match your new title. *Rich*mond."

He glanced down, sheepish. "Don't tease. I'm a duke now. Have to dress my station."

"You've mastered that requirement."

He nodded toward my necklace. "Did you marry an emperor?"

"A gift from King Louis," I whispered. "It didn't have the desired effect."

"Had I known you were here—" He grasped my hand. "I would have waited."

I met his gaze. "For what?"

"I got married again."

I squeezed his hand. "I heard of Elizabeth's death when I was still in France." One of the many exiles living between The Hague and Paris, he had married her in poverty. They'd returned to England at the Restoration, just before he inherited his highest titles from another cousin. "She was the sweetest of women."

He nodded. "Wouldn't have remarried so soon if not for my daughter. She deserves a mother. I might have rediscovered you first, had I waited."

The words rang in my head. Here was my English nobleman. An offer such as this would have prevented every bad thing that had happened. "I would have liked that," I whispered.

He took a deep, bracing breath. "Here we are, then." He glanced at the gathering of nobles. "Look there at Sir Henry Bennet." He tipped his head toward the courtier with the black strip on his nose. "He served the king during exile, mostly as his representative in Madrid. That patch covers a scar he received fighting in the wars. King Charles made him keeper of the privy purse for his loyalty."

"Why do you point him out?" *I had wondered what that patch was for.*

"He knows half a dozen languages. He's savvy. Cunning. He's the only council member who can influence the king. If you can't press King Charles for an alliance with France, press ministers who can."

I gaped at him. "How did you know?"

He glanced at my necklace again. "Met King Louis in Paris. He longs for English connections. Damn shrewd man."

So was Richmond. A circle of influential alliances would get the king's attention *and* rid me of any need for Buckingham. "Can you help me?"

He shook his head. "Going home to Kent before I do something else to irritate King Charles, but I'll get you started." Then he called to the courtier with the nose patch. "Bennet, tell me you know my cousin Frances Stuart."

He bowed to me. "She is better known here as la Belle Stuart."

"What a pleasure," I said. "The court says King Charles trusts you above any other."

"It is an honor to have his favor."

"Has he mentioned the Raphael?" I asked, inspired. "The one he promised to grant me?"

Bennet glanced at Richmond before turning back to me. "I'm afraid not."

"You must ask him about it. And accompany him when he brings it. Why, I'll hold a reception in my apartments!"

The Duke of York, the king's brother, appeared. "You can't hoard la Belle Stuart to yourselves any longer, gentlemen. I've drawn her name as my valentine." He presented me with a gift: a great emerald ring. It had to be worth near a thousand pounds. "I rigged the drawing, of course." He winked. "Had to have an excuse to lavish my cousin, welcome her home from France properly."

"Oh, it's lovely." I slipped it on and admired it. *Mother will kill me.*

Richmond stepped in. "Off to Cobham Hall. Take care of her, rogues." He kissed each of my cheeks and left us. Bennet watched me carefully as I turned back to York. I spoke softly so they'd have to lean in to hear me. "Your Grace, I was just telling Sir Bennet about the reception I'm having. Won't you join us?"

When the day arrived, I arranged for four palace footmen to carry me in a sedan chair to my mother's apartments at Somerset House. "Mother, come to my chambers this evening for a reception. You'll see there's nothing to worry about." She agreed to attend, reluctantly, but wouldn't allow my brother and sister to join her no matter how much I begged. Before we parted, I gave her fifty pounds. It was nearly every bit of my first payment in service as maid of honor.

In preparation for the event, I borrowed silver plates and candlesticks, carpets, and glasses from the Queen Mother's collection. I sent Mary to the palace pantry for fruits and cheeses and Prudence to the palace cellars for more than my allotment of the best mead and wine. I draped carpets over all my tables, lit candles in every corner, and pasted a star-shaped black patch by my mouth.

Cornbury arrived with Frasier, who brought her friend Helene Warmestry. Then other candidates for the queen's household, including Winifred Wells and Simona Cary, filtered in, appreciative for any excuse to come to Whitehall Palace, and awed by the presence of the

Duke of York. When some of my guests called for gambling, Mother handed out a fresh deck of playing cards, hand-painted in France, and Prudence kept everyone's glass full.

King Charles arrived to a genuine fête. "What's this merry bunch? Holding court of your own, la Belle?"

I fashioned my smile to that of an adoring younger sister, and then Bennet presented a large leather volume to me. I let King Charles open it, and my company gasped at the prized drawing within. "As promised," he quipped. He stayed for over an hour, telling stories and making everyone laugh. As he took his leave, I asked, "And when am I to sit for Samuel Cooper?"

He grinned. "I'll send word."

Even Mother looked impressed.

I began to hold receptions regularly. Mother came from time to time but never brought the children. Everyone seemed anxious to attend, knowing King Charles called on his way to, or home from, Lady Castlemaine's King Street house. We gambled some, then built card houses when we tired of card games. We borrowed the king's violinists and danced in my bedchamber. We played blind man's buff, though Wells most certainly peeked under the blindfold, and Cary got so dizzy when we spun her around that she fell on her backside.

Buckingham appeared frequently, flirting mercilessly with new ladies, including Lady Mary Wood, whom I'd known in France, and Katherine Boynton, a colonel's daughter. The Irish Earl of Carlingford attended one evening, and he amused us by holding a lit candle in his mouth without burning himself or extinguishing it. But George, of the numerous and influential Hamilton family, outdid him by holding two lit candles in his mouth and walking around the room three times. Old Sir William Killigrew, who aimed to become our new queen's vice-chamberlain, topped them both when he brought me a kitten, a little ball of gray fluff.

"I know just what we'll name him," cried the witty widow Lady Scroope when she'd ceased flirting with Bennet long enough to notice the feline. "Miss Ment!"

Then we set about teaching my parrot how to call the cat.

One by one, my new friends got their appointments as the queen's dressers, maids of honor, and maids of the privy chamber. By the end of March the painter Samuel Cooper was my honored guest. Mother sat near me and Bennet arrived early, offering to hold candles aloft while the artist sketched my portrait.

But when King Charles joined us, he frowned. "No jewels, la Belle? That won't do." And he presented me with a short strand of fat white pearls. It was fit for a royal and worth thousands of pounds. He tied the ribbon ends behind my neck right there in front of everyone.

I embraced him and whispered, "Now I know you won't forget me when you go to fetch your bride."

He chucked my chin. "Of course I won't. My ministers tell me Madame delivered an infant girl. Both are alive and well. They claim she was so disappointed it wasn't a male, she said to throw it in the Seine."

"She would never say that!"

"I agree. Nor would she have an affair with King Louis as was rumored." He watched my reaction carefully.

"Of course not." And I knew, merry though he was, I'd have to be careful with this king.

When my mother went home that night, I said, "See, not a trace of scandal. Won't you allow my sister to join us?"

"Perhaps this autumn. When you return from Hampton Court with the new queen."

CHAPTER 15

Hampton Court Palace

The queen is brought a few days since to Hampton Court; and all people say of her to be a very fine and handsome lady, and very discreet; and that the king is pleased enough with her which, I fear, will put Madam Castlemaine's nose out of joynt.

—SAMUEL PEPYS'S DIARY
May 1662

Catherine of Bragança landed in Portsmouth at the close of May. King Charles took her appointed dressers and the new clothes he'd bought her, and he set out to wed her and bring her to Hampton Court for the summer. The other ladies and I traveled by barge to wait for their arrival. Wells tripped up the waterside stairs when we disembarked, and we followed her through the privy gate. "The gardens are huge!"

Though pretty with an avenue of lime trees, parterres, and a long canal, I thought they were small for such a large palace. Inside, Lady Sanderson led us through three great courtyards, then showed us the queen's rooms, draped with red velvet and silver embroidery, and explained our duty to stand for the queen's morning toilette, her daily mass, each of her meals, and her bedtime routine.

"That's standing all day," cried Cary.

Wells elbowed her ribs. "We're ladies-*in-waiting*. What did you think we'd be doing?"

We settled into our assigned apartments, while coaches arrived bearing England's most noble families. They filled every court and corner of the palace, unpacking and preparing to pay homage to the new queen. We were giddy with excitement when we finally spotted two rows of pikemen leading a long stream of coaches on the road. Six horses with two postilions drove the royal carriage while men-at-arms, runners, and footmen ran alongside. The royal standards bobbed over the winding train of accompanying peers. The pikemen formed an avenue over the moat, and the carriage drove through the Great Gate into the first court. The king alighted with his new queen, walking her through Horse Guards lining the way to the great hall stairs beyond the clock tower. The lord chancellor and councillors of state kissed her hand and led her through the great watching chamber. Here we curtsied and paid homage to our new mistress.

Tiny, with a dark complexion, she greeted us cordially. She was dressed in a blue French gown King Charles had given her, and we quickly fell into step behind her Portuguese attendants. The dressers joined us and we made a train to the presence chamber to meet the foreign ambassadors. Nobility and gentry were grouped according to rank in one tapestried chamber after the other, and each one kissed Queen Catherine's hand. My cousin the Duke of Richmond was in the first, highest-ranking chamber. One of the lords from Parliament had recently informed me his young daughter had been interred at the Richmond vault in Westminster Abbey, and I'd sent a box of oranges to his home in Kent as condolence on behalf of my family. He seemed forlorn but winked at me as I passed. When finally we reached the queen's bedchamber, her Portuguese attendants ushered her in. "*Sai daqui!*" one said to us, and with that she slammed the door.

Wells and I gaped at each other.

"It was all we could do to get her into that gown for her entry today," said Frasier under her breath, looking tired from the journey from Portsmouth. "Those scary old maids of hers won't let us near her."

"What do we do now?" asked Cary.

"We can go to my rooms," I said with a shrug. "The Duke of Richmond sent a footman up with a lovely case of blackberry wine when he arrived today."

Cornbury cleared his throat nervously a few weeks later as the last violinist packed up his instrument and left my Hampton Court apartments. "Say, Frances, what does the king truly think about Parliament passing this Act of Uniformity?"

"I don't know." *He's furious at your father for failing to secure religious toleration for his subjects.* "But who cares about politics? Look." I held a new pair of pearl drop earrings up to the sconce in my antechamber, making them glow with life.

The eyes of my guests widened. "Impressive."

I watched Bennet calculate the king's regard for me based on the costly gift. *Good.* He cleared his throat. "Didn't you say you are not his mistress?"

"I did." I dropped the pearls into my jewel casket and slammed the lid. "I'm not."

"Then why . . ." He gestured to the casket.

The nature of my relationship with King Charles, whatever it turned out to be, must be shielded from all but Mary and King Louis' ambassadors. "You've seen him dote on me like a sister. I am his cousin, after all."

"*Distant* cousin." Bennet frowned. "I suppose with Lady Castlemaine in hiding, the king has to lavish someone."

The smile on my face was, I hoped, neutral. Inside, though, I fumed because he was partially right. Castlemaine had made herself scarce since the royal wedding. Cornbury shuffled his feet where he stood near the door. "His attention to Frances has increased since he married Queen Catherine. All the royal trappings enhance her beauty."

Bennet turned to him. "Is that the reason? So what will happen when the queen falls from favor? She's wearing those ugly Portuguese clothes again. And she angered the king when she refused to appoint Lady Castlemaine."

Catherine of Bragança was quiet, cheerful, and seemed pleased by everything her husband did. Then King Charles suggested she appoint Castlemaine as a lady of the bedchamber. She passionately refused. Apparently the Portuguese hadn't created one of the richest, most powerful trading nations by being fools. He explained that he owed this honor to his mistress and seemed genuinely surprised by his bride's sudden willfulness. I waved my hand at Bennet. "King Charles smoothed that over."

"Nothing is smooth for King Charles until Lady Castlemaine gets what she wants," he replied as he left.

Cornbury bowed and followed Bennet out, concluding another evening of good-natured revelry, and I fell into bed exhausted.

Hours later I opened my eyes to the blackness of deep night. A hushed voice rose and fell, filled with longing, and I got up, alarmed. A faint glow beckoned from the closet door, and I crept to it.

I saw Prudence kneeling before a tallow candle. She squeezed her lids tight over clasped hands, muttering, "... commune with ye, Jesus ... grant me strength ..." Her whole body shivered as if her knees were rooted in a block of ice. I pushed the door open and she jumped.

"Go to sleep before you wake Mary," I whispered.

She blinked red-rimmed eyes.

"Parliament just passed an act to enforce religious conformity, and that looks nothing like standard Anglican worship. This palace abounds with Royalists. Do you want to be sent to the Tower?" I reached to pull the door shut. "Now blow out that candle."

CHAPTER 16

Late July

The bay windows in Queen Catherine's presence chamber at Hampton Court Palace were made entirely of colorful stained glass, and none of them opened. I used my fan to swirl sweltering summer air toward the pearls on my neck, longing to escape the linenfold-paneled walls for a walk in the garden. But in the presence chamber, anyone with access to court could have access to the queen, and I stayed put because it was the only time her Portuguese attendants allowed her English ones in the same room with her.

When a herald announced the king, the entire mass of courtiers bowed in unison. Everyone gaped at the sight of King Charles entering with Castlemaine on his arm. Murmurs washed across the chamber. It appeared as if he were about to present his mistress to his wife for formal recognition.

My fan arrested mid-wave. I took note of Castlemaine's shoulders, thrust back, and how her breasts bulged forward, accentuating her flat bodice front. *So she has given birth.* She hadn't been hiding in deference to the royal wedding at all. She'd been busy concealing her bastard. I wanted to judge her, but my own mother came to mind and my scorn died.

My fan slipped from my fingers and swung from its bracelet. If the king insulted the queen so openly, she, and everyone attached to her household, would be disgraced. To my right stood Cornbury. Or rather, he slouched. He shot a questioning glance at me.

Bennet's face betrayed no emotion at all. But his eyes, which I'd learned to watch carefully, widened subtly as he scanned the court's reaction, to see how this insult to the queen would be received. Frasier's frantic whisper stirred the hair on the back of my neck. "The king is going to introduce that slut to Queen Catherine!"

I followed Bennet's gaze across the chamber to a clutch of courtiers who had gathered around Wells. She smirked and pointed at the queen. She would ridicule Queen Catherine behind her back after this. She would emphasize the queen's disgrace in order to separate herself from it.

I pursed my lips and looked at our new queen. Catherine of Bragança, queen consort of England, sat on her dais like a twig wrapped in silk. English ladies-in-waiting should have surrounded her. Instead, her Portuguese attendants stood behind and beside her. Their huge farthingales made their skirts jut out several feet to their right and left, so wide they brushed against Queen Catherine's hair.

Today, finally, the queen herself had dressed in a more suitable, English fashion. Not that it helped. Her green bodice, cut to hug her shoulders, seemed to hang off her as she hunched uncomfortably beside the Farthingale Frights. She knew not a word of English and struggled painfully to learn our manners. None of us English ladies could break past the Frights to help her. Although King Charles wasn't deterred. He'd just spoken to her in Spanish and sent the Frights scattering with a wave of his hand. Everyone in the room saw how enamored she was of him, how her eyes lingered on him.

The panic in Fraiser's whisper rose. "We shall lose all the ground we've gained at court if the king does this."

I reached back and squeezed her hand once, but I had no reassurance to offer. I held my breath as the pair breezed past us.

Bennet muttered, "He will not be governed by his wife, and he's going to show her publicly." He nodded his head, an almost imperceptible twitch. "The king will have his way, and the court will follow his example."

King Charles and Castlemaine took their final steps, and Castlemaine curtsied deeply. When she rose, the king made his introduction. Queen Catherine didn't understand a single word. She smiled and extended her hand. Castlemaine bent and kissed it, winning her official welcome into the queen's presence.

One of the Farthingale Frights hissed and leaned toward Queen Catherine's ear, whispering. The queen's face paled as she looked from her royal husband to Castlemaine and back again.

I muttered to Bennet. "He shouldn't have done it."

"Would you dare tell him that yourself?" He didn't look at me. "This is the custom of English kings. Queen Catherine would be happier if she understood that."

Poor Queen Catherine trembled in her green bodice. Her eyes fluttered and she leaned back. *She is fainting!* A bright crimson trickle oozed from her right nostril, dripped off her lips, and splattered onto her chest. Castlemaine jumped back with a gasp that sounded more like a laugh. King Charles stepped forward, but the Farthingale Frights barked at one another in Portuguese, crowding around Queen Catherine and shutting him out. As they bundled her up to carry her away, King Charles pointed at Bennet. "You, come with me. We're sending her Portuguese attendants away."

The king turned his fiery glare on me. A quick shadow of astonishment crossed his features, followed by a little guilt. "Don't look at me that way, Frances," he said. "And do something with my queen. She's innocent to the point of stupidity."

Hours later, when a twilight glow lit the red bricks of Hampton Court Palace, the courtiers within its walls still reveled in the afternoon's gossip. By the next evening they were mocking Queen Catherine openly, while the queen wept in her chambers.

CHAPTER 17

Early August

King Charles was so angry, Queen Catherine was so unrelenting, and the entirety of the English court was so preoccupied with ridiculing her, no one even thought to call her ladies to wait on her in the week that followed. But I tiptoed to her antechamber the day I saw the Portuguese train leave Hampton Court grounds, waiting for the first moment I could enter. I'd help her recover from her public embarrassment and benefit from it by my alliance with her.

Wells caught me loitering. "The queen is hopeless. Dress her when you're called. Stand behind her at banquets. Why bother with her any other time?"

"Duty." I wasn't going to tell her King Charles wanted me to help. I wasn't going to explain I *needed* the queen. No English woman held higher rank, after all.

"She'll never have any respect here. Neither will you if you cling to her side."

Wells left me, and Queen Catherine's priest scuttered out of her antechamber. I slipped in. Sadness and myrrh clung to the air inside. A Portuguese countess, so old and near death that she was allowed to remain with the queen, approached me. I curtsied and hurried past so she could not push me away.

Queen Catherine sat hunched by her open window, bundled in a cotton undress gown. I took in its painted design; limbs and leaves branched out from her back and down her sleeves in a pattern called the Tree of Life. Its happy birds and colorful flowers contrasted with the queen's hunched posture. Items like this gown, and the other exotic wares she'd brought into England, were the only things about Queen Catherine that the court liked. Such foreign goods were a sign of prosperous trade, a mark of wealth.

She turned puffy eyes to me. A gold and silver rosary clinked in her fingers. She wore no cosmetics, no crown, no jewels. She looked pious and pitiful. She should lace herself up in fine new silk, don some diamonds, and order a supper party with violins in the garden. She should get up and start acting worthy of the court's admiration. The stringy curls in her poor attempt at an English hairstyle caught my eye, and I clicked my tongue. She must have arranged those curls on her own. If she wanted to work at it, maybe I could help her.

She reached to me. *"Orar."* Portuguese for "pray."

I shook my head. "English. Pray."

We knelt at her prie-dieu where she whispered in a jumble of foreign words that had no meaning to me, pleas I hoped God could discern. Then I slipped my hand into my hanging pocket and pulled out a small paper fold. "Tea." I opened it and held it toward her.

She nodded and motioned to the old countess, who shuffled to a tall cabinet, lacquered and gleaming, the ebony and ivory inlay on its doors depicting scenes of birds, trees, and little people in strange hats. When the countess opened the doors, a wave of spice filled my nose with the essence and herbs of new worlds. The old woman carried a mother-of-pearl box to me and opened it. It overflowed with tea leaves.

Queen Catherine pointed. *"Chá."*

I shook my head. "Tea."

"Tea," she replied carefully.

We smiled while the countess fetched boiling water. She brightened as I named objects for her to repeat. I would drink tea with her today. Tomorrow I would dress her and, after that, teach her to dance.

Queen Catherine pointed to a small portrait of King Charles. "King."

I nodded, studying her face as it filled with longing. "Yes," I said. "King."

She laid her hand upon her chest, and the rims of her eyes reddened. I felt the emotions swimming in her face: the questioning, the clinging to hope, the longing for joy.

"Love," I replied. "That is love."

At the end of August we lounged under the canopy of flower garlands draping the royal barge as rowers pulled us up the Thames to Whitehall Palace for Queen Catherine's official entry into London. Every boat, raft, and skiff crowded together from bank to bank so one could hardly see the water. All packed with people cheering and waving and welcoming the queen. *If only everyone at court respected her thus.*

"I've never seen you fidget so badly." Cornbury glanced to my twining fingers. "Do you not want to return to Whitehall?"

I smoothed the lap of my petticoat for the hundredth time. In the weeks following the bedchamber incident, the queen's ladies had gathered enough sense to follow my example and had begun a daily routine of waiting on her. The Queen Mother had returned from France and conducted two official visits with Queen Catherine, one at Greenwich and one at Hampton Court, and neither one in enough privacy to speak with me. Queen Catherine was still unpopular, but the Queen Mother's presence had at least quieted the court's ridicule. "The Queen Mother will be greeting us. My mother will be there, too," I said quietly. "I fear she will not be—proud of me."

Lord Cornbury waved a hand. "Parents never are."

"Are yours not proud of you?" I wasn't really surprised. The court said his father, the lord chancellor, had only pretended to be furious when his daughter trapped the Duke of York into marriage. Like any man with power, he was very ambitious.

"Everything I have attained was granted through my father himself."

"But you are a good and dutiful son."

His lips pressed into a grim line while he scanned the crowd bobbing around us on the water. "Nothing is ever good enough for so great a man. If it be impossible to please him, why should I bother trying? I am free to choose my own path in life, after all."

I agreed, thinking of all I'd done to secure prosperity for my family, despite my own mother's wishes.

The Queen Mother greeted the king and queen on a pier near Whitehall, built just to receive them. The evening light made the swaths of gold fabric glow, and a salute of cannons fired across the river. She kissed her son and grasped the new queen's hands, and the commoners on the river burst into cheers. My mother presented my brother and sister, flushed with excitement, and they handed bouquets of flowers to Queen Catherine.

Mother hugged me tightly. "I hear it goes badly for the new queen."

"But she is making slow strides in English, in dancing. All will be well. Now, may Sophia stay with me at last?"

Her smile wavered. "Very well. But only while the Queen Mother stays at Whitehall. She must return with the Queen Mother when work at Somerset House is finished."

I was delighted, but as we made our way to the carriages that would carry us onto palace grounds, the Queen Mother caught my eye. She frowned, and I knew that soon she would summon me. Perhaps our mother was wise to shield my sister from court.

CHAPTER 18

Whitehall Palace
Mid-September

Sophia followed me everywhere for a fortnight. She stood behind me as Queen Catherine sat at her toilette table and peered at her new hairpiece in the looking glass. The queen turned to me with a questioning look. "Good?" She pointed to the masses of wired ringlets falling over each ear.

I nodded from my place among the rest of the ladies in attendance. "Yes."

"King Sharles like?"

"Yes. King Charles will like it."

She stood, and the dressers removed the brooch holding her mantua gown together. She pointed to her hair. "Like you."

"Yes." Of course, I had several hairpieces in the latest mode. "Like me."

Queen Catherine studied me as the dressers laced her bodice. "King Sharles like you."

Frasier, who was waiting to apply the queen's shoes, dropped a slipper on the carpet. It landed with a soft thud. She snatched it up and shot me a quick glance. My sister peeped from behind me.

But I ignored Frasier and all the others. I held her gaze. "Yes. King Charles likes me."

Queen Catherine eyed me a moment more, the one English lady

who served her earnestly, then nodded. "King Sharles like Laydee Casslemaine."

The queen's presence chamber was only full when Castlemaine came. Queen Catherine, who had never consented to appoint her as a lady of the bedchamber, ignored her, but the court made it painfully clear they preferred to flock to Castlemaine's side.

"Milady," a servant whispered behind me. "The Queen Mother's page, milady. He's outside and has a summons for you."

I had been waiting. And, I thought, I was ready.

Sophia followed me to the end of the Privy Garden, dotted with sculptures, and we turned into the Privy Gallery. Halfway up the black-and-white marble stairs, I eyed the huge painting of Adam and Eve and the way they tried to shield their tender pink flesh. Though I'd never dared broach the issue of Catholic conversion with King Charles, I could make it appear to his mother that I was trying. We reached the golden fountain. "Stay right here," I told Sophia. When footmen opened the door to the Queen Mother's temporary apartments, I crouched in a low curtsy. "Your Majesty."

"Get up, girl."

She sat on a stool, stiff and straight.

So she wouldn't see my fear, I said, "I trust Mary brought you reports of my relationship with King Charles." Her eyes widened, stunned by my boldness or my knowledge that she'd appointed Mary to spy. "I trust you are pleased. The king visits me regularly."

Her expression turned sour. "To give you a loving pat, a kind word, a trinket. It is the king's *pleasure* I assigned you to." She stood and turned her back to me. "Why did you not advance on the king when that Castlemaine gave birth?"

"It seemed disrespectful to the newly arrived queen. I believe the king and I established a certain trust—"

"Trust is worthless. If you give yourself to him, then he will owe you something."

"Pardon me, Your Majesty." My voice sounded tight. "I have come to doubt King Charles is the sort of man to trade political favors for pleasurable ones."

"Stupid girl. Do not profess to know my son better than I. Become his mistress. It is the only way to run affairs through him." She looked at me and I saw fire in her eyes. "Now that Castlemaine has a firm grasp again, you must get close to her in order to get closer to the king."

"I have duties to Queen Catherine—"

Her lips twisted. "Do I need to remind you of your duties to *me*?"

"Of course not." I dipped in another humble curtsy. "I thought to better attain your goals through Queen Catherine's help." I rose and tentatively looked at her. "King Charles respects her refusal to submit to Lady Castlemaine's presence. I think he finds it honorable."

"My son is a rogue. He cares nothing for honor. Catherine is childish. She is not artful enough to control him. I've instructed her to cease troubling Charles over the issue and befriend Lady Castlemaine."

I gasped. "But, Your Majesty, that is below a queen's dignity."

She closed her eyes and muttered, "You speak to me of a queen's dignity? I, who endured my husband's affair with that other Protestant Villiers? He granted his lover a title; *first* Duke of Buckingham. That ravenous snake. So you see, I'm weary of that family crowding the English royal bed."

I suddenly saw Buckingham's use of me in a new way; he was trying to follow in his father's footsteps. "King Charles may yet see the strength in his queen's spirit and abandon Lady Castlemaine. That is how it ought to be—"

"Queen Catherine is a prude in a court of rakes and whores!" Her words spilled out in a heat. "She's made herself look ridiculous."

"She is a good and honest woman!"

She sank her nails into my arm. I tried not to wince at the smell of old cheese on her breath. "There is no place for goodness in a court, you fool. Now get yourself to Lady Castlemaine's house and get yourself noticed. Get yourself into his bed where you'll finally be useful for something."

The urge to shake off her grip thundered through me. "Your Majesty, I must tell you something. Something deeply important."

"What?" she spat.

I blurted the first lie I could think of. "I fear Lord St. Albans will be furious if I make myself the king's mistress."

She handed my arm to her footman, who pushed me through the

door. "You don't know St. Albans, then. Go ask him yourself. You never thanked him for the money he gave you."

"My mother will despise me if I cause a scandal."

"I will dismiss *her* from my service if you *don't*." Her door slammed shut before my face.

I stared at the oak, only an inch from my nose. Bile rose in my throat. I placed both hands against the frame and leaned, breathing deeply. King Charles adored me. He respected his queen. I couldn't let her befriend Castlemaine and degrade herself. I turned to run. And met the angry glare of my mother. She'd arrived to wait on the Queen Mother but stood in the deserted gallery, clutching a wide-eyed Sophia.

"What in the name of God did she just say?" Her voice came out in a hiss. "Did she say she would dismiss me? What did she say about Lord St. Albans?"

I shook my head, feeling faint. I *couldn't* tell her the truth. "Sh-she is angry because I haven't presented myself to Lord St. Albans."

Her expression changed. She rearranged the lace around my shoulders. "If she commands it, you must do it. Straightaway." She stepped aside.

Amazed, I turned and started walking toward St. Albans's apartment. All I could think of was getting back to Queen Catherine before she made the biggest mistake in her royal life.

My feet sank into Turkish carpet as I stepped into St. Albans's long narrow council chamber. He had returned with the Queen Mother's train, and by the looks of his stately rooms, his importance hadn't diminished. The dark paneled walls boasted elegant paintings and neat rows of book-lined cabinets. St. Albans stood by the window, squinting at a large parchment in his hands. The scent of sealing wax filled my nose, and I glanced at the writing table. Rolls of documents, maps, and measuring tools lay scattered over the Queen Mother's household ledgers.

"What is it, Frances?"

I dipped a quick curtsy. "I thought I should present myself to you, my lord, to thank you for the silver you provided for my family."

He stared at me for several long seconds before he made a sound. "That money was for you." He paced to his writing table and tossed the document down. "Is it true King Charles commissioned Samuel Cooper to paint your portrait?"

I nodded

"That pleases me."

I met his eyes. "It does?"

"Mmmm. You are much favored at court." He walked around the table and faced me. "Let me know if you have need of anything."

"Thank you, my lord." A rush of questions filled my head.

He pointed to the array of papers on the table. "I've a building project in mind. St. James's Square, I call it."

I glanced at the table and back at him, confused by the change of subject. "Oh."

The edges of his mouth moved up. He looked almost handsome. "Speak a good word of me to King Charles when you have opportunity."

My mouth gaped open. *He is seeking royal favor through me.* "Of course, my lord."

"Good." His smile widened. He reached out and took firm hold of my upper arm, squeezed once, and let go. "Was there anything else?"

When I returned to Queen Catherine's presence chamber, Cornbury pulled me aside before I could approach her. "Buckingham's up to something. Be on guard."

"La Belle Stuart, there you are." Buckingham's voice echoed off the muraled ceiling, causing Cornbury to wince. "I've been waiting an age for you." He flourished an exaggerated bow.

I glanced toward Queen Catherine. "And you look it, Your Grace," I said, sweetly.

He laughed as though it were the funniest joke in the whole realm and gestured to a handful of nobles standing by. "If I am showing my old age, I need only sip la Belle Stuart's company, for she is a fount of youth."

A cluster of people crowded around us. I slipped my fan from the gold cord at my waist, snapped it open, and wove it gently toward my neck. "Then you'd better drink up."

"She's more like a fount of beauty," said some poor gent in need of favor. "If anyone can unseat Lady Castlemaine, it's la Belle Stuart."

Buckingham pulled an imaginary bottle from his doublet, leaned back for a swig, and stumbled around. Even Cornbury laughed at his pretend drunkenness.

I rolled my eyes to the heavens. "My dear lord," I said to him. "It seems you ought to have sought out the fountain of good sense instead."

The courtiers roared with laughter this time, and I started to sidestep them all, hoping to slip away to the queen. Then all heads turned to the door and Castlemaine sailed in on the arm of Henry Bennet. *That traitor!* They stopped in front of Queen Catherine, who nodded tightly. Castlemaine crossed the chamber and perched herself on the stone ledge of a window.

She was practically sitting in the queen's presence! "I cannot believe your cousin's audacity, Lord Buckingham," I said under my breath.

"Then you are as simple as you are beautiful," he whispered back. Then he laughed, the bastard, and the merry court around us laughed, too.

Soon, several people broke away from us and sidled up to Castlemaine. Over the top of Buckingham's curls, I could just see Queen Catherine, looking sad and alone. "His Majesty the King," exclaimed the king's herald, and everyone bowed or dipped.

Life Guards marched in, followed by King Charles. He walked straight to the queen, whose face lit with joy. She stood to greet him and curtsied when he bowed. They shared some soft words, and he clasped her hands. Queen Catherine was nodding and smiling when, abruptly, King Charles took a step back. With a bow, he bid her a kind word, then turned away.

To look straight at *me.*

"The angelic Stuart!" he announced as he reached for my hand.

I smiled. "You do me such honor."

"None deserves it more."

I sensed the quiet observation from Castlemaine's circle. *Ha!* "None treasures it more."

King Charles beamed. Buckingham and Cornbury laughed heartily, keeping up the merry tone, as if life itself were simply a jest.

I caught my breath when I saw Castlemaine moving across the chamber, folding her own throng into mine. But as she passed the throne, Queen Catherine stood. "Laydee Casslemaine."

Everyone froze and Castlemaine started. She looked genuinely dumbfounded as she turned and gave the queen a shallow curtsy.

The queen pointed to Castlemaine's skirts. "Dis is nice gowns."

Castlemaine looked to her right and her left, as if she couldn't believe the queen was addressing her. But triumph slowly festered on her face. "Your Majesty has excellent taste."

Queen Catherine, who knew little English, laughed as if Castlemaine had told a joke. Poor wretch didn't realize she *was* the joke. Courtiers snickered at the queen who flattered her king's mistress, and King Charles frowned. He leaned toward Buckingham. "Just when I was beginning to admire her mettle."

I fanned my face furiously. *No. No. No.* One misguided compliment had given Castlemaine all the power she would ever need at court.

The two groups converged to one large gathering, and Castlemaine planted herself before me. She inspected me all the way from the curls of my partial wigs to the hem of my petticoats, commanding attention without saying a word. I ached to turn my back to her.

Finally she spoke. "I wondered where you'd gotten off to, little Frances." Her smile was slithery. "So good to see you again." She leaned in close for an English kiss to each of my cheeks, turning my gut.

I smiled a huge, innocent smile. "I hear so much about you."

She glanced at King Charles. Her eyes narrowed. "Let me ride with you to Somerset House when the Queen Mother holds her reception there next week. We can get to know each other. We shall even plan a dinner in your honor at my house on King Street."

I held my breath. If I agreed, this would be Castlemaine's first invitation to officially move with Queen Catherine's court. It would make her almost official. I could not delay my answer, or let her see me think. I looked quickly to King Charles, who nodded, obviously anxious to appease Castlemaine's wish to be included. I glanced at Queen Catherine, sitting utterly alone now and almost in tears. The Queen Mother's words rang in my head. *You'll have to get close to Lady Castlemaine in order to get closer to the king.*

I met Castlemaine's expectant stare. "It would be my pleasure."

CHAPTER 19

Lady Castlemaine's King Street House
October

I brought the wine to my lips, sipping lightly, reminding myself, *Befriend her, betray her.* I smiled across the table at Castlemaine, and she nodded, then leaned into Harry Jermyn, a man who thought much of himself because he was the Earl of St. Albans's nephew. He whispered in her ear.

I traced the patterns on the Venetian goblet in my hand and glanced at Castlemaine's home: paintings by the old masters, ornate sculpture, ceiling murals, plush tapestries, exotic plants, and deep velvet. At the expansive table sat the most favored subjects in the realm, telling lewd jokes and getting a vulgar shade of drunk. King Charles sat at the head as if he were master of the house. Which, in a way, he was.

I raised my glass. "I only wish I'd sought you out sooner, Lady Castlemaine."

Buckingham leaned into the table. "One can seek my cousin all the day, but they'll not find her till she allows it."

Everyone responded by calling out, raising their glasses, and tipping them back until they were empty. We plunked them onto the table, and servants jumped to fill them again. My glass was the only one that did not need their attention.

"Thank God she lets us find our way to dinner here," Bennet called out, "else we'd never have cause to see the king!"

Everyone drank and laughed some more, even King Charles.

"Never fear, Bennet, if you need an audience with the king, you can always scramble into the royal carriage for a ride as Lady Castlemaine did on the way back from Somerset House." Jermyn snickered, then checked himself and glanced at Castlemaine.

She shot him a hot look. "I never scramble. I was invited." She turned to me. "Wasn't I, darling? And that simple-minded queen actually seemed pleased to let me ride in her own carriage home!"

"The queen is very kind."

Castlemaine swatted Jermyn, who grimaced and looked confused. "Do not speak ill of Queen Catherine in front of the angelic Stuart!" She narrowed her eyes. "She is a good and dutiful servant, aren't you, dear?"

"If I am here"—I glanced around at the expectant faces—"I don't know if anyone will ever call me good again."

King Charles threw his head back laughing, and everyone followed suit.

Castlemaine dabbed her eyes when she finished. "Now that you're here, little Frances, you really must stay. To new friends." She raised her goblet in the air. "Now, Frances," she scolded. "Tip back that wine and really drink, would you?"

"The Queen Mother says not to drink too much wine in the presence of men."

"Does she?" Lady Castlemaine eyed King Charles, who raised his hands in mock defense.

"She should have taught her son not to drink too much wine in the presence of Lady Castlemaine!" Buckingham called.

"He has nothing to fear from me," Castlemaine cried.

King Charles shouted, "Except an emptied purse!"

"Nonsense." She slapped his chest while the group snickered. "I am the loving mother of your children, and I will protect this poor child here if she finds she's drunk too much wine. So lead us in a health, Frances."

I held my glass toward the slippery Castlemaine. "A health unto His Majesty!" And while everyone gulped, I sipped.

———

When I woke the next morning, a dull ache pounded in my head, though my body floated in a downy cloud. I covered my eyes against the morning light. Or was it afternoon light?

I squinted; I was in Castlemaine's chamber! Sun gleamed off the bed frame, which was entirely gilded. I sat up, peered beyond the red velvet drapes, and saw King Charles hand his illegitimate infant son to Castlemaine. She cooed at him, and when he fisted her mantua gown and yanked, she laughed. The king took his daughter from the nurse and tickled her neck. Her giggles filled the room, filled her father's face with joy. He beamed as the maids carried the children away, then leaned over Castlemaine where she sat at her toilette table. They must have heard my rustling then, for they glanced my way.

"Go see her." Castlemaine turned to her looking glass.

He sat on the edge of the bed and addressed me. "I sent Prudence here this morning with some of your things."

"How thoughtful." I rubbed my eyes, wondering again what time it was. Wondering if I looked more or less of a sister to him now. "Perhaps I can be ready to attend the queen?"

"She is dressed already, though she expects you for tea. Are you well? Do you remember last night?"

"Who could forget Buckingham's impression of the lord chancellor?"

"Did you sleep comfortably here? You are not troubled to stay away from your own chambers?"

"Lady Castlemaine is a . . . gracious hostess." It returned in flashes. She'd insisted I stay the night, insisted on undressing me herself, and insisted I sleep in her own bed. With her in it.

"I am glad. She is a better woman than most people give her credit for." He winked. "She is the most generous and gentle woman at Whitehall." He rolled his eyes to the heavens as he spoke.

I bit my lips together to keep from laughing. *He knows she is neither of these things!*

I leaned back on the bolsters, smiling, and the king's eye fell to the neck of my gauzy linen chemise. My breath caught, and I realized he'd never seen me with less than a mantua gown. He wore an expression I'd never seen on him. It could only be called lustful.

Castlemaine appeared at his side. "Would you like to see the rest of her?"

"I can see quite enough." He cleared his throat and looked away.

"Not the best part." Lady Castlemaine crept on the bed and started to pull the sheet.

I grabbed the corner, pulling it back up.

Castlemaine tsked. "Let me show him." His eyes trailed the silk as she pulled it down. When the sheet's edge snaked around one calf and slid off my foot, Castlemaine ran her finger up the back of my other calf. "See? Long and beautiful enough to rival my own." She nodded. "You have the loveliest legs in all England. Does she not, Charles?"

I looked at them in amazement, at her informal use of his name, her loverlike introduction of my body, and his easy acceptance.

"Perhaps I shall declare it to all the country." His voice was low and throaty.

I shook my head. "If you do that, everyone will know you've seen them naked."

Castlemaine plopped herself beside me. "Looking is not the same as taking. Or touching. Or tasting."

"People will judge all the same," I said.

Charles smiled. "Seems unfair that the world will judge what they will about me and your legs, when in truth I have neither taken, touched, nor tasted."

Castlemaine coiled a strand of my hair around her fingers "That is why we do as we please and let the world be damned for judging." She pulled the strand of hair back lightly, so I had to lean back on the bolsters. "So go ahead, little Frances will not mind." Castlemaine propped her head on her hand and looked down into my eyes. "I know what he likes. I give it to him, and he keeps coming back to me. That is as close as one can get to having a king as a lover."

She was wrong. I could have had King Louis. He had offered more than an exchange of riches for pleasure. He had offered his heart.

She put the ends of my hair in her mouth. "See the king? See how he looks at you?"

I decided to be just what he thought me: innocent, tugging at the sheet. "No man has ever touched me in such a way." I hardly realized it was a lie.

"He is a gentle lover."

"I'm afraid to do more than let him just look."

"A man's touch is no different than your own touch. Or mine." She sat up and pulled my legs straight. "See?" She leaned down and kissed the side of my knee, swirling her tongue in a circle on my skin. She slid her hand between my thighs, then licked up to the hem of my chemise.

It would be a lie to say it had no effect on me, to claim it didn't make my skin tingle. But as I watched King Charles's reaction, the heat in my belly turned to a slow burning ache. He focused intently on what she was doing.

"See, darling?" Castlemaine kissed my thigh, grabbed the king's hand, and put it on my shin. She moved to lie beside me again, pushing the edge of my chemise up. "Now," she whispered. "Let the king taste the loveliest legs in England, and let England wonder if he ever really did."

He glanced to my eyes and saw passion without resistance. When he leaned over, he caught the sensitive inside of my thigh with his lips. It was like an arrow straight through my body.

At that moment Castlemaine pushed her hand up beneath my chemise to slide her fingertips over my most private place. I gasped and unlocked my gaze from the king's lips to gape at her and her wicked, crooked grin.

King Charles covered the wet spot his lips made on my leg with his palm and sat up.

Castlemaine jerked her fingers away and rested her hand on my hip.

He caressed the moist spot on my leg for a second, then stood. "That should please you, Lady Castlemaine."

"You should question whether it pleased the little virgin, not me."

"Let me worry about what pleases Frances." He tore his gaze away from me. "For now I must leave in order to please my council members."

She let out an exasperated huff. "Oh, go work if you wish. We shall stay here and play."

I slid off the bed before she could grab me. "It's my day for tea with the queen."

King Charles laughed at Castlemaine's disappointed expression. "I shall send Prudence in," he said from the door.

"Help yourself." She gestured toward her toilette table and regarded me with languid eyes. "He likes you."

I perched on her stool and yanked a comb through my hair. "Oh, but he likes you best."

"Yes," she said softly.

I nearly cried with relief as Prudence entered with my clothes draped over her arms. I rushed to help her with them.

"You know," Castlemaine said, "if you will trust me, he would come to like you more."

"You mean he would know my body."

"Of course. How else do you hope to please him?"

"I'm sure I don't know how to please him."

"You don't have to do anything. Trust me, trust my guiding hand."

Prudence yanked my bodice ties hard and fast. I kissed Castlemaine's cheek and lavished her with thank-yous and praise as I left her. The sentiments fed her vanity. I slipped from her house through the back door, practically running through her garden and back gate. Prudence trotted to keep up.

CHAPTER 20

Whitehall Palace

December

The Russian envoys, in their long waistcoats and sashes, bowed be-fore King Charles and Queen Catherine. They must have felt at home in London, where Whitehall Palace roofs were blanketed in white, and winter wind pounded the walls. I shivered where I stood in the line of queen's attendants and eyed the thick furs the ambassadors presented to the king.

Winifred Wells crossed her arms in front of her chest. "Look how the queen hangs on King Charles's arm. She's hopelessly in love with him still."

Cornbury leaned in to whisper. "So are you, Win."

"I am not," Wells snapped at him.

"Oh? You practically lie down before him whenever he speaks to you."

Her mouth gaped. "My father was a loyal Royalist. I don't see why I should not accommodate the king." She shot me a look. "Somebody has to."

I kept my expression passive. Which was worse—being ridiculed for being a king's mistress or being ridiculed for not? I was thankful my family was tucked away at Somerset House so they didn't have to hear such talk. I wondered what Richmond would think and longed for his advice, but he spent all his time in Kent.

"King Charles will want a new mistress when he learns about Lady Castlemaine's affair with Harry Jermyn," Wells announced. "And I'm ready to oblige him."

A snorting sound escaped Cornbury. "Did you hear the Earl of Castlemaine was denied leave for Europe? She wants him in England while she's with child. As if everyone doesn't already know he's a cuckold, now he's a cuckold on a tether. Isn't that so, Frances?"

The formal presentations had ended, and I ignored him. To avoid escorting Queen Catherine back to her chambers, I broke rank and slipped to the wall lined with Russian treasures, casting my eyes over them without really seeing them. I couldn't bear her questioning looks; she obviously knew all about my dinners with Castlemaine's King Street faction. But could I keep my place if I didn't try harder to become the king's mistress myself?

King Charles appeared at my side and gestured to the hunting hawks that sat on blocks in a row. "Did you see these?"

He watched me stroke the breast of a small goshawk. A leather mask covered its eyes, and golden jesses hung around its foot.

"You like her?" asked King Charles.

"She is magnificent. So powerful." I wondered how it must feel to wear a leather hood over one's eyes. Such a creature should not be bound and blinded.

"Good." He leaned close to whisper. "She is yours. We must go hawking when spring comes."

"You would take me hawking?"

"Of course." Then he added, "If it pleases the queen, we shall take all her court."

My heart fell. For just a moment, I felt my tight control over myself loosen. I dropped my hand from the hawk's breast and sighed.

"Before we go out, maybe a few lessons on hawking, just you and I?"

Buckingham's voice tore across the hall. "What say, Your Majesty?"

The king and I turned to face a cluster of courtiers.

"The Duke of York here says that Russian women have the most beautiful legs in all the world, but I favor English legs myself. Being king, you shall have the final say."

King Charles shot me a quick glance. He turned to the court and pitched his voice for the whole hall. "Now, you gentlemen know how far I roamed during my travels."

There were a few soft laughs. This is how King Charles referred to his period of exile whenever he told stories of his adventures abroad.

"Across Europe was I forced to wander before God restored me home. Though I saw the turn of many a favorable leg while away"—he paused to absorb the laughter—"I am most pleased to be in England. For here I've found the finest legs in all the world on . . . Frances Stuart."

Curious and jealous stares turned on me. "Frances, show them."

I didn't wait more than a heartbeat. I stepped forward and clutched up the flounces of my skirts. I pointed one high-heeled mule out farther than the other in a pretty pose before I let my skirts fall back down.

Gentlemen applauded, grinning appreciatively. But an anguished expression crossed the Duke of York's face. "Her legs are far too slender and long to suit me. I prefer plump legs, cased in green silk stockings."

Whispers and snickers flew around the hall, gossip about who the Duke of York's latest mistress could be. No one wore green stockings anymore. His duchess certainly didn't.

King Charles pulled me away. "I told you I would declare it."

"It's not that you declared it that pleased me. It's that you think it at all."

He looked troubled, confused. "Forgive me, my angel. I wish you good night." He bowed his head slightly and walked out.

Buckingham headed toward me. I could see in his face that he was coming to gloat in my success, to remind me I owed it all to him. But York cut him off, placed himself before me, and said, "I ought to explain my comment."

"Explanations would be best served elsewhere," I said, and gestured to the Earl of Chesterfield where he had cornered his wife, barraging her with accusations, while gesturing violently toward York.

He glanced at them. "What I mean is, I want to apologize for my comment."

Something in his expression told me to slip away, for, other than the king, no man in England had a worse reputation for womanizing than the king's brother. "No harm done, Your Grace."

I escaped to my apartments alone, never so thankful that my family was away from court. For as long as I was trying to win King Charles's attention, harm was indeed being done to everyone, including myself.

CHAPTER 21

Castlemaine's King Street House
Early February 1663

Y our Majesty is drunk!"

King Charles laughed and lunged for my skirts. "You dare accuse the crown of being unable to handle its liquor?"

I squealed and dodged him, running down the gallery with my curls streaming wildly in every direction. As I rounded the corner, I crashed into Castlemaine herself. She glittered from neck to waist with jewels, Christmas gifts presented to King Charles that she'd managed to wheedle away from him. I'd seen her drink nearly a bottle of wine this night, yet she didn't even stumble when I bumped her. I, however, nearly went sprawling.

She caught me. "Why do you run from the king?"

I ducked behind her, giggling. "The king is drunk and breaking the rules of blind man's buff."

The king leaned against the wall. "There is absolutely no rule stating that the players in blind man's buff must be wearing all their clothes."

Several other courtiers filtered in behind her. "I cannot say there is such a rule when none exists," Castlemaine replied.

The king wrapped one arm tightly around my waist. "I have you now, fair angel. Off with that bodice and commence to play!"

"I'll not shed my clothes, Your Majesty!" I felt myself mold into him.

"I'll shed them from her!" called Bennet.

"Oh, Frances," whispered King Charles against my cheek. "I'm aching for another glimpse of you."

Castlemaine stepped to me. "You've been playing coy long enough."

I realized the room was spinning. Too much wine.

Castlemaine leaned in as though she would kiss my cheek. "King Charles can be a gentle lover. Now, what would it take for you to give him your maidenhood?"

The king wore a half grin. "Anything you require."

"I—" I lost the words when I looked in his eyes. "A wedding," I blurted.

King Charles's face fell. He looked at Castlemaine. "Did you hear that? She wants a wedding, and yet I'm already married."

She tipped her head back, laughing. "La Belle Stuart wants a wedding, so a wedding she'll have." She turned. "Ladies and lords! Frances and I are to be wed!"

The group of courtiers, all as drunk as we, cheered and applauded. Buckingham called out. "I'll send for a minister."

"B-but I've not consented to wed *you*," I stammered.

She called loudly, "Why, Frances . . . don't you love me?"

Buckingham and Bennet snickered. Even King Charles guffawed. I glanced around at the amused faces and knew I either had to play along or be branded a bigger prude than Queen Catherine.

So I reached out to Castlemaine. "Very well. Wed me and protect me from this ravenous monarch!"

She tugged my arm, wresting me from King Charles's grasp. "Come, let us prepare ourselves before the minister arrives."

We traipsed to the bedchambers. Ladies took me into Castlemaine's wardrobe and outfitted me as a bride in a lace chemise, pink silk skirts, and matching bodice. They powdered my face, poured my wine, perfumed me, and smeared Spanish red on my lips.

Violinists began playing, and King Charles presented Castlemaine dressed as a man in doublet, petticoat breeches, and hose. Buckingham marched out, draped in mantuas as if they were bishop's robes, and planted himself before Groom Castlemaine and me. Everyone howled with laughter when he imitated Bishop Sheldon preaching a sermon. He demanded vows. Groom Castlemaine gave a ridiculous speech about manly love, hoping she could "rise to the task" of pleasing her bride.

Ladies ushered me into Castlemaine's bedchamber, plied me with a drink of creamy sack posset, stripped me to my chemise, and pushed me into bed. Castlemaine leaned in and kissed me hard on the mouth as she rolled off my stocking. She flung it over the bed curtains and pulled away, closing them tight behind her.

I lay back on the bolsters and tried to make myself stop spinning. Jokes and laughter filtered into my ears as they supposedly undressed my groom. Castlemaine gave another speech—something about lacking the physical manifestation of manly love. The bed curtain parted slightly. King Charles grinned through its opening. The room was stark silent; everyone had left us. I sat upright, but the swirling effects of wine struck me down.

He climbed in. "Do you need a husband's loving ways to cure you?"

I put a hand to my head. "I did not marry you. It was that other scoundrel."

"That other scoundrel has no—"

"Yes, I heard. No manly parts." I gave him a hard look.

"Entertain me in her stead."

"You call giving you my virginity entertaining you?" I sat up. "And what will I give you tomorrow when you grow bored?" The bed went spinning, and I fell back again.

"One doesn't have to steal virginity to please a maiden." He settled against the bolsters. "I only meant that I'm very sorry if it was she you wanted to bed tonight."

My cheeks burned as I remembered how Castlemaine had touched me before in this same bed. "She is wicked and you know it."

"I am far more wicked than she. That is why I need her." He toyed with a ribbon tie from my chemise, twirling it around his finger. "A man's needs are not always based in good reason."

I didn't move.

"The Bible says when one sweeps a house free of evil, one must replace it with goodness lest the evil find room to return." He eyed me. "You are goodness."

"You do not have the look of a man who has been reading the Bible, Majesty."

He put his arm across my waist and pulled me toward him. "You are so lovely. So fresh. So much better than me. I would need you if I were to get rid of her." He traced a circle on my breast with the tip of his finger. "But I can make you wicked. God, I could make you love being wicked."

My breath caught in my throat.

He moved his hand to my waist, traced my navel, my hips. "I've tried to stay away from you." He rubbed his lips over the thin chemise covering my breasts. "You are such an angel, and I am sordid as hell."

Angel. My mind cleared, as if passion lifted the wine fog and replaced it with scheming. "Oh, Charles." His name was just breath coming off my lips.

He lifted his head and looked into my eyes. "Yes, say just my name."

"Charles."

Passion seized him. He kissed me fiercely and pulled my chest to his. I sighed, filling myself with his scent of sandalwood and wine. My body longed for satisfaction. He grazed his lips against my chin, my neck. When he cupped my breasts in his hands and buried his face between them, tears burned my throat. "Please, no—"

He looked at my face. "No, don't cry. God, don't. I'm so sorry." He pulled away and lifted the coverlet over me. "Please forgive me." He frowned. "You were right earlier." He rubbed his head. "I'm quite drunk." The King of England curled his long legs and lay beside me.

He held my face. "I am a scoundrel trying to have my way with you. Like the angel you are, you put a stop to me." He stroked the back of his hand down my cheek. "But admit one thing to me."

I clutched the coverlet.

"Your body responded quite naturally. Did you like it?"

Heat crept up my cheek, and I forced myself to look away. "Y-yes," I whispered.

"Then I must keep my distance. Not even God can give me strength to stop a second time." He started to move away.

That is not part of the plan. I grabbed his hand. "Wait! W-what will they say? All of them." I gestured toward the door. "The gossiping beasts Buckingham, Castlemaine, Bennet, and all the rest. They'll say that we—"

He shrugged. "I'll tell them you demurred."

"Then, if my reputation is safe will you . . . stay a while longer?"

He groaned. "I have not the strength."

I bit my lip. "I was thinking that . . . someday perhaps you wouldn't have to stop. If you meant what you said before, about me making you better, then—"

"Frances, I'm a rake." He shook his head, turning his gaze to the curtains as if they were foreign and far away. "There is no honor in me, the outcast king who led so many to their doom during the Battle of Worcester, who couldn't save his own father from execution."

"You sent Parliament a blank document with your signature at the bottom to barter for your father's life. What more could a prince do?"

"*Parliament.* They are on the verge of rejecting my Toleration Bill. They have the real power." He scoffed. "Why would an angel want to fall into the mire of London's streets with the likes of me?"

"I won't fall." I touched a trembling hand to his face. "Let me lift you."

His eyes softened, and he turned his face to kiss my palm. "You could." He kissed my hand over and over. "You make me want to be worthy of you."

He touched his lips to mine. Softly at first, then pressing with more urgency, tongue swooping into mine, carrying me into the fog again. He broke away suddenly and pulled the coverlet up tight around my neck as if to shield me from himself. And then he slipped through the curtains. He would do what he promised, protect me from gossip by telling them all nothing happened. A candle gutted, and I felt a sinking feeling that had nothing to do with the wine. It is unpleasant to trick someone you truly care about.

W hen I next opened my eyes I was alone in Castlemaine's curtained bed, and it was very dim but for a dying glow flickering from the direction of the fireplace. I sat up. My head spun, and I rubbed my temple before opening the curtain.

They were naked on her fur carpets before the hearth. His long dark body twined in her creamy white limbs, moving together in a graceful passion. Her fingers followed a path along his back. He pulled away, inched down to kiss her breast and run his hand down her leg. I pulled pillows over my head and let the wine tug me to sleep again.

CHAPTER 22

Whitehall Palace

A few days later

With one hand grasping the handle of the queen's rare blue and white china teapot, and the other cradling its bottom, I tipped it carefully to pour. Steaming water swirled into our dishes, making the tea leaves dance. I inhaled the tempting scent and set the teapot aside. "Every lady at Whitehall drinks tea now. Fashioning themselves after you, my queen."

"Becauze they see tea is rich. Not becauze they like queen."

"Of course they like their queen. And without you I don't think we could even get tea in England. Thanks to the trading port in your dowry, we shall soon have an abundance!" I brought a delicate dish to my lips for a brief sip. "King Charles says he is impressed with your English."

Her face brightened. "Yes. He like my talk. Though I error much."

Silence settled between us. Queen Catherine's expression slowly fell. "I error with King Sharles many ways. He go with Laydee Casslemaine much."

I placed my dish gently on the table. "He shows you kindness before the court and makes the court respect you."

She touched one hand to the straight front of her bodice. "No shild yet inside me. King Sharles go with Laydee Casslemaine too much.

Our Queen Mother explain me the needs of kings in Eengland. I have come to accept."

"You—you accept that the king has a mistress?"

She pointed to her prayer book, open on a nearby table. "Apostle Paul found contentment even in prison. You read that?" She sipped her tea. "My choices are accept and have peace, or be angry and have hate. Portugal need help from Eengland to be safe from Spain. My duty is being the good wife."

I wondered how much she really knew. Had she heard that King Charles spent an increasing amount of time with the irritating Winifred Wells? Did she know how much I struggled with my own attraction for King Charles?

"But must have shild inside me for King Sharles. For Eengland. For Portugal." She set her dish down. "You must help. Laydee Casslemaine hate me, but you like me. If King Sharles have you be his mistress . . . you would speak well of me?"

Stunned, I sat quiet for a long moment. "Are you asking me to be the king's mistress so I can make him more favorable to you?"

She nodded. "I need a shild."

"You wouldn't be angry?"

"I like Frances Stuart better than Laydee Casslemaine." She giggled, and I laughed a little, too.

By late February I was ready to make my move. I sat between Wells and Castlemaine at the King's Theater as Castlemaine grumbled. "Lady Gerard is a wrinkled old prude. I'll make the king dismiss her from the queen's train for her foul treatment of me!"

Wells leaned across me to respond. "She told *me* the king shows very poor taste in wasting time with *you*." She waved her hands, eyes wide with false astonishment. "Though I can't understand why she would dare insult him to my face, knowing my relationship with the king to be so intimate."

Castlemaine shifted in our gallery box and looked as if she would spit venom. Not because of the pretentious Wells, but because her name was being smeared. "Rest assured. The king heard about it from *me*."

I glanced at King Charles in the box to our left. Surrounded by red velvet and silver gilt, he looked thoroughly bored by his own theater company. The whole building had been refurbished from an old Tudor tennis court, and the stage was completely devoid of scenery. The only interesting thing about the production was that women actually played the female roles instead of little men in gowns. Indeed, now that actresses had taken the stage, female characters often donned male disguises, allowing for wild adventures. Theaters were filling with men happy for a glimpse of curvy legs hugged into hose and breeches.

Finally the poet John Dryden bowed to Castlemaine, flattery for encouraging his first play. She gloated while the audience, seated on benches in the rush-strewn pit below, applauded courteously. She sent her languishing-eye look the poet's way, and I fancied this was the only applause she'd ever get from the English people in her life.

As soon as we were ensconced in her carriage on our way home, Castlemaine flopped on the tufted velvet cushions and closed her eyes. Prudence had learned from her laundry maids that Castlemaine was pregnant again, and it seemed to be draining her. Dark shadows had settled under her eyes, and she complained constantly about her aching legs. She slipped off her mules. "I knew supporting that poet would pay off."

Outside the carriage window, twilight fell on the city of London. I was rarely out of Whitehall Palace walls, much less out after dark. I peeped through the heavy leather curtains. Shops were closed, but the city did not rest. Drunken men and poorly dressed women laughed or fought, and everything smelled of the stench of the gutters. When the carriage jerked to a stop on King Street, I pretended to feel around the floor for the discarded mules, and Castlemaine waved Wells out first. *Perfect.*

"My Lady Castlemaine, I was thinking." I slipped her right shoe on. She yawned into the back of her hand. "Send the king to me. You are so tired tonight. I could . . . entertain him for you."

Her eyes snapped open. "Finally going to relinquish that precious virginity?"

I pushed the other mule into place.

"Very well." She paused. "I'll make Winifred brush out my hair and stay the night with me. But you tell him *I* arranged this and that he is to call on *me* with a full report in the morning."

"Yes, my lady."

"Don't taunt him. You must let him have you this time, or he will grow tired of you." She motioned to Bennet, who'd come out to greet us. When he leaned in, she said, "When you fetch the king tonight, direct him to Frances Stuart's apartments."

His eyes widened over the black patch on his nose, but he nodded.

I kissed her, acting as much the silly girl as she thought me to be, and swept out of the carriage, hardly feeling Bennet's hand under mine.

Prudence popped up from a bench when I sailed into Castlemaine's house. I marched directly through the hall, toward the back.

"Oh, Frances," called Wells. "Will you send your handmaiden up to help me unlace this bodice? I want to change into something else before King Charles arrives."

I didn't stop. "Sorry, Winifred. I have a few things to change tonight myself."

Prudence trotted at my side. "Milady, is something amiss?"

"The king is to call on me. Run ahead and have hot diaper towels to wash me, my silk shift, a fresh dressing gown, and chocolate and wine made ready."

She sprinted ahead without a question. Sharp girl.

The dark disoriented me when I walked through the back door into Castlemaine's private garden, but I kept to the path I'd come to know well. Round the shrubbery, past the fountain, down the walk, and through the gate. In the Bowling Green, pages lit torches that flickered from posts every dozen paces, and I soon turned into the Stone Gallery, almost home. God willing, I would never have to take that path again. And God help me on my new one.

He arrived at my bedchamber without a herald within a quarter hour.

"Your Majesty." I dipped.

"Get up, angelic Stuart. Tell me why Bennet sent me here. Why are you not with Lady Castlemaine? Who brought you all the way to your apartments?"

Quietly, I crossed to my table and lifted the wine. I poured with steady hands.

"You should not stalk the palace grounds without an escort. Especially at night."

"I had my maid." I held a goblet out.

He eyed it, then looked at the raging fire, the lit candles, and, finally, my dark blue silk mantua gown. "I shall provide one of my Life Guards for your express use. You shouldn't go about alone. Not even for me." He took a long sip. "Especially not for me."

"We went through this. I shall make you better."

"Wearing that?" He glanced at my thin silk.

My cheeks burned. "You said before you wouldn't have the strength to stop."

"I want you more than I've ever wanted a woman, but I have never cared about a woman's virtue as much as yours."

"Trust my virtue to be strength enough for both of us. I shall stop you. Some pleasure with me, limited though it may be, will prove you are worthy if you stop when I ask. Then someday . . ."

"Go on," he said, voice husky.

"Meanwhile, the queen's apartment is nearby. If you still need physical satisfaction, you can find it with her."

He grimaced and I hurried on. "She needs to have your heir, and I cannot give myself to you in that way. This way can please us both, I think."

With one quick motion he undid the pin holding my mantua gown together. The doubt disappeared from his face. "People will say the worst even if you are not guilty of it."

"Yes." I paused. "If you were inclined, you could deny everything. They won't question the king's word."

He pulled the ribbon tie that cinched the shoulders of my silk shift. With its restraint gone, the shift gaped open, fell off one shoulder, and clung to my breast. "They won't question."

My throat tightened. "They will trust you as I do."

He stepped to me. "Then come to the bed so I can look at you. Look and not touch since you are not to be soiled."

I backed away as he advanced. "Oh, do touch, just a little bit."

"Only if you command me, angel, and only if you have command of yourself."

The sensations at his hand were slow and consuming. He kept all of his clothes, but I let him see my full nakedness. And when I was completely melted by what he did to me, he pulled away. I could see his hands tremble as he struggled to keep his passion reined.

"Kiss me again, then go to Queen Catherine. Quickly!"

"It will be as you ask." He buried his face in my neck and breathed deep. His last kiss was frenzied and brief. And then he disappeared.

I pulled the coverlets over my head. Candles still flickered in their sconces. *Let them burn.* I felt too perfect to move. When I was on the edge of sleep, Mary crept in with a snuffer and extinguished them one by one. My last, most satisfactory thought was that Mary would describe this scene to the Queen Mother. So, I did what candle wax does when the flame is out. It hardens once more.

CHAPTER 23

Frances Stuart is a fine woman, and they say now a common mistress to the king.

—SAMUEL PEPYS'S DIARY
May 1663

King Charles stood behind me in my chambers, softly nipping my neck. I leaned my head back on his shoulder and watched us in the looking glass.

"I love seeing you in just your shift."

"I had no time to dress."

He laughed, his warm breath melting on my skin. "Why do you think I come to your chambers so early?"

I sighed and watched his hands caress my shoulders, trying to just enjoy his touch. I shut out the image of him leaving my chamber every night to lie with the queen. I shut out the memory of him laying his hand on Castlemaine's growing belly when we supped there together in the evenings. I tried to shut out the nightmare of my sister being ridiculed at court if Mother's past was revealed.

His hands slipped from my shoulders and cupped my breasts. "I love these moments before the favor-seekers come calling."

I sighed deeply, lifting my chest to fill his hands. I wished I could surrender fully to the pleasure this spring morning and forget all the rest: the Queen Mother's folly and my oath to King Louis. But the thread of worry was stitched too tightly. "They will surely be here soon."

He groaned. "Then you must dress."

I squeezed his hand. "Prudence," I called.

She tied me into white lace petticoats and skirts while the king scooted Miss Ment from a chair and settled himself at the table, exuding Stuart charm at ease. He ate cheese and sipped water purified with a dash of whisky. Things he liked that I kept at the ready. His gaze traced my body as Prudence squeezed me into a corset's laces, then helped me into a man's shirt. She fastened the gold button at the top of a red *justaucorps* and tied a blue ribbon around the lace cravat at my throat—and why not wear a cravat if I was half garbed as a man already? Wearing male garments made me feel strong, like I could risk being bold. With every actress in London causing a stir in breeches, dressing thus was catching on with the court ladies. I turned about for the king to inspect me. "Well?"

He grinned. "I think I'll have you wear it for your next portrait with Samuel Cooper."

"Another miniature? You like it that well?"

"I like you best with less to nothing, but you won't let me paint you so."

"The Comte de Cominges," Mary announced from my chamber door.

I sighed as the French ambassador swept in and bowed deeply to the king, who nodded. He approached me with a bundle in his outstretched arms. "A small offering to the goddess."

King Louis had not communicated with me since my crossing. But he had told me he would send his men with commands, and those men would be ambassadors. How much did Cominges know? He certainly sensed my favor with King Charles. I smiled sweetly. "Do you recognize this?" I touched the gold lace on my jacket.

"You have turned it into a masterpiece." He opened his bundle. Today's gift was a great length of soft white lace.

"This will be lovely paired with the red silk you gave me the other day."

The man's face flushed. "It is an honor to bestow anything on you."

"Prudence," I called. "Fetch that red and some of the others to lay out."

I considered, then threw open my bed curtains and smoothed my coverlet. Cominges's eyes widened at the intimate softness of my sleeping quarter. Such private spaces were usually kept concealed from anyone other than family members . . . or lovers. Let Cominges assume King Charles and I were intimate. I hoped he would tell King Louis. I took one edge of the lace from the bundle in Cominges's hands. "This is very fine, monsieur Ambassador. Is it from the Netherlands?"

"You have a good eye, mademoiselle." Then, with a keen sense of timing, he turned to King Charles and spoke in French. "Your Majesty surely sees the value of trade with a country that produces such goods."

King Charles downed the last of his water and whisky. "Fine goods or no, the Dutch drive a monopoly on trade from the East. Some English subjects would wage war for those rights."

Cominges responded with a counterargument. I arranged the silks on my bed. I cared not about trade squabbles. I certainly did not care to hear talk of war. I wanted Cominges to tell King Louis I had King Charles's ear so that he would believe I was keeping my oath to him.

"Frances," King Charles called to me, "how do you say 'inherit'?"

Some days, when Charles didn't care for these discussions, he conveniently forgot his French. *"Hériter."* I gripped the lace in my fist.

"Aha, yes," he said, snapping his fingers. He looked back to the ambassador. "Does King Louis feel his queen should inherit the Spanish Netherlands when the King of Spain dies, despite the waiver they signed in their marriage agreement?"

"I believe King Louis is seeking a way around that settlement," said Cominges.

"There you have it," said King Charles. "King Louis will move to claim those Netherlands the first opportunity he gets."

Ambassador de Cominges was left stammering.

"Ambassador," said King Charles, in English now, "I know my cousin. He pretends peace and friendship with the Dutch. But he will change."

Cominges turned to me, both helpless and expectant. Normally I would translate, but I *dared* not translate that. Smiling with gaiety I did not feel, I held lace to my hip and twirled around. "So long as I can still get pretty lace, I care not who claims the land."

The ambassador's features softened, obviously relieved. "Yes, you must always have the best, fair lady. The most beautiful woman I've ever seen."

King Charles beamed. When I held my arms over my head in a ballet pose, he gave the end of the lace a gentle tug. I twirled around the chamber, and the men applauded. I gave an exaggerated curtsy.

They continued conversing in a lighter vein, about the queen's summer traveling plans or some such. I left the lace on the floor and walked to Sir Ment's perch, extending a crust of bread to him. This was what King Louis expected of me. To keep King Charles's favor and bend him toward Ambassador de Cominges. Make England listen to France. To dance and twirl.

CHAPTER 24

Whitsunday

A wet breeze wafted off the Thames and clung warm to my skin as Cornbury and I passed through a courtyard on our way to Queen Catherine's chapel on this bright Whitsunday. A Lord's day—a respite from the ambassador and all my concerns. But as we turned into the queen's presence chamber, Castlemaine stood blocking our entry, face full of spite, belly well concealed by her bodice. "I see you've come like a good little Catholic to mass."

Cornbury stiffened, held up his hand. "Now there." His father and Castlemaine remained locked in a perpetual fight over the privy purse strings. Castlemaine vied for funds, and Clarendon would block her by policy, so Castlemaine slandered his name at every turn. Cornbury probably felt like shoving her through a window.

I dropped my arm from his. "Go, Lord Cornbury." My relationship with Castlemaine was now marked by polite tension. Everyone knew I was the king's new favorite. She invited me to her banquets, spoke to me at court, but said she resented me with every glare. "I come to pray."

"You mean you come to gulp forgiveness down with bread and wine."

"Sounds as if you've added bitterness to your long list of sins."

"If absolution is so easy, perhaps I should convert to the Church of Rome myself."

"There isn't enough bread and wine in England to pardon you."

"Deviousness is as great a sin as fornication."

"Then you are doubly damned."

"Little milksop." She goaded, daring me, a nothing, to insult a countess. Then her gaze fell on my new double-pearl drop earrings, and she quickly registered their value and origin. "Did you hear?" she blurted. "I'm to get an apartment in Whitehall. Above the king's own bedchamber."

"Oh? *Which* of the king's bedchambers?" The fall of her features indicated she didn't realize he had more than one. I could insult a countess without appearing to.

Someone tugged my sleeve. I realized it was my sister. "Sophia." I put my arm around her shoulder and pulled her toward the wall, far from Castlemaine, who stomped away. Thank heavens.

Sophia, Mother, and Walter came to my apartments often, to sup and play with Miss and Sir Ment, but they didn't usually attend court. It was safer for all of them. "Is something wrong?"

"The queens are arriving. I ran ahead."

All residual irritation vanished. "Both queens?"

"The Queen Mother is bringing her train to Queen Catherine's chapel." She carefully kept her expression serene. "I wanted to warn you—our mother's in a rage."

We dipped to a low position when Queen Catherine entered and again when she received the Queen Mother.

My mother's face was impassive as she took a place standing beside me. "I overhear astonishing conversations when your Mary visits Somerset House. How can I help you if you aren't forthright with me? Why didn't you tell me of the Queen Mother's commands?"

I gestured for Sophia to leave us, and made sure no one could hear us. "Because such a reckless plot should be concealed, it would infuriate the Protestant people here. You saw those heads on London Bridge. I have no intention of following through with her demands."

"Yet you entertain the king in private. Gossip about you will bring scrutiny to your family. You know what they'll discover."

"I know *nothing*," I said, trying to hide exasperation from my face. Anyone could be watching our conversation. "Besides, the Villiers you fear are easy to thwart."

"Don't turn your back on the Duke of Buckingham and his sister. They will plot ways to make you more compliant if you do not surrender to the king. It's wrong, what you're doing."

"Enough. If you expect forthrightness from me, then you must reciprocate. Is St. Albans your father?"

Had we been alone, she'd have slapped me. "If you value your place at court, never, *ever* say that again." She turned her back and moved to the other side of the room.

I felt dizzy, overwhelmed. Frasier appeared at my side. "Everyone is queuing up for mass." I gathered my skirts and drifted, in a blind haze, to the line of ladies forming behind the queens. Castlemaine lifted her nose in the air as I passed.

At mass the priest droned on. The only Latin I discerned were the words for *sin*, *hell*, and eternal *damnation*. I tipped my head up so the tears forming in my eyes would drain back, and I swallowed them. Frasier's sharp elbow in my side made me blink. The priest was before me, bread and wine in hand, making the sign of the cross.

I could not receive the Sacrament without heaping burning coals on my own head. I had not asked forgiveness or prepared for absolution, couldn't even remember my last confession. I shook my head slightly and closed my eyes, whispering a prayer as the priest moved to Frasier.

When mass ended, the queens stood. "Go before me," said the Queen Mother to her train. "I shall stay behind and pray." She gestured for me to follow her. The chapel emptied as we knelt before the vigil lights. "You should have taken the Sacrament, you have started everyone talking."

"What are they saying?"

"That it is a sure sign you are the king's mistress."

"Is that not what you wanted?"

She reached up and grasped my jaw in her hand. "That Protestant bitch is moving into chambers above his. That is *not* what I wanted." I thought she would crush my bones. The vigil lights twitched under her hiss. "You've the most beautiful face I've ever seen, yet what good are you if you can't get rid of her?" She thrust my face away.

"H-he visits her only on friendly terms, to see their children. They are the reason he cannot part with her."

"He refused to hear mass at Advent, Easter, and now Whitsunday. Do you know Parliament is ready to pass an act to exclude Catholics from government? Meanwhile Charles stays to the whore's religion because *you* let it happen."

The tears I'd fought to swallow earlier stung my eyes again. She was wrong about everything. King Charles himself had said the English people would never trust a Catholic king. But one cannot tell a queen she's a fool. "Your Majesty, if I may. I have heard him speak very firmly with the lords who visit my chambers about toleration—"

She stood abruptly. The contempt in her glare was like a slap. "My patience is near its end. Do you wish to see your family humiliated before the court? Get rid of the whore before the year is through, or I will discharge your mother from my service."

Two days later, when the king's Life Guard escorted me into Castlemaine's new chamber for a dinner banquet, she turned her head the other way. King Charles sat at the table with his brother, James, the Duke of York, and Henry Bennet. Each man rose as I entered.

Bennet, ever calculating, came to take my hand and walk me to my chair. "La Belle Stuart. You are more beautiful each time I see you."

Castlemaine's neck flushed, and she hid her face in a goblet of wine. I ached to urge King Charles to dismiss her from court, but I wasn't at all sure I'd gained enough standing with him to command such a thing. Bedding him wouldn't make him more comfortable with such a request, either, no matter what the Queen Mother assumed. King Charles signaled for the meal to begin. *I have to find a way to make him want to do it without asking him.*

Bennet turned to York. "As I was saying, if the Act of Uniformity passes in Parliament, I don't see what would stop them from barring Catholics from government offices."

York waved a dismissive hand. "I cannot imagine it coming to that." He stabbed his food. "What really concerns me is the charter for the Company of Royal Adventurers. The sooner we begin shipments the sooner we can fill our pockets. Watch Parliament try to make us swallow their policy when we don't rely on them for money."

King Charles remained silent. I saw he didn't want to think about politics. He turned to Bennet. "Did you see that new *calèche* the Chevalier de Gramont brought over from France?"

"Indeed, there's nothing like it. All fitted with glass so one can see about while riding."

York laughed. "See about and be seen."

"Just like the vain French, wanting to preen," said Bennet with a grin.

York turned to me. "Frances, you knew Gramont in France, did you not?"

"I'm afraid he did not like me overmuch." He'd come from France in the aftermath of a scandal and knew better than to visit me.

York replied softly, "Some men pretend they do not like a thing only when they discover they cannot have it."

Bennet glanced at him, then held up his wine. "A health to la Belle Stuart's tempting beauty."

Everyone raised their glass and drank the toast. Except Castlemaine. King Charles cleared his throat. "Yes. This *calèche* is so fine a thing that my queen has requested to borrow it to ride about Hyde Park. She wants to be the first woman in England seen in a carriage of this new style."

Castlemaine looked up. She leaned one elbow on the table and pressed her weight against it until her breast bulged into her collarbone. "Surely you know the public will mock her vanity if you let her?" She laughed. "I would be glad to go out first in the *calèche*. For the people love to look upon me. And I do so love to be seen!"

Bennet lifted his wineglass again. "A health to Lady Castlemaine, who grows more beautiful with each passing year."

We lifted our glasses, and as I sipped, I eyed the king. He lifted his eyebrows slightly as if he expected me to say something to relieve the tension. "Oh, how I would love to be seen riding in Hyde Park in the new *calèche*."

Castlemaine muttered through clenched teeth. "Then you shall ask for it when I am through with it."

I fought the urge to stab her with my three-pronged fork. "I think *I* should like to be first." I turned to the king. "Your Majesty, may I please be first to ride in the *calèche*?"

King Charles leaned back in his chair. "Would that make you happy, Frances?"

Castlemaine threw her knife on the table. "Are you not listening? I said *I* shall be first to ride in it." She stood, bumping her own belly on the edge of the table. Her chair clattered to the floor. "Damn it all! I swear, if you do not let me ride in that thing first, I shall miscarry this child all over this floor." She grabbed her wine goblet and heaved it across the table. Wine showered us, and the goblet shattered into the looking glass on the wall.

Silence echoed. No one looked as shocked as they ought.

I put my fork down softly. "Well. If I do not get to ride in it first . . . I shall never miscarry."

York got the joke first and chuckled, King Charles smiled into his goblet, and Bennet shoved food into his mouth.

Castlemaine marched into her bedchamber, slamming the door behind her.

York's face fell. "Does that mean there will be no gambling tonight?"

"Praise God," said Bennet. "I have to lose a fortune to her just to get invited back."

K ing Charles spent the rest of that night with the queen. The next day, when I was sitting at my toilette table in my mantua gown, Castlemaine burst through my door with no announcement. She waved a parchment with a heavy seal in front of my face. "Charles finally gave me my patents for lady of the bedchamber today."

"Congratulations."

"With a tidy sum, a suggestion I stay the summer away at Hampton Court, and a kiss good-bye. How dare you use him against me, take him away from our children, after all I've done for you?" She slapped me so hard lights flashed in my eyes. I fell against my toilette table. A perfume bottle shattered on the floor.

Mary grabbed her by the armpits and hauled her back. Her arms and legs flailed around her awkward belly as she struggled, swiping her fingernails at my face. "Let go of me!"

She screamed so loud I thought the king's Life Guards would come rushing from every corner of Whitehall. I sauntered to where her patents were resting crumpled on the floor. I plucked them up, watching her eyes widen with concern. I balled the parchments in a loose wad and continued toward the door. "Follow them, and get the hell out." I hurled the papers into the antechamber. When she cleared the door, she looked over her shoulder and said, "You'll never be rid of me."

Cornbury appeared in my rooms hours later, breathless and wide-eyed. "You won't believe what's happened. Lady Castlemaine gave a great supper at her house on King Street. She said she would never again invite you to her chambers."

"Is that all she said?"

He nodded. "But King Charles had just arrived from supper with the queen. When he heard Lady Castlemaine, he replied, for all to hear, that he himself would never again dine with Lady Castlemaine if Frances Stuart were not present. Lady Castlemaine flew into a rage and stormed to her apartments. She is packing, Frances! She's leaving for her uncle's at Richmond first thing in the morning."

Relief washed over me. And Mary had heard every word.

CHAPTER 25

St. James's Park
July 13

The king and queen followed kettledrums and Horse Guards on return from our ride in the high parts of St. James's Park. Members of her household followed in form, with every maid of honor wearing matching white lace waistcoats and short crimson petticoats. George Hamilton drew his horse alongside mine, and I laughed. "You're out of rank."

He flushed. "I just have to know how you're doing with your new mare." When he'd learned I didn't have a horse of my own, he had gone to considerable trouble to obtain one suitable for me.

"She's perfect. How do we look?"

Hamilton had become a constant dancing partner, an escort to the theater, a regular visitor in my antechamber. He didn't answer, just flushed again.

Suddenly, my perfect horse halted. She whinnied, pranced back. I looked about to see what had spooked her and saw a black snake slither underneath a nearby shrub. "There now," I said, stroking her neck. But the horses crowding behind us frustrated her further, and she took off like a shot into a clearing, with my red skirts flying up around my face. I pulled the reins, called halt, but she only kicked, and I thought for sure she'd throw me.

Hamilton galloped up beside us, this time taking the reins and heading off my mare with his own until we both slowed to a stop. Catching my breath, I smoothed my petticoats down. He reached to help cover my knees and nearly slipped from his horse. He righted himself, grinning, and flushed yet again.

"Perhaps she should go back to the trainer, then?"

I repositioned myself on the saddle. "She's young yet. I think she can at least get me home."

Frasier waved us back into the procession, and we soon saw that the rest of the court and a crowd of commoners had gathered along the canal at St. James's Park to watch our return. Many gallants rushed forward to help the ladies alight, and grooms rushed to take the horses.

"How unfortunate for us all that Lady Castlemaine decided to return to court. A fortnight of her absence was simply not enough." Frasier threw a disgusted look toward the horse that carried the countess's bulging belly, snugged into a tight bodice with low shoulders. Castlemaine had attempted to distract from her wider girth by wearing a tasteless yellow plume in her cavalier hat.

"No one will help her down," said Wells. "See how disappointed she looks."

Instead of looking, I signaled to an orange-girl and fished out a half-penny.

"She is lonely because everyone flocks to your side, Frances." Frasier gloated. "Everyone knows you hold the king's favor."

What you mean is, everyone thinks I'm his favored mistress. I tucked my orange into my hanging pocket, saving it for Sir Ment. "I wish everyone would look at how attentive King Charles is to Queen Catherine and stop talking about me."

We all looked ahead, to where the king and queen ambled with their arms twined together, talking and nodding at their subjects as they passed. They seemed a portrait of domestic bliss.

Hamilton dismounted and stepped forward to help me, but to my dismay, Buckingham headed him off. Hamilton turned to help the others instead and studied Buckingham suspiciously. Wells and Frasier walked ahead, glancing at us and whispering.

I should have worn a vizard mask. Buckingham braced my waist, pulled me down, and walked me back toward Whitehall Palace. He tipped his head in Castlemaine's direction, where she walked all alone on the path. "Some say you coaxed Henry Bennet to take you to Richmond and talked her into coming back."

"Some are saying the king himself went to Richmond to beg her back."

"Did he?"

"He was with me every night after she left."

"Has he bedded you yet?"

"He is weary of her. That is all I shall say."

"It has been over a year. He wants you. He has made that clear."

"Why do you wish to complicate matters?"

"I need his ear to effect my plans." He tossed a pence to a drink seller, who promptly poured a syllabub and handed it to Buckingham, who handed it to me.

"You are aware that our king has a mind of his own? I grant the French ambassador time in my chambers, but he is unable to sway King Charles. What makes you think you can?"

"You do not know him as I do."

"Do not expect me to forfeit my virtue for the sake of political power you *think* you can gain through me." I handed the syllabub back. "You don't know him at all. He has what he wants."

I moved away from him, took up Hamilton's arm, and let him lead me into the palace. Everyone with access to court followed us to the queen's presence chamber. Inside, my friends enveloped me, casting glances at Buckingham, who hung close by.

"Love that lace," said Wells. "Who made your hat?"

"It's French," I said, handing it to her. "Try it on!"

Soon we were laughing, and everyone was trading hats. But mine, with its red plume, seemed to be the favorite.

"You must take this one with you when we accompany the queen to Tunbridge Wells," said Frasier, toying with it.

Wells sighed. "It's going to be boring. What will we do out there in the country? Milk cows?"

"It'll be so romantic," replied Frasier. "We can pretend to be shepherdesses from one of those rustic plays."

"Be glad the court is going anywhere this summer," Cornbury said as he joined us. "Queen Catherine could barely scavenge enough money from her treasury for this trip."

"Good thing Frances is getting away from court soon," said Hamilton, glancing back at Buckingham. "We can't have the king becoming jealous of a duke!"

Thus I avoided Buckingham when we sat at supper and played cards late into the night, and I thought he'd given up. But he caught me in a dark courtyard on my way back to my apartments and pinned me against a wall. "You think you've won," he hissed. "Don't misinterpret Lady Castlemaine's sullen mood as withdrawal. She is too wicked to go down without fighting. While you and the queen are away, she will move on him again. If you don't do something to keep him attached to you, you will lose him."

CHAPTER 26

Tunbridge Wells
Late July

E arly every morn, before the summer heat settled, the ladies of the court emerged from the little huts and cottages scattered about the village at Tunbridge Wells. I followed Queen Catherine out of the cottage we shared. She stretched in the sunshine and smiled, happier than I'd ever seen her. The accommodations weren't what we were used to, but we'd settled into the glorified rusticity with ease. Her household gathered together in *déshabille,* wearing only long shifts, slippers, and light mantua gowns. Then, informal and out of rank, we traveled the tree-lined walk to the healing spring we hoped would enhance the queen's fertility. When we reached the wooden railing, Queen Catherine approached first. The village water dipper curtsied and filled the queen's goblet. She drank deep and then waved us up for our turn.

Wells eyed her water warily. "You don't really drink yours, do you?"

"Of course." I sipped the brisk, refreshing water. "Why ever not?"

"One of the court ladies might be *with child* from it," she whispered.

I cast my eyes heavenward. "Someone should tell the poor fool it is not the water but the rogue she let into her bed."

Wells ambled away, looking for a better gossip partner. I knew more than I'd let on: Gramont was the rogue in the situation, and the maid's brother was George Hamilton. He would force Gramont to marry her, at sword point if required. So much for the "free pleasures of love," as Gramont had put it in France, after he'd grabbed my backside.

We'd been at Tunbridge Wells for nearly a month, and my heart ached rather badly for King Charles. The ache itself surprised me, and with little to do, I would dwell on Buckingham's warning: "she is too wicked to go down without fighting."

Queen Catherine signaled for me to walk with her on our way back from the spring. Her footmen trotted alongside us, holding giant green screens for shade—they also shielded us from curious listeners.

"Your Majesty, do you not wish to go back to London?"

"To heat, to crowd? These woods are . . . how to say . . ." She took a deep breath, closed her eyes, and smoothed the air in front of her with her palms.

"Relaxing. Though, the more time passes, the more I fret over the king."

She shot me a sidelong glance. "You miss him?"

I didn't want to tell her how much. "I worry Lady Castlemaine is taking advantage of our absence."

"Ah. I think it will matter not." She gave me a knowing look and glanced over her shoulder. "I am with shild."

I felt a twist of anxiety and regret that I quickly tamped down. "Oh. Oh, that's wonderful!" I sensed a new confidence in her beaming smile. *Queen Catherine doesn't need me anymore.* "God has heard your prayers, Queen Catherine. There is no more deserving queen."

The breeze rustling in the woods made me think of Fontainebleau and Madame's pregnancy. I felt a longing for my old friend. She hadn't written me, but I knew from her letters to King Charles that her little daughter was well. I wished the same for my queen.

We tossed grain to the hens in our coop, and I felt better when we sat upon blankets scattered about the lawn before our little cottage. We broke our fast on eggs baked with lavender and thyme that we'd picked from the garden ourselves and dried on hooks from the rafters over our beds. This arcadian way of life was almost romantic enough to make me forget everything, including the Life Guards camped along our perimeter.

Wells approached, wearing a huge straw hat, her maid close behind straining with two heavy buckets. "You have to try this milk!"

I looked at the vat she handed me. "Don't tell me you personally milked a cow?"

She just grinned.

A fortnight later we traveled back to London, and King Charles rode halfway out to meet us. Queen Catherine embraced him so rapturously he laughed out loud. They clung together the rest of the journey. I watched him joke with her about how large her belly might grow, and it occurred to me that she might be right. Giving him a legitimate child could well make him love her.

CHAPTER 27

Whitehall

Early August

I was still tired from the recent journey as I stood in the queen's presence chamber, while the king and queen sat head to head chatting with each other. Buckingham swept me an exaggerated bow. He always wore charm like a jewel, and now he turned it just right to catch the best light. "La Belle Stuart. The prettiest girl in all England."

"It's been so long since I last saw you." I frowned. "And yet, not long enough."

"Save your bitterness for the queen. I'm not to blame for the king's change of heart."

I watched King Charles pat Queen Catherine's belly. He hadn't visited my chambers since our return from Tunbridge.

"Come now," he said. "Make peace with me. I'm giving a banquet tonight in my Whitehall apartments. A grand feast! Join us. King Charles will be there. His first supper away from the queen since her return from Tunbridge."

I eyed him. "Truly?" Could this be the plot my mother had tried to warn me about?

He grinned, showing his teeth. He looked like a smiling wolf.

I settled into my seat that evening, glanced at the ordinary banquet table setting, and wondered what was so grand about it. Buckingham's silver plate and Venetian glassware glittered across the tabletop, but no flowers decked the walls, and the only music came from a musician plunking away at a lone virginal.

Buckingham's sister made an effort to stir the stilted conversation. "I lost a wager of ten pounds last month when the Duke of Richmond's footman beat that famous runner in a race at Banstead Downs." But no one replied.

Buckingham's duchess tried to help, too. "You should have known better than to bet against the Duke of Richmond! Don't you remember when he beat that earl in a horse chase this spring at Newmarket? I thought he'd surely break his neck when he almost fell at the end." When no one replied again, she tried a joke. "He must have been drunk!" But everyone just stared at one another.

"The king! The king!"

I jumped at the herald's call and stood with everyone else. Lords and ladies bowed and curtsied as the king entered and took his seat at the head of the table, spaniel dogs scampering at his feet. As he passed, he gave me a searching look: warm, familiar, and somewhat questioning. *What did it mean?*

Conversation in the room remained stilted and slow as servants filed in and placed mutton before us. *A feast?* I stared at the food, and then at Buckingham.

He attacked his meat with zeal, talking with his mouth full. "I cannot stomach the idea of a Dutch ship not lowering its flag to the English when they meet in the Channel."

"They ought to concede those are our waters," was someone's muttered reply.

King Charles forked the bland food into his mouth, then raised his hand. The footman behind him presented him a fresh goblet of wine. The king downed it, glanced at me, then eyed the goblet of wine by my plate.

I lifted the glass to my lips.

King Charles lifted his empty goblet in the air. The footman took it away, poured wine in a fresh glass, and held it, waiting for the king's next thirst.

Why did everyone seem to hold his or her breath? I tilted the wine into my mouth and had to stifle a gag. *Vile. Just like the menu.* I lifted my napkin to my lips, and my cough seemed to echo in the quiet hall. Everyone stared at me.

The king turned his attention to his meat again, with . . . *is that a frown?* I set my fork down and decided to wait for the salad course. If this was such a "*grand feast,*" surely Buckingham would serve salad? With a little oil and vinegar. Hopefully without garlic. Maybe chocolate for dessert. The guests continued to glance at one another, their expressions guarded. How odd everyone seemed tonight!

"The queen! The queen!"

The herald's call seemed too loud in the strained silence. The music fell to a discordant hush. The king looked surprised. Buckingham glanced at his sister, confusion in his eyes. She shook her head as if to say, *I don't know.* Footmen flung open the doors, and everyone scrambled to their feet. The queen's rank gave her the right to attend any event without an invitation.

"Please sit. Sit," said the queen. Behind her, Castlemaine sauntered in, grinning like a smug cat.

Buckingham nodded at his footmen, who jumped to make two new places ready. Then he gave another bow to the queen. "What a pleasant surprise, Your Majesty."

"I hear bery special entertaining be here dis evening."

"My queen. You are welcome." King Charles kissed her hand, and she sat at the place made ready by his side.

Buckingham and Castlemaine crossed each other as they walked to their seats. Buckingham muttered, "Cousin."

"My Lady Castlemaine," I said softly, refusing to appear as irritated as I felt when she sat down at the place set beside me. "I know not why you came," I whispered. "It is quite boring and the wine has gone bad."

She looked out at the solemn faces at the table. Everyone sat dumbfounded.

Suddenly King Charles laughed. "This party is a failure, Buckingham." Buckingham slumped in his seat. "You there, page!" The young pages jerked to attention. "Go to the maid of honor apartments. Tell them the king commands they come to banquet here straightaway. And send for my violinists, for we shall have dancing!"

The poor musician turned and started playing again, and finally the guests fell into easy conversation. Talking about the duke again, the Dutch, and our upcoming progress to Bath and Oxford.

"A health," the queen called as a footman handed her a glass. "A health unto His Majesty!"

We raised our wine. "A health unto His Majesty!" we called. I only held my glass lightly to my lips, and Castlemaine snorted. "Why do you not drink, Frances?"

"How can you? The wine is bitter."

She handed her glass to me and whispered, "Only yours."

I took it and sniffed. Hesitantly, I tipped the wine to my lips. *Sweet and smooth.* I narrowed my gaze. "Why are you here?"

She leaned closer to me. "To rescue you from rape."

"How ridiculous."

"You were coaxed into coming by the duke, who dangled the king's presence as bait." She kept her voice hushed. "Your wine was poisoned so the king could have his way with you, you little fool."

"The king would never hurt me." My stomach roiled.

"No?" She reclined in her chair and took back her glass, swirling the red liquid. "While you've been off in the country I've been his constant company. Even in his bed. His *constant* company. Does that hurt?" she hissed.

My heart thundered in my ears. "You're too far gone with child to go with us on progress. The queen and I will be alone with him."

"I'll not let him come sniffing around your skirts again."

King Charles didn't visit me privately that week before the royal train embarked. In our weeks at Bath, he stayed in quarters with Queen Catherine, supped with her, and met the subjects with her. He was openly flirtatious with his queen, touching her, kissing her hand. I soaked in the Roman pools by day, hoping *this* would be the evening he would come to me. He never did, and my soul drowned in my sin. During our weeks at Oxford he flattered me in front of everyone—danced with me, chatted with me, bestowed every sign of adoration upon me; thus I kept my favor with the court. Then I learned he was riding to the outskirts of Oxford to visit Castlemaine, who had crawled from her childbed and left her infant, contriving to be near the king. *I had lost him.*

CHAPTER 28

Whitehall Palace
Mid-October

For the first night in months, King Charles walked into my bedchamber. "The queen is dying." I leaped from my bed to embrace him, and he draped his arms over my shoulders, holding back tears. "She has fallen with such a fever that she cannot be woken."

"No. She's been perfectly well since we returned," I said. "I waited on her just yesterday when the doctors told her she's two months gone with child!"

"She is bleeding. The child is gone."

Genuinely grieved, I tightened my grip. "What can I do?"

"Keep vigil with me."

So I wrapped furs over my nightgown and followed the king to his quarters. Castlemaine was already there, turning back his bed. She wasn't surprised to see me, and strangely, I didn't mind her presence. She crawled into bed on one side of our king with me on the other, and we kept vigil while he slept.

The king must have an heir." Buckingham loomed in the doorway of the king's secondary bedchamber. An uninvited pestilence in such a sanctum.

I glanced at him and quickly looked back to my sewing. "King Charles has an heir. His brother, James, Duke of York, is fit and hearty."

The king had ordered Castlemaine and me to stay here together so we would be at hand when he felt able to leave the queen's sickbed. Castlemaine had just taken leave to check on her children. "You must go. The king would not be pleased to find us alone in his bedchamber."

"How fares the queen?"

"Her Portuguese doctors have strange methods of healing: shaving her head and strapping pigeons to her feet." I shifted my weight. "Lady Castlemaine will be back soon; she will tell the king you—"

"When she dies, the king will marry you."

My gasp was so loud I feared the king's guards would rush in.

"It is obvious he loves you." He turned to gaze at the wainscoted walls. "Did you know Anne Boleyn designed this wing? She left her mark on England and so could you."

I cringed. That mark had been many things, including a still bleeding wound to England's peace. "You finally concede he loves me without having taken my maidenhead."

"At any rate, do not lie with him *yet*. See if what the people say proves true."

"People also say the queen was poisoned," I said. Buckingham lifted a finger and opened his mouth to speak, but I continued. "We both know how familiar you are, Your Grace, with different poisons."

A door slammed. King Charles entered his bedchamber. "He didn't serve you poison that night at his banquet," he said. "It was merely a sleeping potion." Buckingham's face turned a ruddy red.

I was too relieved to be stunned. "You knew?"

"Buckingham thinks I'll take what I want at any cost."

"You knew." *He should have stopped it.*

"If I had thought you'd accept an invitation from *Buckingham*, I would have warned you." He stroked my cheek with the backs of his fingers. "You trust that I would never have harmed you, don't you?"

It was the first intimate touch in ages. It stilled my breath. "I thought . . . you were cross when you didn't come to me, afterward. That you'd given me up."

"Forgive me for staying away. I was doing what seemed right. The queen needed my attention. I wanted our heir so badly." His smile seemed heavy. "I thought you would see the honor in it." King Charles turned to the duke. "Leave Frances alone."

Buckingham stretched to his full height. "Let me keep her warm for you in case you're to need another bride again soon."

The king did not smile. Buckingham finally bowed and backed out.

Castlemaine talked of her children all day. Baby Henry had suckled the wet nurse dry. Little Charles had taken his first steps. Young Ann had learned a few new words. If Castlemaine wasn't talking, she was pacing. I sat enough for both of us. The windows, closed against autumn's first chills, let in enough light to embroider a nightdress. Thread, fabric, and needle flew through my hands. In the days we'd kept vigil for our grieving king, I'd nearly finished it. "My lady, your pacing is quite irritating."

"How can you sit so calm?" she snapped.

"If you are anxious for the reasons I think, then shouldn't you be a bit nicer to me?"

"To what end? You hate me, I hate you. If he marries you, he'll banish me to the country." She wrung her hands as she crossed the chamber again and again. "You wouldn't really make him send me away, would you?"

"Of course." I viciously snipped a thread.

She plopped into the chair beside me. "Why do you sew—can't you afford a maid?" She twisted her hands in her lap. "Oh, merciful God. If this queen dies, I will be in a bad way. You were not here when that Puritan Cromwell ruled. My father *died* fighting for the Stuarts. I was nothing then."

"I know of suffering. Of penury and shame."

"They confiscated our lands, our estates. We were forced to poach what was once our own property if we wanted supper."

"The only way an English Royalist could get meat in Paris was by selling stolen art works," I countered.

"Then can't you understand? I have to take what I can *while* I can. You have never seen the mood of the London mob. It could sway against King Charles tomorrow and he'd be gone." She crossed her arms. "Don't tell me you haven't any ambition."

"You know nothing about why I do what I do." *Praise the saints.*

"You try to please everyone. Why don't you just live for yourself?"

King Charles entered and we started to rise, but he waved us down and sat on the floor before us. "She is no better," he reported. "She mutters in delirium that she gave birth to a son."

Castlemaine sighed. "She does not know she has miscarried?"

"She cannot know anything in this state. I made the Portuguese doctors leave her to my physician's care. But there is little hope. She deserved a better husband than she got."

"You made her queen." Castlemaine snorted. "How much better can one get?"

Strands of silver caught my eye as I stroked his hair. "I know she forgives your nature, Majesty. She loves you so."

Castlemaine waved her hand. "Why do you pine over her?"

"I care for her. She seems to love me no matter what I do. It's . . . satisfying."

His grief became clear to me then. King Charles needed the type of love that mothers offer. Unconditional.

"She can't fulfill all your needs. That's why you have . . ." Castlemaine glanced at me and hesitated. "Us."

"Yes, Barbara, as long as I have a crown on my head, I know I'll have you."

She pinched his arm. "And that head must be attached to your shoulders, don't forget!"

Watching the banter between them, I understood why King Charles needed Castlemaine. She was *like* him. It was easy to find physical satisfaction there.

And what was my place? What was I to him? *An angel who inspires him to be a better man.* If he knew of my scheming and plotting, it would leave me no place at all.

His hair coiled in my fingers, and I eyed the nightdress in my sewing basket. I realized I'd embroidered flowers of white silk thread on stark Dutch lawn. The pure white garment would be perfect for a new bride.

CHAPTER 29

End of October

The queen's fever has broken. She lives!" Cornbury stood in the king's doorway days later, panting.

At first I jumped; he startled me so. He rushed to kneel at my side. "I've come from her quarters. The doctors just informed the king that she is sure to live. I wanted to be the one to tell you before Buckingham or Castlemaine returned."

I turned my face away. "Praise God," I said softly.

"I'm sorry for you," he said awkwardly. Then added, "He would have chosen you." Cornbury let out a strange laugh. "What should you do now?"

A deep breath, which I did not know I'd been holding, rushed out of me. I slowly folded the gown I'd worked on into a tight little bundle and stuffed it into my sewing box. "What a strange question, Lord Cornbury," I said with a pleasant smile. "I shall wait on our queen while she recovers. And what should you do, silly?"

"Continue waiting for my time, I suppose." He scratched his head. "I'm thankful, indeed, the queen lives. Sorry for you, as I said, but I'm afraid my family wouldn't be pleased if King Charles made you his queen."

"Your father, Lord Chancellor Clarendon, has nothing to fear from me. I would have let you keep your position at court."

163

"It isn't that." Cornbury's face reddened. "As long as the queen has no child, the Duke of York is still heir to the throne."

I understood. "If James is king, you become brother to the Queen of England."

He shrugged. "Our father's power would be enhanced."

"So I am a threat to the house of York because a child of mine would displace you." He reached for me, but I did not want his comfort. I darted toward the door. "I'm shocked you would place all your hopes on Queen Catherine's unhappiness." I wasn't, but I could think of no other way to lash out at his selfishness.

"My father, he has certain expectations—"

"That is the worst part." I paused in the antechamber. "You once said you were free to choose your own path."

Whenever I stepped out of my apartments, a small clutch of courtiers flocked to me and followed me wherever I went. Escorting me to the queen's chambers. Keeping tally for me playing bowles on the lawn. Handing me into a carriage. Inviting me to a banquet. Praising my dancing skills.

Then, suddenly, Hamilton distanced himself.

Frasier told me she had overheard Gramont, who was about to become his brother-in-law, pointing out the folly in "frolicking with the king's woman." Hamilton's desertion underscored how lonely I was feeling. Without his distracting charm, I began to notice the way my faction drifted to Castlemaine's circle and back without explanation. Amid reports of religious risings all over the north, all anyone talked about was what gown was most fashionable this season and who had contracted the clap. People would come to me, asking for this small favor or that, watching my every move. Pretending to take an interest in me while they really groped for daggers of gossip to hurl at my name.

CHAPTER 30

St. James's Park
November

The Queen Mother's page pointed to the edge of the forest where she sat bundled in her open carriage. With my goshawk perched upon my gauntlet, I pulled my horse's reins away from the hawking party, trotting out of the park clearing. No sooner had I sidled by her carriage than she spat her fury.

"Stupid girl. Your time has nearly ended." The Queen Mother's voice came out hoarse and barky. She was alone, wrapped in furs and blankets, though it was not very cold.

I bowed my head since I could not very well curtsy while sitting sidesaddle.

"Buckingham and his faction are forming a party *again* to get you drunk and seduced. It is proof to me, girl, that the king wants you, and you are unconsenting. You have failed the one thing I asked of you. After all I have done for your family, you ungrateful girl. I will die and my life's mission shall perish with me for your ineptitude!" She closed her eyes. "You have never understood the point."

Yes, I do understand. England doesn't need another civil war. My arm tingled, exhausted from holding the hawk, but I held it firm. "Your Majesty," I said, hoping I didn't sound defeated. *King Charles saw an honorable reflection of himself in my eyes. If I offered to lie with him now, it would corrupt us both.* But how could I tell her in such a way that she would hear me? How could I keep her from giving up on me and trying some other scheme? "I've not failed."

She dismissed me with a wave. I pulled my horse's reins and gave him a soft heel. I slipped off my goshawk's mask. If I didn't send her up now, I would never feel my arm again.

She fluffed her feathers and lifted her wings, anticipating her freedom. I untied her jesses, whispered words of encouragement, and threw my arm to the sky. She would fly to the hunt, soar free over England. She would taste the clouds. But when she completed her task, she would obey her training and come back to her master's arm.

"Your mother is wrong," the Queen Mother called.

I halted my horse and looked back. Her carriage lurched forward as she said, "She thinks St. Albans would be disgusted if you became the king's mistress. She has never understood him."

Later, still dripping from my bath, I sat before the raging fireplace in my bedchamber while Prudence pulled a tortoiseshell comb through my hair. The heat would make my hair shiny and soft, and each rhythmic stroke bolstered my resolution. The Queen Mother's deadline for me had arrived like a henchman to the docks. I'd saved enough coin to support my family, but my greater concern was that her next means to pursue a Catholic conversion might meet with success. Civil war had ravaged England before, and Charles I had lost his head in that fight.

My king arrived, as usual, just as I was climbing into bed. "There you are," he said, peeping through the doorway. "My angelic Stuart."

I extended my hand.

He knelt at my bedside, pressed his lips to my fingers. "I wanted to come sooner but . . ."

His familiar scent enveloped me, comforted me. Then I caught a whiff of musky roses on his doublet. *Castlemaine's perfume.* I could not show him my anger. I'd never made him promise he wouldn't lie with her. "Let me guess, you are pressed at every step by those seeking favor."

"Mmmm," he murmured into my palm.

"I well know it. They loiter here, and I haven't the heart to send them all away."

"It seems George Hamilton no longer nips at your heels. I almost feared he would ask your hand in marriage."

I looked down to our entwined hands, grabbing my opportunity. "Feared? It would be easier to make me your mistress if I were officially sanctioned as a married woman. Even an arrangement like that of the Earl and Countess of Castlemaine provides legitimate birth names for her children." I bit the inside of my cheek.

"No, I feared it because I know you. You would devote yourself to a husband." He looked into my eyes. "I would lose you."

I stroked his cheek. "You have no need to fear that," I said, not missing a heartbeat. "Besides, Hamilton was warned away." I sighed, leaned against the bolsters. "For fear of offending you."

"It is only fitting that you should have courtly admirers. Tell them I take no offense."

"Some dare not risk it. They need your favor far more than my attention." I looked away. "Though, it does leave me rather . . ."

The king sat beside me. "What is it?"

"Oh, Your Majesty." I squeezed his hand. "It leaves me terribly lonely. I am merely an avenue to get to you, not available for anything deeper lest they offend their intended prey."

He winced at that, then pulled me into his embrace. "I can scarcely believe this. Lady Cas— *Some* ladies gather such persons about and make demands of them as a fee to seek my favor."

I wanted him to hear my thought: *I am nothing like her.*

"Yet you, my angel, would never think to do such a thing. You pine for true affection."

It is working. The king stroked my neck with his lips. "What is it? What can I do to make you feel less lonely?"

"I do long for you when I cannot see you. Perhaps if I were closer to your rooms . . ."

"I could grant you additional apartments in my lodgings." His breath warmed my skin.

Victory. "Would you?"

"Rooms below my own are vacant. They overlook the Thames. With a little repair, some paint, you could be moved within a fortnight."

I was too elated to feel guilty about what I'd done, the lies and pretending. Part of it was true. I was lonely. I knew, too, that I had not gained true affection in this bargain. How could a bargain made with me be true, when what little of truth left in me was quickly slipping away?

"One more thing." I whispered into his neck.

"Anything."

"When you go back to your chambers tonight, take Mary and show her the space so she can describe it to me." While the king nodded, traced my collarbone with his fingertip, and whispered naughty things, I went through a list in my mind. Of skirts, lace, fans, and extra coin I would put into a basket. I would order Mary to take it to my mother early tomorrow morning at Somerset House. Surely the old spy would report to the Queen Mother while she was there.

CHAPTER 31

Somerset House
December

Every courtier at Whitehall was aflutter over my new chambers. Between the storm of whispers and Mary's errand to Somerset House, surely the Queen Mother believed that her son loved me and I had his ear. She *must* listen to me now.

I turned my attention back to the priest who stood at the head of the Queen Mother's chapel, informing us the heavens had shown signs of God's wrath and that England was doomed to plague and fire. Candlelight flickered over the Queen Mother's grim black costume. Her lips moved in recital of prayers that I'd come to believe she did not understand. I kept my eye on her, waiting for her to look at me.

After the benediction, she made toward the front of the chapel. *At last!* I stepped forward. But she gestured for *Castlemaine* to join her. I joined the procession of maids exiting through the sunlit hall behind Queen Catherine. We were going to the presence chamber where we would stand behind the queens while they drank tea for hours. But I had to talk to the Queen Mother *now.* I turned and rushed back toward the chapel. Where I saw the Queen Mother hand a small pouch to Castlemaine.

The Queen Mother's eyes widened the instant she saw me. In that first second, there was a glimmer of something resembling shame.

"Your Majesty," I whispered. "I must apprise you of my progress in . . . private matters."

"No. I no longer require your services."

Castlemaine tossed something into the air that returned to her hand with a fat, jingling thud. I stared at it. Coin. A great deal of it.

The old royal gasped when she heard the sound and flushed a deep shade of crimson. But Castlemaine gazed at me with triumph on her face. The Queen Mother marched out of the chapel, and the door slammed behind her. "Close your mouth, Frances. You look rather stupid like that."

I snapped it shut. "What is this?"

"Oh, haven't you heard?" she asked. "I'm converting to Catholic." She smirked at the leather purse in her palm. "Seems God wants England to turn back to the Church of Rome."

"You believe this?" My hands went out for something to steady myself, but there was nothing near to grasp. "You've staked your soul on converting the king?"

She snorted, slipping the purse into the folds of her velvet skirts. "I can more readily get forgiveness for my many, *many* sins in your religion. So if I fail as badly as you did, there's not much harm done." She patted the bulge under her velvet and it jingled again. "Nothing like the ring of true faith, eh, Frances?"

CHAPTER 32

Early 1664

The King's Theater had finally relocated to a new building near Drury Lane. Benches in the pit below were padded with green wool, but rushes still covered the floor. Green drapes and gold-tooled leatherwork adorned the boxes and stage, but the movable scenery was still inferior to that in France. Castlemaine sat in a box across the pit with a girl I didn't recognize. She'd just discovered she was pregnant, and so maintained her status as official mistress. But as far as I could tell, she'd made no move to convert the king. She'd had little opportunity, for the king spent more and more of his free time with me.

I sat in my gallery box with a new friend, an heiress from the north named Elizabeth Mallet. She resisted persistent flirtations from the Earl of Rochester, who sat in the box next to ours, while I eyed the ceiling. Partly open to let in sunlight, it would also let in other elements, and I hoped it didn't rain.

The Duke of Richmond's voice sounded behind me. "Keep away from Rochester. That one's a lecher."

Rochester peeked over. "Richmond," he said. "Don't you have a bottle of whisky waiting for you somewhere?" Mallet giggled.

Richmond ignored him and sat behind me. "Did the two of you come here alone?"

I smiled. "The king's Life Guards escorted us."

"Take care when you venture out of Whitehall. Reports of religious risings have made the militia violent. They're arresting Nonconformists in every county and even overturning Quaker burial grounds. Villagers are nervous. Some have even thrown stones at my retinue."

"King Charles told me of the rising. You must watch yourself."

"Not quite as bad in Dorchester. I'm lord lieutenant there. Off now to report on some prisoners in Dorchester gaol, though, where blood was drawn in the skirmish."

"It's kept you busy. How are you?"

He frowned. "New wife refuses to put her funds into my estates. She's appealed to the king, and we're going back and forth about it. All I really wanted was an heir. Not making much progress in that way, either."

"But you have the king's favor. He just granted you that house in Whitehall's bowling green. He will take your side."

A ripple of whispers in the theater caused us to look across the pit. The king had just arrived with the Duke of York. Lady Castlemaine leaned toward their box and started talking to the king. Then she stood, walked out, and reappeared in the royal box! She sat right between the king and his brother. Their displeasure was evident to everyone in the theater.

Mallet exclaimed, "She just did that to prove to the world she hasn't been replaced."

Richmond patted my shoulder as he left. "Be careful on that count, too, cousin."

I attended Queen Catherine when the king opened Parliament at Westminster two months later. I stood behind her among officers of state, who stood behind King Charles. He sat on his throne in his imperial crown, crimson and ermine robes settled around him. The bishops and the lords sat before him, facing one another on benches. King Charles gave the signal, and the House of Commons rushed into the Painted Chamber, stopping before the barrier designed to separate them from the lords.

For the next quarter hour, King Charles read a series of fabricated truths from the paper in his hands. About how he loved Parliament, though he was actually perpetually frustrated at their doings. About how his subsidies couldn't be collected, when really he spent far too much.

I studied the elaborate painted panels on the ceiling, and the vibrant blues, greens, and reds in the biblical scenes painted along the walls, hundreds of years old. Edward the Confessor had died in this room, and Henry the Eighth had slept here. This room had seen more history than we could ever recall.

King Charles explained the details of the religious risings, and then did something he'd never wished to do. He prompted his Parliament to limit the freedom of his subjects. I caught the Duke of Richmond's eye. We both realized this must be done to prevent another rebellion. To keep the civil peace that had barely settled upon England.

A month later I rose from my bedstead in a long shift and mantua gown. King Charles tried to grab me back, but I dodged him, laughing, and fetched ale and cheese tarts from my cabinet. When I brought them back to the bed, he pulled me up, tickling me. I tried to fend him off by stuffing a bite of tart into his mouth, and he settled down to our snack.

But when Prudence came in to light the sconces, he kept an eye on her. "Be sure to keep her in," he said when she'd gone. "The militia will arrest any Quakers they catch meeting together in the same place. Hundreds are in prison. If they can't pay their fines, they're transported to the Americas."

"At least Parliament cooperated with you this time."

"It isn't what I wanted, but I won't have them rise against me just after my Restoration. If nothing else, I'm determined to keep my kingdom."

"The Duke of Richmond told me of the violence in Dorchester. He serves you loyally there."

He took a long swig from the bottle of ale. "Frances, I do believe you're seeking favor for him."

I laughed. "It doesn't really suit me, does it?" I let it drop, but I knew he'd heard me.

W e need a gallant to lead us in a *branle!*" called a lady among the tipsy courtiers in Castlemaine's new lodgings over the Holbein Gate of Whitehall Palace. The end of May was King Charles's birthday and the anniversary of his return to London.

I grabbed a candle from a sconce and stepped to the center of the room. Fashionably dressed as a soldier in pantaloons, buff doublet, blond periwig, and a gilded scabbard hanging from a gold belt, I bowed, and the courtiers made appreciative *ah*s. King Charles smiled approvingly and the violinists began. I held the candle aloft and danced a *branle des flambeaux*. With three quick hop-steps, I gave a little kick and held my toe pointed long enough for the courtiers to clap. Castlemaine watched me with a guarded grin, and I repeated the steps around the chamber.

It was only fitting that the apparent official mistress host his party. But Castlemaine knew better than to throw any entertainment without my presence. Her new apartments had views of the Privy Garden, King Street, the Strand, and St. James's Park. Huge windows were thrown open to the spring warmth, and her violin music carried to every corner of Whitehall. She needed the whole world to believe she was the king's official mistress. I didn't need to prevent that belief, though every part of me wanted to be rid of her.

I presented my hand to her. She didn't hesitate to link her little finger around mine, hitch up her skirts, and dance with me. Still graceful with her bodice laced tight, one could hardly tell she was five months gone with child. When we'd completed one turn around the chamber, I leaned in for a kiss, as if I really were a gallant. She pressed her lips to mine, of course, and her guests laughed. I presented the candle to her, stepped aside, and let her carry on the dance alone. Soon she would choose King Charles as her partner and everyone would be dancing with candles.

I took a glass from a footman and stepped onto the balcony overlooking the Privy Garden. It was enclosed as an aviary, and birds scattered as I leaned against the bars to catch my breath. As I sipped my wine, I caught sight of a lady rushing through the grounds. Something about her gait was familiar, and when she reached the garden door, I recognized her. *Prudence. The little fool will get herself arrested.*

The Life Guards let her slip out, and she turned left toward the King Street Gate, the open city, and Westminster. I moved through Castlemaine's guests as casually as I could. When I reached the stairs, I flew down and went through a closed door onto King Street. She disappeared through the King Street Gate, and I walked in that direction, so as not to raise suspicion from the guards at the Privy Garden wall.

At the gate, I peeped through. The gables on the many taverns and houses towered overhead, making the road seem narrower than it was. I pulled my cavalier hat down tight on my head and slipped out. I ran after her, keeping close to the tavern walls. "Pru!" I called. But she rushed onward.

A scantily dressed woman emerged from the shadows. "Oy gent, 'ere's yer lady."

Startled, I stepped aside, tripping into the sludge of the road. I ran ahead, with only the candles from the tavern windows to light my way. I caught Prudence by the arm just before she rounded a corner. "Come with me."

She spun around, struggled, peered at my face, then looked guilty as sin. "Sorry, milady. I was jest goin' ta meet my friends."

"Your Quaker friends? The militia will beat you! Do you want to get yourself transported to the Americas?"

She tried to break free but I wouldn't let go.

"You're coming back with me."

Just then, two militiamen stepped out of a tavern across the street. The sounds of beer mugs clanking and laughter spilled out behind them. "Ye got one of them Quakers, milord?" one of them called. "We can help ye."

I froze. Should I run? Draw my scabbard? "Nay," I called in a deep voice. The scantily dressed woman reappeared. A tavern window opened. "Nay," I said again. "Just a twopenny whore who thinks she's worth three!"

Prudence stopped struggling and gaped at me. The men laughed and went back inside. I hauled her by the arm all the way down the street, through King Street Gate, through the guards at the garden door, and under the torches of the Privy Garden before I released her.

"Go back to bed," I said, short of breath. "And if you value your life, you won't do that again."

"That's jest it," she muttered. "I do value my life, and I think I ought ta be able to do as I wish. *You* certainly do."

I stared at her a moment. "I promised King Charles I'd look after you. So you can't."

CHAPTER 33

The River Thames

August

The black expanse overhead glimmered with heavenly diamonds that remained stationary as we glided down the Thames on the way home from Greenwich. The queen smiled dreamily, watching violinists pull a melody that echoed off the water. I reclined at my end of the long dining table, sated by the supper we'd just eaten. I may have appeared perfectly at ease, but I could never loosen the tension that waited, coiled around my spirit.

I'd waited for months for the Queen Mother to dismiss my family, but it never happened. I'd become closer to King Charles, and he deflected any slander hurled at my name. I found myself listening for his footfall on the marble floors in my antechamber. I thought of his smile always. But with so little left of truth in me, and with so many duties left unfulfilled, I could not allow myself to love him. I was nothing like the angel he thought me to be.

I eyed Cornbury, lounging across from me. "You've not said two words this whole supper."

"I am in a foul mood." Cornbury gave me an apologetic smile and looked at the stars. "Forget me. I am merely the son of an unpopular man. Everyone hates the lord chancellor who I am obligated to obey. If his enemies unseat him, I have only my sister for my protection. But you, la Belle? You are the picture of perfection in your silver lace ensemble. Every artist in London flocks to Whitehall for the opportunity to paint your picture. You must be the happiest girl in all the world."

He was right. I had every outward reason for joy. "At least your father doesn't want war with the Dutch. The Comte de Cominges presses King Charles constantly to avoid it."

"Louis signed an alliance with the Dutch." He shrugged. "If they go to war with us, he is bound to aid them." Cornbury frowned. "Why should you concern yourself over it? The cabal who gamble and carouse at Lady Castlemaine's house are the ones stirring up talks of war. They want to fill their purses by increasing our trade in the Indies. The Duke of York wants his American colonies."

"Do you think your father can persuade the king to remain neutral?"

He groaned. "The lord chancellor has no more sway over King Charles than his mistresses do." He shot me a look. "Ah, no offense to you, of course."

"I'm not his mistress."

"There is much to be gained if we are victorious. York, Rupert, the king, Bennet, Albemarle, Sandwich. They all hold shares in the Company of Royal Adventurers Trading to Africa and the East India Trading Company. They cannot establish trading ports because the Dutch are overrunning them all. Profit is motivation enough for war."

The prospect of the African trade had been bantered about among the court recently. "So we will go to war for more opportunity to kidnap natives and sell them to slavery? This turns my stomach."

He smiled for the first time in days. "England has changed. How do you suggest we raise funds? Would you have him tax the wool sellers and farmers more than he does already? The people outside London don't have money to be taxed. The world is a new place. Buying cheap goods in the Indies and selling them for more is the only way to make money now. It's how the Dutch have become so wealthy."

"If our countrymen are so poor, who shall buy these goods?"

"The colonies. And the guilds, the companies, the merchants, the ports, the shipbuilders, the captains, all these will increase. The trade process will propagate until the countrymen benefit. And if the king has shares in all of this, his purse will swell. He won't rely on Parliament's grants of money." He pointed at me, all trace of his morose mood gone. "And if he can free himself of Parliament, he can pursue any policy he wants."

"You sound convinced, but I thought you didn't want war."

He sighed. "Without money, how can we become a powerful nation, safe from threat?"

"Are we threatened?"

"The Catholic Church is always a threat. King Louis is a growing threat."

"I cannot speak for the others, but King Louis desires friendship with England."

He studied me carefully. "You sound as if you *can* speak for King Louis."

"I only know he wouldn't want to defend the Dutch against us." And I alone wouldn't be able to stop England from forcing him to do it. I hid my face in my wineglass, wishing I could conceal my many secrets so easily.

CHAPTER 34

Whitehall Palace
September

Autumn nipped the air outside the windows of the Vane Room at Whitehall Palace. It breezed in, lifting my filmy silk sleeve. I looked to my bared breast and watched my nipple tighten. The engraver, Roettier, noticed, too. He cleared his throat and stepped behind his easel, sketching away.

In my right hand, I held a long spear, while my left rested on a shield emblazoned with the overlapping crosses of Saint Andrew and Saint George. The footstool I sat upon would be depicted as a globe. Loose curls escaped the knot behind my head, falling around my ears and down my neck. My shoulders, arms, and right leg stretched from the folds of a belted Romanesque gown.

King Charles had shown me an ancient coin dredged from the Thames. "See the woman here. This is the figure the ancient Romans chose to represent this land when they conquered it more than a thousand years ago. They called her Britannia. I plan to issue new farthings and halfpennies next year. My profile shall be on one side, and you, as a triumphant Britannia, will bare your fine leg on the reverse."

"Is this your way of declaring to all England that mine are the finest legs in the country?"

"Not just in England, my love. You will be gazing across the four seas, sitting on the world, where your beauty will declare our might. Britannia the Beautiful."

King Charles had appointed this honor to me after Castlemaine had birthed him another daughter. I felt triumphant, indeed.

The unmistakable sound of the king's Life Guards marching in the outer chambers echoed against the walls. I turned my head, listening to him command his followers to wait.

"Ahem. Mademoiselle Stuart," Roettier said. "You mustn't move."

King Charles appeared in the doorway, beaming. "We've got it!"

I dropped my spear and jumped up, running to embrace him. "What have we got, my love?" I asked, kissing his cheek.

"New Amsterdam," he said, smiling and waving his arm. "By New England on the coast of the Americas. I told James he could have the land if he could reclaim it from the Dutch. We had it before, but they edged us out for the good ports and trade. Now we've got it back, and he's going to rename it after himself. New York."

"So we shall not have to fight a war?"

King Charles eyed the artist and tipped his head toward the door.

Roettier dropped his tools and scampered out.

The king pressed his lips against mine. They were hot yet soft, and his thin mustache tickled the skin under my nose. I could feel the warmth of him; his kisses were coaxing, searching, opening. Desire swept through my blood. I could not stop it, knew it would come, yet it always took me by surprise. And I suspect he felt it. "Charles," I whispered. We embraced thus for ages, kissing and fondling and unable to do more. *A true angel would do no more.*

He tipped my head back with one hand and used the other to brace my backside. He licked the top of my breast, tracing a path with his tongue up my neck to my ear. I felt the surging need to squeeze my legs around his thigh, which he had planted between mine.

This is where I always halted.

I circled his neck with my arms and looked at the open window behind him. I called on the girl he thought me to be: the angelic Stuart he needed to keep him honorable. I caused the window in my heart to close. I could see him, I could feel him, but my body was not moved by him. I suspect he felt this, too.

Sometimes he would go on touching, despite my stillness, because he wanted to pretend I was his in every way. He would undress me, trace my breasts with his fingertips, mold his hands over my navel. Sometimes he held me so tightly I could swear he was afraid to let go.

Other times, I know he went on because he had a duty to fulfill. He would touch and taste me, beg me to say something shocking. He rubbed against me, breathing me in, not looking at my face. He would kiss me abruptly good-bye, leaving without cooling his arousal first. Those were the nights he went to Queen Catherine's bed.

Yet, more often with the passing of time, he would simply stop when I closed the window. He still put me to bed, kissed me, and talked with me, calming himself before leaving, but he didn't seem to have the desire to go on pursuing me. As if he didn't want to suffer the anguish anymore.

This was one of those times. He broke away, led me back to my seat, and rearranged my hair. "Roettier," he called.

"Your Majesty," I said. "About King Louis—"

"We've gained a footing from the Dutch, a port in the Indies. They will surely concede. All will turn to nothing." He turned, ending the subject. "Roettier, you must put all your English pride into this engraving. It will be la Belle Stuart's legacy."

CHAPTER 35

Woolwich Harbor, England
October

K ing Charles waved his hand gracefully, face lit like a child's at the sight of a new plaything. "It is the bow that makes her so impressive," he said to Queen Catherine. "At twelve hundred tons burden she will carry no less than seventy guns."

With both feet rooted firmly on the deck of the state barge while it pitched and heaved in Woolwich Harbor, I gripped the side rail and stared up in awe at England's great pride. The Royal Navy. Or at least part of it. The newly constructed ship hovered over the water, awaiting her launch.

The river swayed, and my legs moved to accommodate the tilt. I swallowed the bile in my throat. But Ambassador de Cominges approached me, and the bile rose up fresh.

"King Charles plans to paint the Dutch as aggressors in the next Parliament and appeal for money to fund a war."

I tightened my grip on the rail. "He only wants the Dutch to concede a fair share in the trade ventures."

"It will lead to skirmishes, to engagements, to battles at sea. It will force King Louis to aid the Dutch against the English."

I whispered fervently, glancing around to be sure no one heeded us. "I assure you, King Charles desires friendship with King Louis."

"Hatred for the Dutch brews in the London mob, stirred by the talk of war at court."

"If King Charles doesn't want a war, none can force it on him."

"Are you certain?" He shook his head. "They executed Charles the First. I am concerned about the stability of this restored monarchy." I looked away, but he went on. "Every waterman and tiler thinks it his right to talk about affairs of state. They debate in the coffeehouses what should be done at court. Their talk can sway Parliament. Since Parliament controls the money, King Charles must cooperate with them."

"If any king can balance the opposing political forces pulling at England, it is he."

Cominges glanced nervously at the massive hull of the new warship. "For your sake, mademoiselle, for Britain, I hope so."

The tension didn't seem to affect King Charles. He basked in the glory of receptions and dances and supper parties. Then, in the black of night in mid-December, I woke to the sight of him leaning over me, his black periwig hanging down so long it brushed my cheeks.

"What time is it?"

"Too late," he said. "I wanted to show you something, but seeing you this way makes me want to crawl in and stay here."

I grinned, pulled him to me, and kissed him deeply.

After a while he pulled away. "Temptress!" he said, laughing. "Get up."

A tired-looking Prudence entered with my bodice and skirts. Between the three of us, we had me dressed in no time. I donned slippers at the door and wrapped a shawl about my shoulders on our way out. He led me to the Privy Gallery through one chamber after another.

"Where are we going?" I asked, as he opened a final door.

The wainscoted walls and tiled floor were like any chamber at Whitehall, but this was unique in its function. Glass-fronted cabinets lined the walls, housing vials of substances, bottles of liquids, and preserved creatures floating in jars. Books lined regular shelves. Number charts and diagrams of the human body hung from the walls. Tables held strangely shaped glasses and warming equipment.

"My laboratory," said the king.

"Is all of this safe?"

He shrugged and gestured to the door to the Privy Garden, where men from the Royal Society, mathematicians, architects, and physicians stood around the queen. They held spyglasses to the sky while she leaned over a tubular-shaped object. "Go see Isaac Newton's new invention."

A man with short-cropped hair looked up from the notebook where he was scribbling. "It isn't finished yet."

The queen showed me how to look into the tube.

"It's the night sky!"

"Do you see that star with the shimmering tail?" asked the king.

"The comet everyone's been talking about." It was beautiful, strange, like a piece of heaven falling. I felt it had to mean something.

"You think this be a good omen or a bad?" asked Queen Catherine.

I glanced up when King Charles chuckled. "Neither. It's just a star."

CHAPTER 36

Whitehall Palace

February 1665

The Candlemas Masque in the Great Hall portrayed England subduing her enemies, with court ladies dressed to represent the different nations. I peered through a sequined mask and watched Lady Castlemaine and Frances Jennings, a new maid at court, prance on the stage in pantaloons and stockings.

"I'd rather they stepped down, let you get back up and dance again."

I turned from the stage to find the Duke of Richmond beside me. "Where have you been?"

"France. For a time. But was needed back in Dorchester to review the militia at Blanford, Portland Castle, Sandsfoot Castle. Armed and ready. If we go to war."

"You think it will happen, then."

"Imagine so. Best to be ready in any case. Not that I'm eager for it with the new Commission of Prizes."

"Commission?"

"King ordered us all to prey on Dutch shipping. To compensate the English for Dutch greed. I've fitted out small fighting vessels myself and hired captains to move on the order."

"So you're . . . pirating."

"Sounds nicer to call it privateering, don't you think? Fine time for such a thing. They swept out our garrisons off Guinea. The Royal

African Adventurers are ruined. They're raving mad with us in the Dutch states. Demanding New York back and building up their battle fleet. Wouldn't mind seeing some action myself. York promised I could command some of his ships, but the king ordered me to stay at Parliament."

Louis would be furious.

"I've upset you?" Richmond draped one arm across my shoulders. I felt the dragging need to tell him the truth. He steered me through a back door into another chamber.

I pulled off my mask. "It's complicated."

The sconces flickered as he sat me on a bench, and a look of genuine concern lined his face. Longing to tell my cousin something, I knew not where to start. "You deduced that, when I was in France, King Louis made me promise to befriend King Charles."

He gave a half smile. "Been most successful, I'd say."

"If we go to war with the Dutch, Louis is bound by an alliance to support them against us. I failed to unite them in the beginning, when I was—struggling against Lady Castlemaine for . . ."

He raised a teasing brow. "The king's heart?"

"Yes," I said, thankful for his tact. "I'm afraid this turn will cause Louis to be angry with me. I . . . don't want him to speak ill of me to Madame." *Or reveal my mother's secret.*

"Ah . . . there were rumors about Madame and him. His attentions would have pricked her pride."

"Did you see her when you were in France? How are her children?"

"She was well. Her daughter is the prettiest thing, just three years old. Her son not yet a year."

"I miss her so."

"You know," he said leaning back. "Lady Castlemaine has bedded King Charles often enough, but he wouldn't change his policy for her."

"Exactly! The men around her may talk him into appointing cabinet members, granting titles, lands. But King Charles will never waver on matters he considers important." The words rushed out as I waved my hands, excited to know someone understood.

"Religion, for example. He knows his people wouldn't trust a Catholic king."

"He's determined to keep his kingdom intact." I thought of Prudence. "Do you worry about England?"

"You mean will the Restoration hold?" he asked. "It will, I think. Because the king feels strongly about so few issues. He'll sit calm on his throne and not stir things worse."

I must have looked forlorn because Richmond grabbed my hand. "Cousin." His expression was soft, comforting. "No matter the troubles, I have position now, which counts for something. I will protect you if you have need."

It was the first time anyone had offered hospitality to me without self-seeking motives.

You were the most beautiful player, Frances," King Charles said in my apartments that night.

"An honor to you, I hope."

"Mmm." He didn't look at my face but twiddled with the fruit in Sir Ment's dish. "You were gone for some time." His tone froze me. "With Richmond, was it?"

I knew I mustn't hesitate in my response. "He's our distant cousin, you know. He was telling me more about the nations we'd portrayed in the masque. Explaining it all."

"I see," he said, seeming relieved. "And what did you learn?"

"It made me appreciate your task, Your Majesty. I cannot think what I would do with the troubles abroad and at home pressing on me as they must you."

He caught my hands in his. "As long as I do nothing drastic, everything should settle."

I took a chance: "King Louis will be cross if we go to war with the Dutch."

"Truly, Frances. The more you press his cause, the more I wonder." The lines beside his lips deepened. "It is decided, my love. We will declare war within a month."

The news was like cannon fire. "I speak with you about these matters because of your kinship with Louis—"

"As if I don't have enough to worry about with the war itself, I have to fret over your esteem for Louis! How friendly were you with him?"

I bit the insides of my cheeks hard. Everything depended on my answer. I walked away to compose my thoughts. "Forgive me for interfering. It is . . . King Louis asked me to. It is his priority to form an alliance with you."

"I deduced that." His insight shouldn't have shocked me as much as it did. "What I am asking is *why* you press it? You bring it up constantly. Why do you cling to his expectations so loyally?"

Could I tell him that rejecting King Louis had gotten me banished to England? I looked at Sir Ment, eating quietly, and I had to sit down. I couldn't tell King Charles that capturing his heart was my *punishment*. He would see my lies, see my schemes, see me for what I really was.

I buried my face in my hands. I was an inspiration to this king, and for me, he was trying to be honorable. I could not tell the truth now and risk losing him. Wetness smeared my cheeks. I loved King Charles. Even if I had to pretend to be something I wasn't, I would do it to keep him.

"Frances," the king said softly. "Stop now." He knelt. "Do stop, I can't bear this." He rubbed my cheeks, grasped my hands, and kissed each wrist. "I do not think war can be avoided now, but I sent a special ambassador to France to show my goodwill toward Louis." He looked weary. "Don't give up on an alliance yet. I will find a way to make everyone happy."

CHAPTER 37

Early April

Life Guards helped me alight from the king's unmarked carriage two months later, and I sailed through the front arches and sentries of Somerset House. My mother, the Queen Mother, and my siblings greeted me in the courtyard, and I stopped to curtsy. My sister ran to me, embraced me, and asked, "Can I go with you?"

Mother and I were going to the Tower of London to visit the Duke of Richmond, whom King Charles had imprisoned for dueling with another lord. "Of course not," I replied. "The Tower is no place for a young girl." *Nor is court. Nor is anywhere in London.* I wished I could send all three of them to a manor in the country to keep them safe.

The Queen Mother studied me as I chatted with my brother. I wondered what plots she might be hatching now, or had the recent uprisings tempered her ambition?

As Mother and I left, St. Albans appeared and began a promenade in the garden with the Queen Mother, the children following behind them. My mother would never leave the Queen Mother's service. This was a sort of family to her. Indeed, St. Albans might be real family.

"You look healthy," she said as the carriage jostled us through town.

"Sophia and Walter seem well. How go their lessons?"

"Sophia is a beautiful dancer. Walter adores fencing."

She smiled warmly at me and we held hands. "I miss you," I said.

"It's been some time since your maid Mary reported to the Queen Mother. She seems not to press you about King Charles as she once did," she said carefully. "You could leave court."

"You know King Louis wants me here. And we might go to war with his ally. I can't leave now."

"There is less risk to your family if you do."

"Don't worry. I won't do anything to anger St. Albans."

We didn't say anything further.

When our carriage reached the end of Tower Street, we found we had to walk. We passed through Lion's Gate and followed the narrow drawbridge. To our right, a small crowd of Londoners had gathered to look at the lions, growling and pacing in the enclosure below. The keeper threw in a shank of meat, and I had to look the other way. The outer ward rose straight up from the moat, and the White Tower within stretched high and imposing. We came to the Middle Tower, where guards searched our baskets of peas and spring greens. One led us down another bridge over the moat to the Byward Tower, and finally to the Bell Tower. Up flights of stairs, he unlocked a heavy wooden door and threw it open.

Richmond, with doublet thrown aside and shirtsleeves rolled up, glanced from his writing table and groaned. "What are you doing here?"

We entered the vaulted chamber, curtsied, and Mother extended her basket. "To reassure ourselves that you are well, Your Grace, that you hadn't been harmed."

Judging by the plush Turkish carpets, the canopied bed, and the remnants of a fine dinner at the table, he was certainly fine. Prisoners had to pay for their keep at the Tower. Richmond had obviously paid a tidy sum.

He rose. "You came through London for that? Have you no sense of safety?"

I stepped forward. "You are the one who was dueling. Besides, I must ask if you know anything of my friend. Elizabeth Mallet left my apartments the other night after supper. Her grandfather was conveying her home, but a carriage stopped them at Charing Cross. The drivers seized her! No one knows who's responsible or where she is, but

King Charles suspects the Earl of Rochester and sent him here to the Tower."

He saw my anger. "I haven't seen him. They don't let me out much."

"If you do, you must press him for information. Beat it out of him if you have to!"

"Go back now. King Charles will be angry when he learns of this."

I handed him my basket and turned to go. "When he sees you're important enough to me that I'd visit you here, he'll soften and release you."

"I incurred his disfavor once before, on a botched mission to Scotland. Don't sacrifice your favor for mine."

CHAPTER 38

Yesterday I saw one of his mistresses, whom I should not have recognized, she has grown so much taller and more beautiful since she left the Palais Royal; it is of Mademoiselle Stuart I would speak, who is assuredly the prettiest girl at this court and would pass for a very great beauty in any country.

—HONORÉ DE COURTIN
to King Louis XIV, April 1665

King Charles never stayed angry for long, and Richmond was released within the week. My friend was returned to her grandfather unharmed. Rochester was released, too, and the only punishment he incurred for abducting her was not being allowed to marry her right away as he'd hoped. But standing beneath a long row of orange trees that shaded one side of the pall-mall court at St. James's Park, I didn't care about any of it.

King Charles had never spoken about the night I'd cried into his hands. I was left to wonder: Did he think I'd shed tears for a lost lover in King Louis? When he'd returned to my apartments three anxious days later with trepidation in his eyes, I tried not to ponder where he had been when he wasn't with me. Pretended not to worry when Queen Catherine confided he had not been to her bed recently. Now I watched King Charles on the pall-mall court as he wrapped his arm around petite, blond Frances Jennings, the Duchess of York's new maid of honor. The man I loved was holding a pretty girl's waist with one hand, and guiding her playing arm with the other.

Jennings swung her mallet, and her ball landed far from her target. King Charles and she tossed their heads back, laughing. He pressed his body behind hers and began his tutorial again.

"Mademoiselle? Mademoiselle Stuart, are you listening?"

Blinking, I turned to the men who stood beside me. Three pairs of French ambassadorial eyes stared me down, expressing a mix of frustration.

King Charles had been true to his word and had sent a special ambassador to France. King Louis responded by sending two *additional* ambassadors to England. They had gone directly to King Charles to plead with him not to go to war. Then came directly to me.

"I say, Mademoiselle Stuart, are you well?"

I ripped the gloves off my hands and walked past them, heels crunching the cockleshells of the pall-mall court. The gloves were new, one of many gifts the ambassadors had presented to me since their arrival. I wanted to throw them on the ground. If I didn't need them so badly, I would. Mounting war was expensive. Queen Catherine's income was cut to make the fleet ready. Which meant everyone's income was cut. I hadn't been paid my portion in months. Even meals for the court were reduced to fit a new budget imposed on Whitehall Palace.

The ambassadors scampered after me. "Wait, mademoiselle. Slow down!"

The pleading voice put me in check. I hadn't realized how quickly I'd fled. It was time to get hold of myself and figure out "a way to make everyone happy," as King Charles had put it.

I led them to a shaded bench beside the canal. "Sirs, do you mind if I sit?"

Henri de Bourbon, Duc de Verneuil, gestured toward the bench. "But of course, please make yourself comfortable."

Verneuil, a handsome man, was the illegitimate son of Henri IV of France. Which made him uncle to King Louis *and* King Charles. His presence signified the importance King Louis attached to this embassy. He had a sad disposition that made him quiet, which didn't bother me at all. I tried to seem cheerful. Maybe they didn't notice my frustration. I certainly hoped they didn't notice the king's attentions to Frances Jennings. "Who would have thought spring would be so warm already?"

Honoré de Courtin looked relieved. "We shall gift you a supply of fans next."

Courtin was young, but sharp and studious. He was the one communicating with King Louis by letter. He gestured to his companion. "Shall we supply Mademoiselle Stuart a box of fine fans to preserve her comfort?"

Verneuil only bowed slightly.

"Very well," added Cominges, who now heeded Courtin's every command. "We shall bring her the prettiest ones."

Courtin put a fist on his hip and leaned toward me, scabbard tapping against the bench. "As to what I was saying earlier, mademoiselle, about the king . . . he is rather slow in his manner of handling business. He would not meet with us the other day simply on the excuse of it being a Sunday. Lord Chancellor Clarendon is impossible to see on account of his gout. The few times we have spoken with King Charles he is amiable but . . . noncommittal." He frowned. "I *must* convince him not to release his ships from their harbors against the Dutch." Courtin glanced at his cohorts. "King Louis has impressed this upon me." The three Frenchmen hovered closer over me. "You see, mademoiselle, King Louis mentioned, most confidentially, that you owe him a special favor."

My insides turned to ice.

Courtin pressed on. "I'd hoped we could conduct our business without requesting your help, but we have made no progress. So we must ask you to intercede on King Louis' behalf."

It is finally time. I must obey orders or King Louis will expose my family.

I carefully slipped each glove back on and stood. King Charles's laughter drifted through the orange trees, and I glanced toward the pall-mall court. If I'd had any right to pray, I would have asked God to make King Charles still love me once his angel fell.

I sent King Charles an invitation to sup in my apartments that night. He seemed genuinely at ease, leaning back at my table, empty plate before him, wine goblet in hand. "When I marched my army into Worcester, I thought we could hold out against Cromwell's forces. But we fell apart in the fighting. I had no choice but to flee, go into hiding, make my way out of England on my wits and a prayer. By the time I climbed into that tree, I was exhausted."

"And you *slept* in an oak tree!" I laughed, trying to appear relaxed as well, as he relived some of his days in exile. "Thank God you were safe."

"Thank the good Catholic Royalists who hid me and smuggled me out."

I put my hand on his knee. "Truly," I said softly. "Else I would not have you."

As a rule, I tried never to touch him first for fear of teasing him. Now, my hand threw his features into confusion. "I am thankful you are here tonight," I said with a tight squeeze. "I have been meaning to speak with you about . . . matters."

He put his warm hand over mine.

"I—I have missed you." My heart hammered so loudly I could hardly hear my own stuttering. "Indeed—I—I think I've grown quite jealous."

The king burst out, *"Jealous?"*

"I'm afraid of losing you to—to—Frances Jennings."

The king shook his head back and forth, seeming dumbfounded. "You are more precious to me than words can express." He pulled my hand to his lips and kissed it. "But I find I am not able to become so honorable a man after all. Being with you as we have arranged is sweet hell." He stroked my cheek. "My perfect angel. I cannot do this to you anymore. I fear I will wreck you."

"Majesty—Charles—I'm nothing near angelic."

"If you were my mistress, I could commit to you. Queen Catherine must obviously have her place, but I could give you my soul and abandon all other loves. It would be a sort of marriage, bound by the honor in our hearts if not by God and law." He eyed me. "But you place everyone's views, everyone's expectations, above your own happiness." His shoulders sagged as he took my hand again. "I suppose this is one reason I love you. I will keep you any way you will let me have you."

"Truly?" My heart kicked up its pace. "Charles," I whispered. "I cannot risk having a child, but I can give you more." I stood and spanned the short distance to stand between his knees. "Will it damage your opinion of my virtue if I tell you that I want to touch you? I cannot if it causes you to think your angel has sullied herself."

"Is that what has stopped you all this time? As long as you are mine alone, you will be my angel. I am a rogue, unchangeable. And I want you all to myself. Can you promise me?"

"Promise?"

"I will love you alone, and you must promise to forsake all others for me." He grabbed my hips and kept talking, urging me with his eyes. "Promise me. I will worship you forever, my angel, if you will promise to seek no other man as long as we live. Nor any other *king*."

My mouth went dry, and I said the first word that landed on my tongue. "Yes."

He stood with me in his arms and carried me to the bed. He set me down gently, then tore at his doublet and shirt. "You can still stop me. I will not go further than you wish." He climbed beside me and took my face in both his hands. "But you must not shut me out anymore. Do you understand?"

I nodded, afraid and aching for him to touch me at the same time.

King Charles was forceful. "Say it. Promise me."

"If you will still love me, I promise not to shut you out."

He let go of my face and grasped my hand. "Then I will consider you mine forever."

He placed my hand on his chest and I felt the thud of his heart. I smelled the sandalwood on him and tasted the faint saltiness of skin before I even realized I was kissing his neck. I heard his breath catch, and I moved lower to lick his shoulder, his chest. I did not know what I was doing; I just ran my hands along his arms, across his face, touching as I had always wanted. The ribbons to his trousers strained tight. Gold points at the ends of his laces clinked together as I yanked them. I pulled the final lace and opened his pantaloons.

"I'll not hurt you," he whispered.

I touched him with light fingertips. I ran them softly from the base, circled the taut, shiny tip, until it jumped slightly. Amazed, I wrapped the king in my fingers and felt his pulse in my hand. The throbbing between my own legs was almost painful.

Charles lifted his hips, which slid my hand along his shaft. He groaned, and I slid my hand again; he lifted his hips to meet me, and we fell into a rhythm. But I needed to join him, to climb over him and move this way together, over and over. I squeezed him harder and heard myself moan quietly.

He rose up as I fell back. He deftly lifted my skirts and slid his hand up my thigh. I did not release him. I couldn't. He looked into my eyes; he had touched my secret places before. But never like this. His fingers slid in, slowly, on slick flesh. He was slow, searching, moving inside me. "God, Frances, you are untouched, a perfect virgin. I won't take it, I swear, my angel."

He moved his fingers in a shallow pulsing motion. It only heightened my need, and I groaned. I writhed against him, whimpering. His shaft grew in my hand, and I had trouble keeping my fingers all the way around. He thrust hard in my hand, once, twice.

His creamy seed blasted straight up, splattering the breast of my bodice. Some spilled in my palm, slicking my grip, and I slid down easily on the next thrust. Then I let go of him because I felt like I might shatter. I heard myself call out, buried in the tumult, grasping him, holding on while I seized. I throbbed and writhed and held him, thrusting shamelessly into his hand. "*My* angel," he whispered.

CHAPTER 39

June

rudence!" I stood in the middle of my bedchamber in a bodice of salmon-pink taffeta—boned with tight, precise stitches that made my torso a perfect, tubular shape—listening to her approaching footsteps. "I can't find the fan from Ambassador Courtin. Where have you been?"

She entered and headed straight to my cabinet. "With a friend in Pebble Court, come from delivering a message. Admiral Penn's son. I know him from . . ." She glanced to see if Mary was around, then handed the fan to me woefully. "He says tha fleet's positioned fer tha start of battle, milady."

"Indeed it is," I said, grateful she held her tongue, did not mention that the admiral's son was rumored to have Quaker sympathies. Such an accusation was the last thing the admiral needed on the tides of war.

Pink silk ribbon dangled from my shoulders, holding removable sleeves in place. I checked the waist tabs that flared over the draped skirts and the longer tail tab that flared over my backside with more pink ribbons. Palming the bone sticks of my new fan, I spread the kidskin with a skillful flick. When I had accepted this fan, I'd curtsied to Courtin. "I spoke to him for you. He fears Parliament will never let him get out of the Dutch war now and would rather not waste your time belaboring the issue." Courtin stared blankly. "However, I managed to . . . persuade him . . . in private ways . . . to continue to hear your arguments. You will find him more often in my apartments, which you are welcome to use as your forum."

King Charles did sit through Courtin's arguments for my sake. But for how long would he continue to do so? "Thank you, Prudence," I said, as I took my leave. It was time to cut through the throng of insincere admirers positioned in my antechamber and find the king.

Moments later I entered his presence chamber. He stood when I curtsied before him, and he kissed my hand. So for a few beats I held everyone's attention. But the formal chaos that always surrounded King Charles soon absorbed me. Spaniels yapped and scampered underfoot and one tugged at a lady's skirt. The king, with little regard for whoever was trying to speak with him, called the dog's name, then reached down to shoo one away from his own ankle. Lords laughed, milling about, vying for position, power, money. Gossiping ladies eyed them, maneuvering themselves closest to the ones most likely to prevail.

Queen Catherine gestured for me. "Frances," she whispered. "You must attend me at Tunbridge again. Sharles say we can go. So we make to go." The queen then cupped her mouth to shut out anyone who might try to read her lips. "Castlemaine is with shild again and must be staying here."

Bile filled my throat. Since her last birth, the gossips hadn't reported Castlemaine taking any new lovers. *Surely not*, I told myself. *Not King Charles.*

I tried to conceal my shock. "She will be the only one of us left to . . . entertain the king."

She nodded, as if she had already thought the problem through. "She be getting so heavy and sour. Sharles will not be happy with her. But you." She tapped my hand with her fan. "You must go. Else the French hector you to death."

The bellow of a footman sounded from the doors. "Honoré de Courtin, ambassador extraordinaire from France."

The ambassador walked in, gracefully sidestepping the yapping dogs, and bowed before the royals. With his toe, King Charles nudged a growling spaniel away from the edge of the queen's skirts, and absently addressed the ambassador. "Courtin. Still haven't given up your mission?"

Courtin rose with a smile and spoke in French. "I wanted to speak with you regarding the chancellor's request that we continue our negotiations in writing."

"Ah—*oui*," King Charles said. Then he continued in broken French, "You see, I can hardly remember my French and hold my thoughts for as long as it takes me to comprehend your words. So doing this formally—in writing—would be easier for everyone."

"Some of your ministers speak French as well as I do." He eyed me. King Charles noticed as Courtin went on. "I regret, I cannot proceed in writing."

The king muttered in English, "Can't you see that what you want is out of my control?"

Courtin shot a glance at me as the presence chamber doors opened once more. A new herald called, "Her Majesty Henrietta Maria de Bourbon, Queen Mother of England."

She swept in on a cloud of black velvet. The court turned in her direction and bowed. The Earl of St. Albans entered behind her, towering over everyone else, looking down his nose at no one in particular. My family wasn't with them, praise God. *Are you my grandfather? What exactly would you do if I forced that secret out?*

King Charles reached to take his mother's hands; she only allowed him to grasp one. With the other she reached out to Courtin. "I do wish France and England would come to an understanding."

King Charles hid his exasperation well. Then he broke the circle to drape an arm over St. Albans's shoulder. "I can neither convince Ambassador Courtin of the necessity of our war with the Dutch, nor can I silence him, Albans. You must try to do it for me." Without waiting for a reply, King Charles said, "Very well, then, I'm off to supper."

With that, he left.

I realized the man who had promised to love only me must be headed to Lady Castlemaine. Had he lied? I had to know when her child was conceived. I couldn't accept it if I'd committed myself to another untrustworthy king.

During our month at Tunbridge, the queen received regular communication from London. We had news of the first engagements of war: England had defeated the Dutch off Lowstoff but had not pursued them when they fled. What could have been a swift victory was a promise of more battles to come, and our ships had returned with heavy casualties. The Duke of York had come so close to getting killed that the king forbade him from going to sea again.

Every lord and gentleman in the realm hustled about accounting money, moving goods, or overseeing a warship, while every lady sat busy at prayer. Queen Catherine marched us to her chapel several times a day to pray. For the safety of King Charles and the Duke of York, for the bravery and stamina of the poor wretches recruited to man the ships of the Royal Navy, and for delivery of the evil Dutch to England's victorious pride.

When we rolled back into London in Queen Catherine's carriages, we met a grim, quiet city. The summer heat sweltered, intensifying the usual stench. Stores were closed, and few people dotted the streets. Housefronts had red markings across their doors. *Plague.*

CHAPTER 40

But, Lord! To see how the plague spreads.

— SAMUEL PEPYS'S DIARY
July 1665

The plague spread. Alarmingly fast. King Charles placed the palace under strict security. No one came or went unless under royal employment. When there were deaths near Whitehall, he ordered everyone to pack; we would leave London. But I sent Prudence with a Life Guard to Somerset House to fetch my family. I hid every gold coin I had saved within the lining of a jewel casket, wrapped it in lace and petticoats, and packed it into a shabby-looking sack. Then I sat down to write Richmond a letter. I would use force with Mother if I had to, but I was determined to send my family to one of Richmond's country estates. Prudence called from the antechamber, a shrill urgency in her tone. I dropped my quill and rushed out to find her.

"Milady! Tha Queen Mother . . . tha king . . ."

"Speak. What's happened?"

"He's approved her leave, milady! Tha Queen Mother is going back ta France this very day ta escape tha plague. Her household is all prepared, milady. Tha king and queen have ordered tha state barge ta row down tha Thames. If ye hurry, ye could go. Milady . . . milady?"

Mother is leaving. The Queen Mother, too. And taking my brother and sister. "What?" I said in a daze. "Go where?"

"Ta say good-bye. There should be no threat of contagion just rowing down tha river . . ."

I grabbed the old sack, terrified and elated at the same time, and rushed to the privy stairs by the Thames.

Out on the river, rowers brought the state barge alongside the Queen Mother's ship. I stood behind the queen as the royals conversed across the water and scanned the deck of the ship frantically for my mother, my sister, my brother. I finally spotted them midship. I broke rank and walked down the barge so I could be closer. My throat tightened; my eyes started to ache from the effort of keeping tears in. Sophia and Walter were crying; they reached down for me. I stretched up, but their ship was too high for me to reach their hands.

"Mother, put your arms out."

She did, and I tossed the sack up. Praise God, she caught it.

"Don't do this." My mother's face softened. "The Queen Mother keeps us well."

"I need to know you have it," I said. "Just in case . . ."

King Charles put his hand on my shoulder. "I can order everyone to stop at the Nore," he whispered. "You can board their ship and I'll send your things to Paris."

I glanced at the tense lines around his mouth. Somehow I knew that even if the worst did happen, things would still be well between us. "No," I whispered. Regardless of everything . . . I wanted to stay with him.

The king commanded the household to Hampton Court, and we made the brief journey by river the next day. Church bells echoed over the water, constantly tolling the deaths, and the smell of burning frankincense, lit on doorsteps to ward off pestilence, carried on the wind that filled our sails. The French ambassadors' arrival was delayed because no one there would agree to lodge them. The English people considered the French to be friends of the Dutch, and anything Dutch was hated. When their coaches finally lumbered in, they didn't delay their pursuit of me for a moment.

"How nice for you that Lady Castlemaine went on to Richmond," said Courtin to me while King Charles stood at my side under the row of lime trees in the garden.

"You mean how good for *you*, Courtin," King Charles answered for me. "Since the other ambassadors follow her like puppies, and now Frances can help you monopolize me."

I cringed inside at this blunt truth and resented it at the same time. Then he pointed a long finger at Courtin. "As a cousin and a monarch, Louis ought to stop the Dutch rather than help them. They are a mere republic, after all."

Courtin turned red. I took the king's arm and steered him down the row. Courtin stayed behind as we promenaded through the garden. "You're harsh with them."

"Still wielding Louis' standard?"

Letting him see my anger would get me nowhere, so I kept my tone light. "Well, I must have something to hold on to if I learn Lady Castlemaine's baby was conceived after your commitment to me."

"Don't you trust me?" He grinned.

Infuriatingly, I didn't know. I changed the subject. "Will the plague get worse?"

"I don't see how it can possibly get worse." He rubbed a hand over his brow.

"Do you remember that comet we observed? Some are now saying it was a portent of disaster, that this plague and this war are a curse on England. They say fire will be next. Ruination."

He took my face in his hands. "*That*," he said, "is ridiculous."

M id-August, word arrived that at least six thousand people had died in London in one week. Then one of the king's Life Guards fell, seizing and bleeding from his ears, at Hampton Court. Panic rose to a furor. The Yorks decided to take their household north to York, and King Charles ordered the queen's household to Salisbury where it was hot, rainy, windy, and crowded. All of her ladies rode horseback through Farnham in men's riding habits, smiling all the way to cheer the people. Queen Catherine selected me as the only lady to stay with her in the royal lodgings.

The plague arrived in Salisbury almost immediately.

A royal groom fell sick and was shut into his house. All its inhabitants were forbidden to leave; condemnation for all of them. Then another man fell dead right in the street. We all feared our own mortality, and the weeks turned to months in Salisbury. My only solace was word that the Queen Mother's train had arrived, *healthy,* in Paris. We played basset until we could tolerate indoors no longer. We hunted. We played bowles. We did our best to ward off melancholy. King Charles came to my bedchamber often, and I spent every moment devising ways to assist the French.

"Your Majesty," I said at the supper table one evening, reaching for him. "I had a dream that would be amusing to tell the French ambassadors. Call them over so I can tell all of you."

"Indeed?" He didn't take my hand but summoned them.

"La Belle Stuart here has a bit of revealing news," he told them. "She dreamed last night that she was in bed with all three of you!"

I flushed. I had gone too far.

The next day King Charles complained of feeling ill, and the queen burst into tears. I searched his armpits myself but found no swollen buboes to indicate plague. Praise the saints, he felt well enough to gather himself up in a few days to tour the countryside. Leaving me to reassure the ambassadors that he would return soon to hear their constant supplications, and to wonder whether he could ever forgive me for using him so.

CHAPTER 41

Oxford

October

I had the king in my lodgings at Salisbury at least," said Queen
Catherine with a light hand over her belly as I checked the inven-
tory of tea in her India cabinet in our chambers at Merton College. We
had moved on to Oxford so the king could open Parliament away
from the bed of agony and death that was London.

"Merton is not far from the king's lodging at Christ Church, Majesty," I replied. But she was only voicing my own disappointment.
Castlemaine was stationed in a house across the street from Merton;
we suspected her child was due soon, but we weren't sure.

A satisfied grin settled on Queen Catherine's face, and she rubbed
her hand in a circle over her abdomen. "You are right. Sharles not neglect me."

The queen is with child. A teaspoon slipped from my fingers and
clattered on the floor. I bent to retrieve it and hid my face. *I am not
jealous,* I told myself. But when I peeked at her again and saw her happiness, I knew I was.

The Duke and Duchess of York arrived and took house around
Christ Church near the king, who was preoccupied with business. I found myself sitting across from the king's brother one day in

the hall at Merton, playing basset with several maids of honor from his household, including Frances Jennings.

"I had word today from London," York said, tossing a bill of mortality on the table. "For the first time in months, the number dead from the plague has dropped."

"Praise heaven." I eyed the woodcut print of skull and crossbones framing the foolscap and shuddered. "The very word 'plague' frightens me."

"Don't be so serious!" Frances Jennings studied her cards. "All this talk of plague, war, politics, religion. I say any *serious* person should be taken to the pillory and whipped." She pushed a stack of coins into the lot, and the other maids giggled.

"I believe I have a losing hand," I said quietly, thinking of my family and all we had at stake. I put my cards aside. "Pray excuse me." I walked out to a large courtyard called the quadrangle and breathed in the October air, so clean compared to London. I wished the bracing, refreshing autumn breeze were enough to blow away my mistakes, set things to rights.

"Frances." York's voice sounded beside me. "The plague will abate. You no longer have to live in fear."

"I do hope you are right." I continued walking and he kept in step. "Though plagues return. And what of this dreadful war?" I wished he would leave me to my thoughts. "I cannot sit and gamble all day while such uncertainty hangs about me."

"Gambling is a distraction, a sort of solace. Why, every Royalist man is betting on our monarchy's success and drawing winnings from every pot just in case it falls."

A bitter laugh escaped me. "Some ladies play that game."

York looked sidelong at me. "Yet you do not grasp at the drawstrings of the privy purse."

"The things I need are not monetary."

"Artless charm," he whispered. "I've longed to speak with you privately. Your beauty has captivated me. I've long wanted to ask your favors."

Don't damage his pride. My lover's brother was also the heir apparent until Queen Catherine produced a living child. I had to be careful.

He could be the next king. "Me? With legs too long and slender, not even clad in green silk stockings?"

He looked blankly at me for a moment, then blinked when he remembered. "I didn't really mean that." His shoulders sagged visibly.

"Please don't look so forlorn. There are many pretty girls at court who would make you a suitable mistress." He shot me a grievous look. "Look there, Arabella Churchill is a lovely girl."

"How I wish you could find something in me to admire." He stopped, glanced down. "How can I prove my devotion?"

I took a breath to speak, then paused. A risky idea formed in my mind. I took another breath and threw myself straight into it. "Oh, cousin." I took his hand. "There is something." The instant brightening of his face should have made me feel shame. "In France, King Louis spoke fervently of his love for you and your brother. He badly wants an alliance of friendship. You're the lord high admiral. Can you not find a way to secure it?"

York's eyes couldn't have opened any wider. "My trade ventures depend on the acquisition of ports from the Dutch. Friendship with France means no war, no way to expand trade. The French have that alliance with the Dutch, you see."

I let my face look drawn. "Then you put your ventures over me."

"Very well." His gaze flicked away. "I shall concede defeat."

The world seemed to shift. "P-pardon?"

"I shall consider you my victory instead." His mouth twitched.

Is he bluffing? "Y-you will stop the war?"

He stepped close. "May I come to your bed on my word?"

"My bed?" *What have I done?*

He leaned his face close to mine, persistent. "What you ask will take time. Would you make me wait to sample my prize?"

I stepped back, struggling for composure. "You insult me if you think me so easy to win." I couldn't believe I'd taken the risk. My king was a fool for thinking I could ever make him a better man.

CHAPTER 42

*I can assure you, I am on much better terms with Frances Stuart than the Spanish
ambassador is with Madame de Castlemaine.*

—HONORÉ DE COURTIN
to Louis XIV

The French ambassador's carriage rumbled toward me. I considered abandoning my walk and running back into Merton College, leaving the clamor of hoof and drivers calling halt. But I had gambled high and it was time to assess the loss.

The golden-crested door swung out before the footman even jumped down. Courtin stepped out and bowed stiffly. "Mademoiselle Stuart. How fortunate to find you, I was just coming to seek an audience with you. Would you accompany me to Christ Church?"

I paused before gesturing for Prudence to climb aloft. "I am at your service."

Cominges sulked in a corner of the carriage. He nodded when I climbed in beside him. It seemed colder in the little space than it had outside.

Courtin thudded onto the opposite bench and pounded the roof with his fist. I braced my feet against the floorboards, and we lurched forward.

"There may be no pretense today, Mademoiselle Stuart." Courtin stared at me intently across the short distance. "You'll have heard your parliament voted unprecedented sums to the Dutch war. Your people hate the French so much I fear our supplications only angered them. We have pleaded for nothing but friendship, yet they seem determined to oppose anything King Louis wants, so great is the animosity toward him. We are now at an impasse. Today we've been to see Lord Chancellor Clarendon. So obstinate a man! He heard our final arguments and merely shook his head with a sour expression."

"We don't know if he was disgusted with us or grimacing with gout," Cominges muttered.

"Then we went to the king. Amiable, as always, with no answer to give." Courtin pressed on. "We went to the Duke of York. Do you know what he said to us?"

I shook my head. *I don't want to know.*

"He admitted he wants this war. He said he cared not if King Louis joined the Dutch, but war he shall have." *York had been bluffing after all.* Cominges rubbed a hand down his face. "Mademoiselle, we've heard the Duke of York is in love with you. You must talk to him for us."

This is the best gambling loss of my life. "I've already asked him to cease the war."

Both men stared. "You spoke to him?"

"I told you I would serve King Louis' interests. I had the opportunity to ask him, so I took it." A fresh wave of self-disgust rose in my throat. "His mind is made, sirs. You shall get no cooperation from that quarter."

Courtin dropped his head into his hands. "There is one more office to petition." He lifted his eyes to meet mine. "Henry Bennet, the newly made Earl of Arlington. He is one of the king's highest ministers." He put his hands on his knees and sat up. "We will take you there now. You may tell him we will call on him before evening, and we shall send another carriage to take you home."

No! I won't tolerate another day of France coming between King Charles and me! "Of course." I touched his knee lightly. "Dearest Courtin, will you do something for me? I fear losing King Louis' good opinion if I fail. Promise me, even if the worst happens, you will tell your king I was a good and faithful servant to him, and I strove to do his bidding."

He sighed, long and weary, but nodded.

———

When the ambassadors left us outside Arlington's chambers, Prudence was pale and shivering, but I was heated with determination.

Arlington received me without hesitation, black patch glaring across his nose as ever. "What a surprise. I planned on coming by Merton this evening to see Lady Scroope. Perhaps I can escort you back, eh?"

"I hope you will leave off meeting with your mistress this evening, my lord."

Arlington paused, a puzzled look on his face. "You know you can call me Henry."

Good. "Can you do something for me, Henry? It must be our secret."

Arlington was a consummate courtier, even in the face of flattery and the call to do a noble thing for a distressed lady. He dropped pretense, too, but did it with court flourish. "I am at the service of the king's favorite. I will endeavor to please you and ever hope it would please him in turn."

I resented everything about my position, hating my lies and hating my need to lie. "Very well. If you keep this matter private, I shall speak favorably of you to the king." *If the king will ever hear me earnestly again.*

His eyes narrowed. "What do you require?"

I told him precisely and coated it in the guise of charity. "My poor friends from France—the Ambassadors Courtin, Cominges, and Verneuil—they suffer in their plight. They hang on here in hopes that we will cease this war with the Dutch so we can ally with King Louis."

"That will not happen."

"Then ease their path back home. Tell them for certain and end their anguish."

Arlington frowned. "As long as they are here trying to make peace, King Louis has an excuse not to side against us. It would be best to finish off the Dutch before taking on France, too."

"I know. But you've been in trade negotiations with Spain for some time. Do you not think some other country will aid us?"

After silently contemplating, he nodded. "I agree. There's no sense keeping them here; our countrymen treat them with increasing hostility."

The relief made me light-headed. "Let them believe I tried to coax peace out of you. I wouldn't want them to think I was trying to get rid of them." Which was all I wanted at that moment.

He gave his word. No one would remain to force my intercession with King Charles for France. If King Louis ever learned of what I'd done, he would lash out at me by attacking my mother, sister, and brother, all now living in his domain. I had either destroyed my family or fixed everything . . . and the world would be worse for it.

CHAPTER 43

... the factions are high between the king and the Duke of York, and all the court are in an uproar with their loose amours; the Duke of York being in love desperately with Frances Stuart . . . so that God knows what will be the end of it . . .

—SAMUEL PEPYS'S DIARY
November 1665

I took up the habit of waiting for visits from King Charles in the gallery outside my chambers at Merton. While the rest of the court ladies wasted time and money gambling downstairs, I sat by the window overlooking the quadrangle and sewed.

Days had passed without word from the ambassadors. I stood and pressed my forehead against the cold glass window, longing for King Charles, the end of the plague, for some word about France.

"Milady?" Prudence inched the gallery door open and peered apprehensively at me. "Milady, tha French ambassador is here."

"Send him in."

Skipping the formalities, I reached for Courtin's hands. I tried to ascertain his disposition. "I've been so anxious to see you. Do come in and tell me what's happened."

But Courtin clasped his hands behind his back and looked at the floor somewhere near my feet. "The Comte de Cominges and the Duc de Verneuil ask forgiveness that they do not come to bid farewell personally, and they wish you God's blessing."

It was what I had maneuvered for, but I let my tone sound disappointed. I still needed to know if Arlington had given me away. "So, I was unsuccessful."

"Do not blame yourself, mademoiselle. You did all you could for us."

214

My shoulders relaxed. "Surely King Louis will say the same of your efforts here. You must go home in good conscience."

"Ah . . . if only I could."

"What do you mean?" The hair on my neck rose. "You did all you could for King Louis."

"Reports I've received in these last days cause me to reflect on my mission here." He cleared his throat. "I have concluded that I didn't know my king's true motive."

"I don't understand. What reports?"

"You are aware that when King Louis married Marie-Thérèse, he was forced to give up France's old claims on the Spanish Netherlands. Something you may not know, that I should have considered, is that King Louis put his ministers to work at uncovering a way to manipulate the law so he can still claim those lands."

"Still, I do not see—"

"King Philip of Spain is dead. The new king is young and sickly and will soon die. King Louis is preparing to attack the Netherlands, while Spain is weak, and manipulate the law to defend his actions."

"Is that all? King Charles suspected he would do such a thing. He told Cominges of this himself some time back—"

"Don't you see? King Louis distracts statesmen with proclamations of friendship while he claims trading ports. He bides his time, allowing his competition, the Dutch and the English, to prepare to demolish one another while he builds both his trade and his territory."

For a long moment I was silent. "So, you are saying your efforts here were . . . a ruse?"

Humility filled his eyes. "I wasted my own time and energy and, I am sorry to say, yours. I hope you can forgive me."

Ruse. Distraction. Wasted. The thoughts darted through my mind. I felt nothing but the habit to be courteous. "There is nothing to forgive," I said finally.

The lines of anguish in his face softened. After a quiet moment, he took one step back and bowed deeply to me. "I will keep my promise, mademoiselle. I will report to King Louis that you were his good and faithful servant." He turned abruptly and marched out.

Was King Louis' anger at my rejection so great he'd planned this duplicity all along? He could not be trusted to keep my family's secret. Yet I had no justification for the bitterness welling inside me. After all, I'd sworn fealty to him. It was his right as king to use my loyalty to his benefit. But he was also a man. He'd shown me the love in his heart. I'd revealed the honesty and anguish in mine, and he had taken advantage of it.

When I saw the smile King Charles bestowed on his queen during Advent and the glowing look she returned to him, I realized she'd told him she was with child. Queen Catherine was an honest, humble, and faithful woman. She deserved my regard by rights. Still, I revolted at seeing them together.

My mind plotted ways to make it so we could go on as before. But I realized in my anguish that if I had any real love for him, I would allow him to be the man I knew he strove to be. An honorable husband. An honest king. A worthy father. The best, the noble thing to do now, would be to leave him alone.

"Milady?"

The concern in Prudence's tone pulled me into awareness. I realized I was facedown on my pillow, wet with my own tears.

"Are ye well? Shall I fetch a physician?"

"No." I rolled over and faced the cold winter sun streaming upon Oxford.

"Oh." She hesitated. "I thought ye'd want ta know, Lady Castlemaine was brought ta bed of a baby boy today."

I stared blankly at the bed curtains while envy washed over me. "I see." So the child *was* conceived before King Charles had promised to love only me. *Indeed. I've striven in vain to please the wrong king.*

"The queen will know soon. I imagine she'll be calling yer attendance when she hears."

"When she calls for me, tell her I am ill." I rolled into my pillow again. I could relinquish her husband, but I couldn't face her just yet.

CHAPTER 44

. . . Sixteen hundred sixty six is come:
When (as some say) shall be the Day of Doom.

— GEORGE WHARTON'S ALMANAC
1666

K ing Louis declared war on England in January, though he didn't
trouble to attack us. The bills of mortality due to the plague soon
dropped enough that the king felt it safe to return to London. He allowed the queen and her court to stay behind, for which I was glad,
not wanting to tempt the plague too soon. Nor force myself to face
King Charles any more than I must.

I stood meekly behind the queen as she embraced her husband farewell.

Within hours we realized Castlemaine had followed him out of Oxford. Queen Catherine ordered us to prepare for travel. "She'll sink
talons in him again unless I order us go now. Good for me to go be with
him. You think yes?"

"Yes," I replied, reining in my sorrow. If I had to lose the king, I'd
rather lose him to Queen Catherine than Castlemaine, after all.

The morning we were prepared to leave, Queen Catherine started
bleeding. Her dressers fetched me to her rooms. I found her doubled
over on the floor with blood streaming down her legs and pooling
around her nightgown. I sent for the physicians and held her hands as
she passed clots and blood. The physicians told her there was no hope,
and the blood continued to pour out of her. And, finally, a miniature
infant prince. Fully formed and pale, snatched too early from the womb.

"Tell me he lives," cried Queen Catherine. "My babe must live." I touched his lifeless form, dumbfounded and frightened at the fragility of life. I shook my head, and her face crumpled with anguish. I held her when she wailed, and I cried with her. I told myself I cried for her loss. But part of me also mourned things I would never have.

Back at Whitehall in February, the gossips were full of contempt for Castlemaine, and Castlemaine was full of deceit. She tried to convince King Charles that the queen had never really been pregnant. He waved her off; he knew the signs of a woman's body better than anyone. Yet, as reward for his new illegitimate son, she had been given gold plate and new jewels. She amassed a fortune, though there was no money anywhere else. Queen Catherine could not pay her ladies. Sailors—sailors who had escaped the plague, sailors who had risked their lives for England, sailors who had fought without pay—died of starvation outside the Navy Office.

At the end of March, Queen Catherine received word that her mother had died in Portugal, and she withdrew completely into melancholy. "My Queen," I said in her bedchamber one afternoon, "would it please you to go to the theater? Out riding in the park?"

"No." Pale and drawn, she sat wrapped in a dressing gown, cradling her tea dish. "I will observe mourning for my mother, and time heal my grief."

I sipped my tea in silence.

"Physicians tell me wait to conceive. I am weak and tired. I'll no heal fast enough. I want you go to him. You can keep him from that . . ." Her lips turned in a pale, jagged frown. "That . . . whore!" Her china dish slipped from her hands and clattered to the table.

I set it right and wiped the tea up with a cloth. "Forgive me. I cannot do as you command. I cannot continue to undermine you in that way." My hands trembled. "He wants to be honorable to you, to have a legitimate heir, and be a king his subjects can admire."

"I won't blame you," she whispered.

For several minutes I said nothing, just stared at the bits of tea leaves drying on the cloth. "Your Majesty," I finally said, "things have happened between the king and me these last years. *If* the king decided he wanted me again, understand, I could not be satisfied with things as they were before." I stared into her eyes, imploring her to comprehend.

She nodded. "He is kindest to me when he is closest to you."

CHAPTER 45

April

Every member of the queen's household wore black. No cosmetics, no coiffures, no jewelry. We looked very bleak in mourning for Queen Catherine's mother. Castlemaine stood opposite me with her arms crossed, face glazed over in boredom as she watched the queen at her toilette table.

Of us all, Castlemaine looked the worst without her vanities. With dark circles under her eyes and no wig, she seemed positively sallow.

Queen Catherine lounged in the sunken tub of the bathing chamber that morning. She ordered a full hair wash, and oil for her nails. She dressed and redressed. When her hair was combed dry, she had us experiment with modest hair arrangements, and asked our opinion as to which would be most appropriate for a queen in mourning. Then her gaze flicked to her clock. "My Lady Castlemaine, King Sharles has been staying out far too late. I fear he catch cold if you continue to keep him at your house long into the night."

Castlemaine snorted. "He isn't staying at my house too late. It doesn't take long for me to satisfy him." She grinned at me, but I looked away. "He must have another mistress he's sneaking off to afterward." She glanced at me again, as if seeking corroboration.

King Charles was standing in the doorway. He approached Castlemaine and looked coolly into her eyes. "You've gone too far. You are bold and impertinent and you disrespect the queen. Leave court and don't return until I send for you."

She recoiled. "How dare you!"

He spoke in a tone that brooked no refusal. "Get out."

W hen King Charles entered my bedchamber hours later, he bowed.

I curtsied. When I glanced up, I saw uncertainty in his eyes.

"I want to apologize for—"

"Your Majesty has not offended me."

He sighed. "Alas. I could not satisfy you with regard to the French matter. I am sorry for however that may inconvenience your . . . relationship with King Louis."

"It . . . doesn't matter anymore."

He cleared his throat. "As to Louis, I feel I should tell you something which may be of consolation."

I wanted to embrace him, find a way to start over. But I gestured toward the cane-backed chairs. He pulled one out for me, then sat himself. "Do you remember my assertion that King Louis wants nothing more than to seize the Spanish Netherlands?" He studied my face before he went on. "Years ago I told King Louis that I would not oppose his claims on that land."

"I don't understand."

"I tell you in hopes that it will ease your suffering. The French ambassadors have let you think you failed in securing an alliance between England and France. Louis wasn't seeking to gain my friendship. He was only seeking not to offend me so I will keep my word, allow him to advance on the Spanish Netherlands. All the pleas for alliance were meant to impart his goodwill. An outward sign to show his unwillingness to fulfill his deal with the Dutch. Only Louis and I would understand that, I'm afraid. I never mentioned it because I thought he might have told you."

"You thought I . . . was a goodwill offering?"

"If Louis hadn't told you—" He shrugged. "I was unsure how much you felt for him."

"You didn't want his concealment to hurt me."

We sat silently, the new truths echoing between us for several moments.

Years of guilt pressed on me. I had to tell him the full truth without dishonoring his sister. I wanted to be honorable, virtuous. I wanted to be the woman he thought me. I wanted to be the real Frances. I heard myself blurt, "King Louis wanted to make me his mistress. When I refused his proposal . . . he became angry." I gripped the arms of my chair. "He made me promise to seduce you and ensure an alliance. He never told me about your agreement."

"Why did you refuse him?" He leaned forward, so close to my face that I could feel his breath, earnestly seeking my answer.

Madame's face, hurt and angry, flashed before my eyes. "I was so young. And it hurt your sister. She loved him more."

"I always wondered if those rumors were true." He shook his head. "You never fulfilled your promise to Louis."

I held up my hand. "It was plain that bedding you would not ensure your compliance in any political matter. I failed him *and* deceived you." My voice became a harsh whisper. "Now you see me for what I really am."

King Charles stood abruptly. He paced to the window and braced his hands on either side, muttering, "Always be wary of ambitious men."

I ached to follow him, to pull his hands down and around me.

"There is nothing that can come between us now." He turned to face me. "Am I right? Is there nothing else? My mother is gone back to France, the war is decided. Is there anything more that might cause difficulty between us? You must tell me now if anyone else separates us. I cannot stand the distance keeping us apart."

"Oh, Charles." My composure fell.

"Do not cry. Tell me what else remains."

"Nothing at all, and yet so many small things." His image wavered between watery and clear. The small things were my own failures. My dishonesty, my lies, my risks—they reined me in. But he looked at me with such expectation, such hope, that I knew I must let them go. I deliberated and carefully selected my answer. "Two things. Lady Cas-

tlemaine. I cannot see myself fully open with you while she is still between us. The second matter is your wife."

"What of the queen?"

"I will not humiliate her. Much as I desire you, you are still her husband. I am loath to dishonor her by becoming your mistress."

He paused. "How is such sin overcome?"

"She understands you completely and has asked me to replace Lady
Castlemaine as your mistress."

"Did you agree?"

I nodded slowly. "Only *if* you want me alone. I refuse to fight Lady
Castlemaine for you any further."

"Is there anything else?"

It seemed enough. At least all I needed to say.

"You did not contest when I called this sin. What about tomorrow
when the rumors fly? The accusations and the damnation of the people whispering about the king's whore?"

"If we continue with discretion, they will have no reason to say such
things."

"Discretion I can give you. If I take your body . . ." He closed the
distance between us. "I will never return to Barbara. If you give yourself to me . . ."

I closed my eyes and absorbed the fascinating heat his touch always
sparked.

"I may not be able to return to the queen's bed. England will start to
suspect. What will my angel do then? What will you do if you cannot
hide this sin?"

"I—I do not know. But I want you. There is the honesty you want. It
will have to be enough for you."

"Say that again."

"It will have to be enough for you," I whispered.

"Not that." He gripped me so tight I could scarcely move.

"I do want your love."

He grasped my face with both hands and kissed me with such intensity all thought soared from my mind. When he finally broke away, he
whispered, "Will it be enough for *you*?" I tried to pull his head back

down to kiss. "Say it will be enough for you. Say you will finally live for yourself."

We moved without thinking to the bed. Every part of me wanted him to take me. He tugged at my silk, pulling the pearl clasps until he could push the gown away. As he looked down at my body, he threw off his own clothes. When he was completely naked, firelight dancing naughty shadows across his skin, he met my eyes.

I opened my legs and bent them at the knees. Lifting, aching for him to join me, to finally fill me. But he did not touch me. "You will say it." He crept between my knees and placed one hand beside each of my shoulders, not even grazing my skin.

I placed a hand on each side of his face. "Love will be enough."

He lowered to his elbows. "Then I will take you and never relinquish you."

My whole body trembled as he pressed against me.

"It will only hurt at first," he whispered.

CHAPTER 46

Without doubt the king's passion was stronger for Frances Stuart than ever it was to any other woman; and she carried it with discretion and modesty.

—LORD CLARENDON'S MEMOIR

The next morning, King Charles delivered a Dutch cabinet, covered in exquisite tortoiseshell and adorned with the royal arms. He opened it to reveal dozens of little drawers within and said, "I promise to fill each one to overflowing with jewels to adorn my love." He skipped his council meetings, and we spent the entire day alone in my chambers.

As we did many, many times after.

King Charles maintained peace with Castlemaine and continued visits to her, for the sake of their children. But he paid a huge sum to settle all her debts. Severance. Thus, outwardly nothing changed. She was the apparent mistress, but I reigned in private.

I slipped from my bedstead two months later, naked, and opened my tortoiseshell cabinet. I pulled out my pearl necklace and tied it behind my neck. He gestured for me to return to bed. Instead, I let him watch me walk through my dim chamber to the window. I pushed it open to the night sky and the peal of church bells.

I turned to pour wine. "You can see the celebratory bonfires dotting the whole city. This victory will do much to buoy England's spirits."

His smile fell when I handed him a glass. "We had quality vessels, and they maneuvered well. But in a sea battle squadrons pass and repass each other, each barraging the other with cannon until they either sink or retreat. After four days of fighting, we're the ones who retreated."

I put my glass aside. "We'd heard it was a victory."

"We lost ten ships, maybe six thousand men. We must raise money, refit the navy, recruit more sailors, and send out again."

I walked to the window once more. "The streets are nearly empty of men as it is."

"We must prepare quickly, for King Louis has seized our West Indian colony. He may engage us directly."

"Where will either of you get enough of anything to keep fighting?"

He was behind me and turned me around. "Let's not talk about that now."

But I couldn't curb my fear. "My brother is nearly of age. If King Louis finally attacks us, will he be forced to fight? Will my *brother* be forced to fight for France?"

I tried not to seem surprised when the king's men hired merchant ships for battle, called in the militia, pressed a loan from the City, and extracted funds from the clergy. To replace deserters and thousands of dead sailors, troops seized men off the streets and impressed others from the countryside. Old men and boys, the sick and the lame, were escorted like prisoners onto the ships. I pretended not to think of my brother when I heard of it, and instead organized to escape the summer heat on another trip to Tunbridge Wells with Queen Catherine.

In mid-July, while we watched actors summoned from London perform for us, we heard word of the St. James's Day Fight. In August we returned to Whitehall, and news arrived of Holmes's Bonfire. We'd burned nearly two hundred Dutch merchant ships. But our mutilated fleet glided into our harbors like ghosts on water, and we all knew we hadn't really won.

CHAPTER 47

It's so small, a woman could piss it out.

— THOMAS BLUDWORTH,
lord mayor of London, September 2, 1666

Less than a month later, in the first hours of a Sunday morning in September, a small fire started in the city. The dry summer had left London as ignitable as a basket of kindling. I smelled something burning at dawn and stretched from my window to see around the bend of the river Thames. All I could discern was enough smoke to indicate a huge area near London Bridge was blazing.

"Prudence, where is Mary?" I asked as she tied my bodice laces.

"She went out, milady. Her day off. Maybe she went ta hear one of her masses?"

I went to the king's chambers where everyone had gathered to hear his chaplain, when a man bustled in. A secretary for the navy, with access to court; I recognized him from the theater and the park. "Parts of London Bridge are burning. Nearly three hundred houses, churches, and taverns are on fire, and no one's doing anything to put it out."

"What's your name?" someone asked.

"Mr. Samuel Pepys," he replied. "Someone has to tell the king."

King Charles soon emerged, gave the man instructions, and sent him off. But the blaze raged out of control in the warehouses, igniting their flammable goods. The king and the Duke of York took the state barge out to be sure the lord mayor of London was pulling down houses in the fire's path in order to stop it. An eastern gale made

227

things worse, and by nightfall I didn't have to strain from my window to see the red glow beyond the river bend. Sparks of fire shot high into the night and fell down like burning rain.

I was relieved when Mary returned that night, but Prudence cornered her. "Jest where have ye been?"

"Somerset House, at chapel and at rest." She saw the suspicion in Prudence's glare. "What? It was my day off!"

King Charles and the Duke of York organized the city to action. Commanding Life Guards, magistrates, militia, nobles, common workmen, and even members of the Privy Council, they toiled day and night against the fire. They used gunpowder to demolish buildings in the fire's path and handed out gold coins to keep the people working. But the flames only leaped further, past the gaps they created. Families fled their homes, possessions bundled in their arms, to makeshift shelters in the parks. Rations of the Royal Navy's biscuits were dispersed, though they were soon found inedible. Those who had the means took to the river Thames. Every dinghy and skiff bobbing under the smoke seemed piled with poor souls on a doomed journey to Hades. Even the water itself seemed to burn in places where tar and fat oozed onto the river's surface. I thought it might really be hell when I could see St. Paul's ablaze, its lead roof melting, stones from its wall bursting from the furious heat.

From Whitehall Palace, we heard the screams, the explosions, the crack and crumble of walls, and the ceaseless raging roar of the inferno. Eventually we couldn't see the flames through the thick, black, stinking smoke that filled the courtyards and darkened our chamber walls.

Life Guards were dispatched to pack up Whitehall's most valued treasures and move them to Hampton Court, warning the queen to be ready to evacuate at the king's command. On hearing this, Prudence wrapped her belongings in a sack, tied it to her back, then fell to her knees in prayer. Mary recited rosaries in the closet. Too unworthy to approach God or his saints, I packed my art and my jewels with trembling hands and hoped the two of them would say a prayer for King Charles on my behalf.

Finally, on the fourth day, the wind and the city fell quiet.

The queen had ordered all the other ladies to be ready to leave, but called me to attend her while she waited for the king in his ante-chamber.

After an agonizing wait, he arrived, smeared in soot, drenched with water and sweat. He held his arms open and the queen rushed to embrace him, weeping. He wrapped his arms around her, kissed her, then opened one arm and gestured to me. I stepped into them, the weeping queen and the filthy king, and we held one another as if it were all a dream.

"It is mostly out now," he whispered to us. "All will be well."

Late in the night the king sent a page to fetch me up the back stairs of his chamber. When I arrived, he was sitting on the edge of his great gilt bed, dressed in his nightdress. He had bathed and didn't have his periwig. A lone candle made the silver in his short black hair sparkle like salt. His dogs were curled asleep on the red velvet coverlets.

I knelt before him, kissed his knees over and over. "I'm so thankful you're alive." I pressed my face against him.

"Did you think I'd let the fire get me?"

"I—I felt so guilty for indulging in sin as we have and—I didn't know what would happen."

"It was just a fire."

"Just? Much of the city is gone. They say ten million pounds in damage."

He lifted my head and forced me to look at him. "Frances," he said with complete calm. "It is merely an opportunity to rebuild." He smiled the way only he could. For all his exhaustion, he still glowed with confidence. "Now," he said. "I woke up lonely. Will you sleep the night here with me?"

I nodded, not at all reassured. "I shall do anything you want."

He pulled me into the bed beside him. I breathed him deep and curled into his embrace, legs twined with his in a familiar tangle.

"You needn't do anything," he whispered. "Just stay with me. Always."

And it seemed such a small request.

CHAPTER 48

October 1666

Diverse Strangers, Dutch and French were during the fire, apprehended upon suspicion that they contributed mischievously to it, who are all imprisoned.

—The London Gazette

E veryone knows it was Catholics what started that fire!" Prudence said.

"Leave me be," replied Mary. "It was a day of rest. You know I had nothing to do with it. Who's to say it wasn't one of your own kind?"

"Everyone knows the Catholics want ta take over England. Yer pop-ish and ye can't be trusted!"

My antechamber was empty this day, courtiers having gone to prepare for Queen Catherine's birthday ball. "Hush!" I commanded. Both women bowed their heads.

I leaned into my looking glass and affixed a small heart-shaped black patch by my eye: *la passionée.* Testing its stick, I smiled at my reflection. When I'd carefully pinned diamond pendants into my hair, I turned. "If people on the streets of London heard you, they'd attack you or lock you both in the Tower. The whole town is raving with ac-cusations against the Catholics—I don't need you joining the clamor."

Prudence couldn't keep her mouth shut. "I say it was the Cath—"

"I'm cutting both your wages."

Both maids gaped at me.

"Henceforth you shall tolerate each other's religions and neither of you will lord your own views over the other. If you have a strong opin-ion, you shall keep it to yourself."

They sneaked glances at each other, then nodded like errant children.

"I say, Frances, you're beginning to sound just like your monarch!" I turned to see King Charles. He wore a new style: a long vest and coat over knee-length breeches. The look accentuated his height and somehow enhanced his majesty. I embraced him with a sheepish grin. "Don't you mean I'm like your Parliament? They're the ones forcing the laws against Dissenters and Catholics."

"But you're asking for tolerance." He twirled me around. "I'll warn you," he said. "You'll not likely get it." He backed away to study me. "I wanted to see you before I escort the queen to her ball. Lovely!"

I curtsied, elated. The mourning restrictions were relaxed for Queen Catherine's birthday, and I had applied silver-white lace to the low shoulders of my black velvet bodice. My matching petticoat had a long train that my maids bustled up in the back so I could dance without tripping on it.

"I have something for you." He turned me toward the looking glass and lowered a strand of diamonds. I watched our reflection as he fastened it behind my neck, allowing his fingers to graze my shoulders. He put his face beside mine, whispering, "And my love for all eternity."

"They are too much for me to accept!"

"You must accept them or risk my displeasure." He winked.

It didn't matter that the king escorted his wife and queen to the Banqueting House that evening. I was the highest in royal favor. I did nothing to quiet the whispers in my wake. I let them look their fill at my diamonds, my lace, my joy, and took no notice. I did nothing to keep my king out of my heart. I danced nearly every dance with him and pretended not to hear what people said.

CHAPTER 49

Whitehall Palace
Christmas

The king did never intend to marry Frances Stuart to any but himself.

—SAMUEL PEPYS'S DIARY

Queen Catherine and I reclined in the king's presence chamber, tying bunches of holly and ivy into boughs to decorate the hall for Christmas. Company at Whitehall was select this night. The Duke and Duchess of York played with their adorably wide-eyed children, the daughters who might yet become queens. Several members of the Privy Council who kept their families in London had brought them to witness Christmas at court. Most, though, had gone to their homes in the country. To their estates, their children, their comfortable lives.

The presence chamber doors swung open and two Life Guards appeared, crouched behind a great log. They rolled it into the chamber, and King Charles entered behind them. He held out his arms like an actor on a stage and cried, "Let us light the Yule log!"

Courtiers began laughing and dragging furniture aside as the log rumbled past. We jumped up, following them to the fireplace. Greenery spilled to the floor, and the scent of trampled evergreen wafted on the air. The king's pages distributed goblets of spiced wine, and the king's violinists struck up "We Wish You a Merry Christmas." At least half of the group commenced singing. A handful of people added spices to the Yule log; others insisted on burning rosemary branches with it.

"No! You're supposed to pour wine on it for good luck!"

"Seems a frightful waste of good spirits!"

A few lords wanted to lay wagers on how many tries it would take to get the log lit, and soon a flurry of coins and the sounds of gambling mixed with our songs.

"My Queen," Charles called. "Come see this."

When Queen Catherine left my side to see a present someone had given him, I went back to our boughs. As I gathered some scattered branches, I noticed Buckingham in the queen's chair. How I wished he hadn't come! "You caused a lot of trouble in the House of Lords," I said, "obstructing their progress and coming to blows with the peers."

Buckingham made a mocking face. "So *that's* why the House had me locked up in the Tower for three days." The humor fell from his expression. He waved a hand that said he didn't care for the king, for his own wrongs or customary precedence. "Do you know what business is under way at Parliament?"

I snatched up prickly branches. "I make it my particular business to ignore business."

"It's the petition of a broken family. Right now it's just a matter of keeping the Roos title away from illegitimate children. But soon it will be a divorce."

I glared at him. "Why should I care?"

"Don't be dense. If I can push this into a divorce and see it through, it will be a perfect opportunity for the king to press his case of divorce against the queen . . . so he can marry you."

I determined to keep control of myself. I would not let this man see my emotions. "He would never disgrace Queen Catherine with a divorce. I wouldn't let him."

"She's a barren queen."

"She's conceived more than once and may yet produce a full-term child."

"You were ready enough to snatch the crown when Queen Catherine was dying."

"You misjudge my sense of honor if you think I'd glory in my queen's downfall."

"Honor." The word came out on a snort. "Not so much honor that you could keep your legs closed, eh? You wear the pleasure of a worldly woman well. I knew you'd enjoy it once you finally gave up."

I searched the noisy chamber to make sure no one had overheard. My gaze landed on Arlington. He was observant and calculating. In the fleeting second before he looked away, I had seen a coolness in his eyes: much more than my reputation was being pondered.

Holly bit into my fingers and I glanced down, releasing my grip on the bough in my hand. "You shouldn't be at court, Buckingham, much less be scheming to control the life of a king who is far out of your reach. When did you last banquet with him or even speak to him? Stop this foolishness—he won't listen to you."

"He will consider a divorce once he sees it done." Contempt and confidence oozed from him.

I glanced toward Arlington, who was carefully looking at a spot over my head while whispering to Cornbury. I had to change the subject. "Apologize to the king for your misbehavior. Get your favor in the customary ways."

Buckingham jumped up. "You owe me—"

"Nothing." I sliced the air with my hand. *I owe you nothing.*"

"You disloyal daughter of a bastard."

I turned to walk away, but King Charles stood in my path. Buckingham paused, then quickly presented his leg and bowed deeply over it, sweeping his arm full to the side. "Good tidings, my King! I've come to tell you about a gift I'm fashioning for you."

"Which you've no right to present to me under the circumstances." He quietly offered his arm to me without taking his eyes off Buckingham. "Leave court."

I put my hand on the king's arm and watched Buckingham flush with resentment. King Charles led me to the antechamber where a table of mince pies and plum puddings sat steaming. "It was presumptuous of him to come here," he said. He embraced me and kissed me full on the lips. "I have a gift for you." He produced a velvet pouch.

Reluctantly, I broke our embrace to take it from him. I tugged on the silk cords and pulled out a curious piece of jewelry.

"It is a watch," he said with obvious excitement. He took it from my fingers and held it toward the sconce's glow. "Look at the enameled picture on the face."

Beneath a tree in a flowery meadow, a naked woman reclined on a couch while a man in cavalier dress approached. A winged cupid hovered above the woman. "How beautiful! Is it you and I?"

King Charles pointed to the tiny cupid. "See the arrow?"

I brought it closer and saw that the cupid's arrow was wayward. It would miss her and hit the man. "When he arrives, he'll find cupid struck him instead of her. So it is us!"

"Was," he whispered. "I shall visit you tonight. But I'd best get back to the queen. I left her with my brother. She'll be bored to death by now."

Courtiers, who had been dutifully overlooking us, though noting everything with surreptitious glances, now parted to make way for him. He held my eyes until he passed through the doorway. I glanced at my watch, the whimsical portrait of our story, and my heart felt lighter.

"There you are, Frances."

I looked up to see Cornbury approaching with outstretched hands. "I've been trying to catch you alone all night."

Arlington's voice sounded from behind him. "Lovely gift." He spoke coolly. "I know what he's trying to do."

I dropped Cornbury's hands. "You are a man of government. You shouldn't concern yourself with the king's personal affairs—"

Cornbury spoke. "He means Buckingham."

Arlington leaned in. "He can get the Roos divorce through the House of Lords. Buckingham has a way with the king. He could, eventually, convince him to divorce Queen Catherine." I pressed a hand to my temple as Arlington hurried on. "He'd use you as the prize for King Charles in the end." He glanced at Cornbury. "We need to know where you stand on this."

"You don't think . . . surely you don't think this is *my* idea?" I whispered.

Cornbury relaxed. "I told you she wouldn't like it."

But Arlington wasn't convinced. "He would make you queen. Surely you want a crown for yourself?"

All I could think about was Queen Catherine, who trusted me, promoted me. A divorce would disgrace her, barren and unloved, in front of all Europe. "No," I said firmly. "I told that fool Buckingham I wouldn't go along with his scheme, and I'll tell you the same. I would never betray Queen Catherine. I would be no more use to Buckingham as the king's wife than I am now as his—" I stopped myself. "No."

Cornbury, looking shocked, finally addressed Arlington. "What can we do?"

Arlington studied the floor. "There is no way to stop him if the Roos case is in the House of Lords—"

"You must discredit him *before* the case goes to the Lords," I hissed. "Slander him if you must!" Arlington was a clever man. If anyone could pull Buckingham down, it was he.

Cornbury squinted at me as if he were seeing me for the first time. Arlington slowly looked up, nodding. He gave me a half bow. "If you wish, I shall begin tonight."

I told myself all would be well as I climbed into my bed and Mary stuffed a warming pan under the covers at my feet. I told myself, too, the deepest, most hidden part of myself, to *forget the idea*. No matter how much I loved him.

CHAPTER 50

Westminster Abbey

January 1667

My cousin, the Duke of Richmond and Lennox, endured his second wife's funeral with a look of forced composure on his face. When the last of the attendants approached to pay their respects and then filtered out of Henry VII's section of Westminster Abbey, Richmond's stiff posture relaxed. I approached him with outstretched hands. "I'm so sorry, cousin. So sorry."

He nodded to his first wife's tomb behind me. "I knew I'd never find a love like her again. She married me before I was a duke, before I had—" He dropped my hand to wave his around the abbey. "Titles, responsibility." He finally let his hand fall. "Before all this scramble for position and money began." His face crumpled. "Our daughter is buried here, too."

I wrapped my arm around his shoulder. "This added loss has made you mourn them anew."

"When Elizabeth died, I couldn't fall apart because I had our daughter. Our baby—" He broke off, regained his voice. "Not even a year old! Thought my life ended with hers. But I have this title, this massive honor that befell me at the Restoration . . ."

I spoke softly by his ear and stroked his back. "Even great men mourn. It is natural."

He quietly accepted my embrace. We both understood loneliness. "What will you do?"

"Get to Richmond House at Whitehall for a good Scottish whisky. And then, I suppose I shall have to be getting myself my next wife."

Relieved at his lightening mood, I hooked my arm around his. "If it's a wife you want, Whitehall is the place to stay. Tomorrow is Twelfth Night. There are sure to be many eligible maidens dressed in their finest and on display."

"You must help me, then. My last choice was rather poor, God rest her. I'll be glad to have your advice."

CHAPTER 51

Whitehall Palace
February

Straight-faced and serious, Arlington presented his leg and bowed low in my bedchamber. "I've come to apprise you of our mission. I arrested an astrologer under the Duke of Buckingham's employ. We, uh, examined his papers and . . . talked with him."

"Did he confess anything incriminating?"

"He spoke of plots to take over the Royal Navy. The duke also ordered the king's nativity, a horoscope, to be drawn up. It is an act of treason to predict the death of a king, for the acts of men who believe in such things could be deadly."

I gasped. "I know he left when Parliament ended without taking formal leave of the king. It was rude and insulting. But treason?"

"I'll soon present this evidence to the king—"

The Earl of St. Albans cleared his throat in my doorway. Arlington bowed to both of us, eyed me, and took his leave.

"Dear girl," St. Albans said as he bowed. "I've come to say farewell."

Once I would have been perplexed by a visit to my chambers from this unapproachable man. My mother's reverence for him made him too mysterious. The things I longed to ask him were too weighty and made me worry anew about a problem of my own. *My monthly flux is late.*

I smiled from the chair at my toilette table. "Such a short visit this time."

"Back to France to the Queen Mother's service and to do a particular task for King Charles. He holds you in much esteem, you know. I believe you are part of the reason he is sending me to treat with King Louis."

"Please give my family my love."

He cleared his throat. "I thank you for your good word to the king for me. My project, St. James's Square, is well under way." The old earl kissed each of my cheeks and parted, leaving me dismayed that a man could be so warm but wouldn't acknowledge his own child. *What will I do if my flux doesn't start?*

I had not yet bled a month later, when Arlington returned to my bedchamber. "I dispatched men to the Duke of Buckingham's estate to arrest him, but he fled. We'll soon find him and bring him to the Tower."

"Then you are certain . . . his divorce scheme will never come to pass?"

"The king was deeply offended." Arlington paused. "He revoked the duke's offices at court."

I understood him perfectly. "Which will be divided among many hopefuls here at Whitehall. No doubt you want me to remind the king what a good servant you are when he's making appointments."

"No, I think I have that in hand," he said, surprising me. Then he pinned me with a very serious stare. "But there may yet come a time when I'll need you to remember the services I've done you. Congratulations," he said, and the seriousness vanished. "You averted the first true disaster in your reign as official mistress." He bowed, then backed out of the room as if I were royalty.

Looking out my window days later, I saw choppy whitecaps on the Thames, the water a dull reflection of the low-hanging fog, thick with smoke and soot. Wind whipped the watercraft, tipping and swaying the few watermen that dared row out on such a day. Surely they wouldn't risk the rough waters unless driven by some urgency, some pressing responsibility? I wondered absently if what drove them to race the storm was pleasant or grave.

"Milady, it's His Grace, Duke of Richmond and Len—"

"Show him in." Mary hurried back through the chamber door. Fixing my expression, I turned carefully and curtsied low.

He bowed in return. "Mind if I smoke?" he asked.

"Certainly not." I crossed to the fireplace to light a stick. "Sit, please."

"If you summoned me to ask how it goes with Mademoiselle La Guard, you'll be disappointed. She's fair and pleasant, but I don't think she likes me overmuch." He sat at the table and packed fragrant Virginia tobacco into his slender clay pipe. "Made some comment about my love of whisky." He sucked the flame I held for him until he drew a sweet smoke, which swirled into the air above him. "Besides, at the rate I spend, I'll need a wife with an income or at least a good dowry."

I tossed the stick into the fireplace where it immediately blackened and curled. "Would it be very bad?" I asked. "To have a wife with no money?"

He nursed his pipe. "I do have a sizable income myself. Damn generous of the king, really, to allow me so much. My estates do well enough. Hard to get vassals to pay rents during the war, understandably." He eyed me curiously. "Cobham Hall, my estate in Kent, absorbs everything. The improvements cost a fortune. Worth it, though. You should come see it. I'd have to sell another estate just to pay that debt. Rather not do that, though. Rather have another income to balance it out."

"I see."

He lowered his pipe. "Say, what's bothering you?"

"Nothing," I lied, clasping my hands in front of me. "That is, I was wondering, would you settle for potential gains rather than idyllic love in a marriage?"

"I told you before," he said, studying me. "I don't expect to find love again."

"And if you had an opportunity to make a marriage to a girl who had nothing but good blood and a good name and our king's favor, would you consider marrying her for the prospects that might provide?"

My cousin stood. Palming his pipe, he propped his fist on the mantel above my head and leaned over me. "King's favor is more profitable than any dowry," he said, very seriously.

I hoped to God I was doing the right thing. My hand slipped low to my belly and lingered. "And, cousin, do you still want an heir more than anything in the world?"

CHAPTER 52

*I saw Frances Stuart this afternoon, methought the beautifulest creature that ever
I saw in my life.*

—SAMUEL PEPYS'S DIARY

All I had to do was wait. When he cupped my backside, I moaned
softly. I felt a thread of shame at my behavior, but this was the
best way. I wrapped my arms around the king's neck and whispered in
his ear: "I thought it would be good for me to have a husband."

He froze, paused for one small moment. "No."

It was the response I expected. "Now don't answer before I've explained." I spoke softly. "Charles, if we're going to continue this way,
then I need a husband to protect my reputation."

"I've refuted every claim that you're my mistress!" His eyes were a
mixture of pain and irritation. "I refuse to let a *husband* come between us."

"He would be a husband in name only. If I had a husband with
a title, I'd have legitimate status, a sign that I'm not a spinster or a
mistress. What if I anger you? If you forsake me, I'll be alone with
a ruined reputation! I need to know . . . I have a place to fall."

His expression softened. "I could never be cross with you, my angel."

"God forbid it, my love, but what if something happens to you?"

He held his hands out wide. "I will arrange a title and an income for
you now. You'll be a duchess with power so no one can touch you
when I die."

"You may as well wave a flag over my head that reads 'Official Mistress.' I can't wear that title. Please let me protect my honor."

"You can't stand before God, vow to love a man, and not follow through." He hung his head. "You are my light, Frances."

"You're afraid I'll fall in love with a husband?" I leaned close and whispered, "There's no need to fear." Holding his tender feelings in my hands, I pressed even further. "The man has no love for me; he would not be a real husband in my heart."

His arms stiffened. "You already have someone in mind?"

"My cousin the Duke of—"

"Not Richmond!" He released me and flung his arms out, palms up, in an exaggerated, questioning gesture. He opened his mouth to speak but closed it. Then he shook his head. "He . . . is not a man to take being cuckolded well."

I held up a hand as if I could soothe away the biting tension. "The marriage is as convenient for him as it is for me. He's our cousin, a good man, with good estates. And you've made him very wealthy."

"He spends outrageously."

"So do you. Besides, he's one of the only unmarried lords in England."

"If I were inclined to let you marry, I'd pluck a sturdy beggar off the streets and grant him a peerage before giving you to Richmond."

"The man doesn't matter overmuch, just the arrangement. And he's already agreed!"

His brows knit together; then his expression turned thoughtful, and he studied my face and my body with intensity. A shadow of suspicion lined his features.

"I've explained it," I said, suddenly unsteady. "I'm marrying him!"

King Charles pointed his finger at my face. "You *cannot* do so without my sanction."

Of course I *could* marry without the king's permission. But that insult would shatter his pride. I couldn't risk hurting him that way. My love was also my sovereign. All nobles sought the king's approval before marriage, a traditional courtesy. It would be easier if I could find a way to make him agree.

"Charles, my own heart. Please trust me enough to allow it!" *It isn't just me anymore.* I resisted the urge to cover my belly with my hand. "My sweet king," I said, touching soft fingers to his tight jaw. "Let us stop this talk, it is upsetting you so. Take me to bed now, and we can think on it more tomorrow."

He rubbed his hand down his face. "We shall see."

CHAPTER 53

March

I sat by the queen in her presence chamber as she lost a meager sum to a few of her ladies at basset. Unable to focus on games, I tried to build a house of cards with shaky hands. King Charles had begrudgingly agreed to consider the arrangement and had ordered the Duke of Richmond to present his accounts. He was now delaying his approval on the pretext that Richmond's disordered finances were an unsuitable provision for me.

Richmond was unruffled. "Give him a little time," he'd said. "He thinks you'll drop it. When he sees you're serious, he'll let you." And he went about his usual business at Whitehall, which was spending money and corresponding in the management of his numerous estates.

"Are you well, Frances?" Queen Catherine asked with a look of concern.

I smiled weakly at her. "Actually, my head does ache."

She nodded. "You go if you like." She clasped my hand as I stood. "Sharles tell me your plans. Is anything wrong?"

"No," I whispered. "It's an arrangement to suit appearances."

"You not leave me?" Her tone was strained.

"Of course not." I hoped I was right. For her sake and mine.

When I reached the gallery, I leaned against the wall and closed my eyes. I didn't want to shut myself away in my chambers just yet. There would be much of that in my near future.

"Frances, I must speak with you."

Startled, my lids flew open. "Oh, Lord Cornbury." I pushed off the wall and walked down the gallery. "I really have no desire to discuss the Duke of Buckingham."

Cornbury kept pace with me. "Not about that—about your plans to marry Richmond." He looked over his shoulders for listeners. Seeing a few servants and Life Guards in the gallery, he pushed me gently into a passage and leaned close. "My father told me."

Lord Chancellor Clarendon had never spoken more than two words to me in my five years at court. Why would he trouble himself with me now? "And how would he get word?"

"He's lord chancellor. The king seeks his guidance in all matters."

"Why would the king need guidance in a personal matter of *mine*?"

He put a hand on my shoulder. "King Charles ordered my father to investigate Richmond's finances."

I yanked away. "This is no business of yours or your father's."

His eyes widened. "I'm your friend! I'm trying to tell you how things are with him."

"What makes you think I don't already know?"

He tipped his head. "You do?"

"Of course I know. Everyone at Whitehall has outrageous debts. We are at war, it is the age of debt."

He placed both hands on my upper arms. "Then I must tell you, do not despair. My father has told me the king's words in utmost secrecy." He peeked out of the doorway before going on. "He says the king would never allow a duke so highly ranked, especially a Stuart, to fall into poverty." He let go of my arms. "I've come to tell you there's no need to let Richmond's financial shortcomings deter your plans to wed." He stood back, an expectant look on his face, when a shadow darkened the passage.

Cornbury's expression shifted to disgust as his eyes fell on the figure joining us.

I turned my head. *Arlington.* And he was bearing down on Cornbury with a contemptuous stare. The spite exchanged in their gazes confused me, for they had so recently approached me in like-minded accord. I turned to leave. I gathered my skirts to step down the first few stairs.

"La Belle Stuart, a word please?" Lord Arlington called behind me.

Cornbury looked completely panic-stricken.

"Very well," I said, resigned. "Lord Arlington, I will see you in my chambers."

As I moved through my antechamber, Arlington practically trampled my train.

"Lord Arlington, what is so important that you must press a weary lady so urgently?"

"I know about your engagement to the Duke of Richmond."

I snorted. "Of course you do."

"King Charles told Lord Clarendon to investigate Richmond's financial accounts to find some excuse for breaking you up."

"I know all about it."

"I suppose Cornbury told you that and more?" I rolled my eyes to the heavens. "Did you know the king also gave orders to Archbishop Sheldon? To investigate the possibility of divorcing Queen Catherine."

All the breath rushed out of me.

"The king inquired whether the church would allow a divorce if both parties were consenting and one party was . . . barren."

"What did Sheldon tell the king?" My voice sounded far away.

"He asked for time to study it. Sheldon went to Lord Clarendon. Clarendon *directed* Cornbury to talk to you. He was following his father's orders."

He did not come to me in friendship. I rubbed my temple.

"What else did Cornbury tell you?"

There was no sense keeping anything from this man. "He told me Richmond was such a close relation the king would never allow him to be financially ruined. He said I should take heart and not deter my plans to wed."

"Clarendon would give anything to keep King Charles married to a barren queen, you see. As long as the king is childless, his heir is the Duke of York."

"Which would make Clarendon's daughter Queen of England."

"And himself grandfather to the next monarch."

"It is possible that Clarendon only wishes to be rid of me to avoid the scandal of a royal divorce?"

"You give that greedy Hyde too much credit. Besides, he has no right to take the choice from King Charles."

I eyed Arlington cautiously. It was no secret that he hated Clarendon. Arlington had once plotted with Castlemaine to bring the lord chancellor down. When their plans fell apart, he shifted back to the chancellor's side. Now I suspected he was working with her again, trying to make Clarendon fall through me. "Why have you told me this?"

"I know you'll marry Richmond. I know you won't allow King Charles to disgrace himself and the queen."

"So?"

"I've taken Buckingham out of your way. Even now he is locked in the Tower. I helped you with the French ambassadors and arranged for you to see the king privately in Salisbury. All this time I never once asked you for anything."

He was calling in all his favors at once.

"Tell King Charles of Lord Chancellor Clarendon's duplicity. He has a right to know. The truth will mean more, coming from you."

"You want me to destroy the highest lord in office."

When Arlington left, the tension he had created remained. I now understood that Arlington's own ambitions were what drove him to strike down Buckingham. Each of them wanted the power of the lord chancellor's position for themselves. I spent the next hour pacing from one window to the other. I knew King Charles was weary of Clarendon. From failing to obtain religious toleration early in Parliament, to his self-important attitude, everything Clarendon did caused the king to trust him less and less. King Charles had told me himself that he preferred proactive men to run his council. Men like Arlington.

By the time King Charles arrived, I wondered that he didn't see my anxiety.

We ate quietly. Spoke of horse racing a little. Finally, he cleared his throat. "I got word from the Earl of St. Albans. You will be pleased to know I sent a secret promise not to attack France for another year. King Louis will return my West Indian colonies, and I won't interfere with his attack on the Spanish Netherlands." He eyed me. "That means he will turn against the Dutch. It will end our war."

This should have thrilled me, but I could only summon a nod.

"I thought that would please you." He was deliberately avoiding the topic of my marriage. Delaying it.

I knew, I knew with certainty then: he would never consent, never let me go. Had he really asked the bishop to investigate a divorce? As he rinsed his hands in a silver bowl, King Charles studied the skin above my delicate dressing gown. His eyes had that passion that usually melted me. And something else. He was taking measure.

"Dear heart, I'm tired." I pulled my mantua gown over my décolletage. "Will you return in the morning, the usual time?"

"Anything you wish." He kissed me on each cheek, bowed, and backed out of the room.

Treating me with such reverence yet stopping my hand. Aiming for things that would shake the government and church apart. What of England herself? War torn, ravaged by plague, fire, and religious radicals, England couldn't cope with more than it had in the last year. The people and Parliament would revolt against him. *Just as they had against his father.*

CHAPTER 54

Expect that birds should only sing to you,
And, as you walk, that every tree should bow;
Expect those statues as you pass should burn,
And with wonder men should statues turn.

—LORD MULGRAVE'S
"Elegy" to Frances Stuart

R ichmond sat next to my bed later that night, resting his elbows on
his knees. For the first time, he looked concerned. "I could
reform the accounts or sell an estate to prove I can support you, but it
would take too long. By then everyone would be able to tell."

I put a hand over the slight mound of my belly. "The money wouldn't
matter, he'd find another excuse to block us."

"Then we must make plans to elope."

"It would put him in a rage if I left without his permission!" I shook
my head. "He'd never forgive me. It would do you no good, cousin. If
you incur his wrath, he'll never grant you additional income—"

He looked down at his hands and spoke softly. "You're reward
enough."

Brief, as was his style, the gentle words were a soft caress. And I knew
his plan was the only way. I knew I could trust him. "Are you sure?"

He looked at me, clasped my hand. "Quite, lovely cousin."

The intimacy conjured thoughts of my real love. The king had taken
the first drastic step to marry me himself. I had to prevent him from
ruining his country.

"If you do tell the king about Clarendon, surely Arlington will help
you regain the king's favor?" In an absent motion, his left hand went to
his left eyelid. "He will forgive you eventually. He loves you, after all."

251

I pressed both hands to my navel. *Sweet small one, you come first in this.* "Then . . . yes. And, perhaps—if I speak with the queen . . . If I gain her consent, and she grants my leave, we have not wholly disregarded the crown. She would entreat him to forgive me."

"You *must* go to her. I shall make arrangements in Kent and send word to you."

My chamber door swung open so hard it slammed into the wall. King Charles, in a cloud of fury, stood in the opening. His eyes fell on Richmond and filled with scorn. "Get out."

I sat up from the bolsters. Richmond took a deep breath, an attempt to gird himself for the worst. He slowly stood and bowed to the king. When he rose, he chanced a questioning look at me. I gave him a slight nod, as if I were sure I would be able to handle the king on my own. They circled like angry animals facing off with each other, until Richmond's back was at the door. He stopped for another glance at me, then backed out. If only I could have made the same escape.

"What the hell was he doing here? I told you I don't approve of him." King Charles slammed the door shut. "Why don't you tell me the truth?"

In one great stride he was by my bed. He lifted me by my shoulders and carried me to the toilette table. When my feet hit the floor, I started to push him away, but he yanked my chemise ties loose and spun me around to face the looking glass. In my reflection I saw my own swollen breasts and his eyes behind me. They held more than anger. *He knows.*

"I would have to hide away to birth it, then tell the world my baby was someone else's! Or accept the world's scorn if I own it myself and make the child live an illegitimate life!"

"Damn it, Frances!"

"I won't make a child live like my mother," I said flatly.

The anger left his face. "Her situation was different. Your child will have royal blood."

So he has always known. I shook my head. "I cannot express what it is to live with someone so conflicted, so guarded. If I have a bastard, it will likely expose her and my family. They cannot bear the shame." It was so personal and profoundly important I thought King Charles would understand.

He threw his hands in the air. "You win. I love you more than my own kingdom, and I'll not lose you. If you must have our child legitimately, then I will arrange it."

I stepped back. "W-what do you mean to do?"

He grasped my shoulders in a soft clutch this time. He brought his nose within an inch of mine and whispered, "I shall divorce Queen Catherine and marry you as soon as possible. The archbishop is already working on the details. Catherine will consent, and I can easily get it through the House of Lords."

No! No! No! "The queen would be devastated. The people like her. Your kingdom is weak and at war. Such a scandal might make them revolt. They beheaded your father." I shook off his grip and hit his shoulders with my fists. I could hardly feel them connecting, but the blows reverberated through my body. "This is the way to ruin! You will not make me another Anne Boleyn!"

He turned his face, refused to look at me. "Do not leave your chambers. I shall send you to Hampton Court with a small household while I finish this. Then I shall join you and we shall wed privately. I will come to you as often as I can, but you will stay there, secluded, until our child is born."

I grabbed him. "I'll not let you do such a dishonorable thing."

I could see my statement hit him. For an agonizing moment I held my breath.

Then he met my glare. "I'm the king, I'll have none other than you."

CHAPTER 55

By thee fell Wolsey and false Clarendon,
Abandon'd by their kings, but here undone:
Both overwhelm'd for daring to remove,
Or stem the torrent of their master's love.
The one fair Boleyn to his prince deny'd
The other made lov'd Stuart Richmond's bride
And with the Royal blood forever mingled Hyde.

— LORD SACKVILLE

After he left I vomited, the first time during my pregnancy. For days I debated how to stop him. There was only one way, but Richmond—my means of solving this problem—had disappeared after the king found us. I'd sat in my chambers thinking that if I could get to France, to the Queen Mother's chilly old convent in Colombes, I might find refuge. Surely the old nuns might let me keep my child? Then I received a blessed missive from Richmond and sent Prudence to tell the queen I was coming to her. When the doors to Queen Catherine's bedchamber opened, our eyes met. I let her embrace me. "My Queen. I have failed you in every way."

She pulled away to face me. "Not possible."

"I have given myself to your husband and am now with child."

Another woman might have sent me away in a jealous rage. But Queen Catherine, in her generosity, offered reassurance to her husband's mistress. "Did you think I would hate you? I cannot spite you only because I not have my own shild."

I knelt before her. "I have come for your advice, for if I do not remove myself from your husband, this will cause ruination for all of us."

She tried to pull me up, but I only let her have my hands.

"Your Majesty, I leave it to you whether you would have me go to a convent in France or marry my cousin, the Duke of Richmond and Lennox."

"No nunnery for you." She put her hands on my shoulders and studied my face. "Does Richmond know about the shild?"

"Yes. He will make it his heir and hopes for prospects through my favor with the king."

"No favor from Sharles. He will go mad!"

"So you see. You must guide me. Do you think the king would . . . ever forgive me?"

She thought quietly. "I—perhaps."

Minutes later I sent a secret missive to Richmond. And waited.

King Charles came to me each morning, each moment a masquerade. I was memorizing each look, the contours of his face, the feel of his mustache, the tone of his voice. The last night, long after I'd gone to bed, King Charles appeared, as if he'd sensed something amiss.

"Are you well?" he asked. He leaned into my bed and kissed me.

It was all I could do to keep the tears in. I embraced him, and he caressed my waist, kissed my belly, and whispered, "I'll be a loving husband to you, Frances." He wrapped his arms around my hips and pressed his cheek into my skin. "I would rip the British flag apart and use it to tie you here if I thought I could really keep your spirit with me."

Then, mercifully, he slipped away.

With him went my very heart. With him went all I loved and wanted in the world, the childish belief that I could make him honorable and that we could be happy together. It all went with him, and I knew I might never have those things back, never be whole again. I did not sleep. I did not cry. I was a motionless, boneless, empty thing except for the occasional flutter within that reminded me of my purpose, the only part of Charles I would have now. Some recess of my mind was working, and I knew the hour by the waning calls of the watermen on the river, the toll of occasional church bells echoing over London. Eventually I checked my watch, careful not to look at the enamel picture, and knew it was time.

I stepped out of bed and donned one of my best bodices, one that laced in front so I did not have to wake Mary or Prudence. I put on knee breeches and sturdy, old boots. In a sack, I stuffed silk mules wrapped in finer petticoats. Pulling the draw cord over my shoulder, I checked my watch again, then slipped it into my hanging pocket. I tied on my black velvet cloak, lined with fur, lifted the hood, placed the letter where I knew he'd find it, and left everything else behind.

> My own Dearest Heart,
> I beg you to forgive my marrying myself to another, though it
> be the only way I know to prevent you the dishonoring of your
> kingship, your queen, and your country only for the sake of
> yourself marrying me, one who I implore you to believe is ever
> your faithful love and who will return to your side with haste
> and everlasting affection,
> FS

Leaving the king's apartments by the back stairs, I crossed the Life Guards with my head down. Trained to be discreet, they saw no threat in the passing of a lady. There was a long courtyard off the king's quarters, a gate, then another courtyard. I passed quietly by the connecting houses on soft earth, but through another gate there was a cobbled outdoor passage. I crept so as not to wake the doctors, pages, and noble persons inhabiting the adjacent chambers. When I finally burst into the Pebble Court, the quiet, dark openness enveloped me. The massive Banqueting House glowed faintly white despite the cloudy night sky. I avoided the wooden walks and tiptoed on the pavers.

I chose to leave by Court Gate because it would get me out of Whitehall, with its thousands of eyes, quickest. But that route had the most Life Guards and Horse Guards, too. Their hushed laughter subsided as I approached. With my face guarded by my hood, they did not recognize me and did not call me back. And so I slipped through.

Along Whitehall Street I kept to the paved walk by the palace wall. With my face still down, I finally stole past the last set of guards at the gate to Scotland Yard. I held my breath, hurrying on, and hoped I'd given them no cause to follow me.

Their jovial banter faded as I walked toward the city. Across the street I heard the lewd words and laughter of drunken men and coarse female voices making their way to the entrance of St. James's Park. The elegant homes by the palace made this area safer than parts I had yet to pass, but a thundering rush pulsed in my ears and I hastened my pace. If I pressed on and paid them no heed, they might not bother me. I probably had as much to fear from the Life Guards at Whitehall if King Charles discovered my absence.

The open expanse of Charing Cross to my left caused my boot steps to echo in the darkness. I had reached the Strand. I looked up and left, in the direction of St. Martin's Church. If there was a parish watchman in the tower, I couldn't see him. No hackney coaches were out for hire at this hour. I longed for a sedan chair, a carriage, even a carthorse to carry me.

As the road curved, I looked straight ahead and felt a fresh rush of fear. It was so dark. The affluent homes in this area normally kept the proscribed candle lanterns out, but I was shocked at how few were lit.

As I passed under one of them, I brought my watch under my nose. We would just make it to Ludgate before it closed for the night. I had to find a link-boy to light my way.

Male voices floating over the darkness caught my ear, and I searched the shadows. I spotted their outlines several houses ahead, heads together, huddled under a lantern. One of them turned, suddenly brandishing a lit link. The other figure disappeared into the alley.

Every muscle in my body jolted. *Oh, Lord God, what am I doing here?*

The remaining figure called out, "Do ye want light?"

My breath halted. I took a step back. It was a deep male voice. This was not a link-boy but a man. And another man now lurked somewhere unseen. *I have to go back.*

I turned and walked quickly away, back to the palace, back to the coarse-speaking women outside St. James's Park, back to the palace guards.

"Do ye want light?" The voice was louder . . . or was it closer?

I ran. The blood rushing in my ears and my own panting made it difficult to hear, but I thought I heard footsteps behind me. Or was it hooves on the cobbles? I dared not look back, ran harder, faster.

All of a sudden four men on horseback galloped, not from White-hall but from around the corner of Charing Cross ahead on the right. There was nowhere to run. I turned around and the man was no lon-ger following me. So I ran again, this time away from the horses. Som-erset House was at the end of the Strand, if I could just get there . . .

"You there!"

I kept running. If they caught me and raped me, what would happen to my baby? I had to get away.

"Frances!"

The voice and horses were just behind me. Four more men on horseback appeared ahead, blocking Somerset House. *Why have I done this foolish thing?* I turned and shook a gate, but it was locked. I heard myself cry out.

"Frances!"

I raised my fists and turned around, ready to flail at whoever came near me.

He caught my wrists before they fell on him. My cousin Richmond. "Hurry, mount up!"

My breath left me all at once, and I felt myself fall.

He caught me firmly. "What's wrong with you?"

"There were men . . ." My voice sounded weak.

He shouted at the men on horseback. "Payne, your four will flank us. You two close behind. Lee, go ahead with the torch." He turned back to me. "Can you ride?"

I nodded.

He mounted quickly. One of his men appeared at my side, hoisting me up so I was pillion in front of Richmond.

"To get through unscathed, we have to ride hard. Can you stay on this way?"

The only thought I could muster was that straddling a horse might somehow hurt the baby. So I settled in, gripped the saddle as best I could with my backside, and nodded.

Richmond wrapped his arms around me to grasp the reins. He kicked his horse into a trot while his men fell into stride around us. When we were at a canter, I had to lean forward, grasping the horse's mane to keep my seat.

We passed the New Exchange and Somerset House in minutes. Once we were through the arches of Temple Bar and on to Fleet Street, demolished houses and shops rose into view and quickly diminished. Suddenly we were over Fleet Bridge, Fleet Hill, and at Ludgate. But it didn't look like Ludgate anymore. There was hardly enough light to inspect it as we slowed to navigate the cleared passage among the blackened rubble.

I hadn't come farther than Somerset House since the Great Fire and hadn't yet seen the entirety of its aftermath. Every shop and house that once stood was torn down or left a charred shell. I was bewildered by the sight, so unlike what it had been before.

Richmond kicked our pace up again on our way over Ludgate Hill. I almost didn't recognize the cavernous remains of St. Paul's Cathedral as we dashed around it.

There were no lights. By Lee's torch I saw quick glimpses of tumbled brick, burned wood, and ruins everywhere except the street. These were cleared wide and lined with fresh wood pilings staked into the ground: markings for a new road. When we arrived on Thames Street, I realized the air carried ash and singe instead of offal and filth.

We covered ground faster than would have been possible in the city before. With no jutting houses or hanging trade signs to duck, no carts or carriages to maneuver, no apparent sign of life anywhere, our going was clear.

Yet there was life lurking among the ruins. Some of the shadowed shapes resembled shanties. Once, I thought I saw an animal's eyes glitter with torchlight. They peered at us, gleaming from a blackened face. The figure stood, fled through the ruins. I saw it was actually a small boy and shuddered.

Our troop clattered to a halt at London Bridge. Lee doled out coins to a bleary-eyed warden, and we trotted past. Buildings that had once stood on this end of the bridge had burned and were replaced by little sheds.

Richmond's voice behind my ear carried on the open river air. "When you said to meet you at Somerset House, I assumed you'd be there all evening. You weren't waiting. I panicked and ordered a search."

"I stayed at the palace late so as not to raise suspicion."

"Did the men you saw hurt you?"

"No."

"Praise God." His voice caught.

Then we entered the half of the bridge where houses and shops still stood. Horse hooves echoed in the dim tunnel, and we rode single file to avoid the hanging trade signs on each side.

At the bridge foot, I spotted Richmond's carriage. We veered right and came to a halt outside a tavern. Its sign, swinging in the river wind, bore a painting of a chained and muzzled bear. We dismounted, and the men took the horses to the front of the carriage to harness. Richmond pulled me to the wall between the windows of the tavern, tugging my hood around my face as he did.

Just then the tavern door swung open, and a man staggered onto the street in our direction. Lee bumped into him, pretending he hadn't seen the man, then apologized and walked him some paces away, distracting him from us.

"We can't risk anyone recognizing you from court," whispered Richmond as he guided me to the carriage. "Get in."

He closed the door and blackness enveloped us. "We'll take the Dover Road to Kent. It doesn't appear that Life Guards followed you. We should be at Cobham Hall before morning. My chaplain is waiting there." He paused. "You're certain this is what you want?"

"Yes," I whispered, one hand on my belly.

CHAPTER 56

. . . I reflect on the old passion the king felt for her when she was at court as a girl, simply a maid of honor; his rages at her clandestine marriage; Castlemaine's jealousy; . . . and finally above everything else her angelic and wonderful beauty.

— LORENZO MAGALOTTI,
Italian philosopher, author, diplomat, and poet

In the gray of predawn, after a sleepless night, we broke our fast with Richmond's chaplain. The wedding he officiated afterward was brief and clumsy. I was too spent to care. When we left the chapel and entered the central wing of Cobham Hall, I faced Richmond's tired eyes and realized I was a duchess. We looked at each other for a moment in uneasy silence, unsure what to do. What do you say on your wedding day to a husband that is not really a husband?

Without absorbing my surroundings, I had hastily donned the clean skirts and shoes from my sack, and discarded the filthy ones I'd worn through the city. From the little I'd seen, Cobham was magnificent.

"We'll go back to your mother's Somerset lodgings and then send for your things."

I smoothed my skirts and tugged at my bodice. "That would be best. And we shall hear how news of our wedding is received at court." *And how King Charles receives it.* I raised a weary hand to rub my eyes.

Richmond grasped his hands behind his back. "But perhaps we should begin this union with some rest?"

I nodded gratefully, not speaking because I didn't trust my voice not to break, and let his servant show me to my chambers.

———

Cobham Hall was a stately pink-red brick estate sprouting clusters of chimneys all along its roofline. The wings were massive Elizabethan structures, with octagonal turrets rising from each end. The next morning, I saw why Richmond loved the place so dearly. It was easy to be with him as he showed me around. He asserted with pride that Queen Elizabeth had stayed here twice. Both wings were joined by a newly finished central limb. He had completed its construction based on designs by the great Inigo Jones, which prior Stuarts had been forced to abandon during the Civil Wars. Richmond pointed out each detail of the estate with sweeping gestures, but as I walked the length of the elegant great hall, listening to his plans to have it gilded, I could think of nothing but moving on to Somerset House.

When he called up his retinue, they ushered us into a carriage with six fresh horses. A dozen men-at-arms and half a dozen hounds led and flanked us on the Dover Road to London. I couldn't get there fast enough.

Oh, milady," Prudence cried at my feet at Somerset House. "It is so bad! So very bad!"

Mr. Lee, Richmond's footman who'd beaten that famous runner in a race, stood at the door of my mother's Somerset apartment where he had just led my maids through. He wore a look of restrained agitation while they, one weeping and one looking stern, poured out the news.

I hoped my own expression was calm as I struggled to remain composed. "Tell me what the king said when he came into my chambers."

Prudence pressed a handkerchief to her eyes and sobbed.

Standing behind Prudence's crumpled figure, Mary straightened her shoulders and spoke for her. "We had no notion you'd gone and thought we were letting you get some extra sleep, what with all the strain lately." Her eyes shifted to Richmond.

"Go on, Mary."

She looked back to me. "The king arrived first and we admitted him. He—well, he went plain mad! He tore up that letter you left and cursed so much I thought the walls would crumble. Swore he'd never admit you or my Lord Richmond to court again! Then started searching around your chamber. That's when Lord Cornbury arrived for his appointment."

I put a hand on my belly and told myself to stay calm. "While the king was still present?"

Mary nodded. "He walked into your bedchamber while the king was quiet like." She clasped her hands in front of her. "When the king saw him, he blamed the poor lord for inducing you to marry. He raged at him, not letting him speak at all. I've never seen a man so red and angry in all my days."

Richmond turned from the open window where he'd been standing quietly. He swirled wine in the goblet he held—his own goblet and his own wine that his men had carried with us from Cobham—and took a sip before speaking. "Frances has a missive for the queen," he said to Mary. "Can you get it to her?"

Mary nodded again.

"Frances." He looked at me. I went to the writing desk. He was right. The queen would be my first ally. Richmond continued. "Prudence."

She looked up at him then, as if realizing his status for the first time. Did she also realize this duke was bound by his duty as lord lieutenant to persecute Dissenters if he discovered them? I hoped I'd taught her enough discretion to remain undetected. Protecting Prudence might be the only promise to King Charles I'd end up keeping. She scrambled to her feet, wiped her nose, and curtsied for him.

"Prudence, even if we gain the forgiveness we seek with His Majesty, my wife can no longer live in her chambers at Whitehall."

Understanding dawned in her expression. "Ye want I should start packing her things?"

Richmond smiled. "My men will help you."

Mary returned later with a missive sealed by the queen. I took it into trembling hands and read it while Richmond stood before me, apprehension lining his face.

I scanned its words and felt the color drain from my face. The foolscap slipped from my fingers, floated to the floor. He had sworn to her that I'd broken his heart and betrayed every promise I ever made to him. She spoke of fierce anger. She advised me, for my own protection, to stay away.

CHAPTER 57

Cobham Hall

We expected this. The king's anger will cool." Richmond directed the move of my belongings from Whitehall to Cobham Hall and set me up in chambers beside his own. Prudence and Mary hopped to his every command.

He suggested I redesign the bedchamber interiors, and grateful for the occupation, I set myself to the work of selecting beds and buying chairs. The day Richmond presented a cradle to me as a surprise was the first day I didn't have to force a smile.

I wrote letters to my mother and Lord St. Albans in France, telling them of the wedding. I did *not* tell them the reason for it. I forced myself not to write to the king. I tucked the quills and foolscap away so I wouldn't.

The grounds of the estate were my escape. I walked them every day, noticing shoots budding from the earth and green dots emerging on branches. Outside, watching birds busily nesting, I held a hand over my swollen belly as I walked the gravel paths and let the season of rebirth remind me *I still have Charles with me*. The fluttering response made me smile, and a maternal happiness pulsed into my blood. *Sweet one*, I thought, and clung to my first accomplishment as a good mother. I'd ensured a legitimate birth.

"I wrote to my Lennox estate that you are with child," Richmond said at the massive dining table in May.

"Is it not too soon?"

"I dare not wait. I don't want to give them reason to question the child's early arrival."

"Oh, of course," I answered.

"By the time word of it filters down to London, it would be the proper time to make an announcement. None will be the wiser."

I accepted his judgment and whatever comfort he offered each day.

Some nights I cried. Richmond, in the adjoining chamber, dared not attempt to comfort me then.

One day, in late May, my back ached so much I stayed in bed. A few nights later I had more trouble sleeping than usual. While I listened to the light spring breeze blowing in my window, I came to realize why. Pain. A tight ache, it came slowly and faded. Only to return several minutes later . . . worse than before.

I put my hand between my legs and felt that I was dry. I put both hands on my belly and rolled on my side, breathing deep and willing myself to sleep. It didn't help.

Within the hour I could feel my belly balling up under my hands in intervals. *It is a passing sickness.* When one of the pains ceased, I slipped from the bedstead to the closestool, gathered my nightdress, and sat. When I finished urinating, I wiped with a linen cloth, then held it to the faint light of the moon. It was covered in a dark smear

I leaped into bed and lay back down, heart shuddering. *No!*

The pain returned, the worst yet. It caused me to bend at the middle and cry out softly. I clenched my teeth and turned my face into the bolster. *Please, no!*

The pain faded and I took deep breaths. I thought of Charles. If only I could send for him, he would know what to do. He would hold me and tell me the baby would be well. He would kiss me and caress me, and the pain of our separation would disappear. All of this would pass. We would be together again and happy. We would laugh at my big belly and damn what the world thought of us.

When my middle clamped again, I balled the covers into my fists and looked at the corner of the bolster in front of my eyes, focusing on a stray thread, focusing through the pain. *Let the pain pass. Breathe through it. It will stop again.* I could withstand it no more and cried aloud.

"Milady?" Mary's voice was pitched high.

"Go away," I said through tight lips. If she went away, if I could fall asleep, we would wake in the morning and all would be well.

She pulled the curtain open. "Do you need a phys—"

"Go!"

She let the curtain fall, and I heard her feet slapping the floor on her way to Richmond's chamber.

Again the pain subsided and my clenched muscles relaxed. I panted. Rolling over, I stared at the Tree of Life design embroidered into my bed drapery. Scrollwork and vines twined all around me in a symbol of living cheer. An edge of the fabric rustled and lifted in the soft spring breeze, carrying the scent of budding flowers.

Richmond's voice sounded outside my small prison. "My lady, are you unwell?"

A sudden sharp pain beset me. I grimaced with the effort to keep from calling out. Hot wetness spilled out of me, and I reached down, pulling my nightdress.

Red. Red everywhere. The coppery smell of fresh blood filled my bed space.

"Frances?"

A hateful cramp bit through me, but I reached down to the redness pooling between my legs. I touched it, unbelieving, and raised sticky red-black fingers up to my face. *No.* The baby could *not* come too early.

The curtains suddenly ripped apart and there stood Richmond, candlestick in hand, behind my bloody fingers. He shouted orders to the maids. Something about his doctor.

"No!" I heard myself say. It was an order, not a cry. "Go away, all of you, and leave me alone!" I rose to my knees, grabbed the curtains, and yanked them closed. Fresh blood gushed down my thighs.

I heard him order the physician anyway, and the maids ran off to fetch him.

An hour later, I was sweating and panting under my coverlet, curled in the middle of my dark red stain. I had allowed Richmond's physician to examine me. He had shaken his head, given grim news, and I'd commanded him to leave. He handed me a draught to take that would bring down my courses faster. I threw it on the floor.

I wanted everyone out. They had allowed me that. The physician had agreed, saying there was nothing they could do anyway. Richmond was in his chambers. My maids were in the closet. They would check on me, or I would call for them, but they would leave me alone.

Between pains I tried to stay calm, calling on all my powers of control. When they came, I bit the covers, grunted, or cried until they passed again.

When the dim light of dawn lit the Tree of Life draperies, my body betrayed my soul. It wanted to push. I braced my head on the headboard and resisted. Curling up around a bolster, on my side, I squeezed my legs together as tight as I could.

But there was a great, wet release. I moaned, threw the bolster and the coverlets aside. There, floating in blood, lay my tiny baby, still as death. I gingerly tore the sack away. She was no bigger than my hand and made no movement, no stir. Perfectly formed with her large head and thin limbs, she seemed a miniature baby. She looked perfect. Charles's baby.

I lifted her limp little body and slowly tucked my discarded dressing gown around her. She had no hair, but the brows that arched over her puffy eyes were golden red. There seemed nothing wrong with her besides her small size. Why had she come too soon? It must have been me, my fault, something I did. One, or all, of the many things I'd done wrong.

I wished, *so wished,* I could go back to Charles and tell him privately, so we could grieve together. But I had forever altered everything, *everything,* in order to protect this child. Without her I had lost Charles completely. She blurred as my eyes welled.

My tears splashed on her still, quiet face. I delicately reached out and wiped them away, wanting, more than anything, to care for her, do something for her. How could I fail her before she took her first breath? I held her to my body to see what it was like, not wanting to part with her, wanting to feel, know, and have her. I allowed myself to both meet and bid farewell to my daughter.

After a long while there were shuffling sounds in my chamber. "You've been quiet a long time now, Frances."

When I didn't answer, Richmond slowly pulled the curtains open. His swollen eyes were red and wet. A mirror of my own.

My throat, tight with sorrow and coarse from the strain, only allowed me to whisper. "Please fetch a priest."

Armed with money and a mind to bribe important churchmen, Richmond and his chaplain took the baby to London, determined to place her in his vault at Westminster. "It will be a comfort to you someday," he'd said. "No one need know but us."

I left that horrid bed and slept in other chambers. Or rather, I stared, tossing, awake and thinking. Time seemed to blur.

"Will ye wash?" Prudence asked.

I refused.

I walked the halls of the great mansion. My bare feet hit cold floors as I gazed, unseeing, at huge portraits of people who had once lived and were now only painted reflections of the past. They were gone, dead, no more.

Mary pressed me. "You must eat, dear."

I refused.

My mind was wild with broken thoughts, regret, images of her face, longing for Charles. They jumbled together, and I fought to sort them out. But nothing could be changed. All was lost and there was nothing to do. Nothing to do but lie down and not sleep.

At times I bent at the middle while blood and clots spilled between my legs. I drifted near the fringe of unconsciousness when these fits were past, but I jolted awake, clutching empty arms to my chest. Empty arms. A chasm within my arms echoed like my insides. My swollen breasts leaked. Wasted sustenance, too early and too late. I got out of bed because I couldn't bear to lie thinking anymore.

Mary blocked my way. "You must drink this broth."

I put the dish to my lips to appease her and choked some down.

"Now you will change your gown."

"No. I shall go back to bed."

But there was no rest, and I got up when the maids were asleep. Bare feet on cold floors for hours again, and I suddenly couldn't stand the house anymore. I had to get away. A side door—soft gravel crunched under me. Breeze, heavy with spring, filled my nose and lifted my ratted hair. Crusted old robe hung to my body—my body?—as feet fell on wet grass.

Lamplight at the mansion faded far behind. I entered utter blackness. On I walked into darkness. No sound but my feet in the grass. Taller grass, the wet drops sprang to my calves and hem. Not high enough to cleanse me, not cold enough to refresh me.

A sudden whoosh of wings and screeching of pheasants and I tripped. I fell to my knees, my hands hit earth. Another pain struck me, clamping and brutal. I called out and held my belly, my soft, hollow, agonizing belly. Wet globs of warmth oozed out of me and trickled down my leg, sticking to my gown and filling the air with copper-scented sorrow.

Finally, it passed, and I collapsed in the tall grass. Something clinked faintly, falling from my pocket. I felt around and closed my fingers on stones and chain; Mother's old rosary.

Richmond's hounds bayed in the distance, and I heard faraway voices calling my name. I breathed in the spring air and waited, too weak to move. The dogs would find me soon enough.

CHAPTER 58

June

After Mary fed me and Prudence washed me, Richmond walked me to my chamber. The servants had hastily prepared it with the new bedding I'd ordered from London. Everything was swathed in pale pink damask and gold braid. Fit for a duchess. I felt too unworthy to sleep in it, and Richmond heard my muffled sobs because he came to me, climbed in, and held me.

He had lost much by this, too. He let me cry. At times he swiped his own cheeks. "I know too well the sorrow of losing a child. Of losing love," he said. We did not talk about what we would do but hovered over unfamiliar ground. Eventually I busied myself with meaningless things. He did not seem to mind when I began to inquire about the posts from London.

"No word from court today, my dear," he'd say. After one sleepless night, I stared at my untouched plate and asked, "Could you rip the British flag?"

Richmond cleared his throat. "Pardon?"

"Could you tear the flag to make binding strips or would that require seamstress shears?"

He had no answer, of course.

———

Richmond clasped my hand with one of his. In the other he held a glass of wine, something my husband was almost never without. "My uncle Aubigny has died in France," he said. "I could use your help."

I nibbled fruit from the table in his chamber where we sometimes broke our fast. "Oh?"

"His title and the estate were rightfully mine when he claimed it as an inheritance before the Restoration. Out of my power to dispute it then. I was very young. Now it is mine to reclaim. I shall have to go to France to take possession."

"It will be difficult for an English duke to prove ownership of French land."

"Thankfully, my wife knows important Frenchmen." He gave me a half grin.

"The ambassadors?"

"An excellent start. You will write them?"

"Of course." *I lost the child you would call your heir. I burdened you with another loveless marriage.* "I shall do all I can."

He put aside his goblet to hold both my hands. "All will be well. When I get this estate, it will do much to alleviate my debts." He kissed my palms. "I value you above everything else." He looked down at my lap. "If we are never restored to favor, perhaps . . ." He glanced up with pleading eyes. "Perhaps we could make this a real marriage and try for a child of our own?"

This man showed me so much tenderness.

There was an urgent pounding as the door flew open. The steward rushed in without bowing. "Forgive me, Your Graces. The Dutch are sailing along the coast and up the Medway. We must arm against invasion!"

Richmond stood. His chair toppled to the floor. "How close are they?"

"Halfway. Some of the village men rode here to tell you. They and some of your vassals are coming to Cobham to protect it. Everyone is in an uproar."

"Tell them not to panic." Richmond moved to his cabinet. "The

Admiralty docked the English fleet in the Medway at Chatham this year. Not enough money to man the ships. That's what the Dutch are after. Not our villages." He shot me a quick glance, then called out orders. "Go to the armory and start issuing muskets. Order half the horses saddled. I'll take men to the high ground in the park to get a view of the river. Post guards around the house with the hounds and alert all the servants."

Payne ran out without another word.

"Damn," Richmond muttered. "What would possess King Charles to dock the entire navy in one place during a war?"

I sat, hands folded in my lap. The ships weren't *only* docked for lack of money. King Charles didn't expect more war. Because of me, he'd struck an alliance with King Louis through St. Albans. An alliance that had promised to end the fighting. Now, because of me, the entire fleet sat at risk. *No . . . the entire nation.*

Richmond emerged from his cabinet with scabbard strapped on, a spyglass in one hand, and a pistol in the other. He knelt before me. "Go to your chamber and stay. I can see the Medway from the park and will send word if you are to flee." He deftly slipped the pistol under my hands. "Take this." He caressed my shoulder. "I would die fighting to keep them from coming close to you, my love. You shall not need it." He leaned, pressed hot lips to mine, and headed out.

I looked at the pistol. Its gleaming metal seemed to sing, *What do you have now? No child. A disillusioned lover-king. Ruination wrought by your hands.* The weight on my lap was taunting, threatening. Almost promising.

I jumped up and ran to my chambers without it.

The cannon fire shook Cobham even from so far away, as our country's great pride, our Royal Navy, was destroyed.

CHAPTER 59

To languish in love, were to find by delay
A death that's more welcome the speediest way.
On seas and in battles, in bullets and fire,
The danger is less than in hopeless desire.

> —JOHN DRYDEN'S
> song to Frances Stuart, "Farewell, Fair Armida"

The ships at Chatham were burned, sunk, or taken by our enemy. The menacing Dutch sailed up and down the coast. Richmond was ordered to call his militias and arm the villages of Dorsetshire against invasion. He left armed men with me and encouraged me to run the house and manage his business while he was away. I did it with surprising efficiency.

Elbows propped on his wide, gilt writing table, I reviewed a post announcing that a peace settlement with the Dutch had been signed in Breda. I dropped it and rubbed my eyes. The war was officially over, and Richmond would be home as soon as word spread to the last ships. Today alone I had given orders to our workmen to build a courtyard, dismissed one painter and hired another, interviewed one of Richmond's privateer captains, and written three letters. I realized I had not thought of King Charles or the baby in several hours. I quickly snatched up a letter to keep distracting myself. Opening it for at least the tenth time since I'd found it among Richmond's papers, I reread the marriage congratulations from Lord St. Albans.

> . . . I beseech your grace to believe that, in order to the first, I
> take the part I ought, not only in reference to my respects to
> you, but by the obligations of the honor I have to be related to

the person you have chosen, and that I wish you both all sorts of felicity . . .

I'd rounded the subject in my mind. He wasn't related to the Stuarts or the house of Blantyre, or he'd have made it widely known for his advantage. His relationship to me must be through my mother! Was this the declaration my mother had dreaded? After I had done everything in my power to keep the question of her paternity quiet, had St. Albans actually revealed himself?

A light scratch sounded at the door. "Come."

Richmond's game warden returned, hat in hand, and bowed. "Yer Grace, we cannot get an outlier these last hours."

"Very well." Prince Rupert was posted at the nearby Isle of Sheppey, fortifying Sheerness. He'd requested a buck from Cobham to feed his men. "You may shoot one from the herd within the enclosure. Send it without delay."

"Yes, Yer Grace." He bowed and backed out, closing the door as he went.

I folded St. Albans's letter and put it away. I dipped a quill tip in ink, positioned it at the top of a fresh sheet of foolscap, and waited. As soon as the temptation to begin the letter with "My dearest King Charles" had passed, I started writing, continuing my role as a duchess.

CHAPTER 60

Somerset House, London
Late March 1668

"Mary, have the servants light each chandelier." I pointed to the ceiling of Somerset House's Great Hall. "I want this reception to be perfect. Tonight may be the night the king comes."

I glanced at her somber expression before she slipped out, and I knew she didn't believe King Charles would come. Why should he?

"You look tired, Frances."

I turned to Richmond, who walked in, tugging at his lace cravat. "My head aches, is all." I crossed to him, took the lace into my fingers.

He never ceased to express kindness to me. No matter how much I pined for King Charles, he held my hand, patiently waiting. As he watched me, he wore a mixed expression of sympathy and hopefulness.

"There." I finished the knot. "The handsomest duke in the realm."

His face didn't change. "He will come."

"Such is the rumor these three months, yet still he doesn't."

He put his hands on my shoulders, and the scent of wine enveloped me. "Then we will go to France as planned. We shall see your mother. You can help her arrange a marriage for your sister. I will find a post in the navy for your brother." He put a finger under my chin and lifted until I met his gaze. "And do not forget . . ." His words faded as he lowered his lips to mine.

It was not our first kiss. There'd been many tearful nights and even quiet days when Richmond had leaned in to comfort me with his soft lips. He greeted me with kisses and parted with them. Sometimes he caressed my arms or my back, a firm, respectful assertion of partnership. I returned the affection. I was neither stiff nor did I fall into him. Richmond's kisses were a comfort, a reminder of the hope he harbored. Even as my heart ached for my lost love, I accepted Richmond's kiss and clung to his companionship.

Instead of King Charles, Arlington attended our reception. "All the rest of London comes to pay court to you for your beauty's sake. I would be remiss to neglect the Duchess of Richmond and Lennox." He bowed low before my chair.

I waved a hand. "What news from court?"

He shot a glance around to be sure no one could hear. "You'll have heard the Duke of Buckingham is back in favor. My—er—evidence against him did not stand. He regained his offices. He is a nuisance, doing nothing but confusing affairs. It is some consolation that King Charles sees his duplicity and doesn't include him in the ministry councils."

"When I heard the king accepted Buckingham back at court, I was all the more glad I had married. We could not have allowed him to encourage King Charles to divorce his queen."

Arlington went on. "You'll have heard, too, about Clarendon, gone into exile in France. I owe you thanks."

"I did but little in that, sir. I am only glad the king did not punish Lord Cornbury for his part in it. I do not think a son is responsible for the sins of his father."

He nodded with narrowed eyes. "I wondered about that, if you'd arranged Lord Cornbury's appointment to coincide with the king's discovery of your absence. Very cunning."

"I did not do that for your sake but for the king's. He tired long ago of Chancellor Clarendon but could not bring himself to unlock his shackles. I merely provided the key."

"Whatever your reasons, it is a more organized cabinet without him. I'm able to do far more than before. You'll have heard that King Louis invaded the Spanish Netherlands?"

I nodded. "You are to be congratulated on the Triple Alliance. That was a surprise."

"I must say, I'm rather proud of the work between us, Sweden, and the Netherlands to force France into peace with Spain. There is even a peace between Spain and Portugal now. Louis will have to compromise on the Spanish Netherlands and will be kept in check . . ."

He droned proudly on. Nothing would keep King Louis in check. Charles would not stand forever as a blockade against his cousin Louis. I knew these men well enough to know that Arlington, though working admirably, was working himself into his tomb.

I held up my palm. "I am afraid I have no more stomach for politics."

"Forgive me, Your Grace." He glanced around again for listeners. "I thought your return to favor with the king would place you—"

I sat upright. "What did he say to you?"

Arlington looked confused. "H-he said nothing to me regarding Your Grace. But I believe his anger has long since cooled, and he has softened to the idea of readmitting you to court."

I sat back, repositioning myself in the chair.

"Actually, I thought your presence in London indicated your intention to become his mistress once and for all."

I stared at the statesman with growing contempt. He was correct, of course. That was exactly why I had come back. It was why Richmond let me come back. It was love for me, and gains for Richmond. But it was the first time I had heard it stated thus. It made me sound like a whore.

"Lord Arlington, my reasons for being so near Whitehall are personal. As you know, I injured the king. I wish to beg His Majesty's forgiveness and make amends. I had hoped you came to facilitate that."

"Alas," he said. "Only rumors of your reconciliation brought me."

"Tell the full truth. You wish to invest me in your political interests in hopes that I will further them with the king."

He smiled slyly. "I confess." He bowed. "Your Grace is a seasoned courtier to see so clearly."

"Not so seasoned that I will agree. You shall have to seek Lady Castlemaine's aid and be satisfied."

"I beg your pardon," he said, and bowed again. "I only sought Your Grace's alliance because your temper is so much more amiable than the king's other mistresses."

My chest tightened. "Mistress*es*?"

He arched his brow. "Yes. Um . . . the king has dallied with a few since your departure. None of your character, rank, or beauty, of course."

A *few*? No. If the queen had not satisfied him, he would have sought company with Castlemaine. Wouldn't he? My head, which had ached all day, started a slow, frightening pound.

"Your Grace?" He extended a blue velvet box. "I've brought a present for you."

Inside, a gold medal, impressed with my portrait as Britannia, sang out to me of yesterday, a song of hollow victory. Its perimeter bore the legend "*Favente Deo.*" God's favor.

"It is the medal commemorating the Peace of Breda. I think, Your Grace, I could persuade King Charles to finally relent. If you wish, I will intercede with him on your behalf."

King Charles had once called this portrait my legacy, and he has used it now to signify peace. I snapped the box shut and eyed Arlington. "No. If King Charles forgives me, it will be of his own persuasion. I'll not allow you to interfere."

His expression fell.

"I meant what I said earlier. I've no wish to involve myself in politics again. I'll not take part in any matter beyond my husband's affairs." I felt the faint crush of velvet under the grip of my fingers. "I wish only to have my king's forgiveness and to live quietly."

That night I developed a fever. Arlington's words tormented my dreams. Dreams of Charles, and dead babies, and laughing, careless women.

The fever clung. The fitful dreams grew worse. Images of my childhood and Madame flashed in and out of my mind. I was so hot with fever I dreamed I was running through London while it burned in the

Great Fire. I dashed through flaming ruins looking for that gleaming-eyed little boy smeared in black soot. I wanted to help him, but he ran away from me, hiding. He didn't want me. My skin smoldered. Slipping in and out of consciousness, I heard the physician declare I had smallpox. There was commotion in the chamber. I shuddered with worry for Richmond and my maids who had all been exposed to me.

The dreams took over. Now London was a raging inferno atop the ships of the English navy. I, holding my child and cloaked in my Britannia robes, stood on the rocks of Britain, reaching my spear out to my ships, trying to hook them so I could pull them back. But King Louis, Mother, and the Queen Mother yanked at them from across the Channel, and I slipped, losing my balance, almost toppling into the sea.

In a snatch of lucid thought, I told myself not to die without first seeing Charles, to tell him I was sorry. Remembering his anger was sickness again, and I hoped for an end to my torment. Back in the dream, the ships and burning London were out of reach. I planted the end of my spear through the water to the ocean floor, braced my feet firmly on the rocks, and knew I would not fall. The baby was no longer in my arms, but I was firmly planted and would not sink.

Then the pain began.

When I shook the delirium from my mind, it was only to grasp my disaster. My palms and soles were agonized by blisters. My face felt excruciating. I focused on the maid sent in to care for me and noticed her skin was deeply pockmarked.

"I've had the pox and lived, as will you, Your Grace."

"I don't want to live," I said in a gravelly voice. I closed my eyes and wished I could have fallen into the ocean of my dream.

"But you have so much to live for, Your Grace! Just now there's a message from the king himself."

Tears sprang to my eyes and burned so badly I almost forgot my skin.

"He says to tell you all is forgiven." She paused. "Did you hear me, Your Grace? He says all is forgiven."

Much good may it do me now.

CHAPTER 61

At my goldsmith's did observe the king's new medal, where, in little, there is Frances Stuart's face as well done as ever I saw anything in my whole life, I think: and a pretty thing it is, that he should choose her face to represent Britannia by.

—SAMUEL PEPYS'S DIARY

When the hellish blisters turned to scabs, my own maids returned. They kept their thoughts and feelings carefully concealed when they looked at my face. I was too weak and somber to talk.

Richmond smelled strongly of whisky when he came to my bedside. His eyes were swollen and red, with dark shadows beneath. "So relieved that you will live," he said, squeezing his own hands together because I would not let him touch mine. "Could not have gone on without having you as my wife."

It was the only time I'd ever thought Richmond a fool. It would have been much better for him if I'd died. Over his shoulder I could see large cloths draped over all the looking glasses.

One day I opened my good eye, for one was swollen with infection, and saw a figure in the chair beside my bed. I assumed it was Richmond, but when I stirred, the figure sat up.

It was King Charles. "Are you awake?"

I gasped and futilely turned my face away, both astonished to see him and ashamed to let him see me.

"It's not bad," he said, taking my hand. "You don't have very many marks."

I yanked away, thinking only of the danger to him. "You mustn't touch me. You shouldn't even be here."

He held up his hands. "I've had so much exposure to smallpox, I don't believe I can catch it." He grinned, that mischievous grin I'd ached for. "Or do you not want me because you are still so angry with me?"

"Me angry?" I dropped the little shield I'd made with my hand. "You haven't wanted to see me in a year. You were the angry one."

"When I feared for your life, none of it seemed important anymore."

Unsure what to say, I lay silent. In the moment I'd longed for these twelve months, I only wanted to hide my disfigured face from him. But I didn't turn away again, and he did not avert his eyes. He showed no trace of distaste.

"You will not be marked much. But you are ill, and I will not stay if it distresses you."

The next time he came, I was ready. I felt almost healthy when the herald announced his approach. Hair washed and arranged, scabs all fallen off, supper eaten, and linens fresh, I sat up in my bed, with Richmond waiting at the center of the chamber.

I'd insisted Richmond stay. He was so much a part of me now, my closest and only friend for so long, that I had to ensure he was included in my return to favor. He'd planned and revised an apology, then discarded it, admitting to me that he really wasn't sorry he'd married me. Now an air of dignified humility rose about him where he stood.

King Charles entered. His gaze fell on Richmond first, and his expression went sour.

Richmond presented his leg and bowed low over it.

King Charles's entire body stiffened, as if the sight of Richmond were rousing his old anger.

I held my breath. Richmond stood firm. He glanced at me. In his eyes was a message of tenderness, affection, and that old hope that love would grow between us. It was also a farewell. He would leave me alone with King Charles because it was my wish.

The king saw it, too. Richmond turned to the king and bowed again, and this time stayed low as he spoke. "I beg your pardon, Your Majesty. I acted on the inclination of my heart without heeding your commands or considering any injury my actions would inflict on you. I submit myself to your mercy."

King Charles frowned, but I could see his shoulders relax a little. By the time Richmond had risen from his bow, I knew the king would forgive him. He didn't nod or gesture. He didn't need to. He only muttered, "Richmond."

Richmond nodded. Then, with regret, he stepped around the king and backed from the chamber.

When the door closed, King Charles looked at me. "He's in love with you."

"We've been each other's only company for a year."

"And do you love him?"

"After all he has endured for my sake, I would be heartless to say no," I said. "But what I feel for him is nothing like my love for you."

There was long silence. Each of us looked away. I cleared my throat and gestured to the chair by my bed. "Let us spend some time talking of happier things. How is my queen?"

He took off his hat and stepped toward the seat. "Catherine had been very well, dear woman." He paused as he sat down. "It would be best to talk of other things. She was with child again, you see." He looked at the floor. "She is well now, but, alas, she has lost the child."

"I am very sorry," I whispered.

He cleared his throat and looked up. "Frances . . ."

It was only my name, but it was also a question. Vision in my healthy eye blurred. The other was still swollen, and tears welled out of it furiously. I dabbed it and tried to answer him the way I'd longed to tell him. "She . . . came too early. Before the Dutch sailed into Chatham."

There was so much more: the blood, the confusion, the delivery, the agony, the intense need for him to wrap his arms around me and love my pain away. King Charles's fingers slowly twined with mine, and I grasped his hand desperately. His eyes filled with anguish. "I'm so sorry. So sorry."

I clung to him for a long time, taking compassion from the small embrace. "You would have loved her, Charles. I know you would have. She was so small, so perfect. Her hair would have been red. I longed for you so."

"A dog deserves more loyalty than I showed you." He wiped his eyes.

I squeezed his hand and struggled to find my voice. "You have every right to your pain. I acted deliberately. I had quite feared your heart would be irreversibly damaged."

He did not answer that. When I looked at his face, I saw a surprising, sour grin.

Each visit, and they were frequent, we grew easier around each other. We laughed and joked as we used to do. He told me about Madame; she had actually written to encourage him to forgive me. He was glad about the Triple Alliance but said, "I am anxious to show my friendship to Louis again, and I hope my sister can help." I couldn't help but wonder what Arlington's reaction would be when he heard it. I told him of my plans to reorganize Richmond's finances, and he resolved to do the same with his treasury. His favorite spaniel was about to litter. He had hoped in January to attempt another Declaration of Indulgence but said, "The religious fanatics and brawlers will force me to limit their liberties. I'll have to enforce the Act of Uniformity to get control of the mob." He mentioned he'd been enjoying the theater immensely.

We cautiously avoided the discussion of our relationship. Though my heart was lighter, I often wondered about that sour grin. It had been his only response when I'd tried to ascertain how badly I'd hurt him.

CHAPTER 62

May

A spring rain left the London air unusually clear, so I opened the doors to the terrace overlooking the empty Somerset gardens, which rolled down to the edge of the river. I breathed it in and absorbed the calls of the watermen. Their crafts glided on the Thames, ferrying people to the park, home from the theaters, or to church.

I was too well to stay in bed. But I had removed the cloths from the looking glasses in my chamber and seen I was not healed enough to go out. It was not as bad as I'd feared it would be. My face had marks, pink and peeling pits, but not as many as most smallpox survivors.

At any rate, King Charles and Richmond both insisted my beauty was unmarred. I would always wear cosmetics in public now, but I was alive. Alive and in favor with my king once more.

A hat bobbed up behind the gate in the garden wall that ran along the river. I squinted, my vision still a little blurry from the sore in my eye. The hat bobbed up again, and an arm and foot landed atop the wall. A man scaled it swiftly, planting his boots in the garden.

Only one man wore a curly black periwig and stood that tall. King Charles had just scaled my locked garden gate. With no attendants in tow.

I laughed. He heard it on the breeze, caught my eye, and trotted toward me, smiling. When he finally reached me, he grasped my shoulders and kissed me fiercely.

It was the last thing I expected. In my astonishment, I froze. Perhaps it was more than surprise, for a tiny thought snagged in my mind. *Richmond would be devastated.*

I broke the kiss and clung to his neck. "Come to my chambers," I whispered. I glanced around to make sure no one was in the hall.

His mouth found mine again and crushed me with kisses. Hot and wet but not quite as I remembered . . . almost searching . . . questioning.

A tiny warmth lit, deep inside me, and I let my passion fall back on his lips. The empty ache I'd harbored all year reached to him, instinctively remembered his touch, and fell into the familiar curve of his arm. It only lasted a fleeting moment. *Someone might see.*

I pulled away again. "Please, come in with me."

But the gleam in his eye dimmed. "Are you ashamed of me?"

"I just want to enjoy you privately."

"There was a time when you let me kiss you publicly."

"I—I would not want to embarrass Richmond."

He frowned.

I pulled his hand. "Come with me."

He followed the few steps through the hall and into my antechamber. As we entered my bedchamber, I suddenly felt awkward, hesitant. We were so easy together a year ago, surely we could be so again. I turned to him and put my hands on the sides of his face.

His golden eyes held hurt.

Why? Because I could no longer be carefree with him? I pulled his head down, rose onto my toes and kissed each of his lids one at a time, then looked into his eyes again.

They only reflected sorrow.

I noticed the tension in my body. I was trying too hard to be natural. He could sense it. He clenched his jaw, then seemed to make some decision. He threw off his hat and kissed me again. He pressed his hardness against me, and I thought, *Surely we can get back to what we were before.* I kissed him back and tried to forget myself. I pretended I was just Frances Stuart kissing the king again, not the Duchess of

Richmond and Lennox. But I could not find my King Charles. The change in his kiss . . . it lacked the tenderness, the openness.

He pulled my mantua down, coaxed my body. He caressed my breasts, licked my ear. But it was just a physical request without connection. Not a sharing. Finally, he broke our kiss and stepped back. In his eyes, I could see he was aware of it.

"Oh, Charles," I whispered. "If you had divorced her, you would have hated yourself."

"You took my heart with you when you left. So if I am heartless now, it is my own fault. I should have ordered you back from Kent with it the next morning."

But I knew that wasn't all. He had been overjoyed to see me in the garden and I him. Before I'd unleashed my passion, my first thought had been Richmond's feelings. King Charles had been right in his fears all along. My husband had indeed come between us.

King Charles visited Somerset House regularly that spring while the court was in London. He attempted passionate interludes with me a few more times. His lips were gentle, his caresses soft. But he could not seem to carry them very far. Open as I was to his advances, he would stop. He'd look away to hide the hurt in his eyes, then chat with me for an hour or so about inconsequential things, struggling to overcome the damage.

When Cornbury presented himself at Somerset House, I insisted he tell me what he knew about the *other mistresses*. My old friend shuffled his feet and turned pink.

"You must, Lord Cornbury. The queen doesn't want to discuss it, and no one else will tell me for fear of insulting me."

"It is true that after you left, the king . . . sought solace in the arms of other women. He seemed to be searching for relief, distraction. I think you had better leave it at that, Your Grace."

"How many?"

"Ahh—yes." He looked like a rabbit caught in a snare. "Please forgive me for telling you, Your Grace. That I know of—there were at least five other mistresses."

"Five!" I gasped. "So many in such a short span. He could not have shown constancy to any one of them."

"Ahh—yes—that is—no. He is not constant in his attentions."

"*Is* not? Are you saying he continues these relationships?"

"Well—oh, very well. I shall tell you in full if you insist." He slumped. "When you left, he returned to Lady Castlemaine for a time. But the Duke of Buckingham persisted in presenting him new women. He started with a clergyman's daughter. Then there were the actresses. One was a virgin when he bedded her. Nell Gwynn he continues to summon to his lodgings at Whitehall. And Moll Davies he has set up in her own house."

"Actresses. He has taken up with *actresses*?" The information stunned me. "Actresses are prostitutes! They aren't fit for a king's mistress."

"There now, you wanted to know."

"They are commoners. They have no noble blood at all!"

"Some claim to be the illegitimate offspring of one lord or another."

"Bastards aren't worth a king!" I clamped my mouth shut, remembering myself. "You said there were *five*."

"Ah—well. Lady Castlemaine's maid is carrying the king's child."

"Her *maid*?"

Cornbury held up his hands. "She *is* a very pretty woman."

I glared as if he had trespassed on my haven. But of course, none of this was his fault. If blame lay with anyone, it was I. The king was seeking solace without regard for honor. *What have I done to him?*

In June, when Richmond and I hosted a lavish banquet for the king and queen, they announced my new appointment as lady of the bedchamber. With pomp and ceremony, King Charles held my hands before the guests and called me one of his most important friends. But the golden hue in his eye lacked its old warmth. He kissed each of my cheeks, then returned to stand by Queen Catherine, the woman who loved him unconditionally. He seemed not to stand as tall as he once did. Understanding finally resonated within me. I had tried to save him from ruining his honor. Instead, my actions had left him so despondent that I had ruined *him*.

CHAPTER 63

Whitehall Palace

The Duchess of Richmond is likely to go to court again, and there put my Lady Castlemaine's nose out of joynt. God knows that would make a great turn.

—SAMUEL PEPYS'S DIARY

Come summer, Richmond finalized improvements to his house at Whitehall. Richmond House was an independent building overlooking the Thames on one side and the Bowling Green on the other. The prettiest and most private lodgings at the palace, it was fit for the highest-ranking duke in England. And his duchess.

We settled in. And in August, when summer was hottest, I was finally healed enough, with careful application of cosmetics, to be seen at court. On my first day of return to the queen's service, I walked out of Richmond House into the bright expanse of the Bowling Green and turned right—and there was the Countess of Castlemaine.

She turned to go the other way. Her abrupt change in direction threw her attendants into confusion, and they tried to scurry into place behind her again. She was going to avoid me! Like hell. My new rank gave me precedence over any countess. I didn't even have to call her Lady anymore. Once I acknowledged her, she was obligated to show deference to me. With a wicked flash of pride, I called out, "Castlemaine."

She halted, almost toppling in her reluctance to stop. Slowly she turned around, nose high in the air. Servants scurried out of her way again. Her fists clenched as she gave a quick curtsy. "Your Grace."

I approached her, waving her attendants off. When I was several feet away, I extended a kindness that I was not obligated to give. I curtsied.

She eyed me, as if weighing her conceit against affection. "It is good to see you again, Fr—Your Grace."

I smiled. "You look well. I heard you moved to Berkshire House with your children."

"King Charles is very generous." She cast her eyes down as she said it, as if she were not completely satisfied with the new situation. "He is kind to us, visiting the children often. I do not wait on the queen much anymore." Her shoulders slouched as she studied me. "So you shall have no trouble from me as you take my place once and for all."

I'd heard she was very troubled by my return to London, delighted when I fell ill with smallpox, and melancholy again when the king forgave me. I didn't discredit the gossip entirely, but I knew she cared for me in her lofty way. Thus, at my first opportunity to gloat over my old rival, I found I could not do it.

I sighed. "I don't think I'll actually be able to take your place after all. He is distant. As if he only extends kindness without fully feeling it."

"I had never seen him cry. Never seen him so upset over anything as he was when you left. I thought he would never heal."

I glanced at her attendants and whispered. "How could you let him resort to taking in actresses? Why didn't you comfort him?"

"I did all I could. But it was never enough. It was as if he were just . . . broken." She shook her head as if the memory still bothered her. "I hated the idea of your return, but, honestly, I thought you were the piece of him that was missing."

My spirit recoiled at her words because, for all her selfishness, she did know the king well. "It seems there is a part of him that I can no longer reach."

"You are the only woman he has ever loved," she whispered with only a trace of bitterness. "If you can't restore him, then what you did to him is irreversible."

CHAPTER 64

September 1669

After a year and a half of marriage, I became Richmond's true wife. He was a gentle lover, considerate and passionate. We made progress curbing his spending and his drinking. The king tolerated his presence at court, though he never showed him much favor.

Thankfully, my friends in France persuaded King Louis to concede Aubigny to Richmond. Which shocked me, but made me smile to think King Louis cooperated partly out of respect for me. Perhaps he considered my old oath to him fulfilled after all?

Richmond had to go to France for several months himself to take possession. "My precious bride, won't you come with me?"

"I don't think I want to face that court. What is past is past. I shall stay and oversee your affairs."

Richmond met my family at Colombes and sent reports. Young Walter, after all my worry for him, hadn't been pressed into King Louis' army. He'd joined Lord Douglas's regiment, a group of Scottish soldiers stationed in France, and thus managed to avoid fighting against the English. Richmond now obtained a post for him aboard the *Montague* in the English navy. He sent my sister to me by my mother's request. I fulfilled one of my greatest hopes and arranged a marriage for her to the Royalist Henry Bulkely, fourth son of a viscount, master of the king's household. Sophia had grown taller than me, with darker hair and our mother's poise. She told me she was relieved to wed and folded into Bulkely's quarters at Whitehall comfortably. The Queen Mother died while Richmond was there. Thus, my mother returned to England in Richmond's retinue, and I arranged for her to live quietly at Cobham Hall.

I watched her tall, graceful figure step off the ship at Greenwich, and I extended confident arms to greet her. "It is so good to see you!"

"My daughter-duchess," she said.

At Cobham, I sat her down at Richmond's writing table and pulled out St. Albans's letter. She cradled it and read it wide-eyed. When she finally let it fall to her lap, she seemed hesitant to look at me. I waited for her to relinquish her story.

"It is said that before the civil wars, the Earl of St. Albans was the most handsome courtier at Whitehall, the queen's favorite. He wasn't titled then, he was only Henry Jermyn, but many ladies fell in his bed anyway. One of them was a maid of honor to Queen Henrietta Maria, Eleanor Villiers, and she became pregnant. He proclaimed her a slut and refused to marry her, for he was infatuated with the queen. Charles the First sent him to the Tower for it. Eleanor's family sheltered her during her accouchement, and Henry Jermyn's father, Sir Thomas Jermyn, governor of Jersey, sent for the child."

I studied my hands for a long time. "The child was you."

"My earliest memories are of playing under Elizabeth Castle on the Isle of Jersey, and of a man who came to visit me at times. He would inquire about my health and my lessons. I was young when the civil wars began. The Prince of Wales's troops sheltered on our island for a time. Eventually the queen, who had escaped by fleeing to France, sent her vice-chamberlain to collect the prince. The chamberlain was Henry Jermyn, the man who'd visited me before. And this time he took me to France with him."

She sighed. "I was a child when he put me in a convent in Paris. I was a young woman when he was elevated to earl, and he brought me to the Queen Mother's house in Colombes. To present me to your father." She buried her face in her hands. "Walter was studying medicine in Paris, a Stuart, a loyal Royalist. We spoke of marriage, and I could not believe my happiness. I fell into him with every intention of becoming an honorable wife so that I might keep my good fortune, make a real family, a place I would finally belong. I became pregnant." Her hands fell and she stared, seeing a past invisible to me.

"St. Albans was disgusted. He said he should have known I was too beautiful to be anything but foolish. He ordered your father to take me to Blantyre in Scotland to wed me, and not to return until the baby—you—were old enough that scandalous talk could be avoided. I will never forget the look in his eyes when he thought my indiscretion would bring him shame. He couldn't risk losing the Queen Mother's regard; they were lovers by then. I swore I would never do another bad thing." She glanced at the letter. "I was merely too young. He never acknowledged he was my father. I learned his story in snatches of gossip through the years. This letter is the only indication he has ever given that we are related."

I waited a moment. "The Duke of Buckingham knew."

She blinked, as if awakening. "As a Villiers, he would have known Eleanor's story and might have deduced the rest. I always wondered what became of her but couldn't risk getting close enough to that family to find out."

"Did Lady Castlemaine know? The other Villiers? Did they all know what I didn't?"

Her gaze, soft and hurt, fell back to the letter, and I could see she didn't know. Nor did it matter. She reached her hand to me, and I saw frail skin over something that had once been so strong. I kissed her hand and left her at quiet Cobham when I returned with Richmond to our house at Whitehall Palace.

CHAPTER 65

Richmond House

August 1670

The Duke of Richmond and Lennox, my husband and friend, walked confidently into our great room and sat at our tea table. The wall of high windows behind him brightened our space, and I pointed to the watercraft bobbing outside along the river Thames. A skiff full of men craned their necks toward Richmond House trying to capture a glimpse of the royally cuckolded duke and the woman they assumed was the king's mistress. "People are peeking in again."

He grinned. "When they get to their coffeehouses, they will have something else to prattle about. Everyone's complaining about King Charles and his actresses, and how he runs his council members against his parliament."

Prudence poured steaming water into our dishes with a shaky hand.

I studied my husband. "And you still want to snatch an appointment to such a council?"

"Of course." He winked. "I'm a Stuart, after all."

I laughed with him, our ease echoing off the chandeliers and marble floors and settling into the scattered groups of velvet-covered furniture. "Did you order the new coach?"

He nodded. "And six new horses. We shall travel to Dover in style."

A flush of nervous excitement washed through me. Madame was coming to visit her brothers, King Charles and the Duke of York, at

Dover. Everyone important would go: the royals, the ministers, titled lords, the court. All in a festive array of new clothes and general merriment to greet Madame. She wasn't coming to see me, but see me she would. How would it be after so many years? When she saw my face again, would it remind her?

When Richmond retired to his rooms, I started for my bedchamber, but Prudence wrung her hands, eyeing me.

"Is something wrong?"

She nodded furiously. "One of me old friends was arrested fer preaching in public." Her face broke into worried lines. "May I have permission ta go ta Newgate Prison and buy his release?"

I glanced to make sure Richmond wasn't near enough to hear. "Who?"

She hesitated. "Admiral Penn's son, milady. Tha judge locked tha whole jury up with him because they refused ta find him guilty. He was jest trying to prove England's common law heritage, show that people have rights." Her lips trembled.

My eyes widened. "No wonder he is in prison. He is sharp enough to start a revolution."

Her brows pinched together. "Please. Won't ye let me do as I wish?"

I took a breath, waited for the sadness to pass. "I once promised King Charles that I would look after you, protect you. This is a *Royalist* household. I won't let you disgrace our name to chase foolish ideals."

"Royalist?" She straightened her shoulders. "*I* have no use fer kings. Milady, I warn ye, if ye don't let me help him, I won't be in yer service by tha time ye set off for Dover."

I stared at her, trying to decide whether I envied her strength or feared it. "It would be a waste of every farthing you've ever earned." I cut the air with my hand. "You cannot do it."

Within a fortnight, Prudence disappeared.

CHAPTER 66

Dover Castle

September

D on't worry," said Richmond, stroking my hand. "You look magnificent."

So did he. He had, once again, extended his credit to deck both of us in the richest clothing attainable. I gazed from the windows of Dover Castle, down soaring white cliffs guarding the Channel. But I wasn't just worried about receiving Madame. My treatment of Prudence had shaken a regret deep within me. She'd only asked for things I'd sought myself. I longed to know she was well, to apologize, to give her my blessing. *I will never make such a mistake again.*

When Madame's ship was finally spotted, King Charles took the dukes of York and Monmouth and Prince Rupert out in the flagship to fetch her. They disembarked at the port with Madame and a few of her ladies before her ship and household of two hundred attendants had even docked.

At the castle entrance I stood behind the queen in perfect position as King Charles walked up with Madame on his arm. When he brought her into close range, my breath caught. She was so changed. She wore the most luxurious silk ensemble I'd seen in years and a tasteful array of diamonds and pearls. An ermine-lined cloak draped her shoulders, and silver-slippered toes poked from her trailing skirts with each step. She was perfectly poised as she greeted Queen Catherine and kissed each of her cheeks. But her face, sallow and drawn, was missing the crucial Stuart liveliness.

When Queen Catherine stepped aside and turned to walk her into the great hall, Madame's gaze fell on me. My heart nearly stopped. I curtsied low.

She leaned forward, took my arms, and urged me up. Her eyes, deeply shadowed and crinkly along the edges now, filled with kindness.

I wrapped my arms around her and hugged her frail body as if we were children again.

She laughed, dismissing my breach of etiquette. She embraced me, and when we looked into each other's eyes again, we both wore smiles of understanding. I had always loved her, and perhaps she couldn't help but love me, too.

King Charles had Dover Castle adorned with splendors to regale Madame, and each hour was packed with constant entertainment. The Duke of York brought actors in from London to play for her. Balls went into late hours of the night, though she never danced. Through the banquets, games, and receptions, she always sat. And at suppers, Madame never ate. She sipped milk, not wine, and used her fork to toy with food on her plate. Her fatigue, though concealed behind her perfect smile, was evident to me.

She asked Queen Catherine if I could wait on her a few nights. Thus, we sat on her bed sharing stories about Colombes, remembering the years that connected us. I looked at miniature portraits of her daughters with heavy longing in my chest. I held her hand when she told me of her son's death and a stillborn girl. She told me of the Queen Mother's passing with dry eyes. She told me of Louise de La Vallière's children, that King Louis had finally replaced her, and how lonely she now seemed. She'd tried to move to a convent to repent her life as *maîtresse-en-titre,* but he forced her to remain at Versailles to conceal the fact that he had a new mistress. Her replacement was our old friend Françoise-Athénaïs de Mortemart, now Marquise de Montespan. My cousin promised that Montespan would become more infamous in her excesses than even Castlemaine.

At first, we laughed about her husband's preening vanity. "He's wretchedly unpleasant." She pursed her lips. "His fits of rage and jealousy shake the palace walls."

"Does he still . . . entertain men?"

"He treats his men as one would a wife." She spoke plainly. "While he treats his wife like butchered meat." She waved her hand. "I am used to it. If I truly require help, I need only call on King Louis. Of course, my favor with the king infuriates my husband even more, so I must be cautious."

I looked down. "And how are things between you and King Louis?"

"You mean, are we still lovers?" She sighed. "No. That ended between us"—she shot a shadowed glance at me—"long ago. I knew you rejected him."

Shocked, I looked up at her. "You did?"

"Well," she said. "I didn't know for sure. But he seemed so offended by you one day when he had been so smitten by you before. I suspected he made an offer to you."

"Did you know I refused him to spare your feelings?"

"Yes," she whispered. "But my pride . . . I couldn't forgive either of you for a long time."

"Mmm. A trait you share with your brother, I think." I laughed ironically. "At one time, I thought I could brush away all the hurt by telling you King Louis wanted me to conduct important political business with King Charles. He demanded I come here to form an alliance between France and England the moment I rejected him, you know. I thought you might be persuaded to believe that was all he ever wanted from me."

"That was what he wanted even then?"

I nodded. "He made me swear fealty to him. He sent ambassadors with further instructions a few years later. But war with the Netherlands made it impossible—"

"That is why I'm here," she whispered, leaning in. "King Louis has finally gotten his alliance with England. Through me."

I shook my head, thinking I'd heard her incorrectly. "King Charles formed a Triple Alliance to keep King Louis suppressed. He cannot have one alliance against and another for. Besides, it would cause an outrage with the English people."

She smirked. "That is why it is a *secret* treaty. No one must know. Charles will fulfill his end in his own time. I only tell you so you know King Louis truly did want what he asked of you. It was not just some futile punishment."

My shoulders slumped. "It doesn't matter anymore."

"What?" she asked. "Are you surprised at Charles?"

"Yes." How could King Charles be so duplicitous? "Quite shocked, really."

"I have been working on this for some time, and I am rather surprised at him, too." She reclined against her pillows. "He has changed."

"How do you mean?"

"Since your marriage, he has taken a new approach to political dealings. I know I can trust him, but no one else can. Ministers with clear sight complain he is evasive, shifty, steering one man against another. Some merely say he is empty."

I crossed my arms. "If his politics have changed, it is because Lord Clarendon is no longer his chancellor."

"Did Clarendon not fall because of you?"

I changed direction. "If I hadn't married, King Charles would have divorced Queen Catherine. I could not allow your brother to ruin his honor, embitter his nation." My throat started to tighten. "He let bitterness chip away at his own soul in my absence. It was only when I nearly died that he did forgive me and by then . . ."

"Go on."

But I couldn't.

She shook her head. "He is still a good man. He will always do what he thinks is right for his country. Balance the extremes. He is judicious, cautious, and cool-headed."

I nodded. "There is a sort of honor left in him. He is resolute now in his devotion to Queen Catherine. He will not hear of divorcing her. I do think he can yet be a great king."

"You must promise to be good to him."

I put my hand on her arm. "Don't fret. I shall ever be his friend. I promise."

Madame went home from Dover and, in about a month, we received word at Whitehall that she had died. Buckingham raved that her heartless husband poisoned her, and an angry mob attacked the French embassy in London. King Charles retired sadly with Queen Catherine. She was the best to offer him comfort. Richmond took me home, and I cried myself to sleep that night.

CHAPTER 67

Whitehall Palace

February 1672

King Charles wrapped one arm around my shoulder and nuzzled his nose against my cheek. I inhaled deeply to catch that whiff of sandalwood and Stuart. Much as I tried to suppress them, I felt familiar sparks of wistfulness and longing. But no passion. That had long since dimmed.

"I trust your husband knows by now that you have the finest legs in England."

I shoved my hand against his chest lightly, pretending to push him off. "Of course he does. You know better than anyone I couldn't live without some passion in my life."

King Charles tightened his embrace. "You seem well content, and for that I'm glad."

Even if I hadn't made that last promise to Madame, I would have remained King Charles's loyal friend. At times, indeed, we were so friendly it roused the old suspicion I was his lover. As I gazed across the Banqueting House at subtle glances tossed our way, I knew this would be one of those times.

Richmond, standing across the hall with Cornbury, swigged a sip of whisky from the flask in his pocket. His eyes met mine and he grinned. It reminded me not to let King Charles's caresses linger too long, for every time they called me the king's mistress, it was calling Richmond a cuckold.

I'd come to see the king's repeated flirtations as subtle requests. As if he sought reassurances to himself that he still had his old angelic Stuart's regard. "At one time you promised to declare to all England that mine are the finest legs in the land."

"Which I've honored. Your portrait as Britannia will be on the copper farthings minted next year."

My smile widened. "That will make your new mistress flutter with worry."

He tried to stifle his laugh. "Yes."

Shortly after Madame's death, King Louis sent one of her maids of honor, Louise de Kéroüaille, to England to plant herself in King Charles's bed and in his politics. Some said she used my old "trick" of holding on to her virtue as long as she could to enflame the king's ardor. It had worked. The fresh-faced girl was the new official mistress.

"On the other hand, your old mistress will hardly notice. She is quite content with her new title."

"Yes," he said, laughing again. "Barbara started hectoring me to make her Duchess of Cleveland as soon as she learned you were a duchess."

"It won't be long before Louise wants to be a duchess, too."

"She takes jabs from the people for my sake. Indeed, she's incurred such hatred from the people, I'd do almost anything to secure honors for her."

I bit the inside of my cheek. I was a mistress who had refused to suffer for his sake. But he appeared nonplussed, merry as ever, apparently not meaning to slight me by his remark. "Your Majesty, I want to thank you."

"For the coins?"

"For Richmond's appointment."

The glimmer left his eyes. "If anyone can present themselves in a splendor of ostentatious finery to the Danish, it's Richmond. I want them to be impressed by our wealth. The position of ambassador extraordinaire to Denmark suits him."

"He longs to be a credit to England and perform a service for Your Majesty that is consistent with his rank."

King Charles loved to dislike poor Richmond even still. He had accepted his presence at court, dined with us, even drank himself drunk with Richmond at times. But his subtle resentment always pervaded the rest of the court. If the king could really forgive him, Richmond might regain the regard he deserved.

King Charles's gaze landed on someone behind me. He patted my hip and pulled away. Strange, even after all this time, the loss of his touch saddened me. "I'm going to pay the queen a call now, to see if she is feeling better."

I turned my cheek, which he promptly kissed. "Oh," he said quickly. "Be nice to Louise, would you? For my sake." Then he walked away.

"Your Grace of Richmond and Lennox."

I turned to see Arlington, with Kéroüaille hanging on his arm looking tearful.

"Your Grace," he repeated as he bowed low. "You have the best French—would you speak to Louise? I want to catch up with the king to discuss—" He glanced at Kéroüaille. "A personal matter."

"*Oui,*" I said with an easy smile.

He bowed and hustled away.

A terrified expression flashed across her face, but she concealed her feelings quickly. She curtsied to me, then swept her glance up and down my person with a pretend hauteur. Her knuckles turned white as she gripped her fan.

I felt a slight twinge of sympathy for her. "I hear the new French ambassador is taken with you, ever pressing you with beautiful gifts," I said in French.

"All to decorate my new rooms at Whitehall. I'll have the most luxurious décor, the finest of everything. King Charles insists I shall have anything I wish." She gave me a little smirk.

"Yes. King Charles is very generous."

She placed both hands on her flat bodice front. "He is especially now."

Was she with child? All sympathy vanished in a rush of jealousy. Richmond and I had tried to get him his heir. We were disappointed time and again. "Lord Arlington will be a great advocate for you in your condition."

"Do you really think I should continue to allow Lord Arlington to sponsor me?" She narrowed her eyes. "I shall surely need a determined advocate." She leaned her head toward me. "I shall need protection, a title, money, an estate, and a title for my child. And when it comes to the queen, so frail and always ill, I will need someone to negotiate for me. It is only a matter of time before—well—before King Charles will need a *new* queen."

I excused myself, found Richmond, and made him take me home.

I tossed about in my bed that night. I tried fervently to forget Kéroüaille and our differences. *I had placed honor above love.* Was honor all I had left? *Almost all.* I tore open the bed curtains, padded into Richmond's chamber, and climbed into bed with him. "Rich?"

"What's wrong?" he asked, voice groggy.

"Nothing." I tucked myself under his arm. "Will it bother you if I sleep here? Does your head still ache?"

"Yes—I mean, no. You won't bother me, of course. But yes, my head aches."

"Then lean into me—let me hold you."

I did have an honorable marriage with my husband. He would be an ambassador. With time, we would have heirs, a large family to fill our estates. Richmond leaned over me and kissed me, deeply. Perhaps I would be with child even before he took leave. We had our title, and Richmond's reputation would soon be repaired. We were free to pursue happiness together.

I did not get with child in the months before Richmond left. In Denmark he worked diligently and finally earned the praise he longed for from King Charles. We wrote often. I managed our affairs while he was gone. I missed him. I prayed he would fulfill his mission quickly and come home to me so we could build our family.

But before the end of the year, before the mission was complete, King Charles presented himself at Richmond House with a troop of Life Guards dressed in black. I stood before the wall of windows and watched him cross the room toward me. I saw the anguish in his eyes, saw the roll of parchment with huge black seals clutched in his hand. He had come to give me grave news. Richmond had died in Denmark.

It took an age to get his body shipped back to England. When I finally stood on the docks at Gravesend to receive my husband's remains, the chilled wind whipped my black mourning cloak around my body. The Danes sent Richmond in a ship painted black, harnessing the wind with black sails. Watching it approach, all sense of purpose blew out of me.

He lay in state at Cobham for a few days so the neighbors could pay respects. I had him shipped by barge, coffin draped in black velvet, up the river to Westminster Abbey. Most of England's nobility proceeded in the extravagant funeral parade. They placed him in the Richmond vault. With his other wives, his daughter, my stillborn child, and my fragile dreams.

Richmond House
October 1688

I stood before the full-length Venetian mirror in the bedchamber of my home and studied the rows of curls stacked over the forefront of my head. Little gems and pearls glimmered in the *fontange* hairpiece while my natural strands, long and thick, curled down my shoulders and back.

My favorite old style of gown, the mantua, had altered through the years to form a day garment. The one I wore hugged my shoulders and fell down my backside in bustled, red silk drapes. A stacked row of bows, red and silver *échelles* to match the silver flowers embroidered on my skirts, ran down the stomacher that joined it in front. I tightened a sash around my waist and straightened the ruffled sleeves.

Fat pearls gleamed at my neck, and I saw a flash of my younger self, wearing men's pantaloons, posing for the king. I chose to remember mostly the happy memories from my years at Whitehall. But since King Charles passed away, too much reminiscing was an invitation to longings and regrets. Old ghosts were better left to yesterday. I pinched my cheeks and decided I still looked fashionable for a forty-year-old dowager duchess in retirement. And certainly sharp enough to face King James's Privy Council to discuss the controversy surrounding his newborn prince.

Autumn sun filtered through the windows and twinkled against the gold braid on my bed, lit the tapestries and paintings on my walls, and made the toilette set shine on my new chest of drawers. I'd finally achieved my haven, where everything reminded me of the independence I'd struggled so long to attain.

St. Albans had been so proud of his building project. Though he'd never extended affection, he'd offered me one of the first houses at St. James's Square. I'd sold Cobham Hall, and Mother joined me there, grasping that offering as if it were acceptance by St. Albans himself. But Whitehall, the rambling old palace by the river, the court life, soon called to me. Richmond House was mine for my lifetime, and I couldn't stay away. Besides, Sophia's quarters weren't large enough to house her six children, and she needed our extra eyes to watch them.

Mary, slow and gouty with age, padded in. "Milady, your mother wants to know when you are taking her riding in the park."

"Tell Mother we won't ride today. I've been summoned to the Privy Council."

Sophia and young Anne entered as Mary left. Anne stopped to raise an almond to old Sir Ment. He stretched his little body and spread his wings, stirring feathers from his perch. Anne then pointed to my flat slippers. "You're wearing those simple things?"

"Certainly. The toes aren't pointy and vain. They fit well."

She considered this. Sophia had named one son Francis, after me, but of all her children, this one daughter was most like me. She watched, waited, and learned the fastest. If the nurse laid out plans that were disagreeable, she entered into negotiations like a miniature ambassador, securing better terms while her brothers and sisters sat back with blocks and dolls. Whatever came of today, even if Sophia had to take them all into exile, I knew this child would grow to do as I had done. She would ever work to protect her family.

"A letter arrived," she said.

I took it from her, put it in my hanging pocket. "Now, go to the nursery. No telling what mischief is going on in there."

She paused. "Very well. But may I take the kittens?"

I pretended to think hard on it before nodding. She fetched the basket from the corner and carried Miss Ment's granddaughters, mewing adorably, back to the nursery like a prize.

Sophia watched Anne go before she spoke. "Our cousin Lord Blantyre is sure to side against King James."

"He once sought favor with King Charles," I said. "But he is an opinionated Scottish nobleman, we mustn't quarrel with him over it. He is the noble head of our family."

"*You* have always been the head to me. But you won't go, will you? If the worst happens, you will stay here."

I nodded. "Don't worry for me, sister, I will have Lord Blantyre's aid if I need it. I have my Lennox estate. Mother and I will prosper." I paused. "You know, if King James is deposed, he will likely go to France. You remember what it was like before."

"My place is at my husband's side, and his place is in service to King James."

I embraced her so she wouldn't see the tears in my eyes. "Then you must take every farthing we can muster, for they won't allow me to send it to you later." And in my mind I started planning to build a larger estate for the Blantyres in Scotland, where Sophia's family might slip in easily from France if they needed a haven.

Walking through the Bowling Green to the Stone Gallery, I peered at the scratchy handwriting on the letter and smiled. It was the first word I'd had from Prudence in a few years. I broke the battered seal and a long, shiny, black-brown feather slipped from the paper folds, fluttering to the ground.

Years earlier, King Charles had granted her old friend William Penn a mass of land in the colonies. They named it Pennsylvania, and Penn drew up a constitution of governance to promote religious toleration. Prudence now prospered in the new colony. Her first letter from there had said, "May God bless it and make it the seed of a new nation."

Today's letter spoke of a great eagle. It reminded her of me, she said, because she knew I loved such creatures of God that could soar the heights and live free above the valleys. With a dark body and white head and tail, its striking coloring was the most beautiful she'd ever seen. When she'd found an eagle feather, she thought it the perfect gift to send me.

I picked up the feather, touched it to my lips, testing the delicate firmness of its edges. When I breathed in, it had no scent. That was how the sky must be. Clear and clean with whiffs of cloud and blue expanse and never a care. I smiled for Prudence, for the freedom she'd found, and tucked the feather into my hanging pocket. Until we all lived in a world like hers, we must embrace liberty any way we can.

But in England, my old fear of another war had nearly come to fruition before King Charles died. During the Popish Plot, Londoners had gone mad and accused everyone of trying to return England to the Catholic Church. Since James, the widowed Duke of York, had converted to Catholicism and taken a Catholic Italian princess as a second wife, Parliament wanted to exclude him from the succession. King Charles, for all his merriness, managed to block Parliament. He might not have attained the tolerance he wanted in England, but he refused to let the monarchy be dashed again because of bigotry.

I could hardly remember feeling so light. Golden leaves danced on the trees in the Bowling Green and seemed the most beautiful sight, richer than a thousand nations. I patted my hanging pocket, and I realized I was hardly worried about the Privy Council.

My Charles lived his last four years without having to call a Parliament. Trade ports were established, money flowed to his treasury, and he happily dispersed my late husband's titles to his beloved illegitimate children. But his brother was never careful like him. By the time James inherited the throne, England's politicians had learned how to work together peacefully. Yet King James was willful enough to disturb the most tolerant of men. Today's Privy Council meeting was proof of that.

I reached the Privy Gallery, and my pages ran before me toward the councillors' hall. Inside, just as they turned a corner, they tripped to a halt and bowed low. King James stepped into view. The pages backed away, and I dipped a low curtsy. The king extended his hand, and I kissed his ring.

Time had preserved his looks—he still seemed a lighter version of Charles—but every action was pomp and tedious formality. Though I loved him as a cousin, I was glad he did not expect me at court often.

"So good to see you, Cousin Frances," he said firmly, waving away his Life Guards. "I could call you *la belle* still today as ever I did. I presume your mother is in good health." He raked his eyes up and down the length of me in that old, ogling gaze.

I grinned. He had not changed one whit. "Perfectly well, thank you. She would have me express our gratitude in continuing to keep my sister and her husband at service in your household."

"With your brother no longer living, it is the least I can do for your family. Stuarts must help one another where they can. You, though, you've never needed my help."

"I'm thankful to say, your brother and my husband left me in a fair position."

He nodded. "I am glad I've been able to continue that annuity—the one my brother established for you. As I said, Stuarts must support one another."

The hair on my neck rose, and I bowed my head instinctively. "You are a most generous king and kind cousin."

A satisfied smile spread across his face, and he stepped closer to me. "I've never asked anything of you before, Frances."

I immediately held up my finger, both to throw him from his suspicious tone and to tease him. "Ahh. There was one thing. You asked me to become your mistress. Remember?"

All at once he looked flustered. "B-but that was ages ago. How can you even remember such a trivial thing? Not that it was trivial at the time. I meant it when I professed my devotion to you. You were so beautiful—I mean, you are beautiful still. Ahh—" He scratched his neck.

"Be at ease. As you said, it was an age ago, after all. Now," I said, daring to turn slightly from him, "won't you show me into the Privy Council?"

"Wait." He grabbed my arm. "I need to tell you what to say."

I held my breath.

His face was stern and very serious. "They are going to ask you about my newborn son, James Edward."

"I arrived too late to witness his birth, remember?"

"No." He shook his head. "You must tell them you arrived just in time. You must tell them you saw him brought from my wife's body so his legitimacy cannot be disputed. You're the Duchess of *Richmond*. I need you to use your rank, your honorable reputation, to help me."

"Your Majesty, those who were there already when I arrived could refute my testimony. It would not be prudent—"

"Frances!" He glanced around quickly to make sure no one was near. When he went on, his voice was strained. "Everyone is saying she was never pregnant or our child was stillborn, and we smuggled a babe into her bed on a warming pan. It's ludicrous! These doubts are causing a madness among the people, and they'll try to cast me from the throne." Droplets of sweat sprang to his forehead. He dropped his hand from my arm. "Help me prove his legitimacy."

I shook my head. "That is not why they want to overthrow you. They cannot accept the Catholicism you are reestablishing in this country. Open your eyes and see that England will not tolerate absolutism. She strives for her freedom. To rule herself."

"Don't think me a fool. Of course I see. But my beliefs force me. I cannot allow my country to languish in heresy."

"Your Majesty, please consider the consequences. I visited your daughter in Holland not long ago. William and Mary will not hesitate to use the strength of their Protestant army to turn you out of England."

He studied me carefully. "I once tried to stop a war to win your love," he lied. "It is not my fault I failed to do as you demanded at Oxford. Do this for me in honor of the love I once had for you. I beg you."

I'd stood up to powerful kings, managed the largest dukedom of England, and my image was on the back of every English farthing as a symbol of Britain herself. I'd failed to embrace my own liberty in many ways. But I would not fail in my answer to this king. "I, too, tried to stop a war. For love and in spite of love."

"I command you." His eyes narrowed.

I searched his face. "Please, my king, my cousin, believe my love for you. I know the child is your own son. I know your wife was truly pregnant. But I did not see him emerge from the womb. Please do not blame me if I feel I must tell the truth."

He brought his face within an inch of mine.

I refused to tremble. He was the king. He could lock me in the

Tower, stop my annuity, dismiss my sister from service, and seize my property. But he could not make me lie. He could not break my spirit. He could not make me help him force England to do something she didn't want to do. I was bound by nothing. No matter the price, I would never be cowed again.

The stern lines in his face slowly softened, and he backed away. He nodded his head a fraction. My signal to go. I curtsied carefully and deeply, sidestepped while I was still low, and rose to walk toward the council.

Fifty peers of the English aristocracy, the prince of Denmark, the archbishop of Canterbury, officers of the crown, the lord mayor, and aldermen of the city of London jostled and shifted in the Great Council Chamber to witness the deposition. Even my sister stood among the queen's ladies. We were two of forty women who had entered the royal birthing chamber. Because of my high rank, space was made for me to stand close to Dowager Queen Catherine's place, which was at the right hand of King James.

She approached her seat, and I knelt to arrange her train. She sat, giving me a quick, dignified smile, full of the affection of years of friendship, which I returned. Then I glanced at King James, who had seen our quiet little greeting, and backed to stand behind her chair.

King James gave a rousing speech and explained his purpose. Dowager Queen Catherine then gave her word. She had arrived to Queen Mary Beatrice's chamber a little after eight of the morning and never left until after the little prince was born. She signed her name to the transcribed oath, and King James looked to me.

The threat of consequence loomed over my head, yet I was not afraid. In my pocket was a reminder of the strength I'd garnered. A blackish-brown eagle feather.

I had never felt more free.

AUTHOR'S NOTE

King Charles II understood the need for tolerance and was skilled in playing one power against another, but King James II failed to win England's confidence. Despite James II's Privy Council depositions, important members of Parliament invited his daughter Mary and her Protestant husband, William of Orange, to invade England. When James fled, Parliament declared his abdication, crowned William and Mary, termed the change "the Glorious Revolution," and composed the first Bill of Rights. This shifted the balance of power from crown to Parliament and, therefore, the people. American revolutionaries followed this model when forming the United States Constitution.

James spent the rest of his life maneuvering to reclaim his throne, as did his son (the Old Pretender) and grandson (Bonnie Prince Charlie). All failed, despite bloody, tragic battles. The crown passed from William and Mary to Mary's sister Anne, and then to the Protestant Hanovers.

The late Lady Diana Spencer, Princess of Wales, was a descendant of Charles II through the illegitimate son who inherited Frances Stuart's Richmond and Lennox titles. If either of Diana's sons, William and Harry, succeeds to the throne, the Stuart line will finally regain the British crown.

Author's Note

FACTS BEHIND THE FICTION

While writing this novel, I sorted through references, biographies, historical documents, and contemporary accounts, many of which were apocryphal and full of gossip. I used as many facts as possible to fictionalize gaps and address unanswered questions about Frances Stuart's life.

I aimed for accuracy in timing and placement of historical figures, with at least two notable exceptions. First, the Duke of Richmond's and the Earl of Rochester's terms of imprisonment in the Tower of London did not overlap. They were imprisoned three weeks apart, and Frances did not visit the duke there. Second, though Charles II and Isaac Newton did observe the same comet, Newton's observation took place from Cambridge. He did not interact with the king until several years later.

The only fictional characters in this novel are the maids, Mary and Prudence. Prudence's father, Mr. Pope, was real, but he didn't have a Quaker daughter.

The Earl of St. Albans claimed biological relation to Frances in a letter he wrote to the Duke of Richmond, as published in *La Belle Stuart* by Cyril Hartmann. They are not connected through the Blantyre Stuarts, and Hartmann believed the relationship existed on Frances's mother's side. Mrs. Sophia Stuart's parentage is unknown, perhaps because she was born out of wedlock. The Earl of St. Albans was accused of fathering an illegitimate child with Eleanor Villiers before the civil wars. Carola Oman states in *Henrietta Maria* that St. Albans's father sent a midwife for the birth, so it is possible the child connected with the governor of Jersey and made her way into France with the exiled court. Based on the considerable favor shown to Sophia by St. Albans and the Queen Mother, it is not difficult to theorize that St. Albans was Sophia's father.

According to Bryan Bevan in *Charles II's Minette,* Frances spent the glamorous summer of 1661 with her friend Henriette Anne and the French court at Fontainebleau. Though Louis' affair with Henriette Anne received more attention in history books, diarist Samuel Pepys recorded Louis XIV's declaration of love for Frances. I designed Frances's ruby necklace based on a similar jewel adorning her effigy on display at Westminster Abbey. Her stuffed African gray parrot is also on display, but its name and how she obtained it are not known.

The extent of Frances and Louis XIV's relationship is also unknown, but Henriette Anne was jealous by nature and would have resented it. Derek Wilson explains in *All the King's Women* how Louis XIV may have used Henriette Anne and Louise de Kéroüaille as liaisons to Charles II, so it is not unreasonable to hypothesize that Louis XIV attempted the same with Frances. The French ambassadors' correspondence with Louis XIV indicates they found a friend in Frances.

When some historians assert that Frances did not capitulate to Charles II, they are accepting her third-hand account recorded by Pepys, in which she admitted she didn't want the world to think her a "bad woman." But Pepys also reported that Frances did "everything with the King that a mistress should do," and that she was likely pregnant by Charles II. This and the Duke of Richmond's early announcement of Frances's pregnancy soon after their nuptials convinced me to write the story as I did.

Charles II's attempt to divorce Queen Catherine with Archbishop Sheldon's help is further evidence that Frances might have been carrying his child. Why would Charles II, known for fathering over a dozen bastards, bother about this one? Because Frances may have been the only woman Charles II truly loved. Biographer Allen Andrews referred to her as Charles II's "fixed star by which to orientate himself" and says, "her rejection was cataclysmic on Charles' emotions."

A letter from the mother of the maids, published by Hartmann, implicates Cornbury and Clarendon in Frances's elopement. Many believe Frances eloped because she loved the Duke of Richmond, based on affectionate letters she wrote to him. Although written in the stylized romanticism of the day, the letters do seem to contain genuine tenderness. However, all of the letters were written after the marriage, mostly during their lonely banishment from court.

When James II was still Duke of York, Pepys recorded James's affections for Frances. But I consider her failure to follow kin and king into exile to be her true rejection of James II. Her letters to Lord Blantyre reveal her respect for those with a "tenderness of conscience." Her beliefs conflicted with James II's, and I suspect she stood her ground by staying in England.

CLOSING

Frances's sister, the younger Sophia, did follow James II into exile because her husband was his master of the household. She and her daughters lived in France as exiled Jacobites. Frances's niece Anne married James II's illegitimate son, the Duke of Berwick, and provided a home for her sisters.

Anthony Hamilton was intimate with the Berwick household when he wrote Gramont's humorous and often inaccurate memoirs. Why would Frances's family have allowed Hamilton to portray her as an innocent featherbrain? They would have wished to avoid scrutiny in the pious atmosphere of the exiled court, to conceal their matriarch's illegitimacy, to minimize Frances's involvement in Louis XIV's affair with Henriette Anne, to hide Frances's failure to stop England's war against the Dutch, to detract from the likelihood that Frances was carrying Charles II's child when she eloped with the Duke of Richmond, and to downplay Frances's hand in the fall of Chancellor Clarendon.

I believe her family understood and wished to preserve the purity of Frances's spirit. She positively influenced one of England's most important kings, and her sacrifice prevented a political calamity: the divorce of a Catholic queen.

La Belle Stuart lived to attend Queen Anne's coronation, her charm and grace inspiring poets to her final days. Events of her era had thrown the divine right of kings into question, and there emerged a sense of aspiration among the English, a budding desire for civil rights and self-governance. Frances Stuart, who rejected kings, is a symbol of her time. She was also the symbol of her nation on its currency, and the most natural and compelling figure for a novel of Restoration England.

For sources and more information, visit Marci Jefferson's Web site at www.MarciJefferson.com

ACKNOWLEDGMENTS

This novel wouldn't have progressed past page one without the vital support of my prince, Kevin; the lights of my life, Dalton and Delani; my mother and assistant, Deborah Pinckney; and the Jeffersons. I am ever grateful to my agent, Kevan Lyon, who believed in this story before it was finished; to my editor, Toni Kirkpatrick, at Thomas Dunne Books; to my publicist, Katie Bassel; to critique partners, who taught me so much in the beginning, Lisa Wells, Barbara Bettis, Jennifer Jakes, and especially my dear Sara Ann Denson; to local authors Shirley Jump, Julie Sellers, Karen Lynfestey, and Diana Welker; to faithful beta readers Chris Irons, Molly Shoup, and Jill Sloffer who doubles as my gifted photographer; to the numerous professionals within the Historical Novel Society, especially Michelle Moran, Kate Quinn, and Sophie Perinot; to the wise Allison; for the camaraderie of "super-writers" DeAnn Smith, Lisa Janice Cohen, Julianne Douglas, Amanda Orr, Candie Campbell, Janet Butler Taylor, Arabella Stokes, and especially Heather Webb and Susan Spann; to those who inspire and strive for excellence at the Allergy and Asthma Center; to art historian Madeline Archer, may we someday find that Raphael; to the Allen County Public Library system for delivering cartloads of books over the years, especially librarians Donna Rondot and Nancy Saff for finding historical records; to Marjorie L'Esperance and Margriet Lambour for Dutch correspondence; to archivists Alex Richie of the UK National Archives and Rachael Krier of the Lancashire Record Office for help with historical manuscripts; and I must also acknowledge the late Cyril Hughes Hartmann, whose biography *La Belle Stuart* provided the starting point for much of my additional research.